God, I Respect Ya Gangsta

by
TERESA RAE BUTLER

teresarae@text4mpublishing.com

GOD, I RESPECT YA GANGSTA
Copyright © 2006 by Teresa Rae Butler

All rights reserved. No part of this fictionalized book may be reproduced, stored in a retrieval program, or exchanged in any liable form or by in any way possible without the cleared physical written consent of the Publisher/Author.

Published by TEXT 4M PUBLISHING

Text4mpublishing.com is a self-publishing company. The stories portrayed here are fictitious in content. Any characters or events, places and names are of the author's thoughts. Therefore, any resemblance of this material to anything, anyone, or anywhere is coincidental in form. Pictures and cover by Teresa Rae Butler.
Illustrations by VAN ADAMS
Cover design by Yvonne Vermillion, Magicgraphix.com
Copy Editing by Chuck Vermillion, HelpPublish.com

10-digit ISBN: 0-9779207-1-2
13-digit ISBN: 978-0-9779207-1-6
SAN: 850-6299

Library of Congress Control Number: 2006938931

Printed in the United States of America

Dedication & Acknowledgements

This book is dedicated to every ghetto in the world, and to every person found or lost, born into it, or long departed from the mayhem. For the loved ones passed on, and I would say gone but not forgotten; however, that's definitely not my style. So, for every reason that every tear has ever fallen in the hood like raindrops, I will share with you my umbrella and tell you what I know about the weather — It changes. Put your own name on the sidewalk with your own, living hand and celebrate your own life. Make changes. All are what makes the fabric of time. All are eternal. Believe in the love in your soul. For those of us still here 4 the ride, hang on tight, and for those of you just arriving — Welcome to the Universe. Big Love to James Cameron, Mother Freedom Simpson, and the Bronzeville District of Milwaukee WI, both the old and the new one to come.

Table of Content

Dedication&Acknowledgements iii
Table of Content v
Prologue viii
Coraz's Shout Outs xi
Coraz's Forward xiv
Chapter One - City Lotto 2
Chapter Two - Not Now; Not Like This 14
Chapter Three - Two Again 24
Chapter Four - Babbette's House 48
Chapter Five - The State Street Suicide 68
Chapter Six - 43rd and Good Hope Road 86
Chapter Seven - Eyes in Dina's Window 100
Chapter Eight - More Like a Player;More Like a Pimp 110
Chapter Nine - Doin' Up 126
Chapter Ten - Pine Bluff, Arkansas 138
Chapter Eleven - Them North and South Folk 148
Chapter Twelve - Hawrd Dick or Bubble Gum? 170
Chapter Thirteen - Guess Who Got Out? 190
Chapter Fourteen - Is This Love, or Racism? 202
Chapter Fifteen - Is It Racism, or Sexism? 216
Chapter Sixteen - Jack-Pot; Whore Pot! 230
Chapter Seventeen - Weep-Deep in The Struggle. 250
Chapter Eighteen - One Peace 276
Chapter Nineteen - Mind Vacations 290
Chapter Twenty - G'dom in the Kingdom 306
The End? 323
Teresa Rae's Questions and Trivia 324

Prologue

Coraz sat at the kitchen table, concentrating on the gorgeous turquoise and crème-laced, white-gold wedding invitation in her hand. Mill had done such of a professional job at putting everything together. She stroked the fine fabric of her gown which he had so carefully picked out, fingering the eloquent but bizarre beadwork set at an angle on just one of the shoulders. The soft, mesh, aqua material that hung off of the beaded shoulder was captured with a beautiful platinum and diamond-studded brooch. She then tried to twirl her sparkly, yet classy, princess-cut ring on her slightly-swollen ring finger but let out a sigh. It would not budge. She was now too fat to wear the dress, the silver 'Margott'-styled Manolo shoes, or her damned, scrumptious ring. *Too Bad!* It was also too bad that the mother of Mill's baby had caused so much legal drama that his and Coraz's wedding had to be postponed.

Coraz was still so upset that she had to let Mill finish the on-going business for their movie production of, *Honey, You Showed Me What to Look For* on his own. *Just my damned luck. Every time things get to looking up, here comes the hardships. I long to be right with You, but how do I do this? This woman is crazy and is trying to take my man to court for everything we got, and we're not even married yet. She doesn't want just a reasonable amount; she wants it all. God, I hope she receives only what You want her to have, because truthfully, as hard as it is being a sista, I don't mind helping her out. I just wish that she would go to college with somma the settlement or maybe even get a life of her own that doesn't involve hating and trying to ruin us.*

Coraz felt like all she could do was reveal her raw emotions in her tell-all, yet somewhat fictitious, juicy, but complicated book. *I know that it's best we go through this now, b4 we get married, because then she can't come back for more money, no matter what. And with this novel set to be released come the end of the week, and the movie wrapping up, I know that we is about 2b PAID! Poppa and Momma done put it down!*

The words seemed to just flow from her fingertips, as she'd descriptively written of the nightmares and longtime torments she had endured in her lifetime which were caused by poverty, racism, and abuse. So many of the young people she'd known in her journeys were dead and gone already. It was amazing that *she* was alive to tell of it. She'd described, in great detail, her experiences of being caught in the ugly web of inhumane selfishness, social lockout, and the struggle for equality which had been branded on Milwaukee, Wisconsin minorities. For three months she had finger-tapped on the keyboard of her laptop and relived all that had haunted her — 'The Past'.

Although all of the facts of her life were true, the fantasized lottery idea had remained her deepest wish. Now her controversial novel was complete, all the way down to the significance of God being included in the title, the body, and the cover design. She had wanted something positive for Milwaukee's Blacks, and this was her gift to the city.

Coraz got up and waddled to the freezer where she had several slices of the delicious wedding cake waiting. She had been nibbling on it a little at a time, not letting the paid-for cake go to waste. Today she decided to eat a big, honking wedge to celebrate her well-polished literary masterpiece. *Now, if only the proof copy would get here! When it does, I'm sending it, autographed, to Oprah, to see what she thinks.*

Just then the doorbell rang, and she went into the living room, calling, "Coming! Who is it?" she asked, as she peeked through the peephole. *God, please bless me.* She grabbed her car keys just in case she had to fight a bogus delivery guy who was really a murderer or rapist in disguise. In Coraz's world, a service van with UPS on the side didn't mean squat. She opened the door and the man pulled off his shades.

"Delivery for…" he turned the packed right-side up in his hand to read the name and looked up at her, "Coraz Singleton. Interesting name. You wanna just sign right here for me… good!" He punched in some information on the computerized clipboard. "OK, and here you are."

Coraz's soul felt replenished once the package touched her fingers, "Thank you."

He put his shades back on, "You betcha!" Brown socks, shorts, and a shirt disappeared into the brown van.

She closed and locked the door, then, with her pregnant belly leading the way, she 'Fred Sanfordly' walked back to her spot at the kitchen table, package in hand. Coraz sat down and closed her eyes to think, *When I was a newborn baby, these eyelids covered my view of the world, but once they opened, the bullshit began. Pretty little girl done seen way too much. So much that she had to do this memoir. Somma my family members gone be real mad about it, too! Oh well... In the words of 'Ms. Jack', who was a prostitute/ peeping Tom/husband/father/ motherly-wisdomed drag-queen I used to know, "Never suga-coat shit. Tell the ugly, peanutty, corn nibbletty all of it. You can be a stiff cock or just use your boring imagination and settle."*

This new author had decided to be cocky and tell the stiff, hard truth. Resting there at the table of artifacts past and present, she devoured a big bite of cake with her high-class *Mr. And Mrs. Milton Worthy Jr.*, engraved, silver fork and smacked her lips. "Mmm... butter-crème frosting. Alrighty, Almighty. You are what's real. Let's see now." She ripped open the package and pulled the wrapped book out to release it from its cellophane casing. Mommy 2b then ran her hand across the smooth surface and smiled to herself, tenderly flipping the pages, creating a small blow of wind that sent the smell of the freshly-pulped paper to her highly-sensitive nostrils.

She felt a wave of success grab at her heart, causing a warm tear of great self-pride to embrace her tingling cheek. Coraz sighed with confidence, "This novel is jampacked with Eff'd up. What will the hungry readers of the literature that is filling African-American book clubs think of this crazy one? If anyone reads these words from cover to cover, they may walk away with a new-found strength for their own battles. At least, that is what I'm aiming for."

She opened it up, autographed it to 'O', glanced at the cover one last time, and began to read aloud to her unborn child, who, at that moment, had seemed to kick her from the inside, as if to say, "You go, girl!"

Coraz's Shout Outs

    I, Coraz Sade Singleton, a.k.a. Rainia Dae Harris have proposed a view of my own beliefs about the universe, God, and our individual life's purpose in a direct manner, as it is correlated to my own somewhat fictitious, yet graphic and true story. As I grow spiritually, some of theses beliefs are subject to change. In no way am I trying to put my own opinions on others, but I do hope to touch the hearts of people who search for peace in these ugly and unpleasant times. The recognition must precede the reality of this memoir which is destined to be read by various adults and youth across the world who are in pain and who are suffering. The reason you will feel me on this piece is that you know I feel you. All of you! So here we go.

    My first shout out is to You, God, and here's why — I would like to thank You, God, for putting me in my place, for all of the times that I tried to jump bad with You. Universal Mother/Father, I finally have learned to let You deal with everyone like You have been asking me to for the last thirty-three years. I feel so free. I love myself the more I know You got this. I wasn't satisfied with my childhood, and then my adulthood, because I was always trying to dodge the pain that my soul needed to feel. I now realize that You have made a very wise star outta me, and for that, I'm gonna shine for You and for anyone who needs or asks for my help along the way during my life's path. You have turned every obstacle into a blessing.

    My next shout out goes to the beautiful children who You, Dear Universe, have allowed me this time to care for. All around us, the little ones are being murdered, molested, beaten, degraded, deprived, raped, and starved, but many of us still stand with Your Grace for today, facing, feeling, and graduating from the pain. God willing, I'm certain that my babies will be better than You have made me — Eventually.

    To my human Mother and Father; the shout out to you both is — Thank you for loving me, and taking good care of me. Step-Father, it was all of your long talks that made a big difference, so big that I'm 4ever proud 2 call you my Dad. And Momma, it was you, constantly helping me with my kids, bad relationships, and finances that erased any doubts about thinking that you didn't love me when I was a little girl going through so much, right with u, as I stood at your side.

Last shout. For my love and fiancée, Mill — Even though I have fallen in love with you, my soulmate, I know tomorrow is not promised to us. For the remainder of the day, Mill, you are my deepest relationship, human to human. What a beautiful hustle in your real purpose here. You-r-so-fun-ny-2-me! U understand me? Continue to touch the minds of these youngins with comedy and film. Once a struggling, young G, now a kingly Black man I see.

Back to the Almighty — God, You are so Gansta. You've shown us that we, the forgotten, are extremely important. Thank U 4 our great Black mentors who have set excellent examples during our struggle. U are more than a real entity. I can't believe the way that You have blessed our family and the rest of the ghetto people who have been disincluded for so long. Bullets fly, people die, and everyday we say, "Not an arrow by day, nor pestilence by night." Thank You so very much. It is because I believe that life is pretty much a dream in one's head from where we are really living out of anyway, and because I believe that one can dream a life into reality, that I would like to open with this:

"And before him shall be gathered all nations."

(Mathew 25:32 KJV)

Coraz's Forward

For those of you who may have a problem with the title to my piece, I have tried to break it down for you with the help of the very best dictionary to give a little something extra. Be sure to pay attention to the words that are **bold and underlined**, for they hold a secret message, when brought together./

GOD -a being worshiped by <u>monotheists</u>-{those who go by belief or doctrine that there is only one GOD}, as the <u>perfect</u>-{flawless, and/ of relating to, or constituting a verb form, that expresses} <u>action</u>,-{action/ process of doing/ act or deed/ a movement or sequence of movements often/ behavior/ the plot of a story or play}.../me: my purpose in life?/...completed before a fixed point in reference of time. /me: GOD knew what I was going to be, and what I was going to do, and go through before I ever did...or was! /: continued... as the perfect, <u>omnipotent</u>,-{having absolute power or authority} <u>omniscient</u>-{knowing everything} <u>originator</u>,-{one who brings/ come into being/ from root original-proceeding all others in time. New and unusual, inventive. A first from which varieties arise or imitations are made. } and <u>ruler</u>-{the head of state in monarchy/, supreme}, <u>paramount</u>-{of highest rank in power/} of the <u>universe</u>-{All EXISTING SPACE AND MATTER as a WHOLE, THE PLANET EARTH, ALL HUMANKIND} /WOW! That's aptly described as the first definition of GOD. And between the words <u>omnipotent</u> and <u>omniscient</u> is the word, <u>omnipresence</u>- {the fact of being present EVERYWHERE!} /me: so the definition of another phrase for the joined meaning for the term, "Current tense" can correlate to, omnipresent, or, in terms of GOD, is... "He, who is always here right now for me... Hmm... so I can come back to Him," WOW! / ++ **"I"**- is defined as, {*the* self, one who is speaking or writing} /me: God's voice is in my head, at all times, helping me to get back to Him, / ++ **respect**- {to feel or show <u>deferential</u>-(courteous respect for another's opinion, wishes, or judgment) regard for: esteem. To avoid violation of or interference with. To relate to: concern. Deferential regard: esteem. The state of being regarded with deference or esteem. Willingness to show appreciation.} ++ **your** –{of relating to you or yourself} /me:

You are what I believe in? O.k. God, I think I got it. /

++ When you look up the word **gangster-** in the College 'Webster' Dictionary, you'll settle on the word <u>racketeer</u>- look that up and you find in its definition's most powerful word is... <u>extortionist.</u> - Revert to the definition of extortionist and you will find {to obtain by *coercive* means,} so <u>coercive</u>-means, coming from the root word, coerce, {to compel to a coarse of action or thought. To dominate or restrain forcibly. To bring about by threat or force,}. <u>Force</u>-means {energy, strength, power, to move something against resistance. Push to open, or break down by force. To inflict or impose, as ones ... will....} /Me: *So having just come full circle from what is known as a negative word, at the end of its very meaning, I still found God and His Will. God will inflict His Will to open my heart, and it could be at the end... of what is me now, in due time, or... right now, even if I resist it all? Cool, I got to respect that!* /

So critics, question the title to my book if u and the people will, and therefore should. I don't know about you and whatever it is you know in your mind, but this is what "I" tells me, Since God is perfect and created me, then my actions are viewed by the omnipotent, omniscient originator of "I" – me, which is You - **GOD**. So, "I" **respect** deferentially, **Ya-** Your relation to me, even though I am imperfect, undereducated, incomplete, and an immoral born sinner on Your time, using a body that's Yours in Your world, even though I am a racketeer or extortionist who first attempted to direct my own soul, but it is Your coerciveness that compels me, and the most studious and practicing Christians, murderers, molesters, thieves, priests, politicians, all born children, yes, including gays, the deformed, all scientists, and even the *hardest thugs!* For that, I recognize Your power, your coercive force in my resistance still 2 do Your Will, 4 U r the omnipresent voice in my head that knows all of what I am in the universe. Which means that what I do will somehow affect us all, because Your universe includes all of everything, every person, every reason, every question, every action, every reaction, every belief, every religion, everyone inside and outside of myself, for all expanding time. We are in this together and nothing... can be stolen from You, not even the definition for the words gangsta, criminal, racketeer, or extortionist, 4 U own that, too. You own all words, powers, ideas, inventions, diseases, cures, people, places, things, ugliness, beauty, hate, happiness, joy, pain, sunshine, rain, beliefs, thoughts, genius, talents, time, meanings, discoveries, stories, opinions, acts, space, elements, death, dark, life — and Love.

   I will forever owe You, to show You gratitude for even the chance to get back to Your Glorious and Good Presence. So that makes You the biggest pimp I have ever known and I love You, Daddy. Yes, You are my Father. And no matter how much ho-ing I have done to try and get away from You, trying to avoid You with my heathen flesh of confusion, I know I betta have Your money, which is all the good of my life. Yes, I believe in You. I'm scared of You, what You can do to me at any time to make me see You. Yes, I've been on some tough corners, and a lotta johns have done me wrong, but through it all, I keep submitting, to what it is You want me to do, so I can feel more complete as I get closer to what is "I, my purpose", or really, what is really "You, and Your Will be done." You broke me off as a piece of Your complicated Being, without explanation, in Your Image, and You made "Me" and "I" make mistakes. You've allowed me, with Your Grace, to borrow this time to be me, to learn from some bad decisions. You have given me serenity and understanding for what I cannot control. You have allowed me the peace to accept that even the evil in this world will... walk... the... track... 4 U, as Your omnipresent, paramount, pimpin' for souls saved don't stop, and will reverberate all bad things, into Your eventual Plan, which will be completed, as we drift along together in each of our purposes, and You respectfully unfold, little by little, in some strange way, in life or death, now or later, as we become mature and ready for — Your Truth. Even when I have hated episodes in my life, was truly bitter, and questioning if You cared for me, I have found beauty and wonder in You. You are so beautiful to me that I'm hanging up my high heels, and I'm tired of the ho-stroll, and I've got myself a reputable pedicure now, so that we can walk on the beach together, leaving two pairs of footprints in the sand. This time you don't have to carry me, cuz I'm strong enough to reach 4 Your Beautiful Hand. I know that You are holding mine. Even with all of my flaws, You said that I am beautiful, too, and with all the mess around me, I look — and I see You, beauty in Your ghettos, in Your Presence, right smack in the middle of men's wars, in a devastating situation, the peace in my house, and the peace of my mind. And yes, I have always ended up coming full circle, letting go of what I do not really own, respecting Your Alpha and Omega, Your space, and everything in it, Your Grace, Your Will, and yes, Your <u>**Gangsta**</u>,

Signed, Coraz Sade Singleton, AKA, Rainia Dae Harris. Everything is necessary, by all means, when Love is by your side, 2006! And here is our story:

Chapter One

City Lotto

Rainia Dae Harris, or 'Rainy', closed her cell phone and had to grab onto the sleeve of the chairman's arm, as he released the substantial check which was made out to her into her other shaking hand. She felt as if she was in the beginning of the first major drop of a highly recommended roller coaster. Someone may have wanted her dead, but God was definitely making moves in her life. Even though she was still of carnal flesh, trying to find her way toward sanctified enlightenment, God was using her during the journey, and she could feel the presence. With her stomach spastic and her voice crackling with a great emotion of triumph and glory, Rainia began to part her lips to speak to her audience, hoping that the trouble-causing crazy woman hadn't had the nerve to show her face. *She just said that she was coming to kill me. Where the hell is my fiancée, Pooh, at?*

The chairman placed the huge display on its stand next to the podium. It was the major release party for her new successful project 'City Lotto', which was her personal attempt at solving some of the problems of the less advantaged. The lofty funds she now possessed would not only be enough to kick-start the project with a champagne bang, but the amount would also be able to generously cover the donations 2 the correlating programs that would compliment all of the lotto's qualified winner's futures. 'Reraise 4 Praise,' was no longer a dream for the 'Miranda Group', the small community organization that Rainia volunteered for and had also come up with the catchy name, 'Reraise 4 Praise' as their star operation. The lotto promised to turn up great success. There would be at least fifty guaranteed winners a day.

This new tactic would exercise expanding education, work skills, life skills, and morals as an acceptance rule to all winners. Players have to be people who must be in debt, impoverished, under-educated, or disengaged from the morals of society in order to win. They had to prove that they were in this class by bringing items with them to cash in tickets, such as w-2 forms, un-employment papers, or student-loan letters. Friends of 'Reraise 4 Praise' would work with each winner to help that person get back on track with their winnings.

Rainia adjusted the microphone, "This is a way to uplift our down-trodden people for the heights of success by equality. Its main points have already been implemented for every culture in this country except Blacks, until now. For example, the Latinos have gotten their respect from America by us recognizing their language. Spanish is accepted even though it is a slang mix of French and Spanish from their country. And to broaden this point, here in America, we have a little something called 'Spanglish'. Blacks have not been recognized on that same communicational level. For hundreds of years, we have been dissed and called ignorant, and then, later, 'ghetto', because of the use of broken English mixed with the African native tongues passed from descendants who were forced to come to this country as slaves, no less. I represent a slither from the great tribes of people who have been denied adequate and culturally-fitting educations before our generations, who, against their wills, followed the hardships. No mandatory, nationally-placed, continual grants up until now have ever been dispersed for the sake of our natural culture, original language in schools, or common 'must learn if you are a Black American' history classes that are soon 2b an option as a national benefit from lotto winnings. We plan on keeping this thing going until the problem no longer exists, if there ever is such a future ahead of us."

People were clapping and shouting profusely with urgent excitement. Rainia was an exciting, young, African-American woman.

She surveyed the room, meaning business, and spoke again after the crowd had tamed, "Before today, we have been burdened with the cold, hard treatment of, 'OK, everybody, except the African-Americans.' Today, the U. S. has to recognize this race as a diverse and unique culture of people who require certain needs as well as any other people who are accepted for their uniqueness in this great nation, especially when every other class of immigrants, even if illegal, has been getting more rights than Negroes."

Rainia Harris had lived and told the truth. The truth is that the Federal Gov't and the corporate U.S. has consciously and unconsciously still in some ways remained partial to the neglect of this particular race of individuals, and that's the bottom line. A sixty-five-year, heavily-researched, governmental report about a massive number of major corporations who were guilty of having turned down qualified African Americans for positions given to Whites, as well as having a high dismissal rate for the Blacks who they did hire, was published and broadcast over the news as the nations highlight of the week. Rainia had that unforeseen, just in the nick of time, support. The only non-support at the moment was Pooh's ex-girlfriend threatening that this day would be Miss Harris's very last.

She had tried to remain strong on the upside during the event, because in spite of the death threat, she even had the muscle of the famous book, *The Promise to Black Americans*, in translation, the book sitting next to dark folks Bibles. It was being sold in the lobby of the gala representing the sturdy socialites as well as the support of the famous Caucasian author, Tassle Gayle, who wrote of these same issues all the way back to King's day, in his book, *An Author's Love Life*. The informative pieces showed, in high detail, all of the things that revealed the unspoken, slow genocide of negroes caused by unemployment, poor quality of health, the poor healthcare of Blacks, the unfair living standards of the masses, and the mis-education of Black children, therefore providing and guaranteeing the recipe to break the cycle. Information to educate the masses about those details was the golden key which had unlocked this city's highlighting function. It was something that the people could relate to, unlike the White history in schools that their brown babies could not identify with.

Rainia had been a teacher who knew, first hand, that the educational system was a sham for them, for she had witnessed many minority-filled schools being closed in her community. The latest Milwaukee scandal was the 'WI Board of Schooling' fearlessly slapping voucher schools with petty charges and shutting their doors for good. But the only ones who were cut short from this operation were the ones who were predominantly Black. It was as if the board had wanted the outed youth to settle 4 the hard-knocks education of the streets, because they had blocked the kids from going to suburb schools with district restrictions and bussing cuts.

In addition to the brown-skinned bullying were the hand-me-down houses being rented to their guardians that were left over from German immigrants. These houses unsafely function way out of code and burn to the ground with colored children in them every year. The unfortunate urban people even had second-hand, community programs that half-assly took care of their community's needs, like the rundown store-fronts, the barren parks, and the repair of raggedy streets bearing potholes the size of small wading pools. With the approval of new grants stemming from the proceeds of the City Lotto for the poor communities, neighborhoods would finally be able to rise up like what a neighborhood, and neighboring business, should look like. They could ultimately be approved for affordable programs and leniencies for home owners to help them all meet the happy measure.

The timing was perfect, because Capitol Hill was awaiting the outcome of a new law that would help to undo some of the terrible mess. For once, all of the Black voters were at the polls and were not playing games anymore. The numbers were looking really good. It was more than a shoe-in. The state would be ready 2 work with qualifying minorities and unconvicted subjects, such as minor drug traffickers, those who have not stolen properties like purse snatching and pocket picking, parties to bad check writing, and other money-making scams if they were in life-long poverty at the time of the crime noted or the substance abuse. The government had agreed that this notion could be made possible, providing that the funding be dependable and from a strong supportive force. Once the proposed new bill gets passed originating from the New Orleans mayor, the crime-filled cities would forgive the crippling traps by reversing the mayhem.

For example, they could give back drivers' licenses that were lost due to consequences from unpaid parking tickets if people were too poor to pay their fines. They could help those have a fresh start who have gone to jail for being caught driving raggedy-lemon cars without a license. Rainia knew that African Americans had been neglected in the US for so long that they were over flooding the prison systems because they were caught doing illegal things for survival. True enough that in the oppressive ghettos, broken spirited and un-educated minorities have kept each other down, but if the promise of forty acres and a mule would have been fully honored, then old Black money would have done the same wonders as old White money. Had that one lousy agreement been thoroughly fulfilled, more of our original culture would have survived as well. Reparations should have been given but never were. It was a hard, uncoated horse pill of Black pride to have to keep swallowing.

Inner City Lotto would let them and other poor races get the money and the plans which they desperately need, therefore pushing to help one another by the laws of the lotto winning distributions. Rainia may have been worried about being assassinated, but despite this, she delivered her speech with empowerment.

"Before now, no one would admit that poor children were considered only equal to stray animals right here in Milwaukee. The city saw them in constant danger but never did much to safely change their environment. They would often get hit by cars like cats and dogs, or die from lead poisoning in their drinking water and windowsills of their crookedly-leaning, falling-apart, rental houses that had constantly slipped through gapping wide cracks, along with crack rock, all shamelessly allowed in the city. Many minority offspring have died in the crossfires of the drug and gang wars or at the hands of abusing, hopeless products of their trusted, oppressed, overwhelmed caregivers. Some small ones have even been snatched up into modern slavery by strangers, believe it or not, and non-majority teens are often jailed into non-paid labor for major companies due to repeat crimes directly correlated to drastic attempts at surviving poverty on their own. Many have no parents, no home, nor childhood.

I'm telling you, there was once a time here in our old Bronzeville District, when a teddy bear made us happy. Now, with every inner-city street corner and light pole covered in stuffed animals, obituaries, and tear-filled poetry, it's hard to look up and see the street lights without feeling shaded, jaded, downcast, and depressed!"

The people responded with high-rolling, thunderous applause, as she fearlessly continued, "Reraise 4 Praise, the program assisting the lotto, will cover every aspect of poverty-stricken communities by fulfilling every need on an educational, medical, psychological, and financial level alongside the daily winnings. We want to rebuild Bronzeville with new Black businesses and pride, renewing our impoverished people. It's a way to help replenish lost credit by erasing bad debt for individuals as a part of a winning road to a clean slate. This will be done by good deeds like paying off high-interest credit cards and student loans. Utility bill collections will be paid as well as doctor bills." Rainia was literally helping to make minorities catch up to everyone else.

"The books will be kept so straight that they will remain open to the public. This new lottery will finally allow the un-included and eluded poor folk to get on the right track, but mainly focusing on brown skin alongside of any race in poverty. The government understands this grievance solver, to gain *true* economic freedom, just as the Founding Fathers of this country signed the Declaration of Independence, to sever their personal ties to 'European King-isms', only to re-adjust it after the Civil War to suit the rights of African-Americans. Back then, these Founding Fathers *were* the government, and they knew then that there must be equality to see unity. There must not be poverty, if there is to be peace. So the government has decided to allow us our lottery, but we will share it with *All* who are *Poor!* This idea only makes sense, even to the government who would always get their cut," she laughed and paused over the irony, "and was why the idea is being asked to move to other suffering countries sponsored by the U.S. The plan was long overdue, and the balance has already been paid in the blood of the unjust treatment of human life because of racial classifying and segregation. Eventually, there will develop a new, equal-opportunity world where all human races will have dignity, love, hope, and be rich with culture as well as finance, philosophy, medical care, agriculture, and freedoms for peaceful religions. Weapons could then be allowed only for the use of *possible* protection from unknown human destruction. Peace will be our mainstay."

Rainia took a moment to think about the seriousness of the probable, futuristic outcomes for herself and for the people. *My cell phone rings right b4 the speech with a text from her ugly-hearted ass. Had I known she was coming to kill me, I wouldn't have my sweet baby and my tubby behind up here. I would have cancelled. My God! I'm pregnant, for God's sake. I must think positive 4 the occasion. Deep breath... wooo!* She tried, real hard, to dismiss her ridiculous worries of the threatening ex so that she could focus on the event. Rainia felt flushed as she saw the bodyguards make their way to the back of the room. They were walking quickly. Two big guys in all-white scrubs ran through the crowd in that same direction.

What's this foolishness about? I'ma claim in the Name of Jesus that it's nothing! Gotta lighten up! Try to think of something spiritual. "And to think this all started in my head as one crazy wish."

Her emotions were building in an overwhelming way, so she searched for her attacker in the crowd but didn't see her, and she concluded with, "I do not think that I can do anything else at this moment — other than go ahead and cry."

The audience was filled with the finest of the elite world-wide, and those who stood for peace and positive change in the Black communities. Wealthy and not-yet wealthy, alike, had come from all around the country and had traveled hurriedly and haphazardly, like crazed sports fans, to show Rainia full support at the gala. A faceted stream of screams and shouts, praises unto the Lord, a couple of, "Take your time now," and, "That's alright, honey," encouragements started to climb their way up to the podium. All around the room, people were crying real tears of hope and were reinforced with faith.

If I die today, God, then I just do. But it sure feels good working my way back to You. I am scared, but I have faith that nothing will happen that You do not pre-approve! Please let the baby come through this safely. Thank You, also, 4 putting a hospital across the street. I feel better knowing there is help close by in case the unthinkable should occur. Amen. Now I'm ready 4 whateva. She decided to put her trust in Him.

Rainia was standing there, her hands bracing the elegant wood with her head thrown back in a teary-eyed, emotional splendor. After a moment of looking towards the Heavens in awe of this grand reality, she wiped away her waterfalls and make-up, rubbed her pregnant belly, and spoke again, "As you all know, I am very open with my life, my struggles as a mixed African-American, a heathen, a once impoverished, uneducated, and angry child." She laughed sweetly and looked at some of her peers, friends, and family who knew, and said, "Well, I guess I'm finding it funny now that I can say that all of those adversarial moments have led me to seek the feet of the Lord, and have led me into the service of all the lost children we see today."

The audience started to clap furiously and shout to the Most High. Her step-son from a previous relationship, 'Lil' Treasure', began singing softly in the background to polite piano as she continued, "I have lived on the corner of one of the most notorious blocks in this country for seven years now, and I can tell you, first hand, about the major need for change. The block I come from is part of an area where the adults have been murdering the children, and the children have been killing the adults on a record level. They even named this area on the national news as, "Lil' Middle east." I am so glad to be standing here alive and witnessing the time that has finally come to start calling it, "Big, Bad Bronzeville," and have it here to stay! I just know that this is going to work."

She felt uneasy as 5 more people she loved dearly were approaching from behind her. Rainia's oldest daughter 'Cee-Cee, her stepdaughter 'Laiya', joined by Laiya's grandmother 'Sally', Rainia's mother 'Anmarie', as well as Rainy's Auntie Nessara had suddenly appeared behind her to hold her up and rub soft circles into her aching back as she spoke in a now strong and demanding voice, trying to hurry and wrap it up, "I will cut the ribbon to the check now and say this final thing to all of you tonight."

Just then, a large group of teenagers she had helped to graduate shouted in a synchronized boom, "We love you, Miss Harris!"

Rainia stretched out her right hand, palm up, and motioned across with her arm in a sweeping gesture, like a warm welcome to the teenagers letting the audience know that they should also recognize their presence, and continued to close, "As you can all see, it takes more than a village to raise the endangered children of this world. I want all of them to enjoy the new lottery and all of its grandeur to come. God bless this time we have ahead of us, and I thank God and all of you for allowing me to do this for you. May love and inner peace land on the side of every one of you. On the behalf of City Lotto, I bid you all Good night."

She then turned toward the chairman of the nation's wealthiest company, sent by the most important funder and backer of this new project, who was moved by her speech. The red-eyed chairman blew his bulbous nose with his beige hanky, stuffed it back into his maroon, pin-striped pocket, smiled, straightened his suit, cleared his throat, and stood on the other side of the gigantic-sized, hot-pink, bow-adorned, cardboard check that had the words: Pay to the order of, Rainia Harris, founder of, 'City Lotto, Milwaukee Chapter, U.S.A.'-------$500,000,000.00------.

Rainia's mom grabbed her impressive daughter and hugged her, and baby to come, to no end. When Anmarie let her go, Rainia nerve-rackingly rushed them all toward the sidesteps and said to her, "See, Momma, I told you I was going to be a star one day, only the kind of star that comes to shine for the goodness of humanity."

"You will never, ever, know how wonderful it feels to be the mother of a one-of-a-kind creation like you, Rainy," her mother responded with tremendous pride.

"And *always* know that I love you, Momma," She beamed into her mother's eyes, like it may be 4 the last time.

The room started to bustle with a plethora of conversations. A list of itinerary and other plans for every dime of the funding aligned in a spectacular program, complete with a brand-new web address, was being passed among the crowd. There was nothing to hide from the public, for this belonged to the public. As Rainia disguised her fear and panic with a lovely smile, she prepared to mingle with her audience. Her jealous adversary could be somewhere out there, perhaps watching her like an eight-eyed black widow in a dark corner web. The death of her and Pooh's relationship had to have made her heart dead inside to 4get that she had a beautiful daughter to live for, to want to threaten the life of her daughter's unborn baby sister, her only sister. *She probably is here, knowing her selfish self. But where?* Rainia was beginning to sweat profusely and felt her hands and feet start to tremble as people introduced themselves to her, reaching up to the stage on her way down to the rest of the observers.

She again scoped the room for her fiancée, Pooh, but still did not see him. As they were all shuffling to the side of the stage and stepping down the stairs to meet and greet with the crowd, the most unexpected thing happened. There was a very loud, and sudden, "CRACK!" in the air. Rainia's vision started to blur and fade in and out with an obsidian glare. She was thinking, ***Oh, hell, mutha-fuckin' naw! Did this punk-ass bitch just shoot me?*** She felt herself falling backwards, helpless but submissive. She watched, as first chandeliers, then faces, and finally, scurrying, fancy shoes danced her through a slow-motion, mind-numbing "THUD!" And just like that, in her finest hour, Rainia Dae Harris was out of the game.

Chapter Two

Not Now; Not Like This

Ms. 'City Lotto' had always loved to watch those crazy cable presentations about the afterlife, angels, Egyptians, ghosts, and anything to do with the good, but mysterious, possibilities of the forces that you may suspect to be out there but just cannot touch as tangible. She had even tattooed a couple of movies into her questionable thoughts on existence about the search for alien intelligence through a space program, but in the end, the atheistic star finds belief in a higher power, and this other movie about dying but getting a second chance at life by conquering the hell of a soulmate's suicide and then going back to heaven after living a new life over again. This is the way that she had always thought. She believed in everything! She believed in a Heaven for a thug, if it meant that it was the only way to bring a thug to God.

Rainia was definitely the type of person who questioned all aspects of any race, their beliefs, and their religions. She believed in questions, like, *If God was only from the Bible alone, then why are there so many other, older religions? Who was the person there at the beginning to verify that there is only one true religion, and which religion is it? Isn't it possible that even the Bible had certain tailor-designed facts to fit the author's vision to the reader? If Jesus was White, then why did the scripture tell that he had wooly hair and olive skin? If Eve was real and a White girl, then why did scientists find the oldest DNA of a human being to be that of a Black woman?*

Her spiritual quest was always in the terms of, *What is your purpose in life, and to whom do you serve in your heart?* She *truly* believed in GOD and was surprisingly calm when she realized that in this dream-like state that she was in, she was now standing on a glass floor that was over the heads of the people at the gala, including her own, physical, impregnated body surrounded by the masses. Her senses relaxed further when she saw the ambulance medics rush into the room to retrieve her frame. She heard one of them yell, "Her breathing is slowing. Emergency C-section! Take them across the street. The baby is gonna make it if we work fast." Rainia was now comfortable with letting go. With a new form of vision, she looked up to observe an enchantingly and transonic view. From the other end of the room, a spectacular show of pink, purple, and blue refulgent, orb-like lights had started to accumulate from every direction and were now settling opposite from her in the distance. She started to laugh, as one by one these orbs turned into people she had lost along the way. So typical of life; she was dying *AND* going crazy.

***

The first to appear floating toward her, young and beautiful again, was her 'Gramma Marie,' who had recently passed seven months ago after a lengthy life of fine-tuning the family with her honor, her hard work, the life-lessons she gave freely, and her unconditional love. That was the only White woman besides her mother and Sally who Rainia had ever witnessed work themselves into the ground for the sake of loving their families. In fact, the day the old woman had passed, Gramma Marie was at her kitchen table, canning her final jar of pickles and actually writing "Last Batch" on the label when her head fell back like a long-overdue rest — and she was gone. She knew that she was going to die and had proudly served her purpose.

Rainia knew that she would see her again, but not so soon into the middle of serving her reason for being, and not like this. She sort of felt like she was being cheated, even though she had always known that human beings, as an animated, cognitive species, had to come from somewhere, go somewhere, or be somewhere for a cause, for all eternity, as eternity evolves, or so she thought, in any given manner, at any given time.

Gramma Marie advanced in a split micro-second from across the room to Rainia's face and said, "If you do as your good heart tells you to do, then the other side, well, it's somewhat whatever you expected it to be once you pass over! As you can see, I have myself a fresh, new look. What do you think, Rainy?" Gramma twirled in front of her like a diva fashionista.

"Gramma, you are *Fabulous!*" her granddaughter remarked in a wonder-struck thumbs up.

"Oh, please, we were all sent here right away for your benefit. You see, Rainy, the Big Boss feels like you are a prime example of why He still loves us so. You, just like all of us, are one of the many impetus-creating reasons that He allowed the world to receive and mistreat His only son, and help to save every other fool who keeps running from Him. You, my dear, just as we all are, are the reason why babies are still being born, and miracles are given the OK to go," said Gramma Marie.

Rainia thought about any hi-tech pre-natal pills that she may have taken and started to try and remember the name of her now forgotten Dr., so she'd have someone to sue in the court of Heaven once her doctor passes on.

As all of the other people she recognized started to come forward and clap with a thundering strangeness she had never heard before, the glass floor beneath her mules turned into thin air. All that she had known in this life disappeared before her eyes, as the scenery then changed to what seemed like outer space or something. *Wait! I have seen this before, this weirdness, many times, in fact!* It was the same kind of small and speedy, teeny, tiny sparks of lights that appeared to her anytime she would fix her eyes on an object for a while. Sometimes she could see them just staring into a blank, brightly lit white computer screen. She'd always thought that they reminded her of fluorescent sperm cells, or insane, miniscule fireworks rushing to serve someone or something, going a million miles per hour in all directions. She'd even imagined a sound to go along with the visuals.

It was something like — white noise. She'd always wondered if those were actually souls or spirits, or if it was just her needing to see an eye doctor about that, but too afraid to ask out of fear of a cancer scare or something. She even thought about the head injury she had suffered as a child that may have linked itself to the afterlife. Everyone around her had transformed from human form to a strange, electrical energy once disembodied, and quickly joined what had appeared to be a freeway among ga-billions of freeways around them. Still being able to speak with her voice, Rainia asked her Gramma, "So... it's all true, huh?"

Gramma admitted, "Yes it is, dear. Everything you have ever wondered, good and bad, is all true. Every religion, culture, and race is right when it comes to the good of humanity using peace. Ultimately, there is only one God and one Son, and one meaning 4 peace. That's why there will never be another peaceful human being who could be born, knowing and speaking all languages except for Christ. Jesus, even when in the body, was an all-people's person. He proved it in every way. It's true."

Rainia cracked up laughing, "Whatever. And Jesus was Black."

Gramma hesitated, "He was, like in an Arabic or Indian way when he was on Earth."

"I knew it! Now just imagine if he and homegirl Mary Magdalean had really hooked up, had a kid, broke up, and weren't together. What kind of back child support he would owe her? What would the post office picture look like if the Son of God was a 'Most Wanted' for arrears? He'd probably owe universes or something. And to tell you the truth, that sounds like some Black issue. That would explain why the most prominent Black attorney that we have ever seen in the US was called home 2 prepare for this 'Vincci Code War'. He got a brain tumor and died just thinking about the case. Ha, ha, ha!" Rainia kidded. Then a surge of shock and light ran through them all, "Ooooh! What was that?" she wanted to know.

Gramma panicked, "You'd better knock off the Jesus jokes. We can never tell if God is laughing or ticked off, so stop it — just to be safe. Uh... sorry, Almighty. Just a little joke, Johnnie C. She's new to this realm."

Gramma thought about it and laughed at Rainia's humor herself and continued, "I see you wanna be a comedian, so this may take awhile. Let Granny take you to school and to church! Now try to think even deeper than just black and white. Even if God could be married, or had even captured the essence of female in His Image, if you will. No one has ever seen Him, but trust us, He's very much *Real!* He sends out His Love to us everyday to announce His existence. The theory is like this world and the people in it. It's not living without the light and energy of the sun. A woman's egg is round and full of ingredients, like the Earth, and travels through the uterus on one mindless, pre-designed course, and waits for life to fill it up, before it is washed away like a useless unlit rock or a dead planet, period. It's nothing. It ain't much without the light and presence of the lively, but already an entity being, called, 'a sperm'. The sperm is the thinking machine. The carrier of the spirit. It zig-zags about, making right turns and lefts, trying desperately to deliver its enlightened message to the lonely, dark world of an egg. The race against time and space and the fate of what will be will ultimately decide if the soul can unite with the body. If so, the female starts to grow in human form. Somewhere, she decides if she wants to grow up to be an egg bearer or a sperm maker. It's all the same, because she is he, and he is she. They are one for a time. Hey, even the egg lights up when the two unite under microscopic view, declaring the start of a human presence with a purpose. Are you still with me, Rainia?"

Her granddaughter confided, "Ah... no. I'm kinda lost in the dark on this one."

Gramma Marie became even more excited, "That is the grandness of the Great Almighty, because the darkness alone could never, ever, figure out how to make light, or destroy it, and without darkness, the light would not know where to shine. So the light of the sperm cell has no choice but to link itself to the dark beauty of the egg, making us, through our decisions and life experiences, a soul, for whatever roles we need to take. All soul's events have greater reasons. Even miscarriage, still-birth, and abortion. These allowed events are all a part of life and death and actually are the only way in which spirits can move around. The marriage of light and darkness. The foolishness of it all is that the darkness always denies that the Almighty had created the darkness too. Ultimately, it can't win for loosing. Therefore, dark-forces will forever be a servant in the end, no matter how the story begins, as Mother Nature and Father Time are in this courtship romance."

Rainia tried to keep up with her Gramma's logic.

"Opposites attract, and men and women conceive to make more men and women, which, in turn, turns out more scientists, inventions, theories, and facts all designed to try and make us more Godly. We want to fly, kill, create life, and send out a voice of command to prove that we exist. But really, we are only in each of our actions, confirming that God exists, until our spirit passes, announcing death. Life and death are the all-true confirmations of God. Even the biggest Atheist in the world has asked God for something in a time of near death need and has been answered through prayer. An Atheist is, in fact, a person who is just merely undecided, only because they don't trust 'Man's information'."

Now Rainia was truly, 'Buyer Beware'. "Gramma, I'm not sure if I trust your information. Did you go crazy? Does everybody go crazy over here? Don't tell me that 'Heaven' is really 'Shady Acres', plus a shot of heroine, followed by a verse from the King James Version?"

"That's your opinion, Rainia. And rightfully so, because the Bible was written by men, as was the Koran, the Dead Sea Scrolls, and so on. Man has yet to discover something which was not created by man's own hands, as far as the intellectual goes, therefore, each man must be a part of something bigger, but what? The atheist says that he is a scientific evolvement coming from the particles of stars. OK! What better way to admit that God exists? In fact, if you draw the universal image of the star, it resembles a human with its arms and legs outstretched to either side, looking straight ahead. Stars are energy, light and life commanded by a force as is the heartbeat of a man connected to the same force that commands it to operate. So the atheist realizes that the force of energy must have *come* from somewhere, and they do believe that it must *go* somewhere. If they did not believe in anything at all, they would not answer to the call of their own name, nor respond to any human exchange of communication or activity, but would remain silent from birth to death. They would have absolutely no thoughts or opinions at all resembling the non-existence of any worldly ideas, any God, or self that was not self-designed. Total non-communication! And that is anatomically impossible, unless you are born in the woods, left with caring, invisible, non-communicative creatures, and, somehow, you are able to survive to adulthood. There is no such thing as an Atheist. Somewhere, this person has to have heard of a God, or have heard the terms 'Atheist' and 'Christ' to have even formed an opinion. All of this is information, just as complicated as his or her own DNA, which no one can take credit for. The information was passed down from somewhere, and they can't help but wonder, 'Where did the first human get their ideas? Why am I here? How did I get here?' just like everybody else. So what is 'I'? I is a question. WHO, all in the same, but from what point of origin? Hmm...? Free will or having been sent? Of course, we were all made and, therefore, sent from that point of origin which was not of our own free will."

Rainia was thinking, *I already believe in God, so where in the hell is this going? My Gramma is looney!*

Gramma Marie made a throat-clearing sound, "Sweetheart, there is no privacy of thought in this realm; all of us can hear you. *Dumbass!* But like I was saying, once we'd arrived into consciousness here, we then have somewhat of a free will to believe anything we choose, but in the end — when the soul departs from flesh — there will have been a cause or purpose for each individual existence. If a child is born dead, best believe that it could be due to improving the medical research on a disease, malformation, to shed light on another soul in someway, or maybe to just break even. Bottom line? Don't mess with God. Only His Will, will be done, and not a minute too soon. Oh, and to clarify our current whereabouts, we are now in your physical head. Your brain, girly!"

Rainia was now very confused, "Gramma, you just cussed and said about two whole hours worth of bullsh–! Well, a whole lot of mental stuff. So why are we in my head?" she asked. "I always thought that when you die, you go to the Pearly Gates first, and stand there and kick rocks while St. Peter, or somebody, goes through the list on the Golden Clipboard, tediously looking for your name and social security number, and all the shit you did when you were alive, while he's raising his eyebrows, texting Jesus back on his cell phone, and wearing those ugly librarian glasses with the fake gold chain. Oopps! I just cussed!"

"Don't be so damn DUDDISH!" Gramma said to Rainia, in her huffiest, deepest voice. "Why would St. Peter wear a *fake gold chain*? It's *platinum!*"

Rainia and the others laughed, as they made their way to their destination. When Gramma was alive, in the flesh, she had always used this word she made-up to describe someone who acted in an ignorant and un-called-for manner. Rainia recalled the many times Granny thought she was a dud. *Duddish, should be put into planet Earth's English language dictionaries as: Acting Really STUPID>i. e.>foolish. See also the entry for idiot.* "OK, that may have been a smidge country of me, or ghetto, but the purpose of this mind-mission is what, now that I'm dead, in my head?" asked Rainia.

Gramma Marie tried to take it down a notch, "First of all, although you have almost died a few times already, you and baby are not dead. The infant has survived the operation and is doing quite well, but *you* are still out cold in the finest of medical care. So don't even trip — yeah, I like that saying you and your fiancée have been using — but anyway, everything is perfectly fine. Second of all, in order to watch a movie and appreciate it, you have to start from the beginning. We are all on our way to the beginning of your first volcanic, vivid memories, Rainy, and the purpose is to make you remember."

"Gramma... did you just say, 'Don't even trip?' Remember? Remember what?" Rainy asked in sheer denial.

"When you wake up, you will have written the book," said a man's voice which she was sure that she knew well. He sounded like he was talking from way in the back of a room. As she tried to picture who it was talking to her, he added, "This is the book that will help to change the world. God even wants the dirty, the low-down, and the unfortunate to reconsider His Love. That's what this is about. This is your entire, unbelievable, and unique story, and to us, it holds more value than your beautiful lottery."

Rainia turned to look in front of her at a moving group of figures, as everyone said in a singsong voice, "Yes, ma'am, welcome back to 1974, Milwaukee, WI, 29th and Locust."

Rainia watched her long-forgotten memories become clear, in fear of the miscreant and, with major anguish.

"Oh, God, do we really got to do this?" she sighed.

"Yes! Everyone here is going with you, so brace yourself," said Gramma Marie.

***

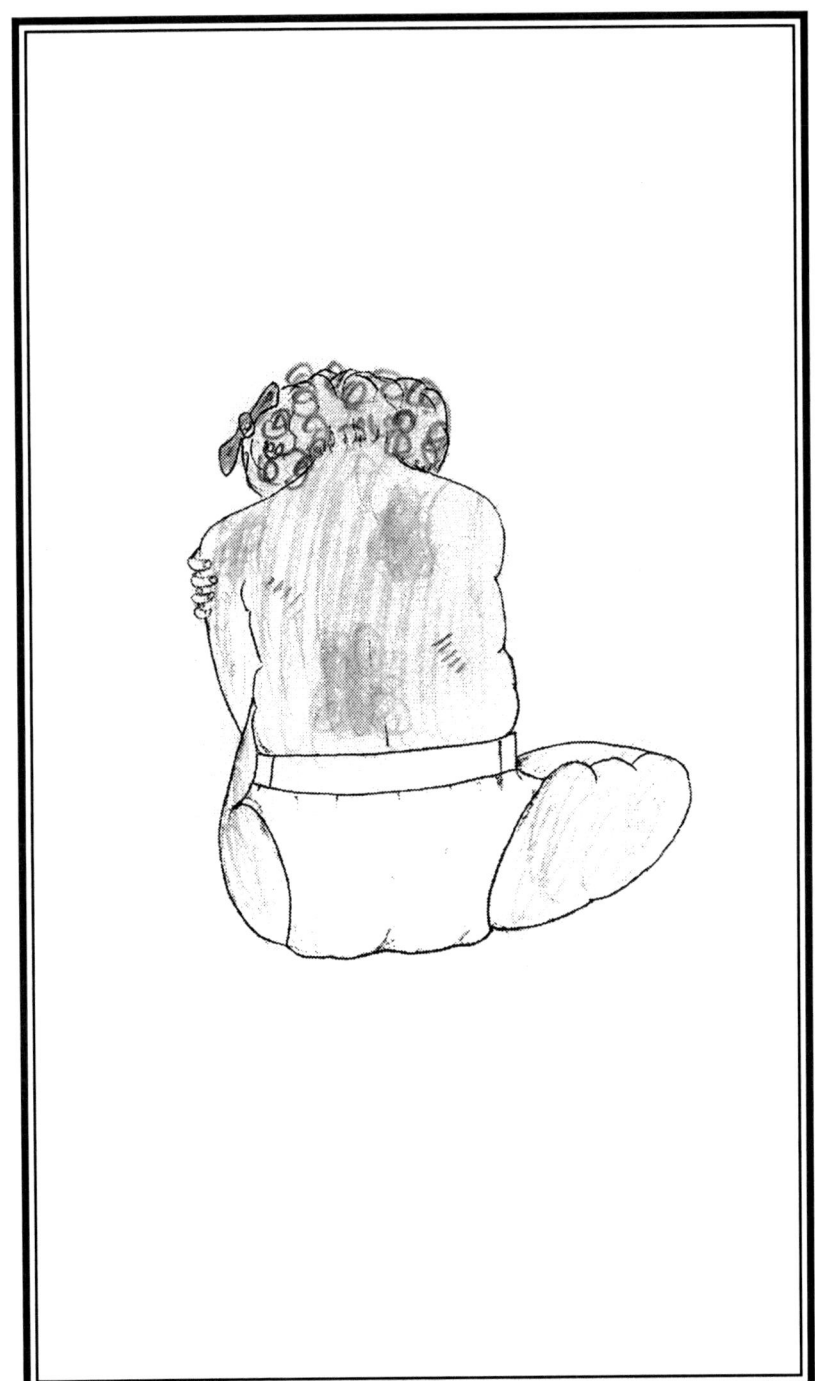

Chapter Three

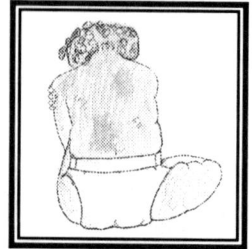

Two Again

She knew right away that it was going to be even harder for her to witness all that she had survived than to have lived it. Rainia didn't wanna see it, "Can't you just send me to hell and get it over with?"

"Shut the hell up and float," demanded Gramma, just floating around the outside of the yellow house with the green awning over the big front window, and going in through the front door was frightening. All of the angels, if you will, that were with her kept explaining to her that it was not fear she was feeling now or then, but the presence of GOD, Himself. In fact, they also revealed to her that the orbs of light were indeed what she had perceived them to be, only to add, they all are a small source from the energy of life, past, present, and future, serving in a purposeful way. "His Will, will be done. This would explain the voice of reason in each person's head," they proclaimed.

The guy unknown sounded like he was getting closer, "Feelings of being watched are constant, even when you think you're alone, because you're never alone. If these words that I am speaking right now were written in your book, and they will be, and the reader was paying close attention, now would be the point of contact where they are actually going to put this book down, and stare into space, until they see us, the little scurrying, zooming lights. Then they are gonna feel like they are totally being observed, more so than ever before, in their whole entire life. Then they are gonna get scared and put your book down for a minute, cuz then they will realize that we have been there the whole time, watching every, little thing. EVERYTHING! Masturbation, stealing, cheating, murders, gayness, eating disorders, sexual abuse, other shamefelt addictions, and whatever they swore that no one saw. We {the scurrying lights}see it all; every moment of every lifetime," said the man's voice.

Rainia became ecstatic, "Hey, I thought that was you back there, Chaz!" said Rainia, feeling the power in his very much-alive voice.

"I look at you everyday, baby girl. I am so proud of you, too! We are all being watched at all times, perhaps by ourselves, or someone assigned to us, past, present, and future. Does this make any sense, Rainia?" Chaz asked.

***

Rainia suddenly stopped observing her two-year-old self and went back to all that she once knew about Chaz, and how very dear he was to her. He was the one that took her to church and held her hand in service when they were boyfriend and girlfriend. Then they would go across the highway and play a game of H-O-R-S-E with their Sunday clothes on, all grownup looking and shit, having a ball. When he was alive and her man, he was spontaneous and unpredictable. She never knew where he would take her, but she always had to go, and he took her many, many places, and showed her many good things about the world around her. He was about 4 years younger than her. He was the one that showed her how people lived when they had money. He came from a good, sound family that had a lot of equity and lived practically in a mansion out in Sussex. The crazy part was that they had both started out poor as all hell. When he was alive back on Earth as a human, Rainia first knew him as a playmate when she was seven years old, just coming from an abusive life caused by her twin brothers' father and from her real dad. Her new abuse at that time was that her then drunken mother would whoop her, about every other day, black and blue.

They were living on 43rd and Good Hope Road. Chaz was only about 3 years old when his mother moved him and his brother there in apt #6 right b4 she had arrived to live in #5. He was taken with

Rainia, and he used to chase her up and down the driveway of the townhouses that they lived in, saying how she was his girlfriend. But at that time, she denied the little White boy with laughter and thought that he was a sweet little guy. His real daddy had left him and his little brother when they were babies, and their momma worked hard in the Army to move them all to higher ground. She was a cute Private Benjihawn type and had the prettiest eyes. She eventually married a guy in the service who ranked over her, and so Chaz's not-so-poor-anymore family moved to Sussex with the new husband.

Chaz told Rainia before he had to move away that she would be his real girlfriend when they grew up. He was right. So she did not see Chaz again until she was older, at her girlfriend Ginny's house, on the run from her ex, J.C., 'Justin Carvey', and plotting to leave the house where she was living with him. Chaz had even went with her and helped her pack her shit, while J.C. was cussing and hollering throughout the house about how fucked up it was that she had some suburb White boy to help her leave him and he was White, too. Chaz reassured Rainia that J.C. could talk all of the shit that he wanted to, but he wasn't gonna stop them, and he was right. Once the rented moving van was packed and Rainia started it up to get the hell away, Chaz tried to steer her clear of running into the house next to the one she was leaving with the van they were in, because J.C. had parked his car in their driveway as a blocking point to try and make her stay. Rainia's old playmate from youth had even cracked up laughing when she killed about 3 or 4 gnomes while going over the neighbor's lawn to get around J.C.'s trap.

Chaz didn't mind helping her escape her unhappiness in that relationship. He didn't even mind that she told him she had a 2-year-old daughter. In fact, he wanted to be her daughter's daddy. Chaz was more than happy to accept Rainia back into his life. He knew that people would have a problem with their mixed-race relationship, her having a kid with some guy already, and her age up over him. But yet, he still displayed the older, colorful Rainia like an ornament of pride no matter where he took her. His family loved her, too. They all remembered her from when she was a small child and were glad to see the two of them together as an adult couple. He was the one who always told her to never worry about money because she would always have it, and get plenty more. He was right. He told her that he could smoke all that he wanted to, because cigarettes weren't going to give him cancer, because he was going to die young. He was right about that, too.

    Once, when they were visiting some of his rich White buddies at Grafton Lake, he played a real bad trick on Rainia in the lake water. They were all drunk off of Rollin' Rocker Beer and partying in the summery night air. The bonfire was going, and the moon glistened off of everyone's skin, showing a dazzling blue display of newly-tanned bodies. There were small, wooden rafts afloat on the shores of the lake, and Chaz, his brother Cid, Rainia, and a few friends were balancing on one, rocking it back and forth. Chaz dived off of the raft that they were standing on into the seduction of the black, slightly-chilly, moonlit, rippled waters, but he never resurfaced. Rainia, his brother Cid, and his other buddy were searching, trying to find him in the relentless, yet self-minding waves that had globs of seaweed feeling on their bodies as they scrambled about. A head would come up for air in a panic yelling, "CHAZ!" then go back under for more than hope. Every time a piece of seaweed touched Rainia's leg, she thought it was Chaz's dead body. Once Rainia started to loose it, yelling for his buddy to go and get help, but Chaz suddenly came out from underneath another dock that was down aways and was laughing, pissy drunk, and said, "It's nice to know that you care so much. At least I know that you guys woulda looked for me."

    Rainia and the rest wanted to kick his stupid ass that night, but they were just too glad that he wasn't really dead from drowning. He was everybody's pride and joy, almost like her fiancée, as Pooh is to her now. *Weird*, Rainia thought silently, as the orbs traveled, and she continued to remember Chaz. The ironic part of the true story she remembered is that Chaz ended up drinking in a boat with his brother and two other girls in that same lake a couple of years after he had broken up with Rainy to be with his ex-girlfriend, only to break back up with the ex and want Rainy back. His friend Jim had just seen Rainia, too, at the carwash a few days before his trip to Grafton Lake, and told Chaz that she wanted him back in her life. Mr. 2Cool was so glad and mad at the same time because he'd turned down riding with Jim to the carwash that day.

Rainia was working a couple of jobs at the time, and one of them was at a J-mart, where 9 days after Rainia ran into Jim, Chaz came in to see her, wearing black shorts and a white, wife beater. He sort of stood there, at the end of the register conveyer belt, looking at her like he was in a trance. He didn't say anything except, **"Goodbye Rainy. See ya on a rainy day."** Once again, he was right, but at the time, she just didn't get it.

She yelled for him to wait up because she was with a customer, but he seemed to have floated out of the door, never looking back.

When she got off of work, she went back to the carwash she had seen Jim at the first time to wash her car and to figure out what had just happened with Chaz. Jim suddenly pulled into the bay next to her and saw her spraying the dirt off of her car. He then got out of his ride and walked over to hers. "Hey, Rainia, I guess you've probably heard, huh?" asked Jim with tears in his eyes.

"Heard what?" She wasn't looking at him but continued with excitement, "Guess what, Jim! I just saw Chaz in the store where I work at, up the street, about 25 minutes ago, and he was acting really weird like he was never gonna see me again or something."

Jim didn't say a word, as if he were in a state of shock, while she went on, "He had on some long, black, jean shorts, a white, wife beater, and he was saying good-bye and shit. He looked totally stoned, man! Is he still doing acid?"

Jim, Chaz's best friend for the last 12 years who was Black and always stayed on 39th and Roosevelt, was breathing real hard, trying not to burst into tears. He walked over to Rainia and grabbed the sprayer from her hand, "That's what he was wearing when he drowned last Sunday, boating in the middle of the night, drunk. He was rowing the small boat that he, his brother, and a couple of chicks were drinking in, when one of the girl's dropped her beer bottle into the water and reached out to get it. The small boat abruptly started to rock, and b4 they all knew it, it had turned over. He was the only one who didn't come back up. The search divers had to net for his body till sunrise." Jim wiped a tear and cracked a big smile, as he continued to blast the water on her tires, "The funeral was yesterday, and it was nice. He looked good like he had made a major business deal. He even had a pair of slick-ass shades propped on his hair like he did when he was hangin' out. You missed him in that suit though. The nigga had on a fuckin' Versachi, and his hands were folded with his pinky propped up, nicely iced. Yep! My best buddy in the world. He's my brotha. He's already buried."

Rainia turned towards him wearing a smile, then her face went blank, as she remembered how many times her and Chaz had washed their car together, having the time of their lives, in the very same 'Do it Yourself' carwash that they were now standing in. That's the kind of person he was; she could wash her car with him and it would always be the bomb. Now she would never see him again. She also thought about how glad she was to have seen Jim the last time to relay her message to Chaz about getting back together. She could feel her sanity starting to unravel.

Jim switched from rinse to soap on the carwash sprayer dial, "He was coming to see you at your job earlier this week at the bus company. He also knew something about your second baby daddy whoopin' on you all of the time, and he was planning to fuck him up and come and help you pack your shit *again,* so you and your kids could come stay with him in Sussex. He really loved you more than u knew. After he and Donna just couldn't go any further, he was always talking about how he wished that he could just find you, and get you back, and marry you, because you were the one. He was so fuckin' glad to know where you were working, but his job at Quaid Grafic Imaging, sent him out of town — the weekend that I told him I saw you. They sent him to Lake Grafton, and you know how Chaz was. Shit! He turned the trip into a party, and there he died. I know that's how he wanted to go, but I know that he really *was* looking forward to getting back @ u. He told me exactly all what he had planned to do to get you to listen to his plight, and how stupid he had been for letting you go. He was gonna send you roses; he knew how much you loved flowers, Rainy." Jim was crying as he told her this. "But I guess he got his wish after all. He got to tell you goodbye, and that is real love. I believe you saw him. I wish I had. I gotta go and get drunk. I can't stay here. Take care, Rainy. Sorry." He hugged her for a moment while she cried, and then he got into his car and left. That was the first time that she could remember being pissed off at God for taking who she swore was her soulmate, right when they were getting back together.

That was the first real, deep, and true pain she had ever felt, of loosing someone who was close to her heart. He was the best boyfriend she had ever had before she'd met Pooh. Chaz was a gentleman, and drop-dead gorgeous, with blue eyes, and wavy, thick, shiny, sandy-blonde hair. He was full-blooded Irish, built like a middle-weight champion, a drinker like she, fun as hell, with a ghetto accent, and big money. She loved him unconditionally, but the sex part of their relationship was kinda lacking, cuz they were always so fuckin' drunk that it was always a bad call.

He was honest with her at all times, though. He would tell her about the girls he partied with and the things that he would wind up getting drunk and doing with them. Chaz was the realest, most honest nigga she had ever met; she had to respect him. He also told her that he couldn't be with her any more cuz 'Big nosed Donna' wanted him back. Rainia loved him so much that she told him to be with the one who made him most happy. He said he hated Donna and knew they could never be happy, but he had been so used to his ex-girl enough to give it one more chance, and he didn't want Rainia to get hurt in their twisted, love-hate relationship, because he loved her too, maybe even more. But Donna had seniority, because he had been with her for so long. She was his high-school sweetheart, and he had to try one last time. Rainia respected the truth and his cause for love, so she cut it cold and backed down to Donna 'The Bitch'. Rainia let him go and find his way.

She was so grateful to God in letting her have that hope to get together again as a couple, after all of those years, and then seeing him earlier that day. But, sadly, it had turned into a last good-bye. He was just a ghost. She wanted to die too. She would come to long for him for the next several years, until she would meet her fiancée, who made her kind of forget about him. Chaz had been dead for nine years now. He was wise beyond his years, and somewhat of a prophet. Up until recently, he was the greatest love of her life at only 22 years old. And she believed it until she was 32 years old.

When she was 22 and they met again at Ginny's on her escape from J.C., he had just left Donna. He was very heartbroken about it. He never let it show, because he always appeared to be happy, funny, and super, reality-show-stopping cool. Something neat or hilarious, or unbelievable in conditions, always occurred when Chaz was around. Everyone wanted to be with him at all times. Rainia was living with Ginny, moving to Brown Deerville, when they hooked back up as boyfriend and girlfriend and were somewhat living together. Between the two of them they partied hard, every single night, with so many people.

Once, when they were high off of acid, her and Chaz were staring at a wall and laughing, while sitting on the love seat in her room, when suddenly, the wall had opened up, and they saw fingerprints off in the distance. "Rain? Do you see the same shit I see?" he asked her.

Rainia, gulped with fear, "Is it a big-ass tunnel filled with," they looked at each other with widened eyes and said simultaneously, "Fingerprints!"

They both ran outside into the night air. When they looked at the trees outside, they saw tiny, green men jumping from branch to branch, as the trees swayed back and forth in the wind. She was getting all freaked out about never doing acid again when Chaz put his arm around her and told her, "The only thing to ever fear, is being thrown from the Grace of God. He sits on a big throne, watching us constantly. If He were to move His pinky finger, everything in the universe would be destroyed. That's how powerful He is. We are just high, for some strange and unbelievable reason, seeing exactly the same shit. I'm sure one day we'll know why."

***

She snapped out of her once-alive memories of him and heard him presently speak to her, "Only this time we are inside the tunnel together, and I get to help you do your thing."

So was very happy to hear his voice again, solid, vibrant and well, and obviously a little more Godly than she was, Rainia stepped out of her trance of their relationship's past and responded to his statement, "Let me get this straight! Because each life is a mission to meet a grand purpose, the only guidance we can follow is the voice in our heads which is coming from Whoever is watching?" she queried.

"Yeah!" said Chaz. "Now that we're here, I want you to know that I am here to hold you up. This will not be easy to watch. I remember when I died and you felt sorry for me. The truth of the irony is that I felt sorry for you, because it wasn't me who died, only you who had yet to live. It feels really good to be close to you again, although I hope your fiancée doesn't mind. He's a stand-up guy. I know I wouldn't a had a chance in hell with you, if I were alive like you once knew me and met up with you now. You guys are soulmates, you know. God only does that for certain people who He makes for one another, to seek each other out and help to change the world with their love for one another, and love with the joy that they seem to emanate like sun rays beaming on everyone. You guys share the same breath of life, blown in by the Holy Spirit to do great and wonderful things together for this world."

Rainia could not believe what was actually happening and how it was happening, but she continued with her response to Chaz, "For whatever good or bad decisions we make, we'll still end up good or Godly as we move forward for answers, therefore filling up the dark, or evil, with love and light by moving on, helplessly searching for truth and divine power?" she again pondered.

"Exactly!" he rumbled. "Although, it is still left up to each sound person to make the decisions of their course of action. The notion that we are never alone is indeed reality. Think of it as a cheat sheet in a major test concerning what the soul needs to move on," said Chaz, his voice laden with excitement.

***

Rainia looked over the scene from her first few years of life as she watched herself like a 1974 re-run of a TV show, her baby body quietly playing with her baby toys in that old, yellow house's livingroom. Her then 20-year-old mother washed the dishes in the kitchen sink while staring into space. Abruptly, the front door to the house opened, and a tall, lanky, young Black man walked in, past Rainia's tiny form without a word and straight back through the yellow house to the kitchen. It was like watching a scary movie. Rainia could literally see the darkness that surrounded her father's spirit as he willed it into the room with him along with his conjured-up anger to try and hide his obvious guilt of being out all night. Anmarie went to the clothes basket to retrieve a pair of peach, silk panties with cum stains in them from Kent's dirty dress pants, "Honey, I found these in the pocket of your pants. Who's are they?"

Kent started to snap, "Wash em and wear em, after you finish those dishes." Anmarie started to feel like a lowly soul but continued with the dishes, because Kent and her baby girl was all she had. Kent was looking in the oven, "Where the fuck is the food, dumbass White bitch?"

Anmarie hurried to the cupboard to try and prepare something with soapy frantic fingers. Kent, Rainia's father, grabbed her mother by the hair and snatched her from the cupboard door, yanking and instantly spraining her finger as it was still caught up in the handle. Baby Rainia was standing in the hallway and watching by this time, recognizing danger and starting to cry. Kent took the thick, black afro-comb from his hair and beat her mother with it, occasionally dropping the comb and punching and kicking her mom with his stylish, low-cut boots in between retrieving the comb.

Once he was tired of beating on her, his rage quickly turned to Rainia. She always tried to run as fast as her little, fat legs and soiled diaper would carry her, but it always ended with the same result. Her dad would pick her up by one of her arms, beat her tiny legs and body senseless, and then he would usually sit on the couch and smoke some weed. This day was different though.

***

"This was the day that inspired my mother to leave him," ghostly Rainia told her peers.

***

As Kent was whoopin' baby Rainia all over with the comb and telling her to shut the fuck up crying, something bad happened, '*Snaaaap!*' Rainia's little baby eyes popped out of her head. Kent had dislocated her right shoulder while she was in midair screaming with no sound because of the pain. Kent suspected, himself, that he may have gone too far this time, so like the punk that he was at the time, he dropped the baby to the floor and he left.

Anmarie was having some trouble, herself, making her way to the living room to see why her baby wasn't crying anymore. She began to pray.

"She didn't know that we were already here watching. How can I help them? I know I'm supposed to be helping them, right?" asked the spirit of Rainia to everyone around her in the spirit world.

The badly beaten woman feared the silence of her baby, who was somewhere hurt in the front room. "Why aren't you making any more sounds?" Anmarie cried out loud and hollered, as she fought with all her might to make her human body overcome the pain and fear to get to her only-born child. Toddler Rainia was lying in the middle of the floor, looking up at the ceiling, motionless. Suddenly spirit Rainia saw her baby self start to turn into an orb of light too and leave her tiny body. Up, up it floated to greet them all, headed right toward the present Rainia as she tried to make the orb go back, "No, not yet, you have so much to do in life!" cried Rainia to her toddler self as the orb lingered for a minute, then floated up to where she was to face her. Older Rainia felt as if she'd kissed her baby self and was flushed with the greatest of love rejuvenated in all of its splendor and glory. The baby's voice giggled. The orb went back to the baby's body and inside the heart area. It was a powerful surge of love that started her physical heart beating once again. Anmarie was screaming and shaking the infant to please not be dead. At first, with a small, faint whimper and then with a full-blown, blood-curdling scream, the baby-Rainia came back to consciousness and also to terms with her bodily trauma.

Anmarie was unaware of Rainia's dislocated shoulder for the time being. Right now, she was grateful and was running a soothing bath as she usually did for her and her baby to soak in, in hopes of adding relief to the instant bruises and branded comb marks that Kent would so willingly leave on their bodies before he eventually, and always, left out again. Rainia could not stop whining from time to time. The pain was a deadening throb that made her little stomach hurt. Anmarie was also having pain in her abdomen, as she was very pregnant by five months.

The bath water was always too hot for 'baby' to sit in with Anmarie, and as always, the battered mom reacted to the tiny, mixed, two year old with, "Shhhhh... it's gonna be alright." Her mother gently rubbed the whelps on her baby's legs. Anmarie moaned and cried so hard, like never, ever before. She prayed and prayed for a miracle or some strength to find a way to leave the man she was afraid of and yet so adored. The baby was trying to play with the soap but couldn't hold onto it. It was too bulky and slippery for her miniature hands to keep a grasp of. Anmarie suddenly had an epiphany. Kent was just like that soap, a slippery form of man made to chase dirt, not even worth trying to hold onto. Besides, the soap would always wind up lost in the bath until Anmarie would retrieve it once the tub drained or she searched for it blindly, passing it several times until she could get a brief hold of it before it was gone from her hands again. And that's the way their relationship was. He'd go out and do his dirt, come home to Anmarie to wash his sins with blame and fury, only to get lost in the filth of the streets again. Since she couldn't throw the baby out with the bath water, she decided to throw him out. Maybe there was a better brand that could caress her heart instead of coast right by it. She had just made herself laugh out loud. *But how would I do it? How do you throw an angry Black man out of his own house? The one time that the cops saw him hitting me, they just shook their heads in their patrol car and kept right on going. I'll figure something out, but right now, I gotta go.* Seeing as though she had to get ready for work at Stratford-Brigums, a factory job she worked third shift as a machine operator, she didn't have much time to think about the process of throwing Kent out b4 he killed her or their baby. She had to pull herself together.

Once dressed, plastered in 'Coverup Girl' makeup, and ready to go to Big Mary's house, Anmarie and Rainia did a small dance in front of the front door before leaving out. This was something that was like a tradition for Rainia; a dance of hope. The baby would always be so happy to leave that miserable yellow house. She would bend a little bit in her knees and bounce with joy, whelps and all.

Her mother caught on to the jig and made up a song to go with it, "The old gray mare just ain't what she used to be, go out and see the world today, maybe things will change for me." Rainia would always kind of hum in that cute baby way because she couldn't sing the words yet. "Come on, Rainy, go bye-bye to Big Mary's."

Rainia grabbed for her mom's hand and started to cry from her dislocated shoulder pain. Anmarie picked the baby up and walked her three houses down to the babysitters. She was running late to the bus stop. Big Mary and her husband Duke were a nice old couple who'd never had kids but were just crazy about their mixed, little cupcake, Rainia.

Since she was a mixed baby, they liked to call her 'Rainbow'. Big Mary was so absorbed with the baby, she refused to take any money from Anmarie to watch her. She said that Rainbow was her baby sent by God that she never had. She loved that baby so much, she was torn between telling the social services about the beatings of the infant to save her, and the fear of losing Rainia forever to the system. She was too old to adopt Rainia herself, according to the social worker. Oh, yeah, the elderly woman had called and asked a lot of questions about the procedure. Big Mary was smart enough to check into things before jumping into them. Since she could not benefit by telling of the abuse, she never missed a day where she would pray for the freedom of Anmarie and Rainia. As the old, heavyset woman sat the infant on the couch next to her, she noticed the baby scream as she took off her coat.

Duke jumped up out of his rocking chair and made his way across the room. "What dat young fool done did dis tam?" he said to his wife looking at his Rainbow with furious and concerned eyes. Big Mary got the coat off of the child and lifted her shirt up. Whelps were everywhere, some with small-scabbed beads of blood, raked across the baby's back. She took the baby's clothes off down to her diaper, and the baby had bruises, whelps, and nail marks on her arms and legs as well. Rainia smiled at them as she tried to clap her tiny hands, but the baby couldn't even lift her right arm up.

The baby was whimpering and trying to climb into Big Mary's arms. "Duke I believe dis chiles arm is outta socket." They both broke into tears.

"MARE! I know you been scared to call da people on dem youngins, but if we loose our Rainbow to da system, it be a damn-sight better din going to her funra!"

Big Mary picked up the phone and called the number she somehow knew by heart. She reported all of her concerns, anonymously, while she prepared a small meal of cut-up fried-chicken pieces for the baby to eat. The three of them laughed and played and hugged deep into the night hours, as if they would never see each other again. Rainia was sleeping soundly in Big Mary's bed when the doorbell rang at 3:12 in the morning.

"What the–" Big Mary went to the door to find Anmarie standing in the cold, shivering, and saying in a whisper, "They sent me home early, Mary; I kept throwing up yellow shit."

Mary looked at Anmarie's face and could swear she was looking at a dead woman. Anmarie was so pale and lifeless that all Mary could whisper back to her was, "If you love that baby dat you getting out my room, den you would take her and run! Run home to your momma or somebody." They were trying to keep their voices down, as Duke was asleep on the livingroom couch, snoring loudly. Mary followed Anmarie to her bedroom with Rainia's coat over her shoulder. She took it off her shoulder to give it to Anmarie, who was about to explain why she couldn't just up and leave 4 her parent's farm in Medford, WI.

"I can't go home anymore. I'm an embarrassment in my hometown. I know it's the '70s, but they don't like niggers up there, not even nigger babies," said Anmarie, as her eyes started to tear up with shame while getting Rainia dressed. The baby whimpered in her sleep.

"Well, I know someone who you can stay wit," Mary huffed, as she put the coat on the lil girl real easy, carefully minding her bad arm. "Her arm messed up, Ann. She need a dockta."

Anmarie gave Big Mary a hug and said, "I'll take her to the Doctor as soon as these damn marks go away, or else they'll think I'm beaten her and probably take her from me, and you. See you tomorrow, Mary. I love you." Rainia was still sleepy in her mother's arms as she wobbled through the snow with a baby in her belly and one over her shoulder to their house.

Anmarie was in so much of a devastated mood that she did not even notice Kent's car in front of their house. Opening the door, she heard a moaning and grunting sound immediately coming from the back of the house toward the bedroom. Anmarie laid Rainia on the couch and went to the closet on the other side of the living room where the loaded .38 cal. special was always waiting for intruders, at the top of the closet in a shoe box, as instructed by Kent to use if a nigga broke in and he wasn't there to protect his pad. Rainia was up by now, and she slid off of the couch and went to the corner where she would always hide at when her dad would have women over.

Many times while her mom was at work, Kent was partying, and Rainia hit her corner. It was also in this corner where Rainia would take little pieces of her hair and twirl them around her tiny fingers until she pulled it out because she was fearful of the unknown, which eventually was about to happen. She was doing this now, scared of what was about to happen. Something bad was definitely going to happen. Anmarie set up the gun to fire as she tiptoed straight through the house towards the bedroom by the kitchen. The door was partially open, and you could now hear the headboard to Anmarie's bed crashing loudly against the wall, faster and faster. Anmarie turned on the light, and two naked, brown-skinned people flew out of the bed and into the corner, frantically grabbing at the bed sheets for coverage. Anmarie separated her legs to be able to stand like she was in an old western movie and cocked the pistol, asking, "Having a good time, dirty pigs?"

The naked woman in her room did a quick rendition of 'double-dutch' in one place, trying to think of something good to get her Black ass out of there alive, "I'm so sorry; please don't kill me," the young lady pleaded. It was Carol. She was really skinny with shoulder-length hair that she always wore in a bun with gold, hoop earrings. She was really beautiful, in a sort of big-nosed, perfect-smile, Black model type of way.

Anmarie was holding the gun with both hands, "Hell, I don't wanna kill *you*, bitch. It ain't your fault. I'm gonna blow me a nigga's brains out all over them white sheets, though," Rainia's mommy chuckled.

Spirit Rainia made a comment to her illuminated companions, "This may have been the time when the '70s term for 'Nigga' started to refer to a no-good Black man, and 'Bitch' was what he called his no-good Black woman."

The purple-eyed White woman waved the gun at Carol, "Wanna stay and watch?"

Carol grabbed what she could and made a break for it, calling back to Kent, "Stupid ass! You don't give no crazy White woman a gun when you beatin' and a cheatin'." Carol ran screaming to the front door and out into the cold of the winter night, barefoot and butt-assed naked with her clothes in her arms.

By this time, Kent had managed to pull on his dress pants and was trying to zip them up when he felt the cold, shaking, steel barrel of the gun being jabbed, real hard, into his temple. "Start walking to the front, you stanken-ass, rotten dog," Anmarie said this with a deepening monotone of execution clearly in the sound of her voice.

"OK," agreed Kent, as he walked in front of the gun, hands in the air, easily, toward the front room where the baby still sat in the corner, twirling curls and too entranced to move her body or cry, not even from the returning pain in her arm socket. Kent walked backwards over to the white drapes and told Anmarie something in a small voice, but she couldn't make out what he was saying.

"Hmmm?" asked Anmarie.

Kent thought about all of the shitty dirt that he had been sweeping onto Ann's heart for the longest time and gave hisself up, "Just go ahead and kill me; I deserve it." Kent started to pray while crying.

A full minute and twenty-two seconds went by of this crying and confessing until Anmarie broke out into a crazed giggle, "You know what, u piece-a shit? You ain't even worth it." She laughed harder now, but never took her eyes or the gun off of him.

He looked confused as he was trying to catch his breath, because now he was the one crying like a small child who had just received a bad whoopen, "Ssshhhhuh, ssssshhhhuhhh, what choo mean, I ain't worth it?" whimpered Kent.

"Like I said, you're not only NOT worth the time I'd have to do, but you're not even worthy of the bullet. NOW GET THE FUCK OUTTA HERE, NASTY PIG!" she screamed at him as he ran out of the house, grabbing his keys off of the coffee table on his way out. You could hear the car start and then burn rubber down the street into the distance.

Anmarie uncocked the weapon, put it on safety, and dropped the gun onto the carpet, running over to the corner that Rainia was sitting in, still twirling her hair so quietly. "My poor, baby girl," the relieved young mother said. She was now sitting on the couch, rocking with Rainia back and forth and singing, "Thank you, Jesus, for not letting me shoot that fool."

Anmarie felt a sharp cramp in her side. She stood up with Rainia and started to walk around the coffee table, trying to figure out their next move, when she noticed blood in a puddle where she'd just got up from. It was now running down her legs, warm and fast. "There's no turning back now. God must be taking the baby inside me back to Heaven 2 lighten our load. We'll be sad, Rainia, but we are strong girls, you and me."

***

Older Rainia watched to see if she could see an orb leave her mother's abdomen area as she dialed for help, but nothing happened. "Why can't I see the life leaving the unborn baby's body?" Rainia asked the spirits.

"Because for one, that person makes the full transition at the hospital in one hour from this moment, and two, that person is almost done serving their purpose which no longer concerns you at this time," said her grandmother.

I don't get it, thinks Rainia.

***

The ambulance came and took her mother and baby-self away. The ambulatory crew had also figured out that the baby's arm was dislocated and fixed it in the emergency room. The next day, her mother snuck them out of the hospital and they went home to grab Ann's purse. They left that yellow house with the green canopy over the big picture window with nothing but their coats, boots, and change of clothes on their backs, like refugees in the city of Milwaukee, WI.

***

"The pain of remembering is all too real," Rainia told her Gramma.

"No use you dwelling on the past yet," said Gramma Marie with a chuckle.

Everyone else joined in silence, and someone said, "We're not trying to be hard on you, Rainy, we just want you to remember what you have survived without being devastated. After all, what has not killed you off by now has made you one of the strongest women I have ever known."

Spirit Rainia tried to place the newest voice, and then she cheered, "Great Grandma Hodggins, is that you?" Since Rainia could only hear the voices of the people she knew and loved at this point, deciphering one orb from the next was like picking out one star from a cluster right now.

"Yes, ma'am. I remember when you were a little-bitty girl how quiet and shy you were. You would come up in the summertime to Medford and just clam up around adults. I often saw you sitting outside by yourself just staring up into the sky. I used to ask myself then, *What is happening to you back home in Milwaukee?* I always made sure I would have a lip-gloss for you or a sample of perfume to give to you, because you always liked my fragrances from the Avonly Ladies Collection. You were as sweet as a rose, but your eyes declared death. I never, ever would have imagined that you were being treated so badly," said Grandma Hodggins.

***

Suddenly, the force of movement carried them all to a motel room. The year had changed to 1976, in the wintertime, where Rainia was only four years old, and she was walking with her mother down the hall to meet her mother's new boyfriend in one of the rooms up ahead of them. It was one of those cheap Holloway Inn types back then. Ugly, dirty, and without the presence of the Bible. The kind with the florescent-lighted bathroom boasting the two plastic-wrapped cups on the sink, the 2 inch by 2 inch bar of soap wrapped in bubble-gum wrapping, and the face towel it was displayed on. The pissy, cigarette-smelling motel room was decorated in horrifying, plastic, dusty foliage, exorcist-puke-green carpet, a big, wicker-back, gold, ripped, vinyl chair next to a wobbly, round table with the dingy, shaded lamp built into the wiggly, scrapped, and burned table, gold satin, faded theater drapes, a dookie-stained, brown and booger-green bedspread trimmed in gold tassels, and one of those metal, fold-out suitcase stands with the rubber straps across that you always would trip over on your way in or out of the room. There was also a ragged TV in the corner of the room, complete with a coat-hanger antenna, close to the door on a little stand, chained to the chrome coat rack that had a new see-through bag for the cleaner's across the street, neatly folded over one of the coat rack's monkey bars like it was the only sane item in the whole room. The bag had made a clear statement for the whole cruddy scene; 'Do your dirt, wash your ass, take your clothes across the street in this here bag, and get the hell away from here 4 good.'

They had spent the night there. Anmarie was getting dressed in the bathroom while Billy was sitting on the edge of the bed with the brown and green floral blanket across his lower body. *Love Is In American Style* was blaring from the TV across the stale-smelling room. Rainia had just woken up in the chair across the room, still in her coat and sweating.

"Why don't you take your coat off?" he said to her. Rainia did not like Billy Jacksin. Something about him was bad. He was about 6'3", 245 lbs. built, with long, permed hair, trimmed mustache, a beard, and he had a gold tooth. Billy Jacksin was a pimp. He reached over to the lighted, wiggly, nightstand table, put one of the several icy, diamond rings onto his pinky finger, and poured some gin into his cup. He turned the cup in circles and poured some orange juice behind it. He swirled the gin and juice mixture and took a sip, making a twisted face.

He then reached for a roach in the ashtray that was clasped tightly with what looked like tiny pliers and fired it up. He got up off of the squeaky bed and inhaled real deep, walked two steps over to four-year-old Rainia and exhaled into her face. Rainia wrinkled her nose and started to cough. Billy sat back down on the bed and laughed.

Anmarie opened the bathroom door fully dressed and was stunning. She wore her strawberry blonde hair like the TV star, Farra Fashion did, with a rose on the side. Anmarie's dress was a black over-the-knee wrap at the waist with roses on it, and her feet adorned black suede stacks with wooden heels. Rainia always thought that her mother was a real-live doll that always had to go somewhere. Rainia started to feel a sting in her eyes, because she realized that her mother was about to "go out" again, and this time she would be left alone with this strange man who was sneaky. Rainia used to cry for her mother all of the time until her mother started to whoop her butt for it.

For the past two years, Rainia would be left over this person's house and that person's. Sometimes, she would wake up to people she did not even know in a house she was unfamiliar with. Although she would always cry by herself when everyone was asleep or not paying her any attention, something about this man was so scary that she could not help the sudden outburst of emotion, as she watched her mother walk over to her to give her the "Goodbye, Rainy" hug and kiss. She put on her brand-new, full-length, faux-fur coat.

Rainia wanted another hug, "Mommy, please don't leave me," she begged, holding onto her mother's neck so tightly, as if her tiny life depended on it.

"Just gone head; she alright." said Billy.

"OK, Rainy, Mommy has to go to the store now, so straighten up. I'll buy you a toy, ok? I'll be right back."

Rainia could care less about a stupid toy. She wanted her mother to be with her and only her. She ran crying all the way to the door, begging her mother to take her with her — but, SLAM!

Anmarie was gone, and Billy had grabbed Rainia up into one arm and sat her in the chair. "Drink some of that; it will make you feel better." Rainia shook her head 'no' as he poured more orange juice into the glass and put the cup into her tiny hands. He made her hold the cup with his large hand wrapped around her small one and said, "Drink this shit; it ain't gonna kill you." Rainia looked up at him and was terrified by the sternness in his deep voice, so she sipped a little bit. "Drink it before I whoop your tail, girl." he yelled at her.

She started to ball again and drink at the same time. She wished she was dead. Everywhere she went, people were yelling at her, being mean to her, and making fun of the color of her skin. This kind of torture was different though. Something was about to happen.

Billy lit up another joint between his long, lady-like, clear, finger-nail polished, beautifully-manicured nails and smoked intensely, strategically blowing each puff toward Rainia's direction. "Come, sit by me," he said after about five minutes had gone by.

Rainia sat there looking down at the cigarette-burned, drink-stained, pea-green carpet and watched her scuffed-white, patent-leather shoes jump herself down from the chair and unwillingly walk her little, skinny, scared legs over to the green and brown, flowered bedspread. She knew that she hated this man. This was Mommy's new boyfriend, but he wasn't her friend. She imagined her real father, as mean as he was, kicking in the door and beating Billy up real bad. Then her daddy would take her to Medford to live with Gramma Marie and her aunt Halle where people were normal. Billy pulled the comforter down off of his-self and revealed red, leopard-print underwear. Rainia being four years old thought that his underwear was the most ridiculous thing that she ever had seen a man wearing in her small life, so she laughed. She laughed so that hard she almost peed her pants.

Billy looked at her like she was a 'Jerry's Kid', "What so funny?" he asked.

"You have stupid underwear," Rainia giggled, bursting out into another fit of laughter.

"Oh, that's funny, huh?" he asked and started to tickle her with long, hard nails. At first she was laughing still, but then the digging of the claws began to hurt her tiny ribs and started to become too much for her. Billy stopped tickling, "Let's play a game," he said, as he put her small hand on his underwear, but she resisted immediately.

"No!" Rainia said.

"Just touch it," he replied, as he pulled out this very strange looking arm-like thing. It was ugly and it stunk like underarms. Billy Jacksin glared at her with stoned eyes, "Just pet it like a doggy." He grabbed her wrist and forced her to touch him. She started to gag and cry. The man became frustrated with the child, "Oh, forget it, then. You ain't no fun to play with, uuhhlll!"

He got up off of the bed still toking, with his fire-popping joint rolled with a few seeds lighting up bright orange and then dying down between his teeth. Billy went over to his clothes and began to put his socks on. He reached into the pants pocket of his blue suit and pulled out some money. Then, he walked back over to the bed with his shoe-boot stacks in the other hand, and sat down. "Now you know what a secret is, don't you? You love your mommy a whole bunch, don't you? Here, take this dollar. No, take this ten-dollar bill, as a matter of fact." The shrunken, fiery joint in his mouth was now hanging from his lip. "Ouch! Shit!" he said, as he carefully peeled the burning roach off his lip and clipped it. "If you tell Anmarie about our game, I will make Mommy dead. You know what dead is, don't you?"

Rainia never said a word. She just looked at the door, hoping and wishing for this to be over soon.

Billy stood up and slipped into his powder-blue stacks that matched his three-piece, bell-bottomed suit. "Ziiiippp, ziiiippp," went the sound. In his stacks he now stood about six foot six or something. He put a fresh toothpick wrapped in plastic into his mouth. "That's some good-ass weed, girl," he said, taking the toothpick back out of his mouth, unwrapping it, and re-inserting it again. Just then, the doorknob started to wiggle, so he said quickly to Rainia, "Remember what I told you, huh?"

Rainia took off speeding to the door. Anmarie came into the motel room smiling, trying not to trip over her daughter who was grabbing onto her legs, "Told you I'd be right back, Rainy." The young woman looked at Billy, shifting the bag in her arms, and smirked, "Why are you just standing there in your underwear and zip-up boots like a queer?"

Billy fidgeted with the toothpick and looked down at himself like he was also surprised at how ridiculous he must have appeared, "Aw… uh… well, I guess that I'm so high right now that I done forgot to put on my pants and shit. Good thing you pointed it out, or I woulda just walked on outta here looking crazy. Heh, heh, heh."

Anmarie sat the brown bag down on the small, round, lamp table by the bed and reached in to retrieve a lemon pie from Authur Treater's on 27th street, handing it to her four year old. Billy rolled his eyes, grabbed his clothes, and went into the bathroom. Rainia looked at the warm pie in her hand and felt somewhat safe, yet somewhat unloved. This treat would normally be Rainia's favorite thing to eat and always put a smile on her sad, little face, but this time nothing could make her feel better than having her mother in her presence. The fur-fitted, lovely lady pulled out some orange juice and some 'TOP-It-Off' marijuana papers from the bag, setting it to the side for Billy, then she bent down and helped Rainia put on her coat.

The small child could feel the fire build in her stomach, as Billy approached them both, tucking his shirt into his pants. Then he took the shiny, long nail of his index finger, now dripping in diamonds, to tilt the paper sack's rim toward him and peek inside, "Damn, baby, you might be the best girl yet. You even remembered to get me a huney-bun. Stand-up and gimme a kiss, and, uh... be dressed and ready for tomorrow. I got some places I wanna take you to to show you off at. You got a sweet lil girl there. Bye, Rainia."

"I know! That's my best friend and my only baby. I'll see you tomorrow, Billy."

Rainia felt utterly betrayed by her own mother. It was one thing to leave her with strangers, all the time, but to leave her with a fraudulent, nasty, scary, evil man was unforgivable. She immediately became angry with Anmarie, as she watched her kiss Billy Jacksin goodbye.

Anmarie and Rainia lived a few blocks away from the motel and walked back to the apartment building on 26th and Michigan Street. "Momma, can you get a different boyfriend? I hate Billy Jacksin."

Anmarie stopped dead in their tracks of the slushy snow, bent down to her four-year-old's face, and said, "I really love him. He buys me everything I want. He gives me a lot of money all the time. He's good to me and you. I see that money sticking out of your pants pocket. He gave you that, didn't he?"

"Yeah," Rainia said somberly, thinking about what Billy had said at the motel about making her mommy dead if she revealed what had happened back there tonight.

"See, Rainy, were going to go a lot of places and have new stuff all the time and have a lot of fun, ok?"

"OK," said Rainia, noticing how happy her mother was about this mean man. She couldn't remember ever seeing her mom this excited about anything, ever. It was like she was a whole new person. Even still, Rainia couldn't help but think that Mr. Jacksin was the devil, and what years of torment were to come.

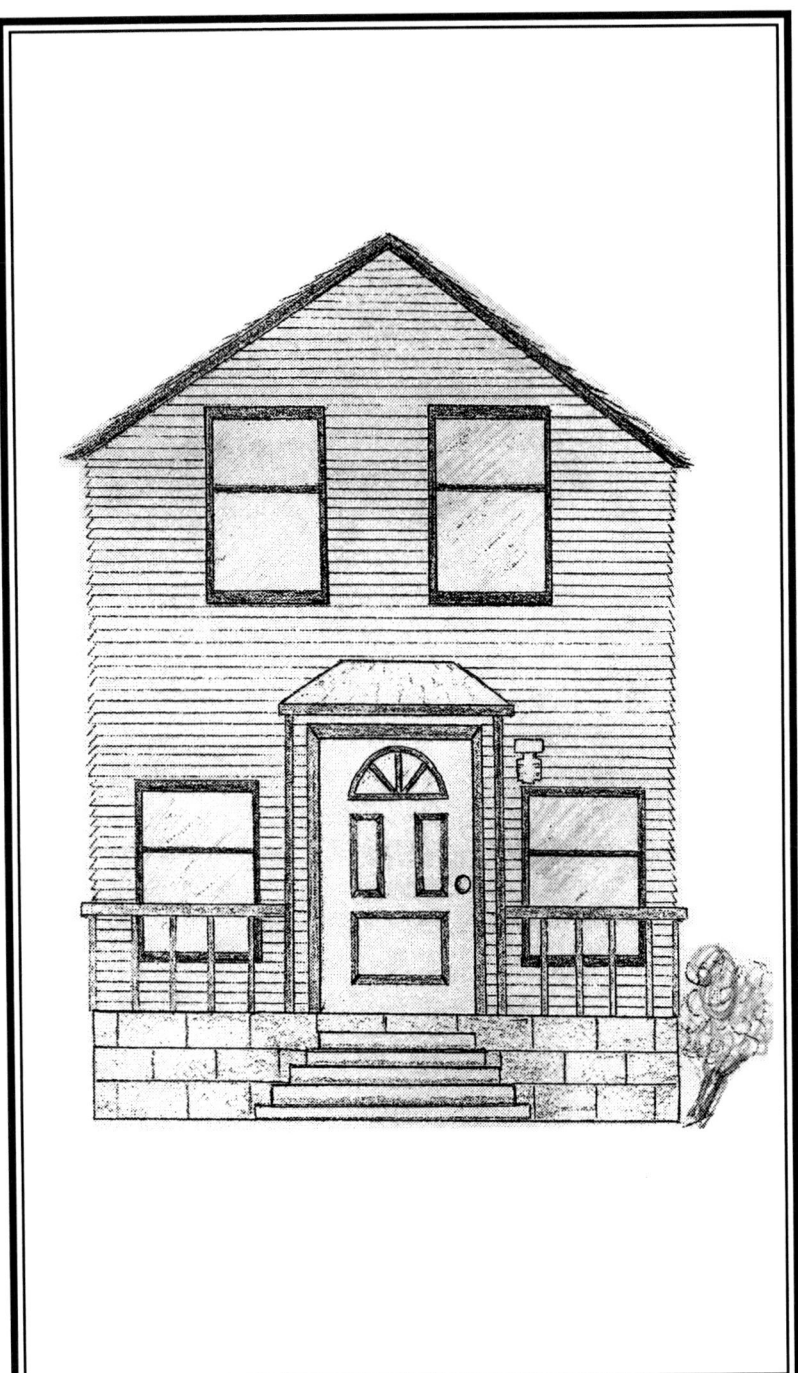

Chapter Four

Babbette's House

  Rainia thought it would be alright to let her mom think the world of this monster, as long as she never left her alone with him again. "Can I go to Babbette's house whenever you have to go somewhere?" she asked excitingly. "I like her doggy."
  Anmarie thought about it. "Sure, that little lassie dog is cute, isn't he?"
  They laughed and skipped through the front doors, through the wet-floored hallway, and got on the pissy-smelling elevator. Once on the second floor, the elevator door opened and they walked down to apartment number 202. Her mother pulled out her keys from her purse and opened the door. Their apartment had been bare until Billy bought them all this new furniture. A new kitchen table was in the corner, with a white leather and chrome bar with matching stools off to the side. The livingroom had a brown sofa-set that had bright-orange stripes that zig-zagged up and down with big chrome knobs on big chrome panels that were going up and down each side of its ends under where the arms would rest. Chrome and tinted-glass coffee tables matched the sofas. Orange, crystal-clear beads flowed from the ceiling by the front door like the early hippie '60s, and a big, black vase with tall, dust-collecting, orange and brown, fluffy feathers dominated the wall by the windows.
  Chubby, blown-glass, orange lamps with orange-beaded chandelier work hanging from their sides graced the side tables. On

the wall was a massive black-background, gold-framed oil painting of a king's palace and courtyard done in bright oil paint, especially showcasing the matching orange colors that stood out in its darkness. There were also tiny, white Christmas lights fixed into the painting that lit it up like a starry night that Rainia decided was the neatest thing in the world. When her mom wasn't looking, she would climb on the back of the couch, stand up on the back of it, and imagine herself as the princess in the painting wearing the beautiful, flowing dress, as she was staring at the moonlit path, off in the distance. Rainia often wondered where that path led to, and if it was a place she would recognize if she ever saw it outside somewheres in her real life.

There was even a neon-colored poster on the wall by the front door with a giant laying back on his elbow, totally stoned. He had little elves coming out of small windows built into his body. He kinda favored the 'Jolly Gross Giant', but he was also smoking a fat-ass doobie lit up with bright pink, and complete with wisps of smoke coming up from the end of it. When Rainia ran her little hand across the poster, it felt fuzzy.

Her mother was really into smoking marijuana. She always had a full or a piece of a joint in every ashtray in the house, and sometimes, after Rainia fell asleep at night, she would wake up to the smell of weed smoke heavy in the air, and people laughing to the sounds of disco. Rainy's favorite song to hear was "Boogie Nights". She would whisper to herself, "Dance to the boogie get down, cuz boogie eyes are always looking around, one two three I see you, dancing, a one-two-three," singing the wrong words while sitting up in her bed, moving her curly head to the beat and trying to silently snap her fingers, and then going back to sleep. She was a lonely child, but she knew how to party by herself.

"Come on up," said Anmarie, as she pushed in the white buzzer for four seconds and ran around the apartment looking for things. It had been a good week. Rainia had not seen or heard from Billy Jacksin and was hoping that he was dead somewhere in an alley. She was turning five tomorrow, and her auntie Nessara was coming up to see her and go out with her mom. Nessara opened the door, "Hey, boogaloo," and Rainia screamed with joy, "Auntie! Auntie! Yay! Momma! Auntie's here!"

Auntie Nessara was always as sharp as a tack. She was the most beautiful Black woman Rainia had ever seen. She was always dressed in a beautiful silky dress with matching metallic heels. Tonight, it was turquoise. Her make-up was always flawless, and even though she wore wigs, her hair was always so pretty and fluffy, like feathers stuck in cotton candy. She had the biggest, brightest smile in the universe, and Rainia knew she was just as crazy about her as she was about her Auntie.

"I saw Billy parkin' that big-ass, clean Cadillac downstairs, girl," Auntie said in a laughing voice. "You know he is a trip, girl. Let me tell you what he did the other night. We was all at the club, 'Cirkiss Cirkiss,' and Cheila silly ass came in, *right*. She was all high and shit, trying to get some money out of her purse to give to him. Girl, why did he start to get into his feelings talking bout, 'Bitch, where's the rest? Did you shoot up the rest of my money, ho?' slapping her all around the tables, honey. The shit was so funny because she would sway back and fourth in slow motion every time he slapped her, but she never fell. It was hilarious, like a scene out of *Carol Burnett*, or some shit. You know, high mutha-fuckas on heroin don't fall too easy? Me and my other girlfriends was laughing so hard I almost missed my turn 2 dance. The owner, Jerry, had to call my name about eight times to go on before I realized it."

By this time, Anmarie was laughing the shade of red right alongside Nessara. They were laughing extra hard after she mimed Cheila being slapped by Billy in slow motion with a spaced-out, one-eye-opened expression on her face, "One day that crazy, drugged-out bitch gonna get tired of his clownin' on her and she gonna fuck around and retaliate. He might even wanna quit dealin' with her, because when a bitch ain't even scared of what a pimp will do to her or doesn't respond to the pimp slap, then it's definitely time to regroup on some new hos. He better watch himself."

Nessara seemed to like Billy Jacksin. As they both sat at the table, wiping tears from the corners of their eyes, opening up bottles of fingernail polish to do touch-ups, and sipping on 'T.J. SWAN' cheap champagne mixed with Colt 45 malt liquor, the door gave a sudden shake. You could hear Billy on the other side, saying, "Why you got the door locked on a pimp?"

They both burst out laughing and Nessara said, "Get the door, bugaloo, before Billy come up in here slapping hisself."

"HA, HA, HA," they both were buckled over on the table with their heads down, their bodies writhing with pain in their sides from heaving into their diaphragm muscles. Rainia reluctantly opened the door and let in the devil himself. Every time she saw this creep, she would miss her mean daddy, more and more. She had not seen him for about three years now, and she didn't like the idea of calling this monster 'Daddy', ever!

"Hey, Rainia! What's happen'n', baby? Give me five."

Rainia looked at her mother, and her mother was smiling at them.

She gave him five, and he then laughed, saying, "On the black side, down low, too slow, " and moved his hand. Then he gave her a five-dollar bill along with a sickening sound that she would cringe just to hear, let alone understand for the next year, "Ehhhhttt, eggghhhh!" was the sound, almost like he was clearing his throat.

This freaky, sad, sick play of sound would come to be known as the "You know what I want to do with you later" sound. Rainia looked at him strangely, as he winked his eye at her and mouthed the words, "Remember what I said."

Tonight he had on his crème-colored, three-piece suit, with his crème-leather stacks, and a Dobb hat to match. His long hair was rolled into long spiral curls that laid on his back. To anyone else, he must have appeared to be a star. Maybe her mother and aunt thought him to be a hero, but Rainia thought he was the devil, and she somehow knew that things were about to get worse, real quick. It was just a matter of time. "Im'ma take yall on to the club and drop yall off. You lovely ladies ready, or what?"

"Billy, quit bullshittin' and fire up a joint," said Nessara. Both of the women stood up and fixed their dresses. Anmarie was wearing a champagne dress that tied around her waist, similar to her aunt's turquoise one. On her feet tonight were some really-cool see-through, glass slippers like the ones in the fairytale. She also had on a wig tonight, as well, and a big ol', perfectly-fluffed bouffant like an old, country/western singing legend. In fact, she even looked like her a little bit. Since she had Billy for a new boyfriend, she had changed a lot. She was even getting big ol' boobs and was gaining a lot of weight. She was still beautiful though.

Billy had taken his hat off and placed it on the table as they prepared to walk out of the door.

"Now you sure you coming right back to watch my baby, right?" she said to him.

"I'll make sure don't nothing happen to her," he assured her.

"Oh! Let me give her a hug and kiss real quick." Anmarie ran back inside the apartment, Nessara following, and hugged Rainia and kissed her cheek, "I love you, Rainy. Be good for Mommy, ok?" Anmarie said.

"Give me my hug, bugaloo," her Auntie said, as she hugged her niece real tight and walked her back to her room. "Just get in the bed and go to sleep."

Rainia got into her bed and lay down while her Auntie tucked her in. She kissed her little forehead and wished her sweet dreams. Rainia lay there with her eyes open, thinking about being the only kid in the house, the only person in the house. She longed for a sister. Somewhere in her thoughts, she drifted off to sleep and was awakened by someone taking off her pajama bottoms and underpants. It was the devil. He had come right back after he had dropped her mother and Auntie off at the club. Rainia was scared as she rubbed her eyes, "I gotta go pee. Get outta here, please. What are you doing?" Rainia resisted in a sleepy, angry voice.

Billy didn't care, but figured that he should let her go, "Hurry up and go pee then."

He let her go, and she ran to the bathroom and tried to lock the door, but his foot was in the door, and he opened the door all the way with his hand. "Get up there and open your legs while you go so I can see," he said, as he pulled out his stuff and started to masturbate in front of her. Rainia really did have to pee now, because she was scared of all the horrible things Billy was doing to her when no one was around, and the gross way he looked at her, and everything about him.

"I'm just a little kid. Why are you being mean to me?" she started to cry, as she looked up at him with teary pleading eyes that started to cry even harder as he started to ejaculate into the bathroom sink. Rainia's face was mortified to see such a nasty, demonic, yucky sight. "What was that — lotion? What is that thing with white stuff coming outta you?" Rainia cried. Why wasn't anybody able to see that Billy wasn't cool; he was a child molester. Oh, but there was much more of Billy to come. He would show Anmarie and Rainia a world of pure hell and torment like they'd never known before.

"Get some tissue and wipe that up for me, and flush it down the toilet. And stop crying, JUDAS!"

Rainia gagged, as he took her hand and made her wipe it with tissue. He slapped her in the head, "Oh, stop acting childish, Judas. It's just cum! Damn!"

"What's a JUDAS?" Rainia asked, in tears, balling and gagging, and looking away as he made her wipe up his sickness.

"You don't know who Jesus is and who Judas is? O.K., Judas was a trader who snitched on Jesus. Bitch-ass mother fucker is what he was. Got Jesus killed and shit, all fucked up on a cross so He could save us wretches, like me and you."

She could tell he was drunk because he stumbled a bit to the side, and she asked, "I didn't kill anybody. Why you say I'm a Judas?" while still crying and gagging.

"Because you're a little snitch. Shit! According to the fuckin' Bible, we are all born sinners. Bastard kids and kids with married parents. Don't matter! Cause we all ain't shit! Especially your little half-White ass. You're gonna try and tell Anmarie what goes on here. This is our business; she ain't gotta know about the favors you do for me. I'm gonna lie and say you're a nasty pig and you gone get a whoopinaghheeghnnn!" He started to laugh profusely and walked away saying, "Get your little nasty, hot tail in the bed."

Rainia ran to her room as fast as she could, put on her pajama bottoms in the dark, and climbed into bed. The little girl was terrified. Her real daddy was a mean man who had liked to hit on her and her mother, but this man was somehow much more evil. Right then and there, Rainia decided to never dare go to sleep or close her eyes around him ever again. She finally fell asleep after she heard her mother come into the apartment.

The next morning, Rainia woke up to a whoopen from her mother. "Get up, you little pig! Get up! I'm gonna beat your ass!"

Her mother had a plastic jump rope from Rainia's toy box and was hitting her legs with it, over and over and really hard. "Why is your pajama bottoms inside out, nasty ass, huh? Billy told me how you were taking off your pants and dancing nasty. You can't do what I do. I'm grown! GET UP, LITTLE PIG! NOW!"

Rainia was screaming bloody murder, "Please, Momma, please. I didn't do nuthin'! Please don't whoop me! I'm sorry for whatever I did! I won't do it no more! Mommy, please! I love you! Don't you still love me, Momma? Please don't whoop me! It's my special day, Mommy!" She held her hands out to try and stop the stinging thrashes, but the rope had a cutting pain that penetrated fire wherever it landed, all the way down to the bone. The little mixed girl hated her mother and Billy to death with every blow. It hurt so bad that she started pissing on herself, leaving the hot urine to run down her whelped legs. Anmarie saw that and became even more enraged. Then her mother grabbed the vacuum from the hall and dragged it into the room, using the cord to beat her with that. Bigger whelps rose from her skin like freshly-dug rows of planted and covered carrot seeds in a garden.

Anmarie beat her so badly that Billy came into the room and said, "Stop now, Anmarie, before you kill the girl." Billy shook his head and walked back into the living room to smoke.

When Rainia stopped making any sound in her crying, because of the overwhelming pain, that's when Anmarie finally quit, "I better never, ever hear about you doing no nasty shit like that again! You understand?" Her mom turned to leave the room and go talk to Billy.

Rainia nodded and silently begged into her pillow that whoever this Jesus was, that if He could be hung on a cross and save wretches, she hoped that He was tough enough to come and save her from this rotten life she was living. She had a real bad headache, and she couldn't breathe but through her mouth because of the snot that would not stop coming out of her little, shiny, red nose. Rainia put her fingers to her ear and cheek and felt that she even had whelps on her face. She hadn't done anything but lived to see another year. Rainia wondered why that was wrong? Was it because she was half-Black? Or half-White? Today was her birthday. She was five today. "Jesus," she quietly cried, as she tearfully lay in her bed, in the shear pain of the heartbreak, more than the unjustified beating in itself, "Jesus, please take me away," she whimpered into her pillow, "I hate this place. My mommy don't love me, and I don't want to be five anymore."

Weeks went by after that, and things just kept getting worse. Billy Jacksin was starting to abide by the laws of a pimp and the case was about the money. Fool in love Anmarie was getting hers alright, and every time she got her ass kicked, she took it out on Rainia. Anmarie was now often receiving beatings from Billy whenever he stopped by to collect money from her or babysit Rainia so Anmarie could go make some money. He would bring her stripper outfits that sparkled and shined with many colors, and some with fantastic beadwork that would make a belly dancer jealous. Many days, she would leave twinkling with black eyes, busted lips, gobs of hair pulled from her head, and a plethora of bruises covered with heavy makeup. Rainia was also whooped from time to time by Billy with his hand on her butt when she didn't cooperate with his sick needs, which was all the time. He had bought Anmarie this really-expensive, massive bedroom set that had a huge dresser with a small door at the bottom. This door provided a hiding place for her twice when her mother left. She stayed balled and crunched up with hardly any air for hours, hiding from Billy. *Jesus, please save me!*

That last time, though, Billy must have heard her gasp for air and snatched the little door open, yanked her by the leg out of her hiding space, and threw her up against the wall over the bed. She hit it so hard that she bounced off the bed and fell on the floor where she laid there in shock for a second. Her eyes blurred in vision, and she could feel the warm blood trickle out of her nose, as she unwillingly focused on a few crumbs on the floor. Then she saw his feet step in front of her, as he picked her up by her arm, shoving some tissue into her small hand. "Jesus, Jesus," Rainia cried.

"That shit don't work, dumbass," he said and took off her shorts and underwear. "Your mom is pregnant with a baby now. Don't you want a baby sister? I sho know I do. More fresh little stuff for me. Because if you don't be nice to me and stop hiding, I'll kill the baby and you'll always be alone, HEAR?"

Rainia nodded yes, closed her eyes, and drifted to that pleasant path in the painting. There it was, like she was out of her body, out of the hateful world, and in the garden that was her own. She tried to imagine a little baby girl who looked like her, playing with a bottle while Rainia pushed her in her play-buggy. She held her baby doll that she pretended was her sister and was silent with her eyes closed, swallowing blood from the back of her throat, as the tears overflowed down into her ears. Going to her painting was always what made the abuse time go by faster. She couldn't wait to have her sister in her arms. A change was gonna come.

Days passed by like a sprinter and so did the life in Rainia's eyes. She was ready to go up North but didn't say but three words for the whole trip, that she never did remember taking, up there or back 2 the Miltown. She was in a dead zone, always staring off into space.

It was the end of summer and the beginning of Fall now, and Anmarie was about six months pregnant with the expectancy of twins. Rainia was doubly happy to be having two sisters on the way, but she still wished for someone her own age to play with. Billy had called to inform them to get ready to go to a picnic at McGovern Park to meet his sister, Earlean. They all went and Rainia had found a playmate right away.

Earlean was a slender, beautiful Black woman, and her husband Andy was a happy, smiling Black man with a gold tooth off to the side. They had three, well-kept, dark-brown kids. Poochie (12), Niecee (6), and Fannie (11). They were so funny and alive with joy.

Fannie took to Rainia's hair. She took it out of the ponytail and combed it down her back with a comb from her purse, "Oooo... you look Puerto Rican, and you got some pretty hair! Anmarie, can I braid her hair?"

Anmarie let her braid it up, but Rainia thought it was a painful procedure that left her head sore, but the braids adorned her head like a crown, and she ran around the park so regally. She felt giddy and saddity as the sisters told her how beautiful she was and wanted to know if she could spend the night. Anmarie said no, of course, but Rainia was glad to have met them and admired the sister's closeness as she got into the red Cadillac to go home. She waved goodbye to the girls who held hands on the sidewalk in the parking lot of the park.

Rainia couldn't wait for her baby sisters to arrive. It would be nice to laugh and play with two cute, little baby girls who she could protect from all evil. It was a good day, except for him trying to stick his hand in her panties while her mother stopped in the gas station for a few things. He was sitting in the driver's seat, masturbating with one hand and was trying to feel on Rainy with the other. "Aw, fuck, Judas, here her ass come already. Act normal now!" Anmarie had come out of the door too soon for him. He shifted his rearview mirror, causing his big, fuzzy, strange, green dice to sway. At first, Rainia saw his eyes in the rearview, then she saw her own, as he spoke, "Just act innocent, Judas," as he fixed the steering wheel with the indigo fur trimming it. So she did.

But the days to follow that one would be severely ugly. Rainia had even developed a series of nightmares about that red car of Billy's. It was the same dream over and over again. She would be a grown woman walking down the street, and up ahead of her on the corner is a band of African warriors with spears, dancing around a giant black kettle over a huge flaming fire. There are several cars parked on the street by the meters. She can see herself putting money into a meter next to a car. The car is red. It is his Cadillac. She looks around in a panic hoping not to see him. She doesn't see him. She hears a small child crying. In the back seat of his car, sitting on the cherry-scented white leather is, herself. She tries to let her young self out, but all of the windows are rolled up and the doors are locked. She tries so hard to get herself out, even by trying to kick in a window, but she wakes up screaming.

***

"To this day, I don't understand that dream. I've only had it a few times since I've been a grown woman, but it still messes with me."

Ghostly Rainia waited for one of the spirits to add something to her comment, as they watched her painful past together, and then Grandma Hodggins said, "You will. You'll get it real soon. In time, that nightmare is going to pay every bill you ever got, and make you so much money that you will be the biggest pimp in the red Cadillac. By the time this journey down memory lane is over, I promise that you will get it."

Present-day Rainia believed in her Grandma Hodggins' words and continued to look on at her mother's pregnancy from years ago.

***

Time ticked on, and Anmarie was starting to show in a big, big way. She had become so big and grouchy that little Rainia really started to hate her mom. The pot-bellied meanie was downstairs talking to Billy, when she came into the house all beat up a couple of weeks later from the McGovern Park venture. Rainia hadn't forgotten what her mother had done to her on her birthday. When her mother started to scream in pain, Rainia secretly hoped that it hurt her twice as bad. She had whooped her daughter for nothing that day, just based on a lie from 'Billy the liar'. She watched her mother scream and yell for her to pick up the phone and call 911. Rainia saw blood start to pour from her mom's legs. For some reason, she had a flashback of her mom doing this once before and someone had died. She felt pity for her mom and remembered her sister's inside her mom's stomach. They needed her, and she wasn't about to let them down.

Now, with panic in her miniature hands, she frantically dialed 911. A woman's voice clicked onto the line, "This is the operator. May I help you?"

"My mommy is bleeding, and the babies are falling out, I think," said Rainia, with a shaking, worried little voice.

Her mother screamed in agony and distress, "2611, Michigan Street, Mitchell Heights, apartment 202. Hurry up!" Anmarie yelled. She sounded like she was dying, and Rainia was terrified that she would. So she prayed for the ambulance to hurry.

As soon as the ambulance arrived, Auntie came into the apartment after they were just getting ready to wheel Anmarie out of the building, screaming at the top of her lungs. Rainia was hiding under the kitchen table and trying to stay out of the way but yet still see what was going on at the same time. She could see the small puddles of blood drip-drop on by as the paramedics wheeled her mother out the door. Her Auntie had suddenly appeared in the doorway, "What happened, Anmarie?"

"Billy kicked me down the stairs; he's trying to kill me and the kids," her mother weakly cried and wailed in fear of loosing her pregnancy.

"I'll be up there later," said her Auntie 2 her half-dead mother with courage in her voice. "Come out from under there and sit with your Auntie. Everything will be alright baby, you'll see," insisted Nessara.

B4 that had happened, Rainia had been staying at the apartment with her mom for a whole week straight and once or twice to the babysitter's down the block. Rainia did not like going to that babysitter's house!

"I'm going to have to take you to Babbette's house, Rainy, and go out to the hospital to check on your mom, ok?"

Rainy hated it over there. Reluctantly, she grabbed her favorite stuffed animal, a big, gray, rat that was built up like, "Mikey Mouse," called, "Ratty," and headed over there with Auntie, hand in hand. Babbette was her White-lady babysitter from time to time when no one was available for free. Her mother had stumbled across her services while walking Rainia to her future school and kindergarten class not that long ago, and Babbette was walking another mixed child to his stop. She asked Babbette if that was her son, and Babbette alerted her that she was just his babysitter.

Opportunity knocked. Babbette had three sons, Steve, Kelsey, and Rodney. Steve, "The fine one," and Kelsey, "The nice one who was cute in his glasses", were teenagers, all heavy into heavy metal and rock, constantly walking through their house, fake playing guitars, as they blasted, 'Pinkus Floydus' and 'Stiks and Stones' and 'R.E.O.'s Red Wagon' albums, with their mother yelling for them to turn down the racket. There they went all day long, back and forth across the livingroom floor, making noises with their feet hitting the plastic, yellow runners Babbette had stretching from the kitchen to the livingroom, as they answered the door for their rocker, metal, head-banging buddies to go in the room, listen to the latest cut, and smoke weed. They wore "Gas-up" brand square-shaped, black, biscuit-toed tennis shoes with letters G-A-S UP on the bottom of the shoe, and tight, faded jeans that reveled how much ass and cock they boasted.

"Owwwww!" They would always be singing a song with an 'ow' in it. The jeans they wore even had faded imprints where their wieners always rested. Rainia thought that they were all cute, but the older boys were nasty for trying to draw attention to their things.

The eldest of the brood also wore T-shirts with 'Allis Copper' or skulls on them. Once, he even asked Rainia to come into his room to listen to his music. He was a seventeen-year-old metalhead/pothead. Rainia just stood in the doorway watching him smoke a joint. He asked her to sit on the bed by him. As she approached his bed, he grabbed her hand and tried to make her touch the crotch of his jeans. Rainia was already hip to that dumb game. She politely said, "No thanks," and walked out of his room, never bringing it up or telling a soul.

All the boys wore feathered, long, honey-blond haircuts and smelled of 'Ireland Summer' soap. The youngest one, Rodney, was an asshole with pure white-blond hair that shined like an angel's. He had an Indian and White friend that lived two doors down from his house that he told to call Rainia a nigger every day after the boys got out of school. One day Rodney did this to her and ran into the house laughing after Rainia was crying on the curb in front of his house. Rodney hadn't known about the bigger Black girl who had beaten her up on the sidewalk earlier that day for being too White.

***

"Hey, I remember that day like it was yesterday. That was the first real day that I was starting to get fed up with the bullshit people around me," said the present and older Rainia. To her younger self, as if her younger self could hear, she called out, "Get up and fight, little girl! Don't let them kick you while you're already down!" She yelled at herself like yelling into a crystal ball.

***

Suddenly, young Rainia was so pissed off and confused when she saw Rodney laughing that she went to beat the shit out of White-ass 'Indian Jerry', dragging him by his hair down the street, him crying, and her calling him a, "Honkey, white-bread chicken shit," and asking, "How you like it?" Little Rainia never did like Rodney one bit after that, or 'Indian Jerry'. Rodney always looked like he smelled shit and said it was Rainia, "The shitty spot." Rainia knew he would rather call her nigger, and she actually preferred nigger than shit. Shit actually stunk, and nigger was just a silly, made-up word for a person with brown skin. His mother wouldn't let him flat-out call her nigger, though, and she would go crazy if she heard him do it. He figured he could say the shit term for nigger instead and only risk a, "Shut up, Rodney! You're a jerk!"

He would come into the living room to where Rainia would be watching "Bug-eyed Bunny and The Road Rage Runner Show" and eating a big-ass bowl of "Johnie Applejohn's Cereal" in her face at 9:00 AM, knowing her mother didn't bring any food for her to eat in his face, right back at him. Babbette provided all the meals when she had a chance to. She was a hip-heavy, short, White woman, with a beetle-bowl haircut, and she wore tight-fitting, flowered, or dark-colored cotton and polyester pocket-less pants with your average, modest cotton shirts that never matched. She reminded Rainia of "Thelma Klue" off of "Shoobie Doobie" cuz of the way she dressed, and cuz of her hair and her glasses. When she had to go pee, she would cross her legs and try to walk that way down the hall to the bathroom, trying to prevent herself from pissing her pants. It always took her a few minutes of strategizing before she made it safely to the commode.

***

"That shit was funny to watch. We called it the 'Babbette Walk' and used it ourselves a couple of times," said the older spirit Rainia to the other spirits who were laughing too.

***

Babbette was a sweetheart, though, and very much into Jesus Christ and Sunday school. She would take Rainia with her to church sometimes, and Rainia loved learning about Jesus with the other children in the basement of the church. There would always be some fun activity to do and color and cut out and paste. No one made fun of her skin tone at church, because everywhere she looked in the basement were pictures of Jesus with all colors of children all around him at his feet.

"Who is Judas?" she asked the Sunday school teacher.

"Shhh! We dare not speak his name in the House of the Lord, little lady!" the woman snapped.

Rainia left it alone and concentrated on Jesus instead. Once, she even dreamed that she went to play on the playground, and Jesus was out there with all of the other kids jumping all around him, laughing and smiling, and Rainia was having a hard time getting through the crowd so she could hug him too. But right before she could get to him, she woke up. She had that dream many times, after that.

Rainia would go to the grocery store with Babbette, as well, besides walking to school and going to church. She was always astounded to see how much name-brand food Babbette would buy all at one time, and she would have this big wad of money to pay for it. Babbette was always on the go outside or inside her home. She even *walked* super-duper fast. She was always hauling a basket of clothes up or down the stairs for the men, while frying slices of ham in real butter, and letting the collie dog back in from his piss, feeding the dog, and eating a dog biscuit or two for herself. Yes, the woman ate dog biscuits, and fed that loud, obnoxious parakeet, while packing her husband's lunch for work the next day. He had the same thing everyday. Fried ham in butter on toast, a pickle, a baggie of plain chips, and a big thermos of coffee.

Her husband "Quincey" was really a prejudice man. He allowed his wife to watch colored kids while he was away at work or sleeping, but he was not amused by their presence. He stood about 5'10" tall, had a shinning, balding head with jet-black, greasy hair slapped over to one side to try and hide the fact that he was really bald, wore prudent, pointed, poindexterish glasses, always blue or gray Dicky pants, a nerd shirt with at least two pens in his front shirt pocket, and proudly adorned a bum leg. His shoes were mismatched because of this. One looked like the dad's shoe from *The Cleaver Show*, and the other one looked like something the long tongued band member from 'Kiss It' would wear. It was a big, wooden stack that he had made himself from his other normal shoe, and 'Herman Monsterous' footwear, molded together in an awful harmony.

Rainia cracked the fuck-up laughing at him the first time she had to meet his grouchy ass. He'd hobbled into the living room bitching about the level of noise, and for Babbette to, "Get those damned, bratty kids in the god-damned bed already! All I can hear is that filthy lil' jigaboo! I'm tryna sleep. God Dammit!"

Rainia thought that his calling her a jigaboo didn't sound cute like her Auntie calling her bugaloo, and she knew filthy meant dirty. When Babbette would tell him that those weren't nice things to say to a little girl and to go back to bed, her feelings were already hurt. So when he would come out to the living room just-a-bitchen, Rainia would sit right there staring him down, and everyone else would "YIKES" and run for cover.

She didn't like him either and thought that he was stupid and ridiculous. She was watching him hobble around the house nagging one night and burst into a fit of the giggles, as she stared at his highly-polished, wooden-wedged loafer, and his straight, stiff leg sitting inside of it. She watched him walk away in disgust of her presence, and it was even funnier to her, to watch him go.

He refused to use a cane, so he looked like he was using his arms for leverage and balance, like he was swimming in the air, like old 'Fred Sanford' off of *Sanford and Son*. The leg had to go out from him and make a circle back in, causing him to use this wide space to walk, for each and every single step, making him appear to be walking very stupidly, waving his arms, trying not to fall or knock things over, for all to see, all of the time. And Babbette made sure no one laughed or they would get it.

Well, Rainia got it that night. "Smack" in the mouth, she got it. "Now knock it off!" said Babbette. But Rainia kept snorting under her hand over her mouth in hilarities as she watched him go about, mumbling and saying everything was damned around his house. Sometimes his shoe would du-fuss-ly clank into something and knock it over or destroy whatever it hit. Like big, wooden chairs that fell into a million toothpicks once his ol' mighty stack hit it. She could even hear him coming without turning around to see who it was, "Slap, boom, drag, slap, boom, drag," was the sound his distinct walk made when Quincy was in motion, even without the shoes!

Once she had calmed down, Babbette had given Rainia a book to read called, *Where's Margie? God's on the Phone For Her!* by Jerry Bloomer. It was about this White girl's mediocre worries about growing up, growing boobs, and wondering if God was watching her, or even paying her any attention at all. Rainia often wondered if God had another plan for her and her mom and now for the babies on the way, as well. She could relate to the book, only in terms of asking God questions in her head, like she had done for so long before the literature was even placed in her hand. The 'Margie' character from the story was living a very sheltered life, and the tale didn't have anything in it about child abuse, molestation, domestic violence, or racism. Even still, she enjoyed it and read the whole thing, wishing she could be the girl in the book, *I wish you would make me a new life instead of this one, God. I am so unhappy in this place.* Rainia could hear someone's heels click-clocking up the front-porch stairs outside the livingroom window.

Nessara rung the doorbell, and Rodney went to look to see who it was. "Oh! Some big, Black, niggary woman is at the door. Must be your real mammy, Rainy, huh? Hurry up and leave, shitty spot. Ma! Rainy's aunt's shadow is here. Time for her to go!"

She was the one more than happy to honor his wish. She had just come home with her aunt from Babbette's house on that church Sunday. Her aunt sat her down on her mom's bed while she was putting on her wig and said, "Rainia, my sweet little niece, you're a big sister now." Rainia's eyes lit up with new life, a new kind of hope. Just as she started to imagine herself with two baby sisters, her aunt interrupted, "Were going to see the baby boys right now; you ready?"

BOYS... Boys!? How could this have happened? Who wanted boys? She hated *all* BOYS! She mo-certainly did not want any rotten brothers to watch. Rainia was pissed but didn't say a word. Once her Auntie was ready, they had walked to the bus stop to catch a ride to the hospital. The city bus was always rim-chocked full of strange people, and there was always a group of prejudiced, old White folk that controlled the front seats.

The bus was pretty full, and there was only one seat open in the front, next to an old bag who made it clear right away that she didn't want Rainia sitting next to her. She did this by scooting real close to her window, fixing her coat away from Rainia and holding her purse by her window. "Hump! Damned coloreds. Can't even sit in peace with my own kind," she mumbled.

Big Mistake! Auntie Nessara had heard the bitter woman's comment and switched places with Rainy, having her stand and hold onto the pole while her aunt sat next to the prude. At first the woman tried to ignore her, then she got agitated, little by little, as Nessara scooted next to the woman, closer and closer. "You don't like Niggers sitting by you, but what about Africans? Shoombubba moom bufu lye, icka doomba yow!" she sang like a tribal hymn. "That's 'Slapfrican' for 'Share your seat with your neighbor for a healthier life, or get slapped.' You got room. Scoot your old, evil bones over." Nessara kept on scooting the hag so close to the window that her wrinkled face was pushed up into the glass, and she looked like a toy cat that was suctioned cupped onto a car window. Rainia was cracking up, trying not to fall every time the bus came to a stop. Then her aunt lit up a cigarette and looked around at the other passengers among them.

One White guy said, "You can't smoke on here!"

Nessara rung the bell cord for her and her niece to get off. A couple of puffs after, she stood up, put the cigarette out in the guy's hand, "I know there's no smoking, but there was so much prejudice smoke thick and heavy in the air, I can't see how yall can tell the difference?" and grabbed Rainia's hand, exiting the bus. "I swear, Rainy. Some mutha-fuckas are so damned ignorant, they will make you act a fool, too. Come on, let's go see those babies."

Rainia was snickering about the events of the bus ride until she had said that. All the rest of the walkway to the newborn floor, she was dead silent.

At the hospital, her mom looked exhausted but seemed happy to see her little girl, "Hi, Rainy! You got little brothers now! Go see them; they're waiting to meet you."

Rainia walked over to her mom and said in a small voice, just loud enough for her to hear in her ear, and said, "You promised me sisters."

Her mother smacked her up-side her head and told her to go see her brothers, because they had been born premature and could die. She also told her that they were hanging on to dear life with tape, tubes, and machines, and that Rainia should ask Jesus to help them live.

Rainia automatically felt bad when she heard the name Jesus again, and felt even worse when she actually saw her baby brothers, laying there helpless, 2 and 1/2 lbs. apiece, bug-eyed, and red all over with junk wrapped all around them, struggling for air in their tiny, visible rib cages. They both lay there looking at her with half-opened eyes, miserable to be in an existence like that. So she put her hands together like the babysitter, Babbette, had showed her to in Sunday school and prayed for them on both knees. She prayed that they would live and that their daddy would die. She prayed that her mom would become nice again.

Chapter Five

The State Street Suicide

Rainia continued to visit the hospital for the next three months with her Auntie. Billy had stopped coming by for a long time now, because Anmarie was so big that he just wasn't interested in her. He also wasn't very interested in his own sons either. He never showed up to witness them being born, never showed up at the hospital to check on their condition, or ever came to see them once they were released. He didn't come by for 5 months, so Rainia had plenty of time to focus on the baby brothers she had now helped to look after. It was the first chance she ever had to forget about her own misery and partake in the lives of others around her in need. She had even forgotten her sixth birthday, and so had everyone else.

Her mother tried to make it up by taking them to 'I-Hop' on 23rd and Wisconsin Avenue. It was about ten blocks away from the 'Marc's Big Boy' on 27th and Wisconsin Avenue that had a giant-sized kid in checkered pants and suspenders, holding a big ol' cheeseburger on a plate over his head, just in front of the little 'Burger Chef' hut out back near the parking lot. All of those restaurants on the Ave were cool, but I-Hop was the girl's favorite. Her mother preferred the, 'Red Barn,' restaurant for its small barn-box of chicken, or the 'Shakey's Pizza Parlor' across from it, where she could order a beer and pour salt in it to watch it froth up, but it was Rainia's day. Just approaching the house of breakfast specialties made Rainia's heart dance. She could smell the aroma of hot syrup, cake batter, and butter being pumped through the heated fans that were blowing over the entrance doors.

They walked in from the chilly wind and through the second door. Next to the hostess podium stacked high with menus, they saw a towering, pink-frosted, ceramic birthday cake, adoring 'happy birthday' in blue frosted letters held by a big, cartoon-looking kangaroo with a winking eye and a smile that was a bit too big. The cake was three-tiers high and had a slot for putting in birthday information cards. In Rainia's eyes, the confection looked so real that she tried to scratch off a piece of frosting with her nail to see if it was sweet until the party of four was seated.

The hostess/waitress, a young woman with a ponytail bearing the name tag 'Bobbie' showed them to a corner table. "Are you ready to order?" asked the snotty, White girl with the discerning eye towards the dark-circled-eyed Anmarie.

The heavyset mom gave her order and pointed to Rainia.

The happy child gleamed with delight, "I want the smiley pancakes! It's my birthday!" said Rainia all excited.

'Bitchy Bobbie,' rolled her eyes, "It's always a birthday for kids like you. How ever else will you eat if it wasn't?" The cold waitress stiffly smiled and snatched up the menus, "fifth fuckin' birthday today, John. We're gonna have to stop this free kid's breakfast, because they are taking advantage of it. What is it? 'Feed The poor Kids Day', or what?" she asked loudly of the chef in the kitchen window, as she slapped the order on the order wheel and spun it around so fast that it practically took flight from it's hinges.

"Just make it, White bitch," said Anmarie under her breath.

"But, Mommy, you are White. Why don't you like her, and why don't you get a White boyfriend?"

Anmarie stopped dead in the middle of pouring salt on the blue and white, plastic, checkered tablecloth to write her name in and squared eyes with her daughter, "Well, I don't like that White bitch, because she's an evil snot to be so mean to you. I don't ever want a White boyfriend because of something bad that happened to me when I was younger. When I was a teenager, on my graduation night, I was snatched by a gang of redneck White boys from my school. They hurt your momma real bad, too. I was a virgin and had never been dirty in my life. I never even had a boyfriend or been kissed or anything. After that terrible night, it was discovered that I had gotten pregnant, and my mother and father had to pay for an abortion. That whole thing had done something to me psychologically. From that day forth, I never looked at a White man the same again. I thought that by getting a chocolate man, things would be better. TAH! They're all queers, if you were to ask me. That's why I'd rather be a fat ass. I'll just be happy taking care of youse three. I don't need a man anymore. They are too much fuckin' trouble. You are just a little girl, but after all that we have seen together, I know that you understand, don't you?"

Rainia agreed.

Anmarie grabbed her coffee cup the waitress had placed in front of her and doctored it up the way she liked it, "Good. Now let's drop it and eat."

The complimentary B-day meal consisted of chocolate-chipped pancakes decorated like a smiley face with whipped cream and strawberries. The last time the little girl had the order, she ate them by herself, but this time she shared them with her mother and a taste of whipped cream for her grinning baby brothers that she had somehow fell head over heels for. It was way more fun. They all managed to enjoy themselves that day in spite of the spiteful waitress. Rainia had come to love those boys from the moment she'd laid eyes on them.

Somehow they had become her obsession, her reasons for endurance. She knew that she had to survive all that was going on, so she could be there for the benefit of the boys. Boys: The essence of man. The species she had come to hate became her lifeline in the mystery of twins. The identical twins, "James and Joseph," or J and Jo for short, were her heart. She played with them everyday, watching them grow to make their first giggles.

By the time they were 11 months old, they both had a laugh that was contagious. It was like listening to *two* 'Woody Woodpecker Cartoon' guys laughing back and forth at each other, causing anyone else who didn't crack-up to succumb until the party-pooper joined in. Rainia found great joy in watching to see what was funny to the little guys about the little things in their little lives. While the infants were getting along well in the 11 months which had passed, their father, Billy, was starting to come around a little bit again, not to spend the night, but to try and nick the struggling family's welfare check that they were now living on.

Anmarie was getting tired of Billy stopping by to beat her ass and take what little money she had, and she was starting to resist his pimping demands. She and the children were home much less often for the sake of hiding out. One day, Anmarie was over Patty's house, another young, White chick who also had three mixed kids, when Billy broke the glass of Patty's back kitchen window by the table where the two women were having coffee. He reached up into the conversation that they were engaged in and snatched Anmarie's purse off of the kitchen table covered in broken glass where the women sat leaning way back in their chairs, mouths wide open, hands frozen to their cheeks, and eyes popping, stupefied with surprise. The monster for money took off running toward the alley but fell and looked back. They all saw his sorry ass real good then.

"How does he even know where I live?" asked Patty.

"Slimy shit musta followed us here," said Ann.

Rainia didn't even really have a chance to play with Patty's kids because Anmarie got freaked out and had all of her own brood in the LTD, Queen Roadster, that she had just bought from Quincey, Babette's husband, to rush home in. Anmarie had to find better strategies to make Billy loose interest and yet be able to take care of her children. The weary White woman had gained a lot of weight during her pregnancy and had to quit dancing for good, so the money that Billy was trying to confiscate from time to time was the welfare money she and her kids needed to eat, and to live. The small, fatherless, husbandless, boyfriend-less family tried to avoid the son-of-a bitch all together. They did this by frequently visiting different friends of Anmarie's, sometimes spending the night at whoever's home welcomed them. They were on the run from a madman in pimp's clothing.

They went to spend some time at another one of Anmarie's White friends' houses. Her name was Francella, and she had four kids at the time and a Black husband. She was always trying to do things to keep him or scare him. She did crazy things, like put 'Viks Methalating Vapor Rub' in her vagina before he had sex with her, or put baby shit in his dress shoes to keep him from going out at night to bars. She eventually gained the name of 'Crazy Aunt Fran'.

Ann stayed a few days with her friend and her hair-brained schemes until she couldn't take it anymore. Anmarie had decided to take her kids home one night to enjoy a hot bath, her own TV, and her own bed. She had all the kids scrubbed clean and ready for dreamland. The twins wanted to dig around in their baby toys that they hadn't seen in days. Because the boys were past crawling and were standing pretty good by then, they were even able to try and get down off of her bed by themselves. Anmarie watched them play around on the floor wearing sleeper gowns, smelling as fresh as the diapers and baby powder on their bottoms. Once the boys tired, rattles still in hand, Anmarie put them and Rainia in the bed with her.

Anmarie was having a thankful moment, staring at the precious, beautiful, light-brown, slumbered expressions of her three children's faces before she dosed off, herself. It was close to the end of summertime and in the middle of the warm, breezy night. All was quiet and ever so peaceful with the family consisting of a mother, daughter, and twins, as the toddler boys were comfortably sleeping in 'Mommy's room', when Billy Jacksin had begun the process of kicking the door in to their dark apartment.

***

"The sound of a vicious man kicking in a door to where you lay your head at is unforgettable!" said the spirit of Rainia to her invisible peers, as they all watched this happening like it was a feature film.

***

Once inside the apartment, 'Billy from the past' hurried through the dark toward Ann's room, "Get up, you fuckin', honkey redneck!"

Young Rainia had already awakened and had jumped out of bed in the pitch-blackened space, frightened by the loud burst of splintering wood buckling under Billy's polished, stacked platforms, as he had forced his way into their unlit home. He rushed to Anmarie's bedside and started right into the startled, exhausted mother. Rainia could barely make out the frame of the big, towering man moving about by the bed, as her mother told Rainia to run. He turned on the lamp next to the bed so he could see how to kick Ann's ass the best way. Rainia was in the doorway of her mother's room watching him grab her from the bed by her hair, knocking over the bedside lamp.

The twins were scared beyond sound, as they were waking up to the insanity of their own father. Rainia was panicking while trying to figure out what to do to help her. The baby boys were now crying and grabbing onto their mother's nightshirt, as he struck her with ringed-fingered fists, over and over, knocking the babies off of her each time his fists and backhand landed.

"Why the fuck ain't you answering your phone? I know you heard me buzzin' that stanken-ass buzzer downstairs! Get the fuck in here!" He was slapping her and kicking her and dragging her into the living room by her hair where he had more room to work her over. He punched her in both eyes, ripped gobs of her hair out, and kicked her everywhere he could get a good one in, even in her nose and mouth. She was spitting up blood and screaming with the salty, red saliva gurgling in her mouth, pleading for him to stop.

Rainia and the babies were scared out of their minds but knew that they had to help their mother. The babies were trying to walk at this point and were crying and combo crawl-walk-falling to their mother's feet with total fear and bravery at the same time, trying to intervene into their father's tirade. Their little feet kept getting tangled up in their long nightgowns, as they portrayed a natural instinct of chivalry. Rainia was punching and kicking Billy in the nuts, and the twins were hanging onto their father's legs, trying to bite him with their two front teeth, making it hard for him to beat their mother.

Rainia was screaming, "Somebody help us! God! Jesus!" Louder and fiercer, and over and over, Rainia made the cry for help.

Someone had called the police, and Billy recognized the sound of sirens over his furious demanding voice, "You gone learn to get me my money, White-bread bitch!" and with a balled-up, bloody fist of gleaming diamond rings, tainted with their mother's DNA, he fled.

He didn't come back that night, as the police questioned the Puffer-Fish-faced Anmarie about the incident. She refused the ambulance, because the last couple of times she had gotten huge bills for the ride. Billy did come back — two nights later. He made the mistake of calling Anmarie on the phone, telling her that he was on his way and to have his money ready.

The barely-recognizable, swollen-eyed, and badly-bruised Anmarie already had the twins at Babbette's house, which Billy didn't know about Babbette or her house yet, and Anmarie was just going home with Rainia to get some things for all of them to wear when she made the wrong move of nonchalantly answering the phone call.

"You got my money, honey?" he laughed like a creep and cleared his throat.

Anmarie blurted out the first thing that came to her mind, "Fuck you, you dirty mother-fucker!" and she hung up, scrambling things into a big and small trash bag and rushing out of her apartment, dropping the keys as she tried to lock the brand-newly replaced door. She practically drug Rainia by one arm down the stairs, because they had no time to wait for the piss-smelling elevator.

When the mother and daughter both got back outside of the multi-colored, brick apartment with the walk-down stairwell on 26th and Michigan Street, there pulled up that long, candy-apple-red, sparkling-clean Cadillac, on white walls, with white-leather guts and the scent of cherry fragrance to enhance the experience of the sight to the smell. He had called her from his strange-looking, high-tech, brand-new car phone he had just gotten installed into the armrest of his car. Billy Jacksin had his powder-blue, sixteen-piece suit on with the powder-blue stacks to match. *This Black muther fucker has a phone in his got-damn car like the pimps in the movies! He's reaaal drunk, too,* thought Anmarie.

Rainia was so glad to see that he was so wasted, stumbling out of his car, and taking a minute to gather his bearings, holding on to his driver's door before slamming it shut. He saw them though, as they both stood there at the doorway, in shock to see the devil himself.

"Didn't know a pimp had him a phone in his ride, huh, ho? — Yea! Now that's real pimpish." He straightened his suit the best he could without falling and looked up at them both as they tried to run, "Un-uh, bitch-shess! Come-mere!" He staggered a bit, and they both flew completely out of the entrance door and hit him with it. With garbage bags of clothes in hand, they hid in the bushes on the side of the apartment.

Billy Jacksin may have been pissy drunk, but he knew they were hiding close to him somewhere out there. He swayed back and forth, stumbled around the corner, and approached the bushes. Anmarie put her hand over Rainia's mouth and held her real still. Billy's powder-blue stacks were standing right in front of their crouching, un-breathing bodies. He was right up over them, moving bushes around, almost touching the bags, while he was mumble-cussin' about how he knew their fuckin' asses was in there somewhere, and that he was gonna kill them both for making him snag his suit in those bushes, looking for *their* pecker-wood asses.

Anmarie and Rainia did not move. Instead, they watched his powder-blue stack shoes go back and forth in front of them, like a game of hot and cold. *Warmer — your getting warmer, Mr. pimp man, awww... Now your cold again,* thought Rainia and almost laughed right there in the pit of terror, lips still under her mother's even tighter grip. After about 9 or 10 minutes, he finally gave up, decided that they weren't there, and started yelling out Anmarie's name, as if she was going to say, "Yeah? What do you want?" like an aggravated barmaid off in the distance with a white towel thrown over her shoulder, ready to take an order.

He finally gave up. He got in his car and left with his adamant, drunk self, and Anmarie stood up to make sure that he was down the street real good and gone before she let Rainia come out of the bushes. "Whew! That was real close Rainy!"

Rainia looked up at her mom and said, "Did you see his shoes?" They burst into laughter and walked quickly to Babbette's house, with their bags, where they remained for the next couple of nights.

The spirits simultaneously let out a sigh of relief. Chaz spoke up this time to the group, "Yeah. No other shoe has declared an era like the stack did. That was thee living shoe of the '70s — and there it died." The watchers from the future, past, and present agreed about the shoe declaration of independence, and then continued to observe Rainia's past life.

Babette's husband, Quincey, had demanded that Anmarie and her kids leave his house with their killer-nigger, pimp problems before drama would claim his doorstep.

Anmarie swallowed her pride and her shame, calling her parents who lived about five hundred miles away from Milwaukee. Then they had all gone up North to her parent's house for a few weeks for a break away from danger. Rainia begged to live up there, but Anmarie didn't feel safe there either. It was an issue of color. Every time Anmarie went into town, old high-school chums of hers, even a few who had raped her years ago, would point and whisper about the kid who left town right after high school to go and have nigger kids. Ann couldn't take it. So the racially-mixed-complected family of four went back to Milwaukee once their Grandfather had given Anmarie a big sum of money to be able to move to a new apartment and pay a security deposit in the fast-paced city.

After they had gotten off of the Greyhog bus back in town, Anmarie called a cab. They sat inside the terminal waiting for it to arrive. There was a snack bar that sold model toy buses, pink, see-through rabbit balloons, travel maps, popcorn, corndogs, nachos, hamburgers, candy bars, stuffed Greyhogs in small bus-shaped boxes, and animal crackers in similar packaging. There was a big vending machine in the bathroom that had twelve shades of lipsticks sticking out from fancy gold tubes behind the glass. The walls in the restroom were of pink tile, and the whole area smelled of strong, lemony-wet napkin packs when they are first ripped open — but mixed with farts.

When leaving the ladies room, the smell of bus tires and hot bus motors filled the air of the terminal lobby lined with rows of orange plastic chairs bolted down to the speckled, white-tiled and scuffed-up floor, as well as the impersonating voice of the guy who did the Emergency Broadcast System commercials. The man's voice on the loudspeaker called the other passengers to the busses outside to have them board it, "Now taking tickets for the departure to, Wausau, Appleton, Marshfield, Green bay, Beloit, and Racine. Please have your boarding passes ready in hand, and be sure that your luggage is secured for the baggage area. This Greyhog will be leaving in 15 minutes. Thank you for going Greyhog."

Rainia had wanted to climb under the bus where their luggage was, and ride up North with the big bags and boxes there and never come back. It was a neat compartment just small enough for a child. The motor rumbled like a song of freedom to a brand-new, better life awaiting all who boarded the mighty, silvery coach surrounded by the dim, pale, pinkish fluorescent lighting where they kept the buses, making the people on the other side of the glass of the lobby think that it was dark outside at all times. The stairs on the bus had reminded her of the sky at night. They were black with white and slightly bright greens flecks on them. The blue seats were tall in their stiff, upright positions with the funny, black, beige, and brown pinstripes going doing the middle of each one. The hard, plastic, aqua-blue armrests were painful to try and sleep on, and the circular lights above each seat were entirely too bright and were set together like eyes when people used them to read. The ceiling on the bus down the narrowest of aisles was cream with gold flecks and sparkles. The windows were tinted a dark green, and the steel trim around them was as cold as the outside when the bus was on the road coasting through the chilly breezes of the summer night.

Going to the bathroom on the bus was some of the scariest shit that Rainia had to endure on the journey. The slender, weird-shaped toilet was made of a cold steel or aluminum material, and the hole seemed to be way down in there. The potent, lemony-green water would splash up and stain her bare butt each time the bus hit a bump. The steel sink to wash her hands was like a lotion bottle pump, and there were soggy, brown paper towels balled up in the basin. After leaving the strange, teeny-tiny, narrowed bathroom, the cream, sparkle, and gold-fleck decorated door would automatically slam shut behind its last customer so that everyone would turn around to see who was the last person to take a shit.

The people on the bus were strange looking with weird glares for her and her small family as well. Rainia hated to get off of the bus and be back in funky-booty Milwaukee. Even as odd as it all was, Rainia had wished that she were leaving right back outta town with the new set of boarding passengers. The cab finally pulled up outside the station, and Ann rode the kids and their bags on a luggage cart to their yellow chariot and got in.

They went and stayed at a cheap motel for a few days, living off of 'Dinky Mo Stew' in cans, warmed up by hot water in the sink. The twins celebrated their birthdays with Hope-Mess cupcakes that they just smeared on their heads and laughed at each other. It was fun for Rainia to go get ice from the ice machine and candy bars from the vending machine down the hall from their room. It made her feel important, and her mother was even being nice to her in her state of depression. Anmarie would sit and cry by the window at night, with the heavy drapes that had the white plastic backing on them pulled back to the side at the 'Billerball' motel, smoking cigarettes and going through the newspaper's 'For Rent' section.

She had finally found a place on State Street, down in the Millville Valley and was secretly planning to move. She had gone to see the house while Babbette had come over to the motel room to watch the kids and quickly fell in love with the privacy alone, as opposed to coming from the constant noise of living in an apartment building. It was a two-toned, green and light-gray duplex with giant, full-grown sunflower stalks that were at least five-feet tall in the backyard. It went right along with the theme of the Indian summer they were having.

Anmarie put down a security deposit and had all of their belongings moved in over one weekend from the storage facility. Rainia could not have been happier in her new home. She was still going to Wisconsin Avenue School, and the school bus had to come to get her and drop her off. When she was at school, she didn't talk. She remained silent there and on the bus each and every day, so she made no friends. But she liked to make pretty pictures for her mommy and had actually learned to read at five when she first got there and figured out how to sound out the letters in the alphabet. She read a lot of children's stories and then moved on to harder stories for bigger kids, as Babbette would bring books to her whenever she could. Rainia read everything that a poor child in America could think of, but never told anyone that she could do this. The only one who knew of her talent was Babbette, and she kept Rainia's secret well.

The warm beginning of the fall days had rolled by with fun and laughter amongst the small family. Once, when her aunt Nessara had stopped by, Anmarie poured a whole pitcher of ice water downstairs on top of her aunt's head, as she waited at the door underneath the upstairs window to be let in. Nessara's wig was all wet,

"You dirty bitch! Wait till I get up there," Nessara charged up the stairs for playful revenge. They had fun throwing glasses of water on each other that day. The pungent smell of crabapples off of the little tree in the backyard had blown its sweet perfume in the wind every day like a 'Welcome Home' sign. There was love and peace starting to grow as the little family bonded, and soon the end of fall came.

All was even more peaceful as the seasons continued to change. Rainia was turning seven in a few months and was looking forward to her birthday this time around. Her baby brothers were walking and running now, and she had a little more playtime to herself outside.

It had now become cold, as the winter months snuck up on them and yelled, "Ha! My turn!" right into their chilly faces. School was about 2 be out for Christmas break. She had never made friends on her bus route over the school year, because they all made fun of her 4 having a White mother. On the last day before she walked to her bus stop with her mom, she asked her, "Mom, can you let me walk by myself from now on? The kids say its funny I got a White momma, and I'm not White."

Her mother looked at her with rage in her face and said, "I'm beatin' your little ass when you get home tonight. Now get on that bus, you little brat."

Rainia was terrified of her mother's whoopens. A cringing shiver made her jerk just thinking about it. She was hoping that her mom wasn't going to do that to her anymore. It had been a long time since she'd gotten a beating from Ann. She had this thing of beating her with the thick vacuum cleaner cord when she did something wrong at the old apartment, but she hadn't whooped her for a while now. Little Rainy wondered why her mom was so mad.

All day, in school, she feared the scheduled beating. When she got on her school bus to go home, she ended up peeing on herself when she saw her mother waiting for her at the bus stop. She had a big pink housecoat on, house shoes, rollers in her hair to match, and was standing in the light flurries of the newly-fallen snow. The kids were dying of laughter when Rainia got off of the bus, pissy pants and all, covered with shame, and shivering with cold and the terror of what was to come.

Anmarie said, "I thought that by embarrassing you with this getup of an outfit, and not the color of my skin, would be enough, and I wasn't gonna whoop you. But seeing how your lazy ass done pissed your pants, I guess I got to now; don't I?"

Rainia was crying uncontrollably all the way up the stairs to their new home. Her mother closed the kitchen door to the house and told her to go into the living room, take off her pants, and lay down. After Rainia peeled the cold, wet pants off of her frozen legs, her mom came into the living room with the baby-blue 'Hooverunner' vacuum cleaner, cord in hand and beat the dog shit out of her till the skinny, little girl couldn't make any more sounds to the sharp, whelping, bruising lashes, as they stingingly pierced her tender skin all over her body.

"NOW GO GET IN THE TUB, AND PUT ON A GOWN!" her mother yelled. Later on, her mother felt bad about beating her and came into her bedroom and tried to hug her, telling her to come and eat, so Rainia thought that it was a good time to talk about what she wanted for her birthday in the next month, and also to tell her about what Billy Jacksin was doing to her at their old apartment, "He calls me 'Judas'. I really hate that when he says that to me. He's the Judas!" said Rainia with courage and self-assurance.

She was having a problem sitting at the table because of the stinging, fat whelps on her butt. Anmarie turned to her, "Why does he call you Judas, anyway? I've heard him say that to you a couple of times." Her mom was now laughing and Rainia was too.

"He made me lick his wiener, Mommy. I was throwing up, but he did a lot of bad things to me every time you left. I hate him and hope that he gets killed. You whooped me for nothing on my last birthday. Remember?" Her mother suddenly dropped the spoon that was stirring the noodles to the macaroni and cheese which Rainia had asked her to make when her mom asked her what she wanted special for the guilty, favorite, make-up supper she was preparing.

"Get your clothes off, all of them!" Her mother beat her again, and this time, she made her go into her room and pray with the Bible, badly beaten, naked, and crying to beg God for forgiveness for making up such terrible stories. She said she better never hear her lying again and wishing people dead.

Rainia, in her Heavenly state, watched herself with an overwhelming sadness at this tumultuous time in her young life, "I never said another word about the sexual abuse that I had undergone until I turned 17."
The group of small, starry orbs all said, "Yeah, we *know!*"

The next day, for little Rainia, it started to snow fluffy flakes, and she asked to go and play outside. Some weeks ago, some new people had moved in downstairs, a White lady, and her White husband. From time to time you could hear him beating her from the upstairs, and each time it got worse and worse. The neighbors downstairs from them also had a little, two-year-old baby boy who Rainia thought was so cute. The woman and her boy had come outside to play with the little girl after a really good snow. The toddler reminded her of a cherub she once saw on the wall in her classroom on Valentine's Day. He wasn't fat in his body. In fact he was too skinny. His face, however, was chubby and ziggy. He had on a coat that was too big, little blue jeans, boots, and a funny hat with a big, fluffy tassel hanging from it. As he ran in the snow, his cheeks wiggled and his tassel flopped around on his giggling, little head. His cheeks were red now, and his little blond hairs that were sticking out of his hat now blew in the soft, winter wind.

Rainia wished her brothers were up to play, too, but they were napping. They would have had a kir-nip-tion fit of laughter with him. He was so very funny to watch. He appeared to be a happy, little guy, so Rainia wasn't sure if his dad was beating on him, too. The lady, who looked very fatigued and sick as she continued to smile, let them play in the yard together all that afternoon. Eventually she joined them and they were all making small snowballs and snow angels and having a good-old time. The mother and son lay on the ground, making a special set of angels of themselves. Rainia watched them bond and admired her love for her baby to try and play with him, even though she looked tired and hungry. Rainia's fat mom was upstairs asleep with the twins. She was too lazy to play with her kids, but the skinny neighbor lady from downstairs acted like there was nothing in the world she would rather do than play with this mixed girl and her own son. She even went inside and brought them both chocolate chip cookies, fresh from the oven and still warm. When the little boy's father came home, the anorexic woman tried to hurry and grab the baby up and go inside before he saw them playing, but it was too late.

He saw, "Didn't I tell you that he can't play with those nigger kids upstairs?" He slapped the frail woman so hard that she lost her grip on their son, who was now crying because he had cracked his forehead on the snowy sidewalk. A black and blue egg instantly appeared on the baby's noggin, and he cried bloody murder. "Get your fuckin' ass in the house," the dad yelled at the tot. The man was a skinny biker type, with chains hanging from his belt, and long, scraggily, dark-brown hair with a beard to match.

Rainia watched as the man yanked the wailing child, with the fresh knot on his head, up by one arm, and told them both to get in the house. He looked at Rainia with pure hatred in his lifeless black eyes, as he slammed the back door. She could hear the man swearing, throwing things, and beating them both. She had felt so terrible for being part Black that she broke down into tears as she listened to the nice lady and the cute little baby suffer because of her skin tone. She held that chocolate chip cookie close to her heart and prayed for them to run away from the man, just like her family had run from Kent and Billy. Rainia was so scared for them both going back inside, that she didn't even notice it when she dropped her cookie.

That night, while Anmarie and her kids were sleeping, there was a gunshot blast that woke them up. Anmarie jumped out of bed, grabbed all of her children, and went into the front room to call the police. Before she could even pick up the phone, there was another shot fired. The small family sat in the living room floor of the cold, dark house silently for two seconds, and then — "Bang!" another shot. Anmarie frantically dialed the call and reported the shots. The twins were crying but still sleepy, so they dozed back off right away.

Rainia wasn't about to go back to sleep until her mother did, and she wondered what the hell had happened downstairs. She hoped that the lady had killed that evil man, as it was real quiet down there. The eerie silence caused Anmarie to get up and go to the hallway to listen. Then she went to the back, opened up her kitchen door, and listened some more. Rainia watched her go outside of the door, and eventually down the stairs. In fear of her mother possibly being shot, as much as she disliked her, the little girl ran downstairs after her mother, crying, "Mommy no! Don't go see!" as her skinny little legs raced down the steps to save her mother from the worst. Rainia stood in the open kitchen doorway down-stairs and could not believe her eyes.

At the kitchen table sat what was left of the family of three's father. His body was slumped back in the chair, and his brains were blown out of his head. Only part of his face remained. Just his lower jaw with his beard and bottom row of teeth were still smoking. Blood, brains, and skull fragments were all over the stove, the sink, the walls, and the table. There was a half-empty, blood-spattered baby bottle of milk sitting in front of him next to a beer and a still-burning cigarette in his other hand. The gun partially lay on the floor under his chair. It was unreal.

Her mother suddenly appeared in a doorway in an adjacent room that must have been the baby's room. She was holding her stomach, bracing herself in the child's doorway to his bedroom. "Oh, God! No! He killed that little baby." Her mother was crying and screaming and almost choked when she saw her daughter standing there just staring at the man's dead body. **"Get your stupid ass back upstairs, now!"** Anmarie roared.

Rainy cried some of the heaviest tears she had ever dropped, because she truly felt like the lady and the cute little baby had died because of her.

Later on, when the cops came, Anmarie and Rainia stood outside of the house and watched as the detectives surveyed the crime scene. They asked them both a lot of questions and wrote stuff down on notepads as they talked, "OK, I think we got everything we need from you guys. Thanks." The detective that Anmarie was talking to gave her a card, and she put it in her pink housecoat pocket. She was still in her nightgown but apparently wasn't bothered by the cold. The coroner was taking the bodies from the home, one by one. Watching them bring out that little, black body bag was too sad to bear for her and her child, so they both went back into the house holding hands.

Sometime during the remainder of the night, Rainia dreamed that the lady and her little boy had finally run away from the man. The lady told her that it wasn't her fault and that they were finally happy and free. They told her that the selfish man was doomed for killing them and himself to be a lost soul to live that night over and over until Judgment Day. The baby boy had real angel wings in her dream, and he flew around with his mother behind him, holding a plate full of chocolate chip cookies. The once-frail woman now looked vibrant, beautiful, healthy, and full of joy. She turned around before disappearing into the snowfall and tossed Rainia one of her edibles, but Rainia dropped it and didn't know where it went. The woman, now turned angel, said, "That's ok. One day, when you need a friend, I'll send you chocolate chip cookies with *rainbow* pieces in them. They are rainbows of hope for you, Rainia. No rain. No pain. Don't cry for us, because we will often cry for you, and one day, when you need us the most, we will save you." She smiled at Rainia, the baby blew her a kiss, and they were gone.

The next day, late in the afternoon, Rainia got bundled up, went outside, and walked to the front of the house where she could see all of the bright-red blood that had spilled from the body bags in a trail leading from the porch to the sidewalk and into the snow. She was thinking about all of the fun that she, the lady, and her baby had yesterday, around this same time. After about ten minutes of missing them both, like she had known them her whole life, her heart was broken and she started to get cold.

As she walked toward the backdoor, tears falling one after the other, she noticed the snow angels that they had made in the snow, a big one that was the woman's, and a little one that was the baby's. There lay the chocolate chip cookie between the angels which appeared to be holding hands. A warm and strong sense of security and peace came over Rainia as she imagined the boy and his mother in Heaven with Jesus. If they were alive in such a place, then there never was a double homicide, only a State Street suicide.

Chapter Six

43rd and Good Hope Road

Things were pretty quiet after the death of Rainia's neighbors and friends. Her mom seemed to be in a bad place because of the triple deaths. She didn't talk too much for about two weeks. Christmas had arrived, and the children were sitting on the living room floor and opening their presents. The twins had gotten an array of clothes, riding toys, and little cars to zoom around with on the floor. Rainia had gotten a couple of 'Barbra' dolls, a 'Super Cherakee' doll, some 'Charlie's Guardians', dolls, an Easy Bake Oven, a Light Bright Game, and a really cool spaceship that drove around on the floor with flashing red, green, and blue lights. She would have to later set up a whole new world of playing with her dolls on the steps. She had also gotten a beautiful, big, red picture Bible with real gold edging and a sweater from her Grandma Lulabelle on her father's side. Her Gramma Marie on her mom's side had sent her some clothes from up North, some patent-leather shoes with a beautiful, small gold bow by the buckles, and a musical jewelry box with a twirling ballerina inside. The little drawer in the jewelry box had a bunch of multi-colored, small, ball earrings in them with a note that said, ' Gramma Loves You.'

Rainia missed her Gramma Marie. She wished that she was up North for Christmas. Up there kids got presents from Santa Claus, and when Rainia was smaller, she'd always had a huge pile of presents to open under the tree, along with every other kid. Gramma kept her tree decorated ever so beautifully, with handmade, beaded bulbs and fancy, colored silk balls. Her Gramma would line up long pins with beads of all sorts, and then design the bulbs to her liking, each one unique from the last. Under the tree were many, many gifts, with the tins filled with wavy, hard ribbon candy, peanut brittle, the chocolate covered cherries, and homemade cookies with silver candy balls sprinkled on them and frosted with an array of colors. The girl could never understand how rich her White grandparents were to buy all of the kids stuff, and how come Santa Claus never missed their house? *If he was real, he'd probably be scared to come to Milwaukee. He might get shot or beat up here,* she pondered. Even still, it was the best time of year, next to her second best holiday that included Jesus. If it were spring, then Rainia would be missing her Gramma's house for the Easter egg hunt, the basket of fun and candy galore, and the wonderful dress-up for church. Rainia use to believe in the Easter Bunny and Santa Claus. She'd thought that they were real. She'd known it because they had always left proof that they had been there looking for her. She'd believed it until she caught her Gramma putting presents under the tree in the middle of the night. Then her Gramma confessed to having put the gifts under there for all of the kids so that they will believe. That pretty much broke her heart to find out that there was no such thing as Santa or Mr. Bunny. Since there was no one else who was left for a desperate child to believe in, she chose to believe in God and Christ.

The doorbell rang. Anmarie looked out of the window and opened it to talk to someone. It was a child's voice, but Rainia couldn't hear what they were saying. Her mom spoke out of the window, "OK, I'll send her now." She shut the window and told Rainia to put on her hat and coat and go across the yard to the old woman's house next door.

Rainia did it, but — secretly she didn't want to. She thought that the old woman looked scary when she would see her sitting at her window at night. Her brown, block siding on her house looked like the witch's house from the story of the witch with the gingerbread house. Rainia walked down the stairs and out the door. As she crossed the big, snowy yard, she could see a little girl playing in front of the woman's porch. She was at least ten or eleven years old.

The old, White woman came to the door, as Rainia approached to walk cautiously up the stairs and look at the little girl who was now ignoring her as she hopped up and down on the last step. "Come here, honey; I got some gifts for you and your baby brothers," said the old lady. The woman reached down on the side of her foot and grabbed a black garbage bag. She gave it to Rainia and asked her granddaughter to help Rainia take it home.

The older girl just said, "That's ok; I got it," and picked it up as Rainia said, "Thank you, nice lady; Merry Christmas." The older girl didn't say one word as she silently followed Rainia upstairs. She sat the big trash bag down and begged Rainia to walk her back downstairs. Rainia was thinking that maybe the girl had wanted to be her friend and play outside or something. This was not the case. As they walked back down the staircase, the older girl stopped suddenly, "What was that? Did you hear that? You guys have ghosts now; I hope you know! I'm getting out of here!" The girl hit the remainder of the steps like a drum roll and was out and letting the screen door slam shut like a symbol. "Patiiiing!" went the door, and Rainia continued down the stairs to shut and lock the main door.

She thought that the girl was silly. How could there be ghosts when the lady and her baby were in Heaven? On her way back up the stairs, she could have sworn that she had seen a dark, black figure move across the top of the stairs. When Rainia finally got the courage to run those last few steps to go into the house, the attic door opposite the kitchen entry door slowly squeaked open. Rainia rushed inside and slammed the door, banning doll playing on the steps and panicking with fright, "Mom, the killer dad from downstairs is haunting us."

Her mother suddenly snapped out of her trance, "Really? What did you see?" Rainia told her mom what she saw, and her mom got up to go see what she could see. As her mother re-opened the kitchen door, Rainia took the bag of presents to inspect the gifts, *I ain't saving your ass this time, Mom*, she thought, as she opened the first gift marked '4 the girl'. It was a Colorformation's 'Happy Hobbie Holly House' made of cardboard that stood up and had a light in back of it. It was made to view from the front and showed each individual room of holly's house. Also contained in the packaging were several small plastic bags that had the Colorforms of Holly and her clothes and furniture that stuck to the laminated surface of the rooms of the house. Rainia stuck a few things on Holly's bedroom, like a lamp, a vase of flowers on the nightstand, and a teddy bear on her bed. She plugged the light in back into a nearby wall socket. It was the neatest thing she had ever, ever seen or gotten as a toy. Once plugged in, there were spaces that the house had that appeared to have been lit up. It was a trick that was revealed with illumination. The inside was made of cardboard, but everywhere that the cardboard was cut out underneath, the laminated scenery glowed, causing the windows, lamps, and fireplaces to be lit up because of the light showing through the back of the pictures of rooms. There was a lamp that was in the living room that appeared lit up. The window in 'Happy Holly's bedroom was lit up with a starry night sky and even had the shadow of the window beaming softly on the rug by her bed, and the livingroom fireplace appeared to be lit with a blazing, warm, and friendly fire.

 Just outside of Rainia's real window, a huge blizzard had come and snowed them in that night. The snowfall quickly left four feet within a couple of hours, and they weren't going anywhere no time soon. The whole Christmas vacation was spent indoors amidst two identical toddlers, a mother, and a daughter who daydreamed about the plastic, cardboard, and paper-laminated playhouse. Rainia sat for hours staring into the different rooms, imagining a new life for herself. She would pretend that she was 'Happy Holly' and that she was a White girl in real life. A White girl that lived up North with her grandmother and aunties on their farm, with the animals and the flowers and the peace of mind brought on by the day's sunshine. Up and down the country roads, in her mind, she would drift away, picking cattails from the creek and breaking sticks to toss in and watch floating in the trickle of the easy flow of the ripples. She would try to catch tiny tree frogs in her hands and throw smooth, fat stones into the water to hear the deepened "Plop" to the bottom. The sound of the wind would bring the sweet, warm smell of honeysuckle around her like a hug, as she danced through the small roadside orchard, making dust-clouds and picking crisp, red apples from trees, enjoying each tender bite taken after she shined them up on the sleeve of her old-fashioned Quaker dress. Once her big ruffled pockets were full, she would stop at the house of Laurie Inga at their little prairie home and skip to school together with a schoolhouse song. Happy Rainia Hobbie and Laurie Inga, studying to grow up to be teachers.

"Rainia, get your little, Black, nigger ass in here, ya brat!"

Rainia snapped out of her secret world and felt a shiver go down her spine and a drop in the pit of her stomach as her mother called her name again. She prayed that she wasn't going to get a whoopen for anything, "Yes Momma?"

"How many fuckin' times I gotta call you to get me a diaper?"

"Only once," Rainia replied and lowered her head, as she quickly ran to get the clean cloth diaper from the baby's shelf. When she returned, her mother threw the soiled diaper in her face, and Rainia handed her the clean one as the tears started to form. She wasn't crying because she'd just had a dirty diaper thrown in her face by her mother, she was crying because she hated being Rainia Dae Harris. Days and days of being stuck in the house had brought out the evil side of her mother full throttle. A whole month and a half had gone by, and Rainia hadn't even been going to school. Several times she'd been spanked for not going fast enough, or for not looking in the right place, or for opening the back door to the cold hallway, which she never had done because the ghost of the evil man did that.

Anmarie didn't believe her though. Her mother was standing in the kitchen and yelling at her one evening when the kitchen doorknob shook. Her mother turned around, as the door cracked open a little bit right before her eyes. "God dammit! Now, I *know* I locked that door." The wind outside was making screeching sounds like a banshee, and Anmarie had fear in her eyes. She closed the door and locked it, "Damned wind. Go in the front room, you all. *The Wizard of Id* is coming on. You will like that movie."

It was as if someone had come into the house and witnessed her mother's unnecessary evil and made her feel shamed. She was clearly stricken with guilt and had totally calmed down. The movie started, and her mother even made buttered popcorn. Rainia had never seen the feature before, so she was not too thrilled when it came on and was in black and white with real actors. She was hoping for a bright cartoon with a catchy song and not the boring "Gone to the Wind" typed selection that was dragging into her ears. Even still, she watched the show. Dorathea from the movie was such of a pretty White girl with long pigtails and a neat, smart face. The little dog was a cute, scraggly, dedicated creature that could seem to understand Dorathea's conversations. The uncles seemed nice and normal, and she'd bet anything that they were not child molesters. Happy was the farm they all lived on until the ugly woman showed up on her busted-looking bike, yelling and making threats. Rainia was terrified of the tornado that came and blew the house away, and she almost burst open with joy and confetti when Dorathea opened that door. It had changed into a wonderful, colored cartoon for Rainia, "Momma, this is the coolest movie in the world!"

"Well, you just sit there and watch your little brothers, while I go downstairs to get the clothes out of the dryer."

She watched her brave mother get up in her flowing, pink gown, leaving the living room like an apparition with the bottom of her gown's material blowing behind her trail. Rainia giggled with the boys here and there at certain characters, as the kids watched the program. Rainia felt bad for the witch in the end when she melted down into a pile of clothes from the glass of ice water that was thrown on her, but she realized that the world was a better place without that mean ol' witch. Rainia believed that she was like Dorathea. She should run away one day to find her real home. One that had a mother of her color and a responsible father who loved her and actually stayed home 4 supper. She felt the sadness in her heart as she thought of her real daddy and wondered where he was.

Getting up from the floor, she picked up the pieces of popcorn that were spilled so her mother wouldn't yell at her. Her mother was like that mean ol' witch in a lot of ways. She would like to throw some water on *her* ass and make her melt — sometimes. She even had times that she'd wished her mother was dead. Just thinking about that whoopen on her fifth birthday made her mad all over again, cuz she'd definitely wished it that day, along with being dead herself.

When she entered the kitchen, a terrible thing had happened. Her wish had come true! It was a few years and months late, but true no less. On the floor by the back door was her mother's gown, swirled neatly in a pile, just as if she had melted into the floor like the witch from the movie. *What have I done? I thought about wishing my mom dead, and it has come true!* She opened the door and called for her mother, "Momma, you down there?" There was no answer. She surveyed the hall and closed the door behind her, running downstairs to the basement, "Momma, Momma, come back; I didn't mean it!" Her heart raced a mile a minute as she bravely entered the musty dungeon of a basement searching for Anmarie, but to no avail. *Where has she gone? There's no sign of her. What if the ghost killed her? What if Billy is in the house hiding somewhere with a bloody Anmarie, ready to get me next?*

Rainia began bawling real hard now. She had caused her neighbor's deaths, and now she had killed her momma with a wish. Rainia now understood why her mom had whooped her for wishing Billy dead, because wishes *do* come true. She wished she could take it all back. She walked back upstairs and closed the door only to find that her little brothers were playing on their riding toys. One was on a slinky, green, winking caterpillar on wheels, and the other one was riding on a bumble bee with a secret compartment up under the seat where he had a car sticking out under his butt.

She walked into her room, since the boys were in the kitchen close to it, and started thinking about how she would miss her mom. She tried thinking about some of the fun times they'd had and some of the nice, once-in-a-while things that Anmarie had done for her. Rainia sat at her little, green and plaid table with the lamp on it. The bulb was hot, so she took her crayons, broke off pieces, and dropped them onto the bulb, watching the colors melt down and creating a strange smell in her room. She remembered the couple of times when her mother had brought her soup to that very table and under that very lamp, when she was sick. Rainia smiled. The twins were giggling and putting crayons on the bulb, too. Down dripped hot wax in an array of blue, yellow, green, and red. They kept doing it until the bulb turned brown and crisp and the burnt wax smell was even stronger than b4. Rainia was wondering what to try and make for dinner. She got up, went into the kitchen, and was just about to turn on the stove.

Just then, the back door opened and Anmarie came in, all red in the face. She had been outside, because she was covered in snow from coat to boots. "What the fuck is burning?"

Rainia was overjoyed to see her mom again, "Momma, Momma, I thought you were dead like the melted witch in *The Wizard of Id*. I saw your nightgown on the floor here by the door, and I looked for you in the basement, but you were gone."

Her mother laughed, as she picked up the gown, "Well, I'm not dead, am I? Make me an ice water, and I'll tell you where I went." She took off her mittens and coat and hung them on the chair. She then went into Rainia's room, where the twins were dropping more crayons on the light bulb of the lamp on Rainia's table. "Aw, shit! You little guys coulda burnt the damned house down! Don't do that!" She grabbed them both and took them into the living room, then she plopped down on the couch, took a deep breath, and asked, "Rainia, where's the ice water? Come on!"

Rainia was so glad that she wasn't in trouble for the light bulb thing that she took off running into the living room as soon as the glass was full from the faucet, sloshing the cubes up and down on the way to her mom. She tripped on the telephone cord, and the entire glass of water and ice cubes went flying into her mother's face, and she just knew that her mother was gonna kill her. Anmarie wiped her face with her hand and asked, "What did you think? That I was gonna melt? If I wasn't so damned glad right now, I'd beat your ass for that."

Rainia saw that her mother cracked a smile, and then she really looked at her mom's face. It was all red and dripping wet, with her hair matted to her head. Her glasses were crooked. She looked like someone had thrown ice water in her face. Rainia burst into a fit of laughter, and her mother and brothers joined her.

Her mom tried to air dry her shirt by waving it back and forth by the neckline, "I went to get my mail from the post office down the street. The good news is that we are moving. I finally got that letter in the mail, and the neatest, low-income townhouses are taking new tenants. I went to go look at the place with Auntie one day before we got snowed in, and they are really neat. I also got a job, Rainy! And the schools over there are nice. We are finally going to live in a nice neighborhood. Aren't you excited?"

"Yeah!" exclaimed Rainy. "When are we going?" The kitchen door started to creak open again, and they all watched it.

Anmarie wiped off her glasses, "As soon as we can move our shit through this snow, we are getting the hell outta here. In fact — we'll try tomorrow morning."

That night, the sound of a man's foot kicking in a door woke them up. Billy had found them. "Open this door, Ann! I know Misty is in here with you! She left this number and address on her nightstand by the phone."

Anmarie stood by the still-standing, green kitchen door, "Go away, Billy. She ain't even over here. She's at her boyfriend's house."

Billy heard what Ann said, ran down the stairs, and flew out of the backdoor. "Who's Misty, Momma?" Rainia asked, as she opened the kitchen door, and from the upstairs back window in the hallway, she watched Billy Jacksin hop into his car, outback, and frantically peel away.

Anmarie looked at the twins who had come into the kitchen, "Misty is his runaway daughter from down South and yall's step sister. She's about fifteen or sixteen, too old for you to play with, so don't get excited. I guess she ran away from him, too. Let's go back to bed. He ain't coming back, and if he does, we'll already be gone."

The morning was a brisk sunny shiner that left the icicles dripping from the gutters above them. Anmarie had only taken about two hours to pack the small things in the house, because they really didn't have much anyway. The moving men had put the last of their things on the back of the truck and started the engine. Thick, black smoke filled the air, and the smell of diesel ignited a fire of anticipation in Rainia's heart. She climbed into the backseat of the dark-green LTD that her mother was driving and didn't even get nauseous at the strong scent of gas that lingered in the backseat, even if the car was untouched for days. Nothing could bring down the high that Rainia was on. Not even not having a party for her birthday already a few weeks past. She had found out that her cousins Niecee and Fannie were going to be living right next door to them. It was strange of her to be glad about it, because they were Billy Jacksin's nieces from his sister Earlean. Rainia had only met them once at a picnic one day in McGovern Park, but thought that the family that they were in was a rare Black-thing of beauty, like an odd, dark pearl. Their daddy and momma were nice, and the children seemed happy. She never forgot about Niecee and Fannie and learned that they would all be enrolled in the same school together, Hawthorne Glens on Good Hope Road. That was the name of the school and the townhouses.

They pulled up into the long, snowy driveway and stopped suddenly. A man dressed in a sequined red skirt, a reddish fox-fur coat, periwinkle-blue, patent-leather, thigh-high boots, a strawberry-red wig, a teal, satin tank-top with one of the foam boobs showing from the bra, and the brightest-red lipstick gleaming beneath his mustache, walked up toward their window as they watched him, speechless.

The man fixed his fake titty as his high-heeled boot slipped away from his switching hips and he almost fell, grabbing onto the hood of their car, "Ooooh, shit, girl, I almost busted my buns and fucked up these sharp-ass 'Ricky James' boots I just got from my wife. She knows how much I like to look superfreaky." Then he lit up a cigarette while squinting through the falling snowflakes and said, "They call me 'Ms. Jack'. Welcome to 43rd and Good Hope, child!" to Rainia. "Make yall selves at home, hear? Yall go to #7 and introduce yourselves 2 my wife and kiddies. I'm running late for a date. See yall." They watched him carefully shimmy down the path, almost slipping and falling several times.

"Did you see that man, Mommy? He was dressed in a woman's outfit and talked like a girl."

Her mother was still watching him in her side-view mirrors, snickering in her throat, "Jesus Cripes! I hope he busts his ass, too. That's what you call a transvestite. It means, well, like when a man likes to wear a woman's clothes — like him. Well, he's one of em. He's a got-damned queer, so we ain't goin't to number seven to introduce shit. Anyway, you ready to see your new house?"

Rainia grinned as bright as the flakes that were falling, as her mother parked the long boat-of-a car, and they all got out. They walked up to the #5 door, and her mother put the key into the lock, turned the knob, and let them in. The guys in the moving van were turning their truck so they could back it up to the door. Once inside, Rainia could see that there was new carpeting, beige, all through the place and up the stairs. The smell of fresh paint tickled her nose, as she held her mother's hand for the full tour. The front room seemed massive, as they passed the basement door straight ahead of them. Across from that door was the downstairs bathroom. It was all clean and pretty with soap-pink walls and tiles. Further in was the kitchen, with brand-new cabinets and a beautiful, laminated, cream-colored floor.

Anmarie opened up the back door to drink in the miniature view of privacy. The flurries had ceased and the sun had come out to say, "Hello" to her. Anmarie thought, *I bet this was a small but lovely backyard until some asshole dog done dug it all up like a snot.* "The people who were here before us must have had dogs. Why don't we all go upstairs to see how nice it is?" Her mother said this but had not moved. Instead, she just stared out the window of the backdoor. Anmarie had an expression on her face that Rainia had never seen there before; it was pride. True enough, she was a White woman on her own with her three mixed kids. And she had missed her daughter's birthday again. But this time she had done good. It was good hope.

Anmarie, Rainia, J, and Jo had settled in nicely. They didn't have that much for stuff, so settling didn't take but a day or two, it seemed. The weather had become warmer and the snow was almost gone. It was a weird, mid-February Valentine's day that had seemed to bring a false spring to the air. The parking lot was wet and icky, as the ugly, little car pulled up into parking space marked #4. Earlean had rung their doorbell. It was about 5:30 PM and the sky was still fairly bright. DING-DONG! Anmarie let her in and Earlean gave her a big hug, "Hi! Happy Valentine's Day! Nice to see you made it in before they got some other family in here!"

"I know, *girl!* I was praying to God everyday to get my fat White ass in here. Shit! I got three kids and no man, and if that don't qualify me, then I don't know what does?"

"Tell me about it. My Black ass also got three kids and no husband. All these little motha fucka's is bad, too. You know, I caught their no-good daddy in bed with my best friend. The mother fucker tried to say that it wasn't him I was looking at. Like I'm crazy or something. Instead of killing his Black ass, I just got the kids and me a new place to stay, and so, here were are."

Anmarie knew the feeling, as she watched Earlean light up a cigarette. Earlean cracked open the screen door, gesturing to her small, orange station wagon with wooden paneling and Volkswagon Beetle headlights, "Yall get yall's rusty, ashy asses on up in here and say hi to ya cousins, hell!" Fannie, Poochie, and Neicee ran through the front as Earlean snatched them by the collar, "Wipe ya damn feet off first on the rug here. Yall act like you ain't got no home trainin'."

They all ran upstairs to Rainia's room where there were already pink, checkered curtains up in the window with a matching bedspread. Her mother had surprised her with the new items to accompany her new, white headboard for her bed. It was Rainia's Birthday/Valentine's day present. She even had a new, pink rug on the floor.

"Dang! Yall rich. Look at how pretty yall's house is. Your room is cute like you," said Poochie. Then he walked out of the room and went to the other rooms. The twin's room was painted blue with a crib in it and a blue rug on the floor. They had an abundance of new and used baby toys which were hanging out of their toy bin. Poochie picked up a Jack-n-the-box and wound it up real fast, "Pop, goes the weasel, whop!" they all sang and laughed.

Down the hall, they went into Anmarie's room. It was decorated in purple flowers with curtains to match the comforter. There was a big, fluffy, purple rug to match. The big dresser sat like royalty taking up one wall. Fannie walked up to it and looked in the mirror at herself. "I'm so pretty. Hey, a good hiding place for the twins!" She opened the small door and looked in.

Rainia became disgusted, "I used to hide in there. I can't fit anymore, though," said Rainia with a somber expression, remembering why she used to have to hide. She would have told them all of everything right there if it weren't for the fact that Billy was their favorite uncle. They loved him to death, and he was like a God in their eyes, so she kept the secret hidden.

The family was all settled in. The older cousins were going to their new school across the street, and the twins were at the babysitter's, two doors down. She was a fat ol', heavyset White lady with long, red hair and blue eyes. Her name was Dina. Dina had a seven-year-old daughter named Ginny with a Black man named Darius. They all lived together, and it blew Rainia's mind. Ginny was instantly made fun of by Poochie and Fannie because she was a chubby kid, but Rainia didn't care about her size. Ginny was also a mixed girl *and* living with her mother and father. That was all that mattered to get into Rainia's club. Members of your own kind, with benefits. It was no wonder that they had become the best of friends.

Anmarie's new job was being the waitress down at the local VFW bar. The veteran's welcomed her busty frame and her now wild, red hair. Anmarie was a pistol, funnier than hell, and she spoke her mind to anyone who asked because she didn't give a shit. That was also the place where she started doing some heavy-duty drinking to keep up with the good ol' boys who had served our nation. The kids would stay at Dina's house while Anmarie tended bar at night, but the fun they had would have made child history.

Chapter Seven

Eyes in Dina's Window

Dina was sitting on the couch, smoking one of her cigarettes, when the scary, Dracula-type movie had started. All of the kids were laughing and pushing elbows as they shook the eight ball for answers.

"Will I be rich and famous when I grow up?" Rainia shook it hard for a long, long time, while Poochie put on Ginny's temperature-affected, color-changing, rainbow-moonwalker boots and turned on the flashing lights to her Zany Zapper glasses. Ginny put another pair of glasses on her face. They were big and blue like huge windows, complete with working windshield wipers going back and forth like on a car. She was telling Rainia to stop shaking the magical, mystifying eight ball when Fannie came back into the room with a small glass of water to mix the packet of pretend-milk powder for the 'Milky, The Marvelous Milking Cow Game.' "Yes, again! See! I'ma be rich and famous when I grow up. Watch!" said Rainy of the toy eightball that held all of the secrets to her future in its ink-blue, watery window of hope.

"Well, who in the hell is that watching us? There, everyone! In the kitchen window! LOOK!" demanded Poochie.

They all turned around, just in time to see a glimpse of the strawberry, pinkish-red wig disappear into the night.

Dina rolled her eyes, "That fuckin' faggot. He's a cross-dressin' peepin' Tom. He's so screwed up that he don't know what the fuck to do with himself. His wife and kids are weird, too. They live in the last townhouse on the far end. You guys met those weirdo-ass kids yet? Tell em how dumb they are, Ginny."

Ginny stood up like she was in a class presentation. Turning off her glasses' wipers and then removing them, she began to speak in a serious tone. "Well, I hate to be the one to tell you all, but they murdered the last family that lived in your townhouse, Rainia. The police had dug up body parts in the backyard for days. Some of us think that they are cannibals, looking into people's windows in search of dinner."

Dina cracked up laughing, "That's right! And tomorrow's suppose to be nice out, so when we all get up, we'll go over to Anmarie's yard with a shovel and see what we can find."

Fannie, Poochie, and Niecee replied simultaneously, "Un–uh! Not us! We ain't nobody's fool."

The movie that came on was, *Love on the First Bite* with Georgee Hamilltin. All of the girls sitting on the floor were smitten by his mole and his dramatic eyes. Poochie was taken with Susan Saint Josh, "Man, I hate being the only older boy in here."

Dina rolled her eyes again, "Well, Cid and Chaz are coming any minute. Maggie should be dropping them off in a second."

The doorbell rang, and a White lady with two beautiful, blond-haired boys, about 2 and 3 came into the living room. Poochie rolled his eyes and huffed because they were little-bitty White boys. The older one was holding a plastic bag of TV dinners, cookies, chips, strawberry toaster tarts, and packets of apple cinnamon oatmeal. All of them were wearing camouflage army outfits.

Maggie tied the littlest boy's boot up tight, "That God-damned fag. I'm so sicka him in my fuckin' windows. I'm gonna start looking in his windows at night; see how he likes it." Maggie was stuffing the loose curls of her just-shy of-shoulder-length hair into her fatigue cap.

Dina giggled, "We already tried that. He's got black garbage bags over his windows, and you can't see a thing."

Maggie threw her hands in the air, "That's probably because the whole god-damned, Black-ass weirdo family is in there running around the house all cross-dressed, with hooker wigs on and shit. Hey, can I pay you on Monday? I missed the bank and I'll be getting off of my shift at 1:00 PM. The bank closes at 12 noon tomorrow. So is Monday alright?"

Dina flicked her cigarette in the tray on the small table next to her, "Well, I guess you're gonna have to."

Maggie kissed her boys, put down the bag of food on the coffee table by the other couch, and went out the door, saying, "Thanks for understanding."

Dina sat there on the couch for a minute, then suggested, "Cid and Chaz, why don't you guys go play downstairs with Poochie on the pool table?"

Rainia thought that Dina was up to something. She watched her sit there as Dina's eyes bore into the little boys' backs on their way to the basement door. She lifted her massive left leg up, rose from the couch a bit, revealing that her heavy, partially-bare, inner thighs had worn away the material between the legs of her black stretch pants. She sat back down with her left leg now pulled underneath her. Dina seemed to find more comfort in this new position. She had a tooth in the front that was discolored. She ran her tongue across it and made a disapproving grunt, "Ginny, bring me that bag over there," she demanded, with her cigarette eloquently held in her chubby hand bearing the gleaming diamond wedding ring her husband had bought her. With her cigarette still in bejeweled plump grip and holding one end of the plastic bag, her free hand rumbled the perishable goods from one side to the other. "Shit, shit, and more sh– Ah! this looks good. This must be some new shit. Strawberry Toast-T tarts." She pulled the full, un-opened box from the bag and turned it around to inspect it under the light of the lamp next to her on the end table. She then tried to get up, and after several unsuccessful attempts to stand up, she'd go down again. She'd almost get up, and then down she would go from the heaviness, for she really was a big woman. She kept on rocking back and forth and finally came to her stance. Finally, once up, she walked her bare, crusted, pie-pan feet into the kitchen. Rainia could see that she was in there planning to eat all of the things that were brought for the boys to eat, as she listened to Dina rip open the pack of tarts and put them into the toaster. After a couple of minutes, the alluring smell of strawberry jam was warm and heavily wafting through the air.

"Oooh… Mom, that smells good! What's that?" pressed Ginny with glee.

Her mother responded with a mouth full of food, "Go watch the fuckin' movie. I'll bring you guys some popcorn."

Rainia could see the hatred in Ginny's eyes. She wanted to try those new edibles, too. The cross-dresser was back at the window, watching Dina eat, as he blew bubbles in his bubblegum and went unnoticed by everyone except Rainia. Ms. Jack winked at Rainia, as she made her way to the stairs to get ready for bed with the other children.

The next morning, all of the kids woke up in Ginny's room. She was the only child and was super spoiled. She had everything a girl could dream of having to do with the Barbra Doll. The 'Barbra,' canopy bed with matching bedding and curtains, the 'Barbra Secret Safe,' that looked like an ordinary portrait of Barbra 2 hang on the wall, but you could open it up and there was a combination knob that when opened revealed that Ginny had a bunch of real and fake money in a rubber band, pretend jewellery, and photos of her and her beloved grandfather in there as her secret stash. She had all of the latest dolls, clothes, fad toys, and board games. She even had a 'Wonder Lady' swimming suit and mint-green 'I Dreamt of Jeanny' genie pajamas with the see-through legs.

With all that Ginny had, she could never compensate the truth of her problem. Underneath that beautiful Barbra bedding was a thick rubber sheet. Ginny pissed the bed at night. Rainia wondered why? *Was she scared to get up and go? Did she see something?* Rainia, waking up to the syrupy smell of piss and giggling around her, just knew that whatever the reason, it was because Ginny was scared of something or someone.

Ginny's mom yelled up the steps, "Come and eat, you guys." Dina was downstairs cooking eggs and bacon, cinnamon and apple oatmeal, and pouring the new 'Dwarf Berry Cereal' with the pink, magical midgets into bowls.

Rainia sat by Ginny and Neicee in front of a bowl filled with blue and red balls. She dug around for a marshmallow midget, but all she found was one little, pink elf finger.

Dina watched Rainy, as she sucked her dead tooth and lit a cigarette, "One lousy finger of marshmallowy fun, hey? We should sue. Speaking of limbs, you ready to go see those body parts, Rainia?"

Dina cracked up at Rainia, who was now choking with blue milk and spit coming out through her fingers.

Rainia refused, "No, that's ok." She didn't want no part of dead bodies. She didn't even want to talk about dead people at the kitchen table. It wasn't that long ago that she had seen an actual headless man at the eating table. In fact, she had instantly lost her appetite.

After breakfast, every kid in the household had cut through Earlean's yard to go to Rainia's with Dina last in line. They all walked in the fifty-four-degree weather, straight to the portion of the yard that was dug up with a shovel already in the upright position.

"Go ahead and dig, somebody," said Dina to the 9 children, the twins paying no mind to any of them, chasing one another around the yard.

Poochie grabbed the shovel like a soldier and proceed to scoop dirt where someone had last left off. It only took a couple of clumps thrown to the side before he jumped back and yelled, "Aw, *shit!* It's a *foot!*" and he took off running towards Dina's house.

Compelled to watch Dina, as she picked up the shovel and moved some more dirt around, the remaining children circled in with caution. There, on the shovel, was a White woman's, dirt-covered foot — complete with pretty, pink toenails.

"Come and look closer, you guys! It's the foot of the dead lady that haunts your house, Rainia!" declared Dina. She lifted it and flung it from the ground, making the girls scream, but a rubber cheeseburger flew into the air with it.

The children gasped for air — then went, "Huh?" The kids concentrated on the mound and could see a hotdog in a bun, a newspaper, and a giant Hershey Bar. "Dog toys?" asked the children simultaneously.

Dina and Ginny sat down on Anmarie's stoop to laugh it out, "Oh, my God, that was some good shit. You should have seen all of your faces! That was the best trick I ever played on you kids," Dina was gasping for air while trying to pat herself on her own back, but failing to be able to reach and settling for Ginny's back instead.

"I had you guys going, acting all scared with you like I was in shock, too, didn't I?" said Ginny to all of them.

"We will get you back on April Fool's Day, and again before the spring and summer is over with!" said Fannie, who was still trying to calm down, for she was temporarily mortified. "Put those nasty toys down, J and Jo! You don't know what kind of germs they got on em!"

Fannie now had a grudge to carry out, and she was going to need all of her cousins to pull it off. As the days went by and Fannie tried to come up with plans to get Dina and Ginny back, the more fun they all seemed to have.

The whole clan had become close like a gang. In # 3 was Dina and Giny; #4 was the Fannie, Poochie, and Neicee combo; # 5 was Rainia and the twin's; # 6 was Cid and Chaz's house, and # 7 was the cross-dresser family. Everyday that they (With the exception of #7) had gone to school, to church, to the park, to Mc Denny's, or to the laundromat, they all had fun. Especially at the kid's playroom in Mc Denny's where they would play and flavor-save their Happiness Meals for later. By the time the kids got home, they would try and eat stale hamburgers and fries in front of the TV along with the Mc Denny's commercials that would air. Dancing shakes, fries, and nuggets of chicken lifted their Mc Denny-the-Clown-filled spirits. The fact that Anmarie was now considered an alcoholic was never discussed. Rainia pretty much kept her bruises covered up and acted like nothing was wrong, in fear of loosing the only fun and friends that she had.

Anmarie had her good days where she would be just as fun as Dina if not better. She even ordered a jukebox complete with a disco ball spinning in the upper middle part of it, and it was also equipt with red, yellow, green, and blue moving beams that made the livingroom look like a skating ring when the lights were turned off to play the records. Ann had brought home all of the latest hits that were played at Skate University on 'Mix-It-Up Sundays' at the skate ring, like 'The Manhattan Transfer's' song, "Boy From New York City", 'Eddie Rabbit's' "I love a Rainy Night" that she would sing especially for Rainia, 'Juice Newton's' "Queen of Hearts", 'Blondie's' "Tide is High" and "Rapture", and the all-time favorite of the kid's that they memorized like The Pledge of Allegiance, 'The Sugar Hill Gang's' "Rapper's Delight". They would crack up every time they heard *"The macaroni's soggy, the peas all smushed, and the chicken tastes like wood!"*

Anmarie even let Rainia join the Lil Lady Scouts with Ginny and switched her from Hawthorne Glens to Our Lady of Hope School just down the block from Hawthorne. It was like Ginny and Rainia were sisters. They played together every day and filled the void of being the only girl in their households and different from the other children at school. Our Lady of Hope was a Catholic School of course, so they would have in-school communion services. Once, when Ginny and Rainia were in communion, Ginny convinced her to go back up to the priest to get seconds like they were at a buffet. "Here, Ginny, another juice and a handful of crackers." After she and Ginny downed the small snack, the sister standing up the isle suddenly appeared next to their pew with a ruler. She instructed them both to walk with her. Once inside the girl's bathroom, she proceeded to have Rainia bend over to receive her ten whacks. She was about to strike when she noticed a small bruise on Rainia's lower back peeking out from the space between her shirt and the waistline of her crème corduroys. The sister lifted the child's shirt up and gasped. There were a great deal of bruises, old, yellowed ones and fresh, purple ones.

The mixture of bruises wrapped around to Rainia's chest, and the horrified nun finally found her voice, "Sweet Lord of the Divine! What demon has laid hands against you, you poor sweet child?" Rainia stood there like she was deaf. The sister shook her, "Tell me, Rainia Harris! Who has been beating you?" Rainia began to cry.

"Her mother," said Ginny, who was also crying.

Immediately, the office called Anmarie, and for some reason beyond Rainia's understanding, her father showed up at the end of the day. At 3:00 PM, the office door opened and there sat Anmarie and Kent. They both looked at Rainia in a guilt-stricken way. They said nothing as the two sisters in command spoke to them both. The salt and pepper parents simply nodded their heads in agreement. Anmarie dropped remorseful tears, and Kent kept looking down at the keys in his unsteady hand. He had long braids with beads like 'Steve Stevie Wonder' off of the latest "Key of Life" album, and Kent's cologne was overburdened with a Jovan-musky hue.

The sisters did not approve of him, "The Bureau of Child Welfare will hear from us if we ever see such of an insane way to manage a child from either of you in the future. Do we understand each other? You will loose your daughter."

Anmarie shifted in her chair, "It's been really hard for me to raise three children by myself. I've just been having a tough time, is all." She looked over at Kent and said, "It's not like the kid's dads help me out. I don't even get child support from either of em."

Kent suddenly snapped out of his trance and cleared his throat, "Ahem — yes, I plan to be in Rainy's life from now on. I would like to help Anmarie by taking Rainia off her hands any time she needs a break."

Rainia, only seven going on eight, was smart enough to know that he did not want to pay this alleged child support issue, for he'd said nothing that would lead Rainia to believe that he simply missed her and wanted to be a "Dad." She suddenly realized the selfishness in what her father had just said. She remembered what she could about him as she studied his clothes, his face, and his hair. Flashbacks of raised fists, afro combs, soaking in the tub, and her mother being badly beaten swarmed her head. Screams of anguish and pleading for mercy echoed in Rainia's distant memory. What good would it be for her to stay with him sometimes if he was simply switching with her mother to beat her little ass? Rainia was tired of getting beaten and felt like taking off and running into the street outside. But there was nowhere to go. She tried to be the optimist, *At least Billy Jacksin is still out of our lives. I'll just try to be real, real good. I can be better. Stupid communion crackers and juice! Next time, I'll just think about the belt before I do something stupid.* Looking at her mother and father sitting in the same room trying to keep her from being sent to child welfare made Rainia feel guilty, *God, I deserve everything I get.* She felt sorry for her parents and all of the embarrassment of the afternoon behind her communion greed and foolishness.

After the long meeting/reunion that seemed to never want to end, Rainia was happy to get in the car and finally go home. To her continued horror and dismay, Billy Jacksin's red Cadillac was parked in the driveway in front of #5's stoop, and he was ringing their doorbell. He never turned around to notice them in their car. Anmarie was pissed, "Old, Black mother fucker! Fucking Earlean has a big mouth just like Nessara! I swear, I can't tell your aunties shit,

Rainia! Now I got both of these old, Black mother fucker's knowing where we stay. It's your fault, too, ya know! You act like I'm a bad mother," she said, as she broke down crying and backed the LTD out of the driveway the same way she had come in.

Rainia really felt like shit. Now she was really going to suffer, and it was all her fault.

It was the weekend, and Anmarie was glad to see that Billy had not come back since the other day. She really didn't need either one of the babies' dads coming around again, unless they planned on shelling out some cash to help her raise the brood. Kent had said something about coming by to drop off a couple-a-hundred dollars for her to take Rainia school shopping, but Anmarie had plans for that money, so she never told Rainia about the deal. Instead, she sent all of the kid's with Dina to go visit Ginny's grandfather in Menominee Falls, a few towns over. She thought that it would be good exposure for the kids to go to where the rich, White people lived as much as possible and see how they were living.

A silver, drop-top Rivera pulled up in the driveway. It was spanking-brand-new, and "Yearning" by the 'Gap Band' was filling up the lot with melody and bass. The speakers and sound system sounded real good. Kent got out of the car dressed in a leather biker suit, complete with the gloves. His hair was freshly braided with crystal-clear beads, black beads, and white beads. He walked up to the door and Anmarie cracked the screen door.

"Well, I guess I owe you a lot more than this," he handed her five-hundred dollars, "But you know how shit is. I meant what I said up at the school. I wanna start coming around for Rainia, if that's OK with you?"

Anmarie laughed, "Hell, I ain't God. She's your daughter, too. You have a right to see her."

Kent opened his car door and looked up at her, "Thank you. I appreciate this. I know you need most of it, but at least buy Rainia a few outfits with that money."

Anmarie shut her door. She felt like she wouldn't need a lot of things if Black-ass niggers weren't so fucking self-centered.

Chapter Eight

More Like a Player; More Like a Pimp

It was a fine summer day. School was out, and the water hose danced from stoop to stoop, washing living room windows and doors in its lively wake. The parking lot was filled with brown, caramel, and vanilla legs running up and down the blacktop. Water balloons were splashed against cars and into wet, stinging backs and heads. Little pieces of blue, yellow, and pink were sprinkled here and there, all around the grounds. Rainia, J, and Jo had just come back from their Gramma Marie's after yet another fine vacation. There, they had played every day in the playhouse that Grandpa built, in the tree house and getting poison ivy, in the creek where they came out of the water covered in leeches, in the old rusted cars out in the pasture where they had fat wood ticks sucking the blood from their scalps, in the hay loft where they got itchy skin and red eyes, and in the garages where they got glass in their feet or almost fell off of the rooftops trying to jump from one garage to the next. In the garages, they wrote their names on the walls in silver spray paint, pissed behind the tractor, and climbed on top of it and played, "Pirate Ship." Old, soft, cardboard boxes contained damp clothes from Gramma and grandpa's wardrobe of youth. There was a collection of 1950s dresses, navy sailor gear from World War Two, and jewelry accessories. One day they were playing dress up in the moth-eaten wardrobe and Rainia had gotten more than ten bee stings, for she had put on a dress that had a hive in it. She almost died, but she recovered like a champ under Gramma's wing and a baking soda extravaganza. In no time, Rainia was ready to go back out and play with her Auntie Halle who was only two years older than her and the twin brothers. They even played Indian Chief and accidentally set the small patch of woods across from the house on fire.

The kids on 43rd and Good Hope listened to Rainia's description of her trip to her Gramma's house, "Boy, did we get our asses kicked that day. We had to pull weeds out of Gramma Marie's garden for hours." The 43rd street bunch all listened as Rainia told them of her fabulous adventures with the exciting, White cousins up North. Ginny rode past on her new bike and bombed Rainia in the face. She had on her Wonder Lady swimsuit and was yelling, "Wonder Lady!"

Rainia was trying to fill up a blue balloon when Chaz ran up to her and kissed her. "Yuk! Boy germs!" Rainia wiped her cheek, and her mother took the hose and sprayed Rainia in the face with the water and teased, "That was so cute. Rainia's got a boyfriend. There! A little more water in your face then, if you think Chaz has cooties."

Chaz kissed her again and said, "You can't wipe it off. You're my girlfriend. I'ma marry you, Rainy!"

Rainia rolled her eyes. If it weren't for the birthday party for the twins and Cid and Chaz going on, she would have hurt that little boy, cute or not.

***

"I remember that day well," said the haunted Rainia to the spirit of Chaz, who was laughing next to her.

"So do I," he chuckled, and the orbs felt all warm with love as they watched the past.

***

"Here comes Anmarie's new boyfriend, playing that dumbass song again," said Ginny. While Rainia and the boys were away, Anmarie had managed to come up with a new boyfriend. His name was Jody, but people called him, "Big Jody." He had a white car like the star from *Superemly-fly*, the movie, and kind of looked like the guy, too. Turning down the music, the words, "That cat named Jody" was all that the kids could hear before Big Jody stepped out of the car. He was real tall, with long, curled hair, wearing a white hat with a speckled feather in it, a white suit, and a long, white, leather trench coat.

Poochie ran up to him, "You a pimp, ain't you? You look like you hot in all of them coats you got on. I understand the pimp game, though. You gotta look clean. My uncle Billy is a pimp, too. Give me five, man."

Big Jody smiled and flashed a gold tooth, pulling the pina-colada lollypop from his mouth, "I'm more like a player, son. I know Billy Jacksin. He's more like a pimp. He likes to whoop on women; I like too put good lovin' on em instead. Ain't that right, baby?"

Anmarie had the biggest smile across her face, and so did Big Jody when he looked at her big chest. He glided over to her with a limp, swinging his drapping trench coat off of his shoulders, holding it like a cape. He drawed up some slob around his sucker and stuck it in the side of his cheek with his tongue and swallowed, "Com'on in here girl, and let me talk to them big ol' titties sticking out your wet shirt fo a minute."

"Yall stay outside and play, hear?" said Anmarie before she locked the screen door.

Rainia heard what Big Jody had said before they went in, because she was still by the stoop filling up the now burst balloon while ear hustling. She wondered, *What's a 'player'? The pimp I know is a dude who beats up his girls, sends them out to dance, sends them on the corner, molests kids, leaves some of his own kids with nothing, kicks in doors, and robs purses — all while smoking weed. Is a player any better? That cat named Big Jody sure is cute, though. But why is he with my momma? He must just like fat, White women with big boobs.* Rainia sat there thinking to herself for a moment when the sky turned on them all. The clouds rolled and the thunder boomed, as it was followed by lightning bolts.

Anmarie stuck her head out of the window and laughed at all the kids, as Big Jody ran to his car to leave, "Here! Wash your asses," said Anmarie, as she threw bars of shamrock-green soap at the children below. They grabbed the bars and started to soap up the speckles of dirt that were splattered on their legs from the heaviness of the downpour.

As Big Jody's car was leaving down the driveway, Billy Jacksin's was on its way up. He jumped out of the car with a black garbage bag full of something, calling J and Jo into the house after him. Anmarie was coming down the stairs, cussing him out, as Billy pulled fire trucks with long ladders and real working sirens out of the wet trash sack for his boys. He also had two little kittens in the bag. Rainia thought that his gesture was the nicest, most genuine thing that she had ever witnessed him do.

"Alright, Ann, I just came to drop this off, and here's some money, too." Billy smoothed back his wet perm and went into his pocket. He gave his babies' momma some money, turned, and then gave Rainia a twenty-dollar bill. He then kissed J and Jo on the top of their curly, two-year-old heads and left.

Rainia was happy to see her mom ecstatically counting the bills, as Anmarie remarked, "Well, the nigga musta finally had a guilty moment. He would usually take from us, and a hundred dollars is a hundred dollars. Let's go to J-mart when the rain dies down. I gotta buy clothes for the twins and some catfood, and litter and shit." Rainia was up for that. She had been longing for a pair of those see-through, blue jellie shoes or 'Dyna-Kiddies yo-yo sandals' with the hole clean through the rubber high heel, or even a new pair of blue 'Zips' tennis shoes.

As the weather began to clear, revealing the sun and even more heat, the 'Kroft Hour' was coming on again. Rainia pulled herself away from the TV set, "Aw, man, we gone miss 'Dr Shrinker', 'The Bug-a-loos', 'Sigmund the Sea Monster', and the 'Land of the Lost'. Dang!" Anmarie made sure her three kids were walking to the car and then closed the door to the townhouse.

The next day Billy came back, jumped out of his parked, running Caddy and took the fire truck toys from the boys right as they were playing with them by Ginny's stoop. "I got them the wrong thing." He snatched the fire trucks up off of the blacktop and hopped back into his ride, swerving as he was backing out of the driveway.

Anmarie ran to get the histerical tots, shaking her head and grumbling, "Dirty mother fucker. That's what that bastard is," as she scooped up her crying boys, walked them into the house, and took them to the play area in the basement. The shadow of the crossdresser's wig was moving away from the basement window. Anmarie shook her head and yelled out, "Ms. Jack! Get a good stare, why dontcha? You get a good eyeful yet? Do you need to see my ass, too? Cuz I can always whip out these big ol' White titties and put your face in between em, and suffacte your fuckin' ass straight. Yeah, that's right. Move to the next neighbor's window, you human channel changer. We are not your personal soap operas!" She laughed to herself, "Look at that hairy bitch. He's got to be the nosiest drag-brawd I have ever witnessed! I'ma get ready right quick, Rainia. Watch the twins for your dear mother while they ride around the basement."

Rainia didn't even laugh and did not feel like going anywhere. She was really sad about what Billy had done to her baby brothers. True enough, her daddy was a selfish ass, but her brothers' daddy was more of one — by far. He was an asshole. *Literally.* Not the ass itself, but the actual hole inside the ass. The foul black space that the shit passes through and the chamber doorway of gaseous, foul, and hot wind. Billy Jacksin was a mother fucka! By the time Anmarie had come down to the basement, Rainia had snapped out of her daze of trying to figure out, *Why does he always got to terrorize us?*

Anmarie picked Jo up off of his bumblebee riding toy. A tiny paw was sticking out from under the seat compartment. Jo had ridden around with the kitten under him and had killed it. The other twin had climbed up the stairs and was in the bathroom trying to flush the other cat down the toilet. Anmarie ran up the steps with one boy under one arm and a dead kitten in her free hand, "God dammit, I need a drink." She threw the deceased feline in an outside trashcan, saved the struggling kitten from the swirling waters of the swirling commode, put it soaking wet on the basement steps, and shut the door. Then she opened the door again, "Rainia, get your Black ass up here! Were leaving."

She put the kids in the car, and they rode to the Northside. They went to a bar called ROSEBUD'S. Inside the tavern was an empty scene. At the end of the bar was Big Jody. He was already loaded and appeared untalkative. Behind the bar was a thick, Black lady that kinda looked like Pam Green, the famous Black actress of the seventies Blacksploitation movies, except this chick had a short curl with a red rose on the side. The kids sat up on the stools while Anmarie ordered a few drinks, "Hey, Rose, can I get a scotch and soda and three kiddie cocktails for the kids? Why don't you give them some of those 'Old Dutchman' sour cream and onion chips, and I'll take a pig's foot in vinegar."

Rose smiled as she served up everything, while Big Jody staggered out the door, then Rose walked over to the jukebox in the corner and played them all a few songs. Rose came back to the bar and wiped it down. Anmarie tried to pay her but Rose refused. The song "Woman 2 Mistress" came on by 'Shirley Brownie', and Rose had a heart to heart with Anmarie about her husband, Jody.

Anmarie was in a state of shock. She did not know that he was married to the woman and was misguided enough to believe that Rose was his bartender and lady friend. Wasn't he was the one who had introduced them both a few weeks back, and now, all of a sudden — Jody and Rose are married?

Rose gave Anmarie a smile from another place, far away and beyond from any envy or jealousy. It was powerfully genuine, like Rose was a queen. She continued to tell Anmarie all about what she knew about the Black man in America. According to her, a Black man can't be a man in this country, because he is forced to hustle for his. He does this by peddling drugs, his dick, and his spoken words, running game to survive. The Black woman has to accept this if she wants to be with him, because at this time, that's the only way to let him be a man, and there are no alternatives for the misfortunate minority. So how does she manage? She has to go through whatever channels to try and help take her man higher. In Rose's case, it was running the bar that was theirs, but in her name. She was doing what she had to do to keep her man. Rose turns her cheek to whatever he has to do, because he is *all* hers, and the little thing that he and Anmarie are having didn't mean shit to either Rose nor Jody. She explained that between business to ease the reality of the human, heartfelt side effects like tonight, she fucks around on him, and he fucks around on her, and it was no big deal, as long as the money was steady. Her main message was for Anmarie not to get too close, coming in the bar too often, bringin' her mixed kids up in there and shit. She also said that Anmarie had beautiful, light-skinned babies and to not let the door hit any of them in the asses when they left.

Anmarie was at a loss for words, and in tears, as she started up her car. Never before had she heard such game. And it was coming from a *woman*. It didn't matter to Anmarie that she was Black, but it was the way that the woman had opened Ann's eyes. She had got borrowed and had given Big Jody money, her body, and even rolled his hair for him a few times. But he was obviously in love with his wife, and it was bittersweet.

Rainia now understood what a player was; just another term for a mother-fuckin' dog. Now, whether or not what she heard Rose tell her momma was justifiable, what mattered 2 the young girl was her mother's tears. She promised herself that when she grew up, she would take men's money, never let a nigga get out of child support, kill any man that put his thing on her kids, never just take an ass whoopen off of a dude, or get real fat. This was the beginning of a new way of thinking for Rainia. She knew that this Big Jody dude had a lot to do with her mother's calmness lately, but now, thanks to him and Roses's open bullshit relationship, it was gonna be all drunk Mommy with plenty of ass whoopens for Rainia. She already *knew*!

School was getting ready to start real soon and the summer was trickling by. J and Jo's older sister, Misty, had showed up on the doorstep one day with a bag of clothes. "Damn! You runnin' away again?" asked Anmarie.

"Naw, I just wanted to bring my lil sister some clothes. She should be able to wear the tops and the shorts. You know how tiny I am. I don't ever wanna get fat like you, Ann," Misty laughed. "So, this is Rainia?" She walked into the house and set down the bag of clothes, surveying their home. Misty picked up J and gave him a kiss and then Jo. She twirled on her heel and gave Rainia a hug, "Hi, nice to meet you. I'm Misty, your fat momma's sons' step sister."

Anmarie slapped Misty on her butt, "Up your ass. Where's your stinkin'-ass daddy at, anyway? And how did you get over here if he didn't bring you?"

Anmarie eyed her with concern and mistrust, as the teen replied, "I walked. You should let Rainia come spend the night with me this weekend. Neicee will be there. Fannie and Poochie are going to a big kid's party, so they won't be there. So, whadaya say? Can she go?"

Anmarie thought about it, and her daughter did, too. Rainia was thinking that if she had a big sis around her and her brothers, Billy would be shamed and act right. If she spent the night with her and Nee-nee, she would be safe and could get to know her step-sister.

Anmarie started to look through the black, plastic garbage bag of clothes for her little girl, "You never did answer my question. What about the twins? He needs to get to know and feel shitty about these little guys he denies. Make your dad watch yall, hear? Sit down for a while so I can get the kids ready. I really need a break from these kids. I'll drive yall over there. Besides, he knows where I stay, so I wanna know where his slick ass stays, too. Son bitch!" Anmarie walked away with the boys.

Misty giggled at Anmarie's comment and walked back out to the stoop-porch and rang the doorbell of Earlean's, right next to Anmarie's. "Hi, Auntie Earlean. Is Neicee ready yet? Cuz Ann gonna take us up the street."

Earleen took a deep breath and flicked her cigarette out toward the parking lot, "Nee-nee, come on down with your stuff to go with ya cousin."

Neicee was all ready to go in a dress with clouds and suns on it. Her hair was done with blue and white puppy and bunny barrettes, and she even had a little too much grease on her partially shined-up face. Misty and Nee-nee both walked into Anmarie's house just outside Earlean's door. Anmarie only took five minutes to shovel the whole crew into the car. Sure enough, Misty pointed out a grey and beige, brick, town-house-styled single unit just 6 blocks away from Hawthorne Glen.

Misty got out of the car and went up to the screen, opening it. She turned her key and opened the house door. After about a minute, she yelled out of the screen door, "Come on in, yall. He ain't even here." Anmarie didn't have to be told twice. The inside was beautiful. White carpet and sapphire-blue plush furniture graced the massive front room. There were black and brass coffee tables and a dinette set to match.

Misty, a come-from-nothing country girl, became even more excited in her seventeen-year-old skin, "Come on, Ann! Let me show you my room."

They all followed her to share her joy. Upstairs were three bedrooms and a bath decorated in navy and gold. Misty opened the first door that they came to. The master bedroom had a fine, cherry and mahogany, master-crafted bedroom set shining underneath the glow of a red light bulb in the ceiling. The eerie glow of the ruby luminescence surrounded by mirrors glued around it like an amplifier to its power was clearly used as a sex enhancer so the bed occupants could see themselves performing. A picture of some very young, skinny White girl with fluffy, curly hair who was sitting in a wicker chair on Billy's lap was propped up on the nightstand.

Anmarie was not impressed, "Typical! Next! Where's your room?"

Misty led them to another door, and behind it was an all-white lacquered and mirrored bedroom set on pearl-white carpet, enclosed by eggshell-toned walls and sheer, silver-flecked curtains blowing softly over open, sliding windows. The whole house was filled with white carpeting.

"Wonderful! What's this last room about?" Anmarie passed by Misty and the hallway bathroom, opening the last door. It was a little boy's room. It was painted green and had several shades of green waving up and down the wall. Pictures of a little White boy favoring the beanpole in the frame by Billy's bed graced the walls. There was a bunk bed that had matching covers to the plaid, green curtains giving the carpet a greenish hue. On the floor were a few cars on a racetrack. Off to the side and under the window was a big, green toy box filled with every kind of toy, including, 'Jawson' the killer shark game that would snap shut on your hand and hurt it for real. The twins ran toward two brand-new fire trucks with long ladders shoved among the toys in the green bin. Billy was a mother fucker beyond. He had given his own son's birthday gifts to a White boy that already had everything.

Anmarie was too disgusted to let her boys stay there, "Com'on, J and Jo. Yall ain't got no fuckin'-ass daddy here. Rainia, you can stay with Misty if you want."

Rainia thought about the fact that Billy might not even come home, or if he did, surely he wouldn't try anything if she hung on to Misty's hip like a newborn baby. She decided to stay and check out her new big sister and see what she was about. After her mother left with the boys and their toys, Rainia, Neicee, and Misty ran through the house, jumped on the furniture, played dress up, and made cookies. Misty played her 'Donna Summertime' and 'Johnny Guitar Westson' albums. "Ain't that a bitch, somebody stuck up in some shit," they all sang.

"What the fuck are yall saying?" Billy had suddenly appeared .They all stopped short.

"Uncle Billy!" yelled Neicee. She ran and gave him her biggest hug.

"Hey, Nee-nee, stop now before you mess up my roller set." He fixed his hairnet over the green, plastic rollers and gave her a dollar. Then he turned to look at Rainy, and her stomach soured as he asked, "What's happenin', Judas?" Rainia ignored him as she watched him go kiss his daughter, "Misty where's my clothes that Roxy picked up from the cleaners?"

"I don't know. Her boney White tail ain't even been here for a few days," she admitted.

Billy went up to his room to change after a shower. He came back down the stairs dressed in royal-blue silk. It was a dressy shirt with matching pants, and into the garbage he had tossed a balled up 'Jonathan Walker's' bag. He had on a pair of royal-blue gators to match. "Look here, Misty. I'ma go over here to where Roxy is hiding out at and bring her stupid ass back here. Yall clean up yall's mess." He grabbed a cookie and bit into it, as he jingled his keys on his way out.

Once the door closed behind him, the party continued until the girl's got sleepy. Hours later, they were sleeping in the bed with Misty when the door cracked open. Rainia could see Billy's faint, overbearing shadow as he tried to get her attention. "Eght-ehh," Billy called his perverted signal over and over. Rainia recognised it, but she ignored it.

Finally, he turned on the hall light, "Misty, get up and come in here for a minute. Come on now; quit acting childish." Rainia was in horror with her back turned to them under the covers and Neicee was sound asleep. The bedroom light had clicked on and Rainia turned over to prepare for a fight. She put her hands over her face. Billy walked over to the bed and snatched the covers off of them. It didn't help the fact that all of them had on negligees, because that's the only sleepwear that misty had owned. Billy's dick was so hard after seeing that, he just started to stroke it.

Misty saw him and instantly became nerve-wrackingly horrified, as he was letting his demon take over him so openly. Keeping her voice low, Misty warned her father, "Get the fuck out of my room, Billy. I'll cut your dick off tonight, and I ain't playin'. You see my lil sister and lil cousin here. Get the fuck out before they wake up!" She tried to keep her rage down to a whisper, but Billy just grabbed her arm and yanked her out of the bed.

"Get up, you little bitch. After all of the new shit that I buy you. I just need to tell you something, right quick." He dragged her into the hall, but she had managed right before the yank to grab a knife that she had stashed under her pillow with the forced clench of her slim bicep. They tussled in the hallway. Rainia could hear them struggle. "No, I said," Misty would demand.

"What's your fuckin' problem?" Billy returned.

"I said I don't want to," said Misty.

"Ow! You dirty, Black, bitch, you!" Billy slammed the door to his room, and Misty walked back into the bedroom with her hair all over her head, her gown ripped exposing her breasts, and her mother-of-pearl, blood-stained knife in her hand.

Rainia just wanted to go home, as the burning tears streamed down her frightened cheeks. "Is he coming back?" Rainia asked, like they were in the trenches of a sickening war meant to be seen by no man's eyes, let alone a child.

Misty jammed the sticky, messy knife into the frame of the door, 'Jerry-locking' it tight. "Hell naw. Everything's alright. He's just drunk. He'll be asleep in a minute. Com'on and go back to sleep."

Rainia now understood why Misty had wanted someone to spend the night with her so badly. *Her own daddy, too! Fucked up! I swear to God, that man is evil! There's no way I'm gonna be able to sleep now. Thanks a lot, Billy Jacksin! ASSHOLE!*

Rainia didn't go back over there again, nor did she reveal to Misty the things that Billy had done to her. Rainia was grateful just to get away from that shit. In the meantime, back at her momma's house, her own black-ass daddy had shown up during the last few days of summer. He had to introduce her to his new lady and show off his new house. Her name was Dee and she was a beautiful Latino-Rico woman that didn't mind taking Rainia everywhere, just her and Dee. Dee would later turn out to be one of Rainia's favorite cooks, because she could burn on some serious Puerto Rican dishes. Aside from her special cooking, she liked to do things with Rainia, like ride bikes, go ice skating at the indoor rink, take her shopping and to Showoff Bizniss Pizza Place. She was light-skinned like Rainia and didn't have any kids of her own, so she made a special place in her heart for the little girl.

Present day Rainia choked up as she cleared her throat to say, "I really miss that lady's cooking. Once she made me–"

"–Green Eggs and Canadian Bacon, and you were my 1st daughter," Dee finished Rainia's sentence, as she appeared next to the current Rainia and shared the moment.

The blast of the passed-on loved ones reunion just kept getting better and better, as they both looked on at her distant father, Kent.

Kent wanted to take his daughter to Texas to meet some of his people. He didn't bring Dee, though. He had good ol' Carol waiting for him in Chicago. She wasn't as pretty as Rainia remembered her to be when she was only two. Now Rainia hadn't really cussed until recently, but, *Got Damn! I ain't seen this brawd since I was two. Time has done a number on her ass. She must have wore the shit out of the last hairstyle I saw her in, because the sides of Carol's head are bald-din a bitch.* And she wasn't all petite like back then, either. Her face looked old from drinking and running the streets butt naked. Her body now consisted of something like Dina's top portion sitting on top of the cross-dresser's spindly, hairy legs. Straight up mick-mack, or, some would say, mitch-match. Her back rolls stacked up neatly like dual, radial tires, and her 'pack-a hotdogs' neck matched just right. Her booty was flat, and her voice had gotten deep like the cough of a German shepherd with a cold. Her breasts were big and all, but they hung down like long socks with puffy, fluffy, wet house shoes in them. She wasn't cute in the face at all anymore, and her shape was fucked up, but it was her.

Rainia had to meet her kids that stayed behind and more people along the way. One of those people was her older half-brother, Kent Jr. He was about five years up over her and was mixed, too, but he had longer eyelashes over big, brown eyes. His hair was a little thicker and coarse, and he was tall and skinny. They had to dip off over to Downer's Grove to scoop him up before they got to St Louis and then down to Texas. Rainia studied Kent Jr. for any likeness of his mannerisms to hers. The way that Jr. talked was real funny sounding. He sounded like he was a White boy from the City of Chicago. They barely even communicated, and the whole trip was boring as hell. Meeting people who they never even heard of didn't thrill either of them, and they didn't have too much shit to relate to each other, because they didn't know each other, either.

They met the Texans, who were all grownups, and watched TV whilst Kent and Carol visited. The 'Ivy League Gum' commercial came on and they laughed. All the lawyers in the courtroom were stuffing huge wads of shredded, brown gum into their mouths before speaking to the judge who couldn't understand any of them and dismissed the case.

Jr. fell off of the arm of the couch he was sitting on, cracking up with hilarities, "The irony in this commercial is that lawyers are full of shit and therefore talk a lot of crap. Rainia, doesn't it look like they are shit eaters? It is good gum though. I got soma that in my duffle bag. Want some? There's more stuff, too," said Kent Jr., so they chewed some Ivy League gum mixed with some Gold Nugget gum and shrugged their shoulders. That was their only big bonding moment, and they were both *so* ready to go home.

The best part of the trip was coming home, stopping at the Scandalous House for Swedish meatballs and going to Jack N. Markus for a few school clothes. This time they dropped Rainia off first. No long talk, and no, "Hey, daughter, by the way, this is why I've been out of your life," just a, "Be good. C-u later."

"Bye, Pop, bye, brother," she said, waving to the distant-behaving relatives and shutting the car door. She held back the urge to cry as she reunited with her momma and baby brothers, telling them of her strange and boring journey. Then she went up to her room to weep. Once Rainia had sat down on her bed, she realized something, *There's really nothing to cry about. My daddy is more like a played-out player. Especially making that old-ass Carol pay for everything the whole way.* Rainia had checked it all out. She also had to check something else out. Her coochie itched. She opened her panties under her skirt, and there it was — one hair.

Chapter Nine

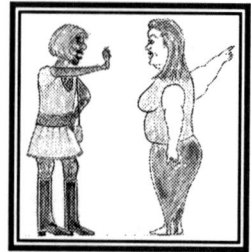

Doin' Up

Another night of being babysat was all Rainia and her brothers knew. This time it was Fannie and not Dina, because Fannie was new to baby-sitting, and she was a heck-of-a-lot cheaper.

"Look, Rainia. I got hair on my stuff. My pussy hairy, ain't it?" said Fannie to her and Neicee in the hallway.

Rainia was jealous of her boobs *and* her full bush, "SO! I'M GROWIN' ME SOME HAIR ALREADY!" Rainia stood up and showed the girl's her area. She now had a hair and a half. "And I can show you a whole bunch more when I come out the bathroom." She went into the bathroom and locked the door. After climbing up on the sink counter and opening up the medicine cabinet, she pulled out the green mascara bottle with the bright-pink top. She unscrewed it and smelled the black mascara. After jumping down to the floor, she pulled down her panties and stroked the brush down her stuff to make it look like she now had a low-trimmed, hairy coochie. She pulled up her 'Underoozies' yellow underwear, fixed her matching training bra, and went into her room. "SEE!" she flashed the girls.

"Come here, Rainy! What the fuck you got on you?" Fannie laughed.

"Dag! It's magic!" yelled Neicee.

"Ain't no fuckin' magic, and Anmarie gonna beat your ass for going in her makeup, so you better go wash that shit off in the tub." Rainia got into the tub after Fannie ran her a bath. "Now here," she handed her the soapy rag and the soap. "Scrub, and no playing in the water." She shut the door.

A song had come to mind, as the little, light-skinned girl soaped up her washrag, "Red, red, you pee in the bed. Green, green, ya booty ain't clean. White, white, we goin' out tonight." The color white. There they were, though, two skinny, caramel, light-brown legs. If only she could be the Barbara Doll, she would have everything and be happy. Blonde hair, blue eyes, the bedding, the safe with her picture on it, the Barbara Car, the Barbara Boat, the Barbara Clothes Collection, with every color shoe in the world. Then she dropped the soap by accident and made a wish, "I want blue eyes and blonde hair and white legs, hell, I wanna be Barbara on a tropical vacation!"

Rainia scrubbed the mascara off, and then she took a deep breath and stuck her head under the water to pretend-play scuba diver looking for the soap. Once she spotted it, she grabbed at it, but it slipped from her hand again and hit her open eyeball. The instant burning sensation made her take a giant gulp of water, and another — and another. She tried to sit up and cough but her flinging arms sent her backwards in the tub, cracking her head and yet causing her to inhale more water. Her lungs were stinging and full, and she quickly became tired. She stopped struggling. The stinging in her eyes and nose and the fatigue in her chest started to fade as she relaxed.

She began to drift upward, and the ceiling disappeared into a cloudy mist. Beyond it was the night sky filled with stars and the twinkling of different colors off in the distance. She saw a beautiful pair of ebony eyes. They were so familiar to her. This angel, or woman, or whatever she was, was definitely someone who loved her. She could feel the mighty power of the endless amount of love emanating from the non-judging, yet compassionate and knowing smile of the woman's eyes. Rainia could feel herself being drawn closer to this fulfilling and warm sensation as she got closer.

***

"Here comes my soul again," said the Heavenly Rainia to her company of lights.

***

Just then Fannie burst into the bathroom, "You done yet? Yo momma gone be home any min— RAINIA!" Fannie grabbed her up into her arms and slapped her cheeks. "Oh, my God! Aw, shit! Rainy!" She laid her on the bathroom floor and gave her mouth to mouth, pumping her chest. It was a desperate combination of tears and air as Fannie's heart raced. Rainia seemed to be long gone already, and it just could not be. Fannie wouldn't accept it. "OK, God," she declared, as she pulled herself together. She pushed on her cousin's chest and repeated the whole CPR procedure.

Anmarie appeared in the doorway, as Fannie lost it again and started to scream and panic. "What the hell happened Fannie? Is she dead?" cried Anmarie.

"Don't say that!" said Neicee, who was now in the doorway and on her knees praying in a quickened whisper. Fannie continued and Rainia coughed up bubbles and bath water, gasping for air. She was alive!

Anmarie had questions, "How did this happen? Where the fuck were you?"

"In your room trying on swimming suits," said Neicee.

Anmarie looked confused, "But I don't have any swimming suits." Anmarie asked Rainia if she was ok, then she got up and went into her room where the old stripper outfits were on the floor. Anmarie beat Fannie's ass all through the upstairs and then down the stairs, causing her to trip and break her leg while trying to stop her Auntie's blows. By the time Rainia had gotten to the bottom of the stairs to try and help her cousin, her mom was gone, and the damage had already been done. Fannie couldn't even get up off of the floor.

"Oh, Fannie, I'm so sorry. Sometimes I hate that fat White bitch. She's so mean."

Fannie stopped crying and looked around, "Shhh, she might hear you. If she hears you, she'll whoop your ass, and you know it."

Rainia laughed, "How she gone hear me when she left to go to work. She's gone again. Can you get up? No, no. That's ok; just lay there. I'll go next door to see if your mama is home."

Fannie grabbed her arm, "Don't tell my momma why Anmarie

whooped me; I don't want her to know that I was trying on stripper clothes," said Fannie in a worried state.

"Don't worry; I won't. I'm just glad you told me to wash off the mascara. That would have been embarrassing. And thank you for saving my life, Fannie. But what about my momma? I think she gone tell it on you."

Anmarie did tell on her — the next day. Earlean wasn't even mad about it after she found out. She just took her oldest daughter to the hospital to get a cast as if she had done it everyday and it was no big deal. Fannie was thirteen now and was starting to become a problem. She and Poochie wanted to go live with their daddy, anyway, so Earlean sent them to live with him. The single mom had been mainly responsible for the two teenagers since birth and was sick of them as well. Her words to her ex as he stood on his porch with his two teens and their belongings were, "I did my mutha-fuckin' fifteen and thirteen. Now tag! You it!" Earlean tapped his hand like in a childhood game and left the teens with their dad, him standing there with his mouth open.

Earlean was keeping her baby girl with her. Neicee was now the biggest baby in the world. She clung to Earlean like an infant and really didn't want to play with Rainia and Ginny too much. She was clearly sad from her sibling separation. Not long after Fannie and Poochie had gone to go stay with their daddy, Earlean was preparing to move away. Day by day, she was loading up her ugly, orange and wood-paneled station wagon with stuff and taking it somewhere else.

Anmarie was outside helping Earlean put the last of her things in the car. She had found herself a White man to go live with for free, and now Neicee was really going to be all alone.

"You promise to come and visit us?" asked Neicee.

"Yes, Neicee, we will come c u."

"Just call me Nee-nee from now on. I like that better."

"OK. Bye, Nee-nee." Rainia gave her cousin a final hug, and now # 4 was empty and things got weird.

A year went by, and Cid and Chaz were the next ones to move out from #6 but made frequent visits as the babysitter's best customers. The whole gang was deteriorating. Rainia and Ginny were glad to still be together though, until one day when Dina and Anmarie and Ms. Jack got into a big fight in the parking lot.

"I saw your son and daughter in the fucking shed on the end humping on each other," informed Dina to the testosterone diva. "And I told your lil powdered donut hole in the ass that I don't want them freaks down by my door!"

He pulled his purse up onto his shoulder and flared his nostrils, puckering pursed, pissed-off red lips, "Who in the fuck are you to tell my kids where they can play? You betta lick my ass like the chocolate and caramel off of a Marathon Manly Bar! Kiss my sweet, lovely, long, and friendly. My boy and girl can play down here with yall's kids. Yall ain't too good, you know. You White bitches always thank yall too damn good to be bothered with niggas' problems. Yall got funky-ass problems, too. Hell, yall like that Black dick enough to have these half-breeds, so yall betta get used to niggas for a lifetime. What u so scared of?" he barked back. He had to scratch his nuts under his panty hose, so he went for it, "Besides, All kids, and I don't care what kuh-luh they are, play, DO UP, at sometime. Shit! It's perfectly natural." He fluffed the back of his blushing bob-cut wig like he was conceited and full of all-knowing knowledge, popping a piece of gum.

Anmarie joined in with, "Yea, but brother and sister doin' up ain't natural. They could at least be cousins, and even that's pushing the envelope. It just ain't natural, man!"

He fixed his new hot-pink wig just right and re-applied some Blazin' Red-Hot lip gloss like he was fed up and said, "Neither is beating the dog shit out of your daughter because your son's cussing already at 3, going on 20. Why does she get beat down because they both tell you that they don't want no muther-fuckin' corny flakes? Yea, that's right! Ms. Jack heard and saw everything. Why are you two pale-booty bitches standin' up here tryna save face? Nev-a suga coat shit. Tell the ugly, peanutty, corn nibbletty all of it. All the shit comin' out yall's asses stank, too. Yall's kids fuck around, too. Yea, that's rite. It's been a lil gayness and incest in yall's basements, too. But it is no big, lousy deal, cuz that's what kids do. Play doctor, play do-up and hell, mock what they saw Mom and Dad do, pose like the hos in the Playerman Books. Hell! All natural! The girls be looking to see who pussy got the most hair on it, and them little White fuckers, Cid and Chaz, they be trying to hump the girls when they are sleeping with they lil, pink cocktail weenies. Tuh! But yall thank they some fuckin' angels, right?"

Rainia giggled. She had just developed a new respect for who she had thought was the oddest man in the universe. Ms. Jack had said some truth, but somehow he seemed to know much more about the whole-wide world than just looking into windows and playing male and female roles all day. Rainia decided right there that she liked him. He was honest.

Dina lit up a cigarette, "That's the fuckin' problem, too; you're a peeping Tom."

Ms. Jack rolled his eyes and snapped his fingers, "So what? I can tell you about how you are always eating up the food that people bring for their kids to eat while you're watching them. Ya fat ass be plugging up toasters and microwaves, and you even be having shit cooking in the conventional oven and on all four burners! Um, hmm! Yet them kids go to bed sniffing the fucking aromas of a full buffet made just for you, while they are hungry with their little stomachs rumblin' on a handful of dry-ass popcorn. Why you think I ain't never let you watch mine? Hell, they would starve, messin' wit chur fat, greedy ass."

Dina blew second-hand smoke in his face, like she wasn't buying into anything that he was selling.

He spit his gum out to the side, "You always smokin' and chowin' in somebody's face. Gimmie a cigarette. Hell! Share, some got-damn time!"

Dina rolled her eyes, and just then Billy pulled up. Mr. 'All That' fixed his lipstick and with a raised eyebrow got real indignant, "Fuck yall sideways, anyways. Here comes my ride," and he switched-walked over to get into the cherry chariot.

Anmarie and Dina looked at each other.

"My eyes don't believe what they are seeing. You see this shit? Where are they going together?" asked Anmarie.

"Probably to go do up, "said Dina. The prostitute/husband/peeping Tom/Father of two with the drag queen, motherly wisdom slammed the candy-apple-red car door that matched his overly-glossed lips and stuck out his tongue, "Don't get jealous. Don't get jealous. You can be a stiff cock or just use your boring imagination and settle. Billy, baby, take me ova here to this guy's house. This old White fool said he got some money for me."

The two women were glued to the pavement as they watched beauty-booty and the beast back out of the driveway. Anmarie took the cigarette that Dina was now offering to her. "Billy really can't come around my boys now. He's a wiener licker. Or maybe he likes his wiener licked by gay men? Damn! The pimp game is getting that desperate that you gotta pimp fags? I don't even give a shit no more. I gotta fuckin' move again. That little, spying, fruity nut-butt knows all of my business," Anmarie declared with a shudder.

A couple of weeks later, as said, Anmarie found them a new place to stay. Ginny and Rainia cried when it came the day that Anmarie and her three kids left to move. Rainia took Ginny's phone number down but knew that they would never be able to get a phone. Things were gonna get a lot worse, and Rainia had a gut feeling that she would probably never see Ginny or Cid and Chaz ever again. She watched through the back window as her friend cried into her mom's, Dina's, arms. She also saw her mom push her away and shove an ice cream bar at her. The rest of the long drive took the family-of-four to a neighborhood that looked familiar. The place where they went to was on 21st and Michigan, right in behind the Eagle Eye's Club.

"Back damn near to the place we left, huh, Rainy?" Anmarie laughed. The house was a small one-family, with only two bedrooms and no upstairs. Earlean and Niecee were living in the Ambassadorial Hotel around the corner, because the White man that was suppose to be her Prince Charming went back to his White wife. Earlean and Anmarie soon joined households. Neicee and her mom moved in with the family of four, making it six, shortly after Anmarie got settled in. It was no surprise when Rainia saw Billy Jacksin one day when she was playing outside. He looked down-trodden and skinny. His hair was sticking up, and he seemed *pathetic*. She started to turn and run away, but it was something that he said that stopped her.

"I'M SORRY, RAINIA! I'm sorry for everything that I did to you. I just wanted you to know that." He turned to walk up the block to where his car was parked. It was still clean and pretty.

This time Rainia spoke, "I'm not scared of you anymore, and you're going straight to Hell. One day you are going to die like the piece of shit that you are. Stick your sorry up your ass, you creep. AND STAY AWAY FROM ME, MY BROTHERS, AND MY MOMMA." She felt like she had more power than he could have ever taken from her.

Rainia could hear him say, "I deserve that," as he never turned back around, but continued to walk to that red Cadillac with the top he never, ever let down. He got in, cranked it up, made a Y-turn, and disappeared. Billy never did come back, either.

It was a beautiful, seventy-degree day when the doorbell rang, alerting them that there was an unexpected visitor. There was a strange look on Auntie Earlean's face as her ex-husband stopped by to drop off the bad news that day, "Nobody knows where he is either. Misty has been home every day, and he hasn't come back since the day that you probably last talked to him. He's your brother. Don't you know where he could be at?" asked Nee-nee's daddy.

"Naw, um… (Earlean looked over at Anmarie.) I had told him to bring some money by, even though I wasn't supposed to be letting him know where we are living at, but that was over two weeks ago. Damn!"

Anmarie rolled her eyes at Earlean, "Well, I haven't seen him either, so don't look over here. Shit, you know how I feel about him, and I know you and your kids think so much about your brother." Anmarie sat on the couch playing with a book of matches, listening carefully to hear all of the details of Billy's disappearance.

Earlean shifted her weight from one foot to the other, as she continued to concentrate really hard on the words coming out of a man's mouth that she had swore that she would never face again. Flashbacks of him cheating on her tried to sneak in and rule the bulk of her thoughts, but, somehow, the thought of her brother possibly being gone for good just seemed more important. It was true that Earlean knew her bro was a real go-getter, but all that she ever really saw him do was pimp. She never saw him beat any of his girl's down, but she had seen Anmarie all fucked up a couple of times. She also knew that he did not take care of J and Jo but took Misty in without a doubt in his mind. She did not agree with the way that he let his daughter dress and run the streets, but her Southern-belle, teenie-bopper of a niece damn sure wanted for nothing in this world. Earlean had called her sibling a little over two weeks ago to have him bring by a thousand dollars. Her nephews had needed clothes, and there wasn't any food in the house. On top of that, the struggling mothers were behind on the rent, and the bills were still high from being transferred from the townhouses when they didn't pay that last round to have the extra money to move. He didn't ask Earlean any questions, and he clearly had his own problems that he wanted to share with her. So she listened to his troubles and offered what advice she could — like — "Get out of the game then."

Her brother got high-pitched in his voice with, "And do what, Earlean? Pimpin' is all I do. That's just me. Billy Jacksin from Milwaukee, Wisconsin, baby."

"Whatever, man. Just keep the snow out cha nose," said the concerned sis.

Billy laughed and said that he was on his way with the cash. Desperate for the extra money in route, Earlean waited for him on the corner for at least three hours, but he never showed. She called him several times after that, but the phone would just ring and ring; even Misty didn't answer. Earlean just assumed that he was probably out of town, breaking in a new bitch or something. But it never took him two weeks to wine, fuck, and dine a brawd into his game. That usually took about a weekend, tops, because Billy wasn't about to stay away from the rest of his flock for too long. He always said that was how they go astray. He had to be around to make his rounds quite frequently. This included fucking them all from time to time and stopping by on the regular to get his money. Once in a while, he had to kick a little ass, but the new hos that he was getting were easier to manage. They were all pretty much cocaine users. Billy was too, but he did it recreationally, not faithfully. His dames would do anything for the new way that drug dealers were fixing the coke into tiny rocks for their customers to smoke in slender, glass pipes. Billy had a connection that allowed him to buy just enough to keep the bitches hooked.

***

All of the orbs of light watching the past of Rainia's life were transfixed on the suspense.

"Back then, when crack first came out, you just couldn't buy crack; you had to know somebody," said the spirit of older Rainia to her twinkling peers, as they all looked on, waiting for Earlean to continue with her statement.

***

"Billy don't have to spend a fortune. He just buys a little bit here and there to pass out like candy. He's more paid than ever, according to Misty," replied Earlean. The only one of his women that didn't use cocaine was good old Cheila. She had been locked in a heroine dream for the past four years, but as the heroine started to dry up, Cheila started to sober up. She didn't trust cocaine or crack rock. Heroine was her choice of poison, but if she couldn't have that, she didn't want shit.

Billy had been trying desperately to convert her because she had quite a few rich, old White men for tricks. True enough, he still had his Black-ass, drag-queen bitch to pass among them, but those conservative men liked their White pussy, too. These men had been coming to her for years, and Billy couldn't loose that kind of dependable security. She did not care anymore and had wanted out of that lifestyle. Cheila had started to talk more shit, and she had gotten herself into college. She never had any children but was even putting on weight. She wanted to be free and live a different life.

Earlean tried real hard to remember all of the things that Billy had on his mind the last time she had talked to him, "He really was the closest to Cheila, his main vanilla bitch from the sticks, for she was the one who he had started out with, and for every pimp, there is something about that first bitch if she's down like Cheila was. It was like she was his wife — or first love — and Billy was talking like she was dead and the dream was over. Times were definitely changing on him and he did not like that. Has anyone been by any of his girl's houses by way of a house party or birthday jam or something? I mean, there's Roxy and Cheila for sure. I know that no one would know about the new girls' places of residence, but those two bitches had to see or hear something," said Earlean to the both of them.

They both looked at her, and Andy said, "Well, I wouldn't know about that. How about you, Anmarie? Do you know where those two women live?"

Anmarie looked at her nails with boredom, "I'm so sure the one yall need to be asking is Misty."

Chapter Ten

Pine Bluff, Arkansas

After Nee-nee's daddy left, Earlean, Anmarie, and the kids all piled into the big, green gas guzzler and drove over to Billy's house. Earlean rang the doorbell, and Misty answered it in a panic, "Oh! Hey! I was hoping that you were my daddy," said Misty, who looked like she lacked in sleep. She had dark rings under her eyes and her lips were chapped. She opened the screen door for all of them, and then she plopped down on the couch and covered up with her blanket.

"Misty, where does Roxy and Cheila stay at?" asked her aunt Earlean.

"I think Roxy went back to Florida with her son for good, but I heard that Cheila was living somewhere by the Harvey Davidster factory. Why? Is my daddy over there with her fat ass? Shit, he better try and come home to pay this rent. We gonna get put outta here in a hot minute. Hell! I can just go back to Pine Bluff, cuz I can't pay no $800 rent for this lavish kingdom he got here." Misty's country accent was emerging in her frustration.

"The Harvey Davidster factory, huh? Where's that, over there by that Mc Denny's on 35th street?" asked Earlean of Anmarie.

Anmarie answered, "Yeah, over that way. Wanna ride over there and see what we can find out?"

Earlean replied, "Yeah, if you don't mind? Misty, give your Auntie about two or three dollars for some gas, so we can find ya daddy."

Misty ran to the freezer and pulled out a stash, "Here, take $50, but please find my daddy."

They drove up and down the streets over in that area, asking the people on the street if they had seen a fresh, red cadillac parked for days. Finally, off of Highland and thirty-fifth, around the middle of the block, was a group of drunks partying on an apartment stoop. The sloppy, drunken men had shopping carts filled with cans lined up on the sidewalk next to a detective's car.

"Earlean, if anybody has seen a red Caddy, it's these street-roamin' clowns. Just go ask the drunken cruddy-crew if they seen somethin'."

Anmarie parked the car, and her and Earlean got out. Earlean asked the first question, "Hello, *gentleman*. How yall doin'? Ah… have yall seen a red Cadillac parked in the neighborhood on any of your can runs?"

The stinkiest-looking man stumbled to his feet and swayed, with his bagged, brown bottle in his hand, "You mean that clean set a wheels dat the police towed away dis mo'nin'? Yeah! We all saw it!" They all laughed real hard. "Naw, naw, naw, baby girl, I'm just having me a good time. But I thank that sumptin' done happened. Cuz we don't eem shtay roun here, but dey say dey found a body up in dea in dat buildin'. Ain't dat how dey sayin', Ronnie?"

The next-most-funky dude stood up to join them, "Dats right, Carl, and whoever it was, it was big, cuz it took a couple of cats to carry the body bag out. Don't nobody know if it was a man or a woman, but somebody ain't gone be drinkin' today, that's fa damn sho!" They all cracked up real hard.

Earlean could feel the tears in her eyes start to burn, as the detective came out of the building, rolling up some yellow crime tape. "Excuse me, officer, ah, sir, but what happened in there?" asked Anmarie. The pale-faced, hard-looking, blond-haired, blue-eyed man looked her up and down and said, "I can't reveal any details to the public, but I can talk to family. Unfortunately, the victim's body left no identification; the license plates left no clues, and we are still looking for the suspect who fled. Why? Do you have information about this crime?"

Earlean was now crying full out, and Anmarie just held her, "She might. She could be the sister of the killer or the victim, depending on which is which."

The cop took out a pen and pad, "I'm listening."

After a short conversation, they all followed the detective downtown and then over to the morgue. Earlean had to identify the body.

"Dammit, Ann. If the plates were ran, and the dead body didn't give a tying clue, then maybe he had killed her. That would mean my brother is going to jail for life. A nigga cannot just kill a White woman and get away with it. He is going to have to watch his back everyday if they catch his ass. I wonder where he is on the run at?"

Anmarie watched, as Earlean was content with accepting the possibilities. They pulled up to the coroner's office and Earlean got out. Ann's eyes followed the confident Earlean into the morgue wearing a hopeful expression, and yet felt a shock, as Earlean ran out of the glass doors, screaming and falling to her knees after only being inside for a short ten minutes. Ann got out of the car and rushed to her side, holding her, rocking with her, and trying to help her get her hysteria in order. Once Earlean could walk again, Anmarie helped her back to the car and helped her to get in. She then got back behind the wheel. It was confirmed, "So, Billy is dead, huh? Well, what the fuck happened to him?" asked Anmarie.

"That fat bitch, Cheila, stabbed him to death in her bathroom. I guess that he had been staying over there on a crack binge and went to whoopin' her ass last night, after she refused to take a hit of crack so she could trick for him like she used to. She said she didn't cooperate with him, and then he started acting like a madman. Cheila had taken at least a hundred major ass beatings off of my brother in the past, and it never phased her cuz she stayed high. But last night she finally cracked. She was the only one who must have known he was using so heavily, because we sure didn't. The police said that he tried to choke her and she retaliated with a knife. She gave it to him in the chest about a hundred and seventeen times, near and in the heart. She stabbed him until she got tired. A wound for every ass kickin' she ever took. Then reality set in and she ran for it. She had called in the information about an hour ago, but she's too scared to turn herself in. She thinks she is going to jail, but you and I both know that White bitch ain't gonna see no time for killing my brother. She was so much in a hurry to get outta there that she left her door wide open, and a neighbor found my brother. He was curled up around the toilet, drenched in his own gelatinous, yellowed blood. The coroner said that he was so zooted that he probably didn't feel a thing. How in the hell am I gonna tell our momma, and his daughter? This is really fucked up, Ann."

Rainia thought about the last thing she had said to Billy. She never reported his last living sighting to her mother or to her aunt but concentrated on staying strong during their rough time. She did not cry either, because she was glad that he was gone 4 good. Neicee was crying, but the twins weren't. Their daddy never gave a fuck about them, and even as little guys, they knew this, so why should they care about the way things had gone down?

Anmarie turned to look at Nee-nee, then she looked at her daughter who was silently looking out of the car window, and finally, at her two beautiful, little boys, who seemed to be occupied with driving small cars up and down the backseat. "I'll be right back, Earlean. I gotta go up in here to ask these police something," said Anmarie, getting out to go inside. She opened the glass door, approached the counter, and gestured for a cop to come by her, "Excuse me, but how do I get a death benefit for my sons from their dead father? Can I get a copy of his death certificate here or at another building? He just came in this morning."

"What's the name?" asked the coroner.

"Ah, Billy Jacksin," said Ann.

The man behind the counter raised his index finger in the air with, "Oh, yeah, that guy again. He's pretty popular today. He had us in a mystery down here. The plates on his car were registered to Billy Jacksin, but his dental markings and skin tone revealed a whole different fellow. The real Billy Jacksin has been dead for at least thirteen years, and — he was a White man. The problem is, we didn't know who this guy was until a few moments ago. We would have had to ship out a missing-persons John Doe file with his teeth to see if anyone was missing anyone, and frankly, that kind of thing can take weeks, or years, or could just go unsolved." He threw a clipboard at Anmarie with filled-out documents on it, "Well, you can start by his real name, Dameon Jefferson from Arkansas. You should have known that if you have sons by him and that's the name you put on the birth certificate."

Anmarie didn't know what the hell was going on, "Dameon Jefferson? But his sister's maiden last name is Jonson, without the H. How could it be different?"

The man said, "I guess they had different daddies. His sister is the one who told us, or else we would have buried him listed under Billy Jacksin if no one claimed the body after a certain time and the dental markings couldn't tell us anything. But here he is, back there with his real name on his toe tag, thank goodness. Different names, I tell ya! That's not uncommon for people of color. In fact, it's quite normal."

It all became clear to her now, "So, what you are saying is, if I don't have the real name on the birth certificate, then my boys don't get shit?"

The coroner put his hands together like he was going to pray 4 her, "You don't, unless you have the money and the power to investigate his whole life, dental records, blood samples and court time to prove that he was their dad. I assume that you are not getting child support, because then the process is automatic, but the only children we have listed as surviving family are two girls from Pine Bluff, Arkansas." The coroner cop raised his eyebrows, tightened his lips, and shook his head, "Sorry, ma'am," and walked away.

Anmarie kicked the bottom of the counter, "Got damn you, Billy Dameon Jefferson Jacksin! You slimy mother fucker, you! You managed to get out of helping me even in death, you rolling stone, child-hiding, name-snatching son-of-a bitch. Ain't no telling how many kids you really left behind."

Billy's body was shipped back to where he was born, and his mother requested that everyone come on down there, including Anmarie and the kids. She said she never even knew about her other grandchildren, and she was getting to be an old lady, so they might as well come and spend some time with her just this once.

Earlean's ex-husband, Andy, had a new, yellow-gold, and brown van. He offered to take all of the family down South. There was Poochie, Fannie, Nee-nee, J, Misty, Rainia, Jo, Earlean, and Anmarie in the van with the observation bubble in the roof. The dashboard lit up with pretty, green, digital numbers, and brown carpet was on the floor and up the walls. The van was really used, but it was new to all of them. The kids played and joked and got riled up every time Micky Jacky's pop hit song "Roll With You" came on the radio. It was a very long journey. By the time they pulled into the town of Pine Bluff, they were all achy, stiffy, smelly, and sick of each other.

Rainia tried to take in the small, rural, Southern town. It was a boring place. The most exciting thing was the Sunbread billboard that had a pretty, canary-yellow, blonde-haired girl actually mechanically swinging back and forth on her swing, smiling and winking about the big, toasted loaf of bread under the sunbeams next to the flow of her baby-blue dress, white stockings, and black, patent-leather shoes. The roads were red dirt clouds that they left behind, as they continued to Earlean's mom's house. The sounds of small stones coming off of the spinning tires and hitting the sides of the van had mocked popcorn popping. Big, mighty pine trees towered over the roads and had massive spider webs up in them and some that were hanging down. "Dang, yall, look at those big ol' spider webs! They must got tarantulas out here!" said Rainia.

Uncle Andy said, "Tarantulas? Hell, a tarantula ain't got shit on a Southern spider. If you thank that the spiders is all you got to worry about, then you must ain't heard-a Pine Snakes and June bugs, either. The snakes are so fat and long that they need all afternoon to cross the roads out here, and the June bugs are chubby, gold, corn-nut-looking things that hit you in your forehead over and over until you run away, crunching them up under your feet. Shit! The mosquitos are so big that they fly with a nurse so she can put a cotton ball on ya arm after they bite, like you was at a doctor's office. Ain't that why we niggas leave the South? To leave the damn bugs, right, Earlean?"

She looked over at her ex-husband and smiled, "Yeah, that's right. Yall gonna see what we talking about."

Once they got to the old house, people started coming out of the front door, jogging down the front-porch steps. "Hey, yall! It's our cousins! Come see!" There were so many kids and people coming out that Rainia just stood to the side.

Misty grabbed a pretty Black girl's hand and brought her over to meet Rainia. "Rainy, dis ya sista, Trease. She got long hair like you. She was Daddy's favorite and pride and joy."

Rainia wondered if he fucked with her, too. She was about 14 and had big breasts. Her smile was as bright as a hundred-watt light bulb, and her skin was a shimmery, dark, dark brown. Her hair was long. It was jet black and was real wavy. In fact, she had waterwave hair.

"Hi, Rainia! Nice to meet cha!"

"Hello. You too," said Rainia.

They walked up the porch to hug Earlean's momma. She was a heavyset, smiling woman with a gold tooth. Rainia could tell that she was Billy's momma. They gave her a hug. "Dese Dameon's beautiful boys? And this here girl is as pretty as a peach. I wonder; why was he shame of dem and never brought them to see Big Momma? Well, can't ast him now, can I? Yes, sah! Dameon gone to the pearly gates."

Yeah, right! You mean the gates of hell marked with 6-6-6, thought Rainia.

"Well, he showed dem White boys that tried to kill him when he was a boy. He had all the White women he could stand in the city; didn't he, yall? He was the man! Come on, yall; I want my family to meet all the rest a my family, White, yella, Black. Hell! We all family," she said, as she grabbed Anmarie's arm and pulled her into the house, linking arms with her and smiling.

The children were introduced to all of the other kids, and then they all walked down the dirt road to go to the soda machine on the dirty old man's porch. Peach Knee-Slap was the only thing poppin', and they didn't say soda; they said, "Pop." They ran up and down the roads playing tag and telling stories, or "sturys" to one another and went to other relatives houses to meet and greet.

"And this here are Billy's boys and his other daughter, Rainia, from Milwaukee. Big city folk, here!" Rainia did not like to be called that man's daughter, but she just played along with the shit to keep the peace. Besides, he was still dead.

Nightfall came, and Just like it was told to them earlier, the June bugs attacked. The kids went into the house, but the teenagers stayed out longer, watching the fat bugs pile up under the single fluorescent street light that they were drawn to. The TV was on, and something called a music video was playing Micky Jacky's hit. He was dancing in a sparkly outfit with beams of lights coming up from behind him. He had a big Afro, and he was cute with his fat nose. The older girls caught a glimpse of the music and ran inside to drool. The boys ran in after them, crunching June bugs under their feet along the way to mock the way he was dancing. Micky Jacky was the '*Shit!*' As the night died down, they all slept on the living room floor and talked all night long to the sound of crickets and a lone firefly that was circling the room.

In the morning they woke up to eggs, grits, bacon, toast, and pancakes with brown and white syrups in jars. Rainia thought that the brown syrup was maple, but it was molasses. The white syrup was corn syrup and was only good for making popcorn balls at Halloween, but still, some people liked it in their grits.

It was the morning of the funeral. Everyone ate well and got dressed in their finest attire. They all gathered in the vehicles which were lined up outside the house and two men had to walk Big Momma to the limo. The kids went in the van, but Misty and Trease went in the limo with Earlean and Big Momma.

Another woman pulled up in a pretty car, "Wait for me, Momma! It's me, Ruby!"

Even Anmarie wasn't aware that there was yet another sister of Billy's to meet. No one up North ever talked about any of their family down South. Now that this man was dead, she was starting to understand a little bit more about the mystery of his family. She paid special attention to the stories about the White boys that had tried to kill him often and had threatened to hang him in a tree if they ever caught him looking at one of their White girlfriends again. She had heard about how they whooped him after school, sometimes leaving him spitting his blood out on the lawn. They had eventually caused him to quit school at about 16 and leave town. His momma said that the day he left for Milwaukee, he decided to change his name and make a new life that allowed him all of the White women he could handle. Anmarie wondered about the White Billy Jacksin who had died and how Billy had got a hold of his identity info. Anmarie kinda felt sorry for him now.

Once they got to the church it was real hot outside, and the inside didn't have much for air conditioning. Big cardboard fans on sticks with a picture of the funeral home on them waved about in a frenzy. Up ahead, in the middle of the aisle, was a big, black, shiny casket. It was open, and Rainia could see the top of his hair. She really didn't need to see anything else. She believed he was dead. Once the service was in full throttle and Big Momma was wailing and laying on the casket, the wheels underneath the casket started to give. One side of the braces underneath had broke, sending the casket to the floor on its side, and Billy Jacksin's body came out and rolled onto the floor.

Rainia was horrified! She looked down at him laying there on the floor in front of their pew and started to get up on the pew and scream like he was some kinda huge rat. She could have sworn that his eyes opened up and looked at her.

Misty and Trease lost it, too, "My daddy, my daddy!"

"Get these girls outta here. They can't see the man like this. Send them home," ordered Big Momma.

Rainia joined in to get the hell out of there, "My daddy, my daddy!" She couldn't take another minute of her precious life being spent in the same room with the corpse that had taken so much innocence from her living body.

Earlean's ex-husband drove them back to the house, bought them all three bottles of peach pop apiece, and cut on the air conditioner. He cracked open a beer, "Damn! I hate that I believe in Karma! The shit you gotta do and go through to make amends with people is too much on a man! Yall ok? Yall gone be alright?" He was glad to be away from the scene, too.

They spent one more day after that with Big Momma and the rest of the family. Then they all piled back into the van and headed back up to Milwaukee.

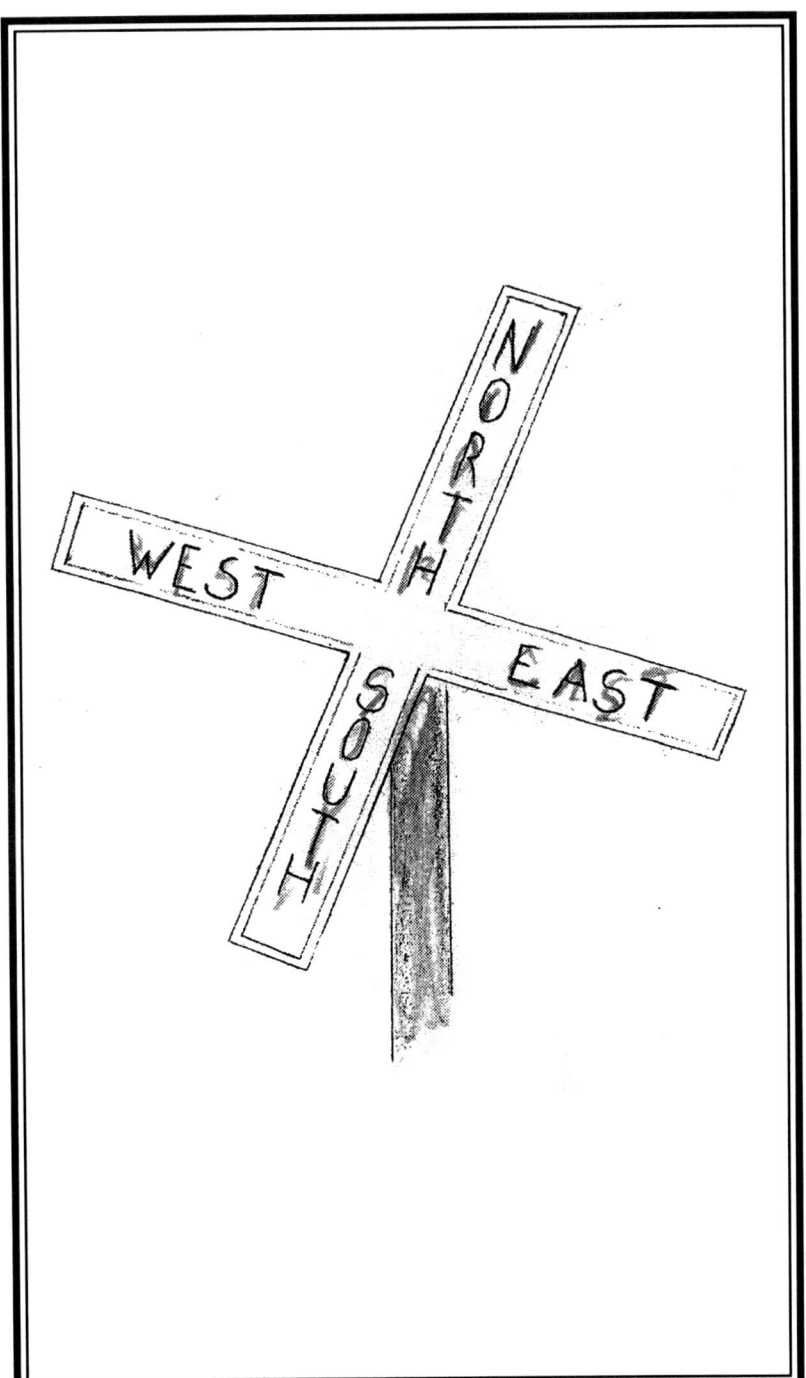

Chapter Eleven

Them North and South Folk

Times were going to get even harder. Even with both women working, the rent was hard to make, because it was high and not a low-income deal like the townhouses. The two mothers knew that they had fucked up by leaving. There was no way to get the now occupied townhouses back. They were really poor now. There were days when they could not even eat. Anmarie had come up with a hustle for cashing in cans. Rainia, J, Jo, and Nee-nee would collect cans from the local taverns' garbage dumpsters so that Anmarie could cash them in, just to be able to go to the Mc Denny's up the street. Sometimes when it was real-real hot, and the garbage was extra funky with maggots and God knows what, Rainia would let a few tears of self-pity fall, because she knew that they were as bad off as the kids on the 'Feed Kids Worldwide' commercials, right here in America, and that the only kids that were doing lowlife acts like that were the minority kids. Never hardly ever the White kids. Her mother was determined to cash in all the cans that they could dig up, "Come on, you guys — faster! And stop throwing full cans of beer in here, because the shit is dripping in our car."

Nee-nee had to pee, "I'm finna go in here and pee. Yall comin'?"

Rainia, J, and Jo stopped digging through the garbage and climbed out of the big green bin of stench.

Anmarie was shaking the overly-stuffed bag of cans when she looked up, "What the hell is this? We got six more places to hit before the recycling place closes."

"But I gotta pee real bad, Auntie," and Nee-nee ran into the tavern.

There was a big fan built into the wall where you could see the floor inside. As they all walked up the stairs to follow Nee-nee, Rainia could hear the beginning of "Hot Child in the City" playing on the jukebox. The place smelled just like a stale beer can. There were fat White men with their hairy, smelly, sweaty, pimpley 'plumber cracks' showing, as they sat on stools and looked over their porky shoulders with a drunken, red-faced, judgmental eye at Anmarie with her children of color.

Rainia heard one of them say to the other, "Aw, forget about it. She only likes dark meat. She's got a nice rack on her, though. Cheers to big tits." They were right about her mother's choice of men. Rainia never saw her mother with a White man — ever.

Anmarie had come up with a chain of ridiculous boyfriends to get them to give her money to help her pay the bills. The twins and Rainy ran them all off. They had even given them names like, Redcap, Chinaman, and Old Indian Chief. The only one of them that didn't need a name more goofy than the one he already had was Ezra. Ezra looked like Eugene Lefty off of Second Town TV in Canada and tried to stick it out by bringing over beer and pizza. The twins put popcorn and napkins in his glass and poured beer on his crotch and on the pizza he was eating. He left, complaining to Anmarie that her kids were too much trouble and that she had mice. It was true! The house was filled with mice, and they were all coming from the dumpsters of The Eagle Eye's Club.

One night Anmarie bought some poison to get rid of them. The next morning, Rainia, Nee-nee, and the twins woke up to spaced-out mice jumping around on the bed and spazzing out on the floors all throughout the house, "EKK, EEK, TWEEK, SQUEEK, EEK, EK," squealed the mice. Some were going in slow motion across the bed like they were wounded soldiers on a field, and some were twitching and jerking on their sides. Others were shaking their heads back and forth, as they ran around the bed in a daze.

"*MOMMA!* Get them outta here! They on the bed wit us! They is on the bed wit us! Aw, shit! We finna get bit and die from rabies. God dammit! *MOMMA!*" screamed Rainia.

Anmarie finally came into the room with a broom, started swatting them dead, and said, "Nonna yall ain't shit. A bunch a little pussies. Earlean, get your ass back here and help me!"

Earlean jumped off of the couch where she was sleeping at and came running to the back of the house, "What, Ann? What is it? *OH! — HELL NO!*" and just ran right back into the front room and out the front door.

The whole ordeal made Earlean move out after hooking up with yet another White man, taking Nee-nee with her. Then Anmarie and the kids ended up moving to 19th and Atkinson by the time the next rent was due. Rainia had gone from Wisconsin Boulevard, to Hawthorne Glens, to Our Lady of Hope, to Lancaster Len, to Gardenia Homes in just a few short years. They lived on 19th for only a few months, then they moved in with one of Anmarie's good friends who also had mixed kids.

Patty and her kids, Tanette, Vanzell, and Lil Kelly stayed in their turquoise-blue house with the white trim on 35th and Walnut where Rainia now went to 37th Avenue School for a minute. They were all welfare kids, and the two checks going toward one rent wasn't even enough.

While staying with Patty, they had the experience of living in a house full of roaches and mice. The roaches were into everything and at all times. They flew from the light fixtures and dominated the sweaty pipe underneath the bathroom sink. They controlled the TV and laughed at the threat of roach spray like it was merely some cologne for them to wear to the roach nite-clubs in the cupboards. When the kitchen light was turned on and the cupboards were opened, they didn't scatter away, they just yelled out, "Hey, there you are!" and invited you to join the party. If you opened the sealed plastic prize in the 'Good cereal' box, you would only find the roach that had gotten to it first, poplocking, roboting, and rapping about how late to the show you always are.

The mice were just as notorious. They could climb up the frame of the door, sit at the top, and just wait. Patty's mice were so hood that they waited for a person to walk into a room and then jumped down on them from the doorframe. If their tiny arms were just a lil bit longer, then you would be in a full Nelson every time. They had a lot of gangsterous personality to be rodents, because that's what they did for kicks. That and running out and stopping in front of the living room floor when you were watching TV at night. They liked to watch the creature-features, too.

Patty, who was never the least bit bothered by any of her small, space-controlling roommates, was an 'Allot-More' cigarette smoker, the brown square with the extra tar. All she ever made was pinto beans. The kids had to eat sugar on bread cooked under the broiler part of the oven. The flame kept the roaches away. On the days when Patty and Anmarie got their government cheese and butter, them was the days of some good eating. There would be the bombest macaroni and cheese on the block stirring in the pot, as everyone was required to stay in the kitchen with a shoe in hand, posted on roach killing duty. They would all be damned if roaches took over that food, too.

At Patty's house, they could run up and down the stairs with her three bad-ass kids — and no one cared. Vanzell could jump down a full flight of stairs and land on his blackened, dirty feet like a cat. He could even go into his closet and climb to the top using his feet and hands on opposite walls until the walls were covered in black footprints on either side.

Rainia discovered his 'Spiderguy' talents one time when they were playing hide and seek. She could hear him laughing in the room that she was looking in, but when she opened the closet door, it was empty. After checking about eight times, she finally looked up to find him up above her, slobbering spit down on her with laughter. Then he jumped down on her, knocking her to the floor. After her butt bone stopped hurting, she learned how to climb up there, too.

They were so poor that they would make up shit to do even though their surroundings were barren. Sheets were over the windows for curtains; plates of crusted food were wherever they pleased to r.i.p.; the couch was all black and dingy from the barefoot children's filthy feet. None of them ever wore shoes and had built on protection due to the dirt of their black-ass feet. Their bathroom reeked of piss and had a sink that always ran cold water non-stop cuz it was broken. The kid's would fight like they were at a bubbler that pumped 'kooljuice' just to climb up on the toilet seat, lean over to the sink, and put their lips to the faucet to get them a good drink of the best, damned, ice-cold water in the world.

Yes, they were without, yet it was a time to always remember. They were the definition of "The American Poverty Struggle", but they sure had fun doing it. The morning cartoons would come on, and away the children's imaginations went. There was a lot of life among Tanette, Vanzell, and lil Kelly, named after Big Kelly, and those poor kids were more imaginative then the adventures of the 'Great Space Drifter' show's whole crew. They all had different daddies, and Big Kelly was the only one of them that showed up for a booty call from time to time 4 Patty. He liked to call her "Shortcake."

He was a drunk with huge, crusty hands and had a heart of gold. He would give the kids anything he could for the days that he would stay, just don't cross him. If they did, he would beat the kids' asses with a big, wooden paddle, dubbed, 'The Ass Flattener, by Acmeus Inventions' if they acted up while he was around. Everything that Big Kelly said ended with, " — and shit." He would say to lil Kelly and Patty, "I love yall — and shit, but Daddy just needs to kick it with the big boys — and shit. You know how we stay into trouble — and shit. That's why I try to do my dirt away from the house, so my boy don't start getting ideas — and shit." Big Kelly's hobby with the big boys was stealing cars.

Patty had a knitting hobby. She put together some Barbara clothes and some crocheted dresses for Rainia and Tanette to wear to school with their White-girl tennis shoes that turned yellow around the toes after trying to bleach-wash them clean. The girls had taken bright-white, leather shoe polish and over-drenched the yellowed canvas, while trying to revive their shoes. They both would have white feet with dirty black heels when they took those shoes off. They looked like damn fools with sweater skirts and tops on in the egg-cooking heat, but they knew that Patty's pride and love in her crocheted work was worth more than being in style, like that song, "Coat of Many Hues" by 'Dilly Pardon' the country singer whose songs she would sing when she went to knittin'. She liked country songs and also had an obsession with Melvis from Graceland.

Tanette had a 'Misses Beesley' doll; Vanzell had a 'Meany Green Machiney' with a cracked wheel that wobbled when he rode it, and lil Kelly had a snotty nose all of the time and was built like a man but only three years old and still wearing a diaper. They ate down the street at the church on Tuesdays and Thursdays and got on the mission bus after school on Fridays. They even had clothes, shoes, and free food delivered to their home from the missionary. Everyone made fun of them. Rainia and the twins worshiped them. They were poor and happy together. The 'J.P. Nickle Catalogue' had come in the mail and they would sit and circle all of the things that they knew that they would never get, dragging it around until the pages fell out of it and it went from 200 pages, down to the 17 pages left showing tools for 'The Handy Man's Garage'.

They lived with her for about 2 ½ years. Rainia was about to turn eleven and had gotten her period. The whole event was nothing like the White girl's from the story, "Where's Margie? God's on the Phone For Her!" because it was one of the most embarrassing moments of Rainia's life. She was at school, and she was called to get up and pass back some corrected assignments to her class, when the other kids started laughing and whispering. Mr. Washington called Rainia into the coatroom, "What the hell's the matter with you? Ain't you got no home training? Go get your sweater off of that coat hook over there and tie it around your waist, and then take the pass from off of my desk and go see the nurse."

"Why? What did I do?" asked Rainia.

"Girl, yo tail is flowing like the Red Sea; now git!"

Rainia went to the nurse's office as instructed and showed the school nurse her problem. The lady gave her a super big pad and pushed her into the bathroom with the full length mirror. Rainia turned around to try and see what everyone else was talking about. Right from the onset of it, she was a heavy bleeder. The puddle was bright red and had spread all over her backside and was even coming through her yellow sweater she had tied around her. And to top it all off, her birthday was tomorrow. Her mother was so poor that all she had bought for her special day was a box of 'Klotex' maxi-pads for her birthday present, which lil Kelly had confiscated and climbed out on the roof of their house, sticking all of the pads all over the outside of the girl's bedroom window. They were all wasted, germy, and uselessly unsticky after that, so Rainia would have to use tissue, which she would later discover to be painful. She would learn that using toilet paper to catch the flow sticks to the hair and hurts too bad to pull off, so it must be bathed off.

All of the neighbor classmates saw what lil Kelly had done, too, and made fun of her at school. Some of the jokes consisted of 'The Maxi-pad pre-teen', 'Klo-ee Flo-ee', and 'Red Rain', replacing all of the, 'I fucked yo momma on a pot of peas. Her booty backfired and her pussy sneezed,' and the old, 'Abraham Lincoln was a good old man, jumped out the window with his dick in his hand. He said, "Pardon me, ladies, I'm doin' my duty. Now pull down ya pannies, and gimmie some booty," jokes that usually circled the playground. Rainia was never so humiliated by another child in her already lowered state of shame.

In the meantime, Anmarie couldn't be anymore shamed than to share a place with so many bugs and vermin any longer and had rented the downstairs level of the house next door to them. Needless to say, they still had to kill a few pestilence pests every now and then. Anmarie had been single and saving money for a couple of years now. She was trying to go to school to be a nurse.

She had even gotten a new boyfriend that the kids nicknamed, "Karateman." He would play 'Jimi Hendrix' albums, get drunk and stoned, and go into Vietnam War tirades. He was a Black Veteran who'd got fucked up in the head from his real bad experience over there in Nam. He would try to kill Rainia's cats, he wore a leather coat that smelled of old ladies hair grease, and it was peeling really bad like the hardtop of his old Seville parked out on the street. He wanted to skin the felines because they had clawed up the stiff, crinkly leather that must have reminded them of genetically altered catnip. They literally attacked his coat on sight. Once he walked through the door, they magnetized with claws to his back. He'd kick and swing at the cats, "Hy-Yah, mutha fucka!" Then he would slip, with a leg high in the air, ripping his crotch and busting his ass on the floor. That did it. He was ready then, piss-steamin' mad he was. He would get all pumped up after Black-Belt Theater. The kids would be kicking and jumping in the air, pretending to be Jackie Chan and walking skillfully over rice paper on spiked sticks as instructed by their pretend master when he would interfere, "Naw, you little, yella motha fuckers. I'll skin every one a yall Jew-Jap asses. I'm gonna catch yall slippin'. I'ma sneak up on yalls' asses."

Anmarie feared that he might be crazy for real and couldn't let him stay. They had to get rid of him, too, but that nigga wasn't gonna go that easy. It finally took Big Kelly to beat his balding head in and throw him, his shredded leather, and his Hendrix albums out into the street. He didn't come back, but it had been too much like the Billy nightmare.

They moved again after their mom hooked up with a short, little Black man who the kids called "Jimmy Stacks." *Oh, wonderful! Another moldy-looking boyfriend. He's a real loser, too. If he has any kids, he is probably the uncle and the daddy to them.* They moved in with the man and were enrolled into Cass Street School. Another one of Anmarie's longtime friends with mixed kids had lived on the next block. Her name was crazy Aunt Fran and she was bitterly divorced from her Black husband and now had five kids. The oldest girl was near Rainia's age. Her name was Reedi, and Rainia had already met and hung out with her a few times in her life. She remembered Reedi and her siblings well. They were even poorer than Anmarie's little family, and they had all shared moments like riding down to the lakefront to have ice cream, while their mothers talked about how much they hated Black men, especially back in the days when her mom was hiding from Billy Jacksin. Reedi was now into playing hooky from school and having boyfriends. She also smoked cigarettes and stole stuff from the drugstore.

One day Rainia and Reedi were walking home from school when a crazy White man jumped out in front of them with something in his hand. He was masturbating with ketchup and mustard. "Come and get some hotdog, dirty girls!" he demanded. His penis appeared to be green and crusty, and he looked like he had been living on the street. Reedi cracked up laughing, while Rainy made a break for it,

"Come on, Reedi, run away like me, dumbass." Reedi just stood there laughing harder and harder. Rainia had to turn around and go save her friend from the queer with the old corroded, green wienee.

The weird things that would happen to Rainy seemed to revolve around poverty, and her family moved from one poor situation into the next. The crazy pedophile was just a part of the deal. The fear of strangers and child-molesting guys was putting more stress on her every time she walked to and from school, thereafter. She tried to stay street smart and strong to hang in there.

As bad it was, Rainia knew the game by now. Her momma had bills to pay, and Jimmy was just a stepping stone. He was about five-foot tall, even wearing platforms, and he lived on Arlington Place off of Brady Street, just a block from Reedi's house.

***

"He looks exactly like the guy who gets shot in the head in the *Harlem Nights* movie who swore that kids gave him lice and bad luck," said Chaz.

"Yeah, he does, too," laughed the Heavenly Rainia at the visual memoir.

***

Jimmy was, in fact, his real name. He was a crazy drunk and was missing his front teeth, too. He had a whore named Jerry living with him that kept crabs, and he would get mad at Anmarie and break up his own stuff. The big, picture-window apartment next to the park on Arlington place had a crazy, tiny, alcoholic nigga yellin' in it every night. The day that he took a hammer and busted his own TV signaled that it was time to move again.

The twins climbed into big, wardrobe, U-Haulem boxes in fear of the chaos. The vagabond family travelers hadn't even had all of their shit unpacked and it was already time to go. So the kids were pulled out of Cass Street School and were sent up North to live with their Gramma Marie for a while. Rainia was now going to Jefferson-Johnson School in the town of Medford. She hated the name of the school, for very personal reasons but enjoyed the peace of mind. Out there she didn't have to fight about being too cute, in fact, none of the White boys even noticed her at all. They did not like chocolate, caramel, or blackberry anything, beyond those concerning food.

Rainia and her little brothers stayed up there for a while and liked the change of scenery. The whole town was quiet and friendly. No police chases or ambulances nor fire trucks zooming around from night to day. No bums and drunks and crack heads to scare the kids back into the house. No roaches and rats, no mangy junkyard dogs, and no terrible, bad news on the five o'clock report.

The kids would come home from school and have chores to do on their grandparents' farm. Some chores were unpleasant, like killing and boiling chickens. That was more like a horror movie. The chickens would be picked out for the upcoming dinner, rounded up, and executed — one by one. Out back of her Grandparents' house was a cut-off tree stump with two nails in it. Between those two nails, the chicken's head would be neatly secured to a tight fit. One of the kids would then have to hold the chicken's feet as it struggled to get away. Grandpa would raise his mighty axe high over and behind his head and bring it down with a clean chop! Blood would instantly squirt everywhere, the kid holding the chicken would instantly let go, and the headless body of the chicken would run around the yard squirting blood until it collapsed. Then the kids would have to walk the poultry corpses over to Grammas' big, burning black cauldron, bubbling with hot water to dump the birds into. This procedure would loosen the pores of the feather so the kids could feather-strip the birds clean with ease. Rainia would gag from the smell of a freshly-killed bird, from all the blood, and from the guilty feelings she would have about her part in the kill.

The twins were terrified and would always run around with the headless chickens and collapse right alongside of the unfortunate flock. They just could not take it. They eventually got more dream-friendly chores, like bringing in logs for the winter with Grandpa and his tractor-trailer haul of chopped-up trees that often went down in storms. They refused to get wood too late in the evening because of the bats that would come out and fly into them and flop around at their feet. They could care less that bats were blind and couldn't help but fly into them. They hated it when the cats would come and eat the bats as they lay stupefied in a silly daze. Once in a while, Rainia and her aunties would be terrorized by the nocturnal creatures as well. Somehow, the bats would get into the girls' room at night, and Gramma would have to come all the way up the stairs to kill them with a broom.

On one particular night, Rainia was asleep when she was awakened in the dark bedroom by the sound of crickets, a dog howling at the moon, and a real-obese bat crawling up the curtain. She was peeking out from the covers with one eye in disbelief. The bat kept making a squeaking and chattering sound, and Rainia was so much in horror that she couldn't even scream. When it turned around and started to make its way down the curtain, threatening to walk on her legs, spreading its wings over her head and body, she finally found her voice, "AHHHHH! AHHHH! AHHH! A BAT! A BAT! TURN THE LIGHT ON! GET IT OUTTA HERE! ITS GONNA BITE US AND MAKE US VAMPIRES!"

Rainia and her aunties, which were only a few years older than her, jumped out of their beds, turned on the light, and ran around the room with covers over their heads, screaming too. That time, when Gramma came up the stairs with the broom, she had to hit the bat and then hit all of the girls in the head to calm them all down from hysteria.

Rainia had to clean the shit out for the cow she was assigned, help feed the chickens, bunnies, and geese, and then take the leftovers from dinner to the dogs and cats.

Dinnertime was always like a buffet. There was salad which had been picked fresh from the garden containing every vegetable in it from spring onions and tomatoes to radishes. The potatoes were real mashed potatoes, not boxed. On any day, there might be pork chops, maybe even meatloaf, country fried steak, or spaghetti and giant meatballs. The green beans were crunchy yet simmered in butter broth, and the chicken was so fresh, one might even find a feather. There would be freshly-baked pies on different days from the berries, apples, strawberries, and peaches they would pick, canned pickles, beets, and four big, blue and green glass pitchers of Kooljuice placed around the feast filled with ice cubes. Gravy, rolls and butter, real see-through, blue glasses to drink from, and plates with a full silverware set for each person.

The kids even *liked* going to the school up North. They didn't have to fight on the playground, or worry about getting jumped or beat up after school. It was nice until the White kids got the idea that they were niggers and not to associate with them. Rainia believed that the schoolyard songs from Milwaukee that she had passed down to her little brothers had messed it up. The White kids on the school bus were singing, "The wheels on the bus go round and round," when J and Jo followed with, "Batman stepped on Robin toe, Robin said, 'Don't do it no mo!' Robin called the FBI. Batman said, 'You a Gotdam lie.' Momma in the kitchen stirrin' that rice; Daddy in the tavern justa shootin' dat dice; brother in jail raisin hell; sista on the corner sellin' fruit cocktail. Grandma, Grandma you ain't sick. All you need is Grandpa's dick, Rockin' Robin, Tweet, Tweet, Tweet, Rockin' Robin!"

Rainia sunk way down deep into her seat, *AW, SHIT!*

All the parents at the school were in utter shock. Their kids started asking questions and singing the chant, and they wanted to know what was a Grandpa's dick. It may have been normal for the colored children from Milwaukee's ghettos, but it was disgusting for their Caucasian, well-protected culture. It was pure Niggerdom, and the song had become a bit much for them to handle.

One day Rainia's mother showed up to take her and the twins back to Milwaukee, and she wanted them to meet someone.

On the road home Rainia cried tears. She hated Milwaukee and would have rather been jailed than to be going back there. She silently wiped her tears, as she watched the scenery outside go from the innocent, serene beauty of the country, to the dirty, worldly evil of the concrete jungle. *I swear, I don't wanna meet another one of her dumbass niggermen. I wonder what this guy's problem will be? Will it be drugs? Alcohol? Women? Damn! I'm sicka living like this. Why do we have to come back to Milwaukee? Couldn't we have moved to another town? I hate it here! — God... Why couldn't we be White and at least get to be going home to the good ol' White side a town where it's quiet and clean and there are pretty houses? But, nooo... We gotta go back to outrageous colors of paint on raggedy shacks, no grass on lawns, garbage, drunks, sirens, shootings, burning buildings, and stranger danger. I wonder where we are going to be living at?*

When they got back in town, Rainia was near twelve and their mother had come up with yet another man. His name was

Fred. He owned a house of his own off of 26th street right around the corner by A.O.Smithers. Rainia and her brothers thought that he was just another asshole who wanted to do up their mom. Fred had a Southern style about him that said nothing but 'Family First'. His ex-wife wasn't shit and was trying to take away a daughter he'd raised and the damned house, yet she was the bitch who couldn't stop cheatin'. When he found out that his daughter wasn't even his, he really considered killing the woman, but he figured, "Why? For what? Then she still wins." He was too hard working of a man to give her the house, so he had enough against her to file for divorce.

He was lonely for a good while — then he met Anmarie. He figured that they could put their raggedy shit together and make something nice.

Rainia couldn't help but admit, *He ain't nonna my daddy, but he's got a nice house here. I hope we can stay for longer than a season. At least he ain't short, or crazy, or violent, or evil. I hope he ain't a queer or a child molester or a woman beater, either. I like this one for my momma's sake. She has put up with enough dogs to deserve a good Black man. At least, I think he is a good one. We'll see, God.*

The kids moved right in with their mother and him in the duplex. He lived in the lower level of his bungalow-styled home, and Anmarie was clearly in love with him. She was cooking meals everyday, and even though she was always neat and clean with her own houses, she was doing extra shit for him, like cleaning out his cupboards and peeling off the months of scum from the bathroom shower and sink. Those two spent a lot of time in the bedroom, and once when Rainia had to walk back home because of a school bus that didn't show up that morning, she had caught Fred running into the bathroom, ass naked. All she saw was his butt, but she thought he was precious for running away, and not running towards her.

Fred had things that the kids had never heard of or that their mother could never afford alone. He had HOBO, 'House Open Box Office' theater, where the kids watched *Brainy Games, Purple Storm* starring 'Princey', and he had a 'Betcha' video machine/recorder that played movies. He only had two movies though, and they were both pornos that Rainia had snuck and watched pieces of when the adults left the house. She was at that stage. He even had a piano and had paid for Rainia to take lessons at her new school, Auer Avenue, until his ex-wife's daughter demanded that Fred had given it to her, and should let them come get it. He gave it up for the girl's sake, and Rainia never touched another piano again. She didn't hold it against him either, cuz he had solid love for a child who was not his own. He was a Southern sweetheart who Rainia saw as a genuine man trying to make sumpthin' with her momma, and it kinda made her believe that a better life was on the way for them all.

She never got her hopes up too high though, because she had already seen and heard too much bullshit to fall for what may just *seem* to be true. Still, she went along for the ride. She would call the man Fred, and hope that he was sincere, leaving time to tell.

Fred's life had been rough. As a small boy, he'd had to drop out of school to help take care of his extremely-ill momma. He grew up in a household where their daddy whooped on the momma and the kids. He said his daddy wasn't even his real daddy, and after his momma finally died of a tired and broken heart, he'd come to Milwaukee to search for the man who they said was his biological father. When he found the man, this man didn't want him either. So at 16 he got himself a job in the city and kept on working until he bought himself a car and that house they were in. It had taken him ten years to do that, then he thought that he had a good Black woman, so he married her. She turned out to be so nasty and evil, he figured that he better get ridda her before he died of a tired and broken heart. "After all, you only get one life, so you might as well enjoy it while you can. If you ain't happy with where ya at, then change it if you still gotta chance."

He was a wise man. He was the first man to ever sit at the table with Anmarie and the kids and really talk to them. He told them about racial indifferences that he had endured from Tupelo to Jackson Mississippi, and he had even known Rainia's father, Kent. "Yeah, I used to work with your daddy at Allis Chomers. I worked with him for a long time. He never talked about yall, though. I just thank it's a damn shame. But if yall daddies didn't want yall, then hell, I do. Yall are my kids now." Every time they had supper, they listened to Fred's philosophies. He would speak during the AM channel of N-O-V's Blues Sunday, listening to the disk jockeys' named O.C. White and Jim Frazier and then later, Wayne C. K. and D. J. Homer Blow. Fred loved to hear the skit called, "Where's my biscuit? Who ate my biscuit?" about a family supper gone wrong over missing biscuits and gravy. He said that dinnertime was family time to share the hopes and dreams of each person sitting at the table. He talked about how a family consists of who's there for you. Who's gonna stick it out with you? Who's gonna fight for you and steer you right? According to him, a family does that for one another, without hurting one another. "Hell, until yall came along, only person I had to talk to was Tommy, and that burrito sum bitch don't speak too much English."

Upstairs from him was a Mexican man who was renting from him named Tommy. He had a big mustache and a heavy Latino accent. He knew how to make small figurines and animals out of paper. He also saw Rainia as a piece of ass. One day when Rainia went upstairs to take him a plate of lasagna from her mother, out of good-neighborly sharing, he tried to kiss her. He was grabbing on her booty and trying to stick his tongue down her throat. Then he pulled out his red-looking dog dick, and Rainia ran downstairs screaming.

Fred took a shotgun out of his closet and ran upstairs to set that mother fucker right. He musta scared the shit out of him, because Tommy left and didn't even come back for the stuff he'd left behind. Strangely, he had the nerve to call Fred's house, asking to speak to Rainia. He was obsessed. He finally got a ticket for harassment and then he decided to stop it.

The event hurt the financial status of the home, by loosing the additional funds from the rent to pay the mortgage. As hard as that first month with no tenant was, the good part was that Fred had allowed Rainia and her twin brothers the privilege of living upstairs, unsupervised. Then the following month had brought the promise of his cousin, Weezie, from his hometown, as a new tenant. She only stayed about a few weeks, so the kids didn't even have to move out. Then she found herself a low-income place, but the word was that her daughters were on their way up to take her place.

Rainia was twelve and had started kicking it with Fred's cousin Weezie's little daughters, from down South in Mississippi. They ended up moving into the upstairs duplex. Only the twins had to move back downstairs to create the space.

The two girls were of sweet nature, warm, and friendly, like every down-home spirit from the South. They took to Rainia like she had always been in their family. They were ages 17 and 18, Reny and Eva. According to Reny and Eva, things moved quite a bit faster in the South than in the big city, because it was so boring there that there's nothing to do but fuck. Teens got their driver's license at 15, and kids could get married, drink, and drop out of school at 16. They revealed that down there girls were broke in by somebody as soon as they had come up with titties, a fat ass, and a hairy cat.

"Well, shit!" said Rainia, "I guess I'm damn-near grown to yall then, huh?"

Eva laughed so hard that she almost fell out of her chair, "Rainy, you ticka me! You realla do. Honey, down there, Black folk would die in becauza you. You too White to be Black; you too Black to be White, and everybody would want them a piece till it ain't none lef. Naw, guh, stay ya ass rightchen he-a. Me and my sista gonna watch you so's you can go to college. Pretty ain't jackshit witout smart, and you can't do a lot wit chillen runnin' up ya ass all day. Hell! Looka me!" Eva had a little baby boy and had just had a little girl in behind him. She was a big, beautiful, tall young miss who had both of her kids with one guy, a little itty-bitty Black man, too. They had a love/hate relationship and would be broke up and back together every other week.

Reny had gotten her an older White man. She had real pretty eyes and some of the most beautiful, healthy hair that would take even the raggediest of relaxers like it was the best. They didn't deal with their men more than they stayed up under each other. They were close and were Rainia's mentors.

Rainia didn't have anyone else close to her age to hang out with, so she hung out with Reny and Eva. They would take the bus over to their friend Angie's house off of Lisbon and 39th by Washington Park. Angie had an older brother named Mike who was about 19. He also had a car.

One night, they were at a house party and were all playing a game of Bullshitter, a drinking game designed to get everyone fucked up, when mike was supposed to be taking everyone home. He took Eva and Reny to Angie's house and another friend of his home. Rainia was in his backseat, drunk as a skunk. It was the first time that she was ever bent, and she had not realized that she was in the car with this young man by herself. He had then driven over to 24th and Center and parked his car. Mike climbed into the backseat and started to kiss her. His alcohol-drenched breath had a hint of vomit to it, causing her to try her best to snap out of it and set shit straight, because she knew she was in trouble now.

She opened her eyes and started to struggle with him. *Please, God! Tell me Imma walk away from this?*

Mike sat up and punched her lights out. He stole her hymen-virginity with a violent rape while she was out like a baseball player. *Are you still there, God? Am I still here?* Rainia woke up in the backseat of his car with a stinging pain between her legs. Her jeans were still pulled down around her legs and her panties were ripped and stained with blood. She knew enough about sex education and personal experience against her will to check for crabs or nut. She couldn't smell or see anything, so she prayed he had the guilt to at least use a condom and hoped that his dick hair was shaved off. He had hurt her pretty bad. She touched her hand to her cheek and it was swollen. She pulled up her pants and looked into the rearview mirror. Her eye was black and blue with a purple line underneath. The mother fucka had clocked the shit outta her. *Where in the fuck had he gone to?* Rainia did not know. She looked around her and it had to be about six in the morning. She looked around the car to see if he had at least used a condom, but all there was, was a dollar on the seat 4 her to catch the city bus home.

Raping son-of-a bitch! she cried out loud, with snot and tears as she walked real funny to the bus stop for her dollar-fare bus ride and went straight to Angie's house, mad as hell, kicking and screaming, still crying, and snapping about how she wasn't nobody's dollar ho, and that she was gonna have Fred shoot Mike's ass, but Angie said that she hadn't seen her brother, and that she better not start no shit because she felt Rainia was a high-yella skank.

Reny and Eva were in shock at the shiner on her face and took Rainia's side when she showed them the blood on her jeans, "Bitch, she is hurtin'! You mean to tell me that don't matter to you as a girl?" said Reny to Angie. "Looka here, imma put my foot clean up Mike's ass when I see him, and yall foul. We can't eem fuck witch yall no mo. Com'om Rainy, les go!"

They rode with her home on the bus and knew that they had to explain everything to her mother and Fred, but on the ride, Rainia had a few questions, "Eva, when a man goes all the way in you is when you actually loose your virginity, isn't it?"

"If you listen to a doctor, it is. But it's all what's in your heart. Some folk are messed wit before they can even know what sex is, and that ain't gotta be no goin' up in you. You heard of molestin'? Well, shit like dat don't count. In or out. Neither does rape. Even tho that shit can steal your joy, it's still your cootie-cat, and you're in charga wats wat. I say until the day you willingly give it up, then that's the day you decided to be womanly and not a mutha-fuckin' day b-4. I'm sorry this shit happen to you, but you alright, still fresh. Some may say you tainted now. But like I said, it's on you. You might wanna do up now, and you might never even want to be with a man again. You got your rights still, so chin up, gal!"

Eva knew that she had made her feel better, but she and Reny couldn't help but feel like it had been their fault. They were so fuckin' wasted that they never saw the shit comin', nor did they even remember getting back to Angie's. The older teenage boy had really hurt the pre-teen girl.

They took her home and told her mother. Her mother and Fred went right over to Angie and Mike's house, but their mother said that they didn't live there anymore. Fred wanted to call the police on the woman's son, but she begged him not to. She gave them $500 to pay for any possible abortion, disease, or if the girl needed stitches. "My baby boy ain't shit, and I know it. He got what they callin' two strikes. If he go back, my boy ain't getting out till he 99 years old, and he jus turned 19. Please, 4 give me for beggin' you, but my other son had got killed only last year. Mike and Angie all I got in this world. Just tell the doctors that the girl had voluntary sex."

Fred and Anmarie figured that the boy would get his one day, and they let the shit go. In the meantime, she was checked out and was diagnosed as ok. She got counseling and her stepfather gave her fifty dollars to buy some new outfits and a book he made her get about teens who drink and the dangers of sex.

Rainia kept on running with the big girls, even after that. A few weeks later, after her eye healed, she was with them up at Washington Park one day when she ran into a young man who was pretty-good looking. He was about 5'10" and had a curl like the lead singer from 'Ready 4 the World' down his back. He was built up real nice and looked like a dark-skinned Princey. His name was Meechie and he played football. He wasn't swole like a football player though; he was more slender and cut up like a diamond. He wasn't dressed like all of the other boys. He had on some baggy pin-striped pants that were rolled up, a wife beater, and some sandals on.

"Excuse me, but are you ok?" he asked Rainia.

"Yeah, I'm fine," she said.

"Yes, indeed you are." Then he walked away, all the while looking back over and over.

Rainia was in an emotional jam. She had just been raped by an older teenager and was now smitten with another guy who was not that much younger than the rapist.

The next weekend they went up there again to go swimming. Rainia was about to dive into the pool when she realized that several men were standing there staring at her hips, thighs, and ass. She felt like going back inside to change and go home, until she saw Meechie running with his football gear on with his boys to come and see the fine girl in the pool.

When Meechie got up to the fence, he dropped his football helmet and yelled, "Hey! yo! Come-mere for a minute!"

Rainia grabbed her towel and put it around her. "You again! Dang! Yall men is some perverts, trying to go with a twelve-year-old girl."

"TWELVE?" cried Meechie in disbelief. "Shit, I woulda thought that you were at least sixteen with a body like that. Say, what's your name, cuz I ain't never seen a girl like you before. Ima Southern boy myself, from Texas, and they don't got too many high-yella niggas, especially stackin' in the back like dat! You got long, pretty hair and caramel skin, and you act like a woman. Ain't no way you no twelve years old. I know that you are just bullshittin'. You know you like me, so stop frontin'! What's your name, girl?"

"Twelve! Now go away!"

"You ain't no twelve hanging with those old-ass brawds I be seeing you with. But that's ok. I'mma get-cho name, and you gone be my girl before the summer is over with." He picked up his helmet and walked away. His smile was contagious.

"Damn! Rainia," said Reny. "Why you keep on turning that fine-ass boy down? He really likes you. We were up here a couple of days ago — and we saw him — and he broke his neck to ask about you."

"Ask what?" wondered Rainia, just out of curiosity.

"Shit, like was you Puerto Rican, and was you involved with someone, and what high school you went to. He really thinks that you're older than you are. He said that a girl like you would make him spend all-a his money."

That last comment was the straw that broke the camel's back. Rainia had decided to become a player and pimp all of the niggas in the hood. She was gonna start with his ass. He had made the mistake of coming back to the pool and was ready to go swimming. He walked through the gate, and Rainia could see his body in its entirety. He had on some blue swimming trunks, and he had hair coming up his belly from his crotch area. His fat, gold herringbone glimmered in the sunlight. His long hair was not greasy, but curly and somewhat dry, like he was trying to make people think that he was born with good hair. He had a little mustache, a goatee, and a blinding smile like Eric Estradav from the cop show, *Chipdip*. "I'm back, Mamacita," he said with a smile.

"I see that, but the question is, how?" asked Rainia.

"I drove. Why?" said Meechie proudly.

Rainia looked around him, "Drove what, your bike?"

He cracked up laughing, "Naw, girl, my Audi over there in the parking lot. See that pretty silver car over there with the sunroof open? Yeah! That's me! That's what your future husband rolls in. The silver lean with the brains blowed out."

Rainia laughed at him and thought, *That may be true, but you sure in the hell ain't my future husband, you fuckin' pervert!*

He grabbed at his herringbone and licked his lips, "You got time to take a ride later on?"

Rainia dove into the water and swam across the bottom. Once she came up, she had a whole audience on the other side of the fence waiting to watch her come up that ladder. Meechie was sitting on the side of the pool with a stiff one, justa grinnin'.

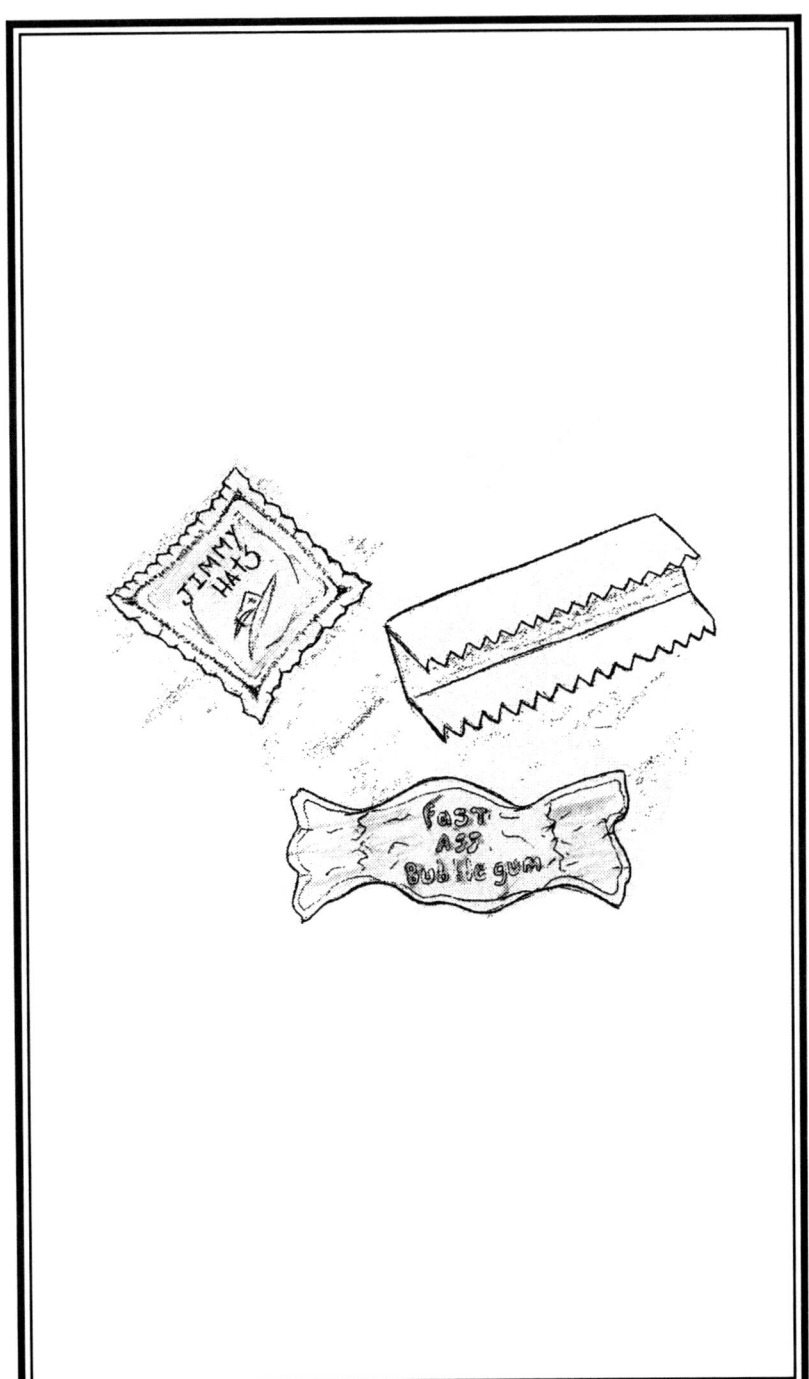

Chapter Twelve

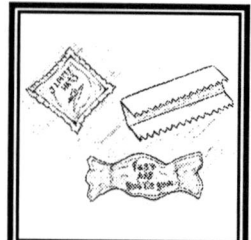

Hawrd Dick or Bubble Gum?

Rainia figured she could play his ass for that necklace he had on, so she said yes to his offer. They left the pool and went for a ride. He had the subs and the bass, making "She's 4 Ever and Always in My Hair" sound like it was live in concert.

"So, Rae, um... how about going to the lake with Daddy?"

Rainia laughed at him, "Boy, please! My real daddy might be down there on his bike with his Puerto Rican girl and decide to play 'Concerned father'. But you can ride me down there anyway; it's all good. Just have me back by 7:00 P.M. so I can leave with my cousins."

"Them two big bitches is yo cousins-nem?" asked Meechie.

She was offended, "Yea, nigga! And don't be callin' them out they name."

"I geh," he was mumbling.

"What?" She was confused.

"I guess. You so proper when you wanna be. I like dat. Daddy gone show you thangs, guh!" Meechie smiled like he was in charge.

She played dumb because she was about to show him the flip side. He took her down to Nigga Rock. Translation, the part of the lakefront where the brothas and sistas showed out at, and he bought her ice cream, played music, and lit up a blunt. She sat and got high for the first time with him, listening to all of his mindless bullshit about Texas and how much money he was making by selling dope. Then he took her back to the park at 6:45, just in time, too. Her unsuspecting mother and Fred showed up at 6:57 to pick the girls up.

Once the teens got home and had a chance to ask Rainia about her first date, they realized her eyes were glassy, "Girl, you high!" Reny elbowed Eva to look at her under the bedroom light.

"So! Who ain't?" said Rainia, like it was no big deal.

"What he give you? White shit or green?" asked Reny.

"You know I only smoke green." Rainia scratched her lip.

"That's my girl, cuz the white will have you sucking dicks in the alley. You ain't suck no dick fur the green though, did you?" Eva wanted to know.

Rainy rolled her eyes, " Hell naw! I ain't stupid! That nigga got money, too. I'm finna get some new thangs up outta him."

Eva rolled her eyes back, too, "Well, you know that you gone havta give up that booty, just don't trick out for him."

"Don't ever worry about that. He gone give to me," the light-skinned girl coolly said.

Eva had gotten serious, "Rainia, be careful though, cuz guys like dat ack all nice at first, and then they ain't got nuttin' fa ya but hawrd dick and bubblegum. Then they asses get all funky on ya cuz they run fresh outta bubblegum, and you know what that leaves, don'tcha? He know how old you are?"

Rainia rubbed her red eyes, "He thinks that I'm 15. I told his dumb ass my real age, but he insists that I'm a lie. So fuck it then, shit! If 15 is the magic number, then 15 it is! Imma play this shit out until school starts."

He ended up with her at his auntie's house off of 25th and Brown one day claiming that he had to bag up his product. He asked her to come inside and learn sumthin'. She followed him up four flights of stairs to the attic where his room was. There was a couch and coffee table with a small scale on it, a bed off to the side, new clothes piled up on a chair with the tags on, and new tennis shoes lined up by the wall. There was a big set of eyes on the wall like in, *Purple Storm*, the Pincey movie. Underneath the orbs was a stereo with big house-speakers double-stacked on top of each other.

"Well, sit down, Rae. Don't ack scary." He took out a baggie from his pocket and set it on a mirror on the table. The razor blade next to it was carefully picked up so he could sift and chop the balls. There were three.

"Do you know how much money this is?" he asked her.

She looked at the drug, "No, and why do I need to? Its not my hustle."

He sifted the white, powdery substance around, "Well, what is, cuz this is a sexy hustle right here."

Rainia could have cared less, "Nothin'. I go to school. Then I'm going to college after the twelfth grade."

"To do what?" He started to kiss her. He kissed just like in the movies. Her nipples got hard and her panties got real hot. Then he put his fingers in her shorts. He swirled her clit and she instantly got wet. Then he put his middle finger in there, in and out. "Then what, Rae? What you gone do as a profession when you do get to college? And believe me, you are going." Everything that Meechie was doing had felt a brand new good. She didn't want to have sex though, because she was scared. He knew exactly what he was doing.

B4 Rainia knew what hit her, he was pushing himself inside her with a condom on. His dick did not feel good to her. It was skinny and hard and long. She was in pain and begged him to stop, but he wouldn't let her go. "Naw baby, your pussy is too sweet and tight, and I'm finna cum." He humped faster, then let out a bitch-like sigh... "Uh!"

He had totally fucked up now. She had a steaming fire in her eyes, and it wasn't desire; there were tears. "What's wrong, baby? Was u a virgin or something?"

She just wiped her tears away real hard and said, "Take me home."

He did, and before he let her out of his car around the corner from her house, he gave her $200 and the fat herringbone off of his neck. "I was your first, wasn't I?" He waited for an answer.

She didn't say anything but was thinking, *Maybe I'll stick to bubblegum, like a young girl should.*

"Well, that means a lot to me. Are you ok? Did I hurt you? I'm sorry if I did, and I won't pressure you though, but I got it bad for you. I can wait as long as you want me to. I want to take care of you. Anything you need, you just call on Daddy." He kissed her hand and opened the door for her from his driver's seat.

School started, and Meechie kept his word. He would leave new stuff for her at Reny's boyfriend's house and take her shopping up to the mall. When her mother asked where she was getting the stuff from, Reny and Eva would lie and say they gave it to her, or one of their girlfriends bought the wrong size, or shit like that. Meechie kept Reny and Eva hooked up, too, with weed and Gold Rush Chicken, and even VIP passes at Unca Sonny's on Broadway, which was a hot club for them at the time.

He didn't try to have sex with Rainia at all. After that one time, Rainia battled with the idea of her virginity all through her parent's home, *Is it still there? Does forced sex really count? Did Billy Jacksin take away everything precious that I had at a tender age of four years old? What the fuck is a virgin, God? Do I have a disease?*

Her side was hurting so bad that afternoon while she was downstairs straightening her mother's afghan on the back of the living room couch that she fell to the floor and buckled over with intense pain, "Momma! Come and help me, please! I don't know what's wrong!"

Her mother ran into the room and found her daughter rolling on the floor, holding her lower abdomen, "What the hell's the matter? What hurts?"

"Momma, something is bursting and ripping inside. It feels like I'm being stabbed over and over." She was crying and screaming with intense pain.

Anmarie questioned with motherly worry, "Well, can you get up? Here, take my arm, cuz I can't carry your big ass. I'm taking you to the emergency room!"

Rainia, her mother, and her twin brothers got in the car and were on the way to the hospital, when — "BAM!" — out of nowhere, a car slammed into the front of their car. Rainia's head went into the windshield, and the glass cracked like an eggshell.

She started to fade out of consciousness. Up, out, and into the street she wandered, then back into the car, where an ambulance tech was in her face, flashing a light into her eyes and yelling at her. She couldn't hear shit that he was saying. Then things got dark.

She saw outer space, and stars, and those eyes. Those familiar eyes that reminded her of her own. A white light inside of a tunnel, with loud, obnoxious clicking sounds brought her attention to the smell of a sterile environment. She started to realize that she was in a hospital.

A man's voice cleared his throat and spoke to someone else, "Well, her head looks ok; she just has a mild concussion. She should be coming out of it real soon. It's too bad that we've got to prep her now for surgery. A car accident *and* an appendectomy is quite an agenda for the last two days, but they are about to burst according to this X-ray. The X-rays have also revealed that even though Rainia will be fine once she wakes up, according to normal brain activity, somehow there is extra room in her brain. It's not a tumor or any kind of damage, but more like a thickening of myelin sheath material for some kind of protection. It's a strange abnormality, but perfectly harmless. Maybe one day God will have a purpose for it, I'm sure. In fact, the only dangerous situation is the appendicitis. Funny, but we wouldn't have known it was that serious, because according to the urine sample we took yesterday, it says she has a bad bladder infection. We would have given her medication 4 that and sent her home, where she probably would have died. But... God does work in mysterious ways now, doesn't he?"

She could hear her mother crying, then she heard her brothers crying, and then she was pulled from the X-ray tunnel machine used for brain and spinal injuries and briefly laid eyes on them. "I'll be ok." She reached out to them and touched a hand. She couldn't tell whose it was because a nurse had shoved a needle into her IV and injected something that was putting her back to sleep.

When she woke up, a pregnant White woman was screaming in her face on a rolling patient bed next to hers. *Why is this pale ho going off in my face? What the fuck is this PAIN?* Then Rainia felt a sharp, mind surging, singeing throb and screamed back into the hollering face of the woman in labor.

The nurse pulled back the sterile curtains and yelled, "Who in the hell did this girl's anesthesia? You didn't give her the right dose, and she just got rolled in here from the operating room. She's feeling the fresh cuts the Dr. made, dammit! Get that damned pain killer, now!"

A young man in green scrubs made his way toward Rainia and inserted a needle of pain meds into her IV. She was out again.

By the time she came to, her family was in her room. They were polishing off the dinner trays that they had bought from the cafeteria. Her whole room smelled of roast beef and mashed potatoes with gravy. There were flowers and balloons and a card.

"Welcome back, stranger," said Fred. The glimmer of his gold tooth and the smile in his eyes made her feel close to his heart.

The drugs had made her mellow out, "Thanks, Dad. Hi, everybody. I'm ok."

Fred continued his conversation which had been interrupted by Rainy's coming n2 consciousness. He confided to the family his fear of hospitals, doctors, dentists, and the DMV.

Rainia just had 2 ask, "Why are you afraid of the DMV?"

Jo spoke on the matter that he found to be amusing, "Daddy say funeral homes and organ donating on the back of drivers' licenses is a scam to make money off of people's body parts."

Fred tried to defend his theories, "Shit, yeah. As bad as shit is 4 niggas, the way we killin' each other, Leo Wilkerson funeral home workers will be waiting on you to turn the corner and hit you with a hearse, bring you to the morgue, and wait on your body out back once the organs are delivered."

Rainia cracked up laughing, "Ow! My stitches and staples are going to undo. Don't make me laugh, it hurts! That was funny though. Daddy, you tickle us with your conspiracies."

He was dead serious, "Shit! You laughing now, but when you discover that you only got one kidney ten years down the line, you won't see shit funny. They got yo ass laid up in here thinking that they done helped you, when really they done helped theyselves to ya kidneys. Well, hell! Who's to say it ain't no truth in it? That's why I say 'Hell naw!' to organ signing on my ID. Hell! It's eight o'clock already? Damn, that little visitin' time came n went, didn't it? I guess we'll be back by here to getcha once'n they kicked ya out."

They all hugged her, and her mother kissed her head and told her that she would be going to a new school was she had healed.

Once home, again, Rainia took the time to heal, and all while Meechie would call Reny's boyfriend's house leaving messages for her to come and see him. She just ignored the invites and wanted to get on with her very fragile, teenage life.

    This went on for a few months while she was at Parkman Middle school, until Meechie went to jail for selling dope. After that, Reny and Eva moved to a low-income house across town, and Rainia went into being a normal teenager, truly sticking to bubble gum. Her favorite kind was Charmers Blowup Pops, square-shaped suckers with gum inside of them that she would stick in her hair for decoration, and then eat later. She really didn't think about Meechie, and it was strange. She had always heard that people are so in love with their 'first' that they write songs. It was the other way around in her case. He was in love with her. She had never even shed a tear over him or written him one letter. She had even got a boyfriend her own age just to kick it with and guard her back, because Parkman was one of the worst schools in Milwaukee, period. She pulled the most built, strong-reputation-havin' nigga she could find, "Darnell."

    He was a big, light-skinned guy who looked about Meechie's age, and he was as giving as Meechie was, except he worked for his uncle, delivering the *Milwaukee Journal* before and after school. Darnell was in love with her just like Meechie, too. No matter how much shit he bought her, she didn't give up nothing. He would take her skating up at the Palace and to the Starlight Skating Ring off of 76th street. The Starlight would hold drill-team competitions with groups like, 'Purple Mack Funk' and 'Pink Lace'. The "Planet Rock" song would come on and kids would fall out. "Boom, scat, scat, boom, scat!" went the drills, as the boys would flip over one another and the girls would do the "Fight Dance". Then they would get into it with other schools, and drama would break out at Parkman because of gang rivalry. Darnell was an L.L. Cool-looking dude and was in a gang. There was always rivalry between 1-9 and 2-7. And the feud was heated day by day between the "Gangster Disciples and Vicelords".

    Rainia didn't know shit about no gang. She was a straight-A student, but because she was Darnell's girl, she was a marked target. One day the space shuttle blew up and the whole school was surrounded by young, riled-up gang members, waiting for the 1-9 crew to be dismissed from class. It was after the detectives told her mother to come and get her and to never return that she ended up loosing Darnell and going to John Murial Middle School.

When Rainia got to John Murial, she was considered to be a P.A.T. kid. "Program for the Academically Talented". She continued to act like a teen without all of the drama, but she got hooked on 'Run D.M.C,' and the 'Beastey Boys'. When Doug Fresh and Slick Rick made *The Show*, it was over. Rainia had become an "In school rapper". 'Roxanne Shante' and 'The Real Roxanne' didn't have shit on her. Rainia was a M.C. Lyte fan. She would stop in the yellow-tiled corridor on their way to shop class and take the boys and the girls on a lyrical battlefield against the other rappers in a challenge of wits to a beat provided by a 'beat boxer'. A 'beat boxer' was the kid who kept a beat made up with sounds coming from his mouth like background drums so the snapping fingers and clapping hands could keep in time. Only the most clever of tongues with the coldest verses could walk away with the daily title.

The crowd consisted of a faithful group of 'ribbers', the kids who talked about other kids for laughs, pointing out holes in socks, dirty collars, and terrible raps. The group of humorous judges consisted of Bernard, Black Tammy, Dre, Kim B. Darsha, Keeba, and Alicia C, who was really more like the preppy nerd and one of Rainia's closest friends. In them, Rainia had her faithful followers. She battled every time and would walk away a winner most days, then before she knew it, school was out. She was thirteen and had started her first job at a Youth Development Center on Dr. King Drive. There, she learned how to model and be a mentor. It was a wonderful place to keep her away from the streets and to earn some extra cash for school clothes. She took A.O.D.A. drug prevention classes and became a Peer Most Positive.

Her mother was going to school at night to be a nurse at a school on the corner of 6th and Wisconsin avenue, and all of the late-night studying and hands-on training started to make Anmarie mean again. She was poor, even with Fred's income, and would ask Rainia for twenty dollars to put gas in her car every time she got her check. Rainia didn't even get rides from her mother but caught the bus. Her mother had only agreed to let her have the job because her grades were so good and she did all the housework by herself without even asking for or getting an allowance. Rainia kinda resented her mother for that, but she gave the money to her anyway. Her mother would come home and nag and be real cold. If Rainia ever forgot to do anything, her mother would do something that she called, "The eleven fifteen". That was the time that Anmarie got home from her apprenticeship job, and when 11:15 P.M. would come, she would kick open the bedroom door, while banging pots and pans together, and having Rainia get up and do whatever she'd missed plus some stupid shit like rearranging every cupboard until 2 A.M. She didn't whoop her, but she was like a drill sergeant, relentless.

Then, she wouldn't let her go anywhere, anymore, because the Chicago gang shit had spread to the next block with "2-7", and kids were coming up shot and dead every couple of weeks. The flyest concerts would come to town with a monster lineup of hip-hop, rap, and R-n-B, but Rainia could never go. Her mom wouldn't even let her have a mushroom bob, but she cut her hair anyway, fucking it up while tryna have her a bob.

The city shut down the Palace and tore down the Starlight, so she couldn't even go skating. Except for the youth center during summer break and school, she couldn't do shit else. The only good part about the closed-in lifestyle was the close family bonding that was starting to take place. One fine morning Rainia woke up to the smell of country ham with the bone inside, scrambled eggs with cheese, French toast, fresh-brewed coffee, and toast. She couldn't remember ever waking up to such aromas in her momma's house. Maybe her Gramma Marie had done it big up North like that, but never Anmarie.

Rainia jumped out of bed and ran downstairs, "I gotta see this shit! Something ain't right!" When she got down the steps, everyone else was at the table and just sitting down to eat.

"Good morning, Rainy! Sleep well?" asked Fred. He had just taken a thick, warm slice of smoked ham and placed it on one of the twins' plate. After he passed the plate to Anmarie, he said, "Well, sit down! The food ain't gonna jump up off the table and come to you, ya know. Besides, we all need to get a healthy start, cuz we fixin' to go to church this mornin'! You ready?"

"Church? Who's church are we going to?" asked Rainia, as she made her way to the bathroom to tinkle and wash her hands. The bathroom was right outside the kitchen.

She could hear her mother talking, "The one around the corner. They are having a 'Welcome All Sunday Service' today, and Fred and I thought that it would be nice if we all went together."

"Oh... well... ok..." said the teen, as she approached the four of them, then scooted herself up to the table to eat.

The meal was a Southern-style comfort complete with homemade syrup and jam sent by Gramma Marie, the queen of canning fruits and vegetables. They family of five then all got ready for church and piled into the gold Citation that Fred had shined up all nice. They only had to drive a block and a half, but as they got closer to the building, they could hear the loud beating of the drums and the mighty shouts of praise. The twins were leery about going in. Anmarie and Fred held hands first before they entered.

The door opened, and an usher grabbed them all and rushed them to a pew in the back. He then handed them all collection envelopes, three apiece, and asked them to share one church service flyer and one ripped, flopped-over fan on a popsicle stick. The preacher was up front screaming and jumping up and down. He had a long, white towel that he kept twirling around as he yelled, "And God don't care whatcha got on, long as you give up whatcha got. That's right, church people, gone give it up to God. Can I get an Amen? I said, can I get an Amen? Can I get a Benj-a-men? A Jackson? A Jefferson will do just fine! Now, church members, don't forget that we have several more pastors as guests today, so don't be shy to go to the bank machine in the hallway, ok? See, cuz I coulda been dead a long, long time ago, but here I stand with long, long pretty hair. I said I used to be a pimp with long, long nails. Now I'm pimpin' souls for Jesus who was nailed to the cross. Don't worry about this $600 suit, and never mind my clean but stanken Lanken, just catch the holy spirit and let loose! Drummer, gih-me something heavy!"

The drummer started to play fast with the organist, and people started to clap and step in time, falling out left and right. The twins were officially scared; Fred wasn't buying into none of this shit, and

Anmarie was already in the car waiting on the rest of them to come back out. Just as Fred had gotten the three children safely to the door of the church, the preacher spotted them, "Stop the music! Stop the praise! Lock that door ushers! Look like we gotta couple a people dying to go to hell!"

Fred cut him off, "Then good! Maybe we are going to hell, but we sure are getting the hell outta here! I betchu that! Now move, fool! Open that damned door, 4 I raise hell!" It was the funniest moment that they had ever shared together as a family. They may have had that bad experience in trying to get some Jesus in their lives together, but the five of them had made a fine family, indeed.

Anmarie suggested a little trip to her hometown where she grew up, but Fred wasn't too happy about going up North, to what he considered as redneck nation, but to please his lady, he agreed. All of the kids were calling Fred 'Dad' by now, so when it was time to introduce Fred, the twins and Rainia had proudly done so as him being their father. The family up there was always so sweet. They never were with that racial shit anyway, maybe because Rainia was always their pride and joy. They called her 'Chocolate Drop'. And then when the twins were born, and they went up, the aunties in the family would fight over them. Their scrumptious nicknames 4 the boys were Hershell and Nestley. Anmarie's family loved Black people and idolized Black football players like gods. They took trips to Greenbay, WI just to see who the new picks for the football season were going to be, so Fred, just being a Black family man, was welcomed with open arms.

The only bad part about going up North, though, was having to go into town. All there was to do was travel to the J-mart and walk the isles. It was a dead town. Fred and the boys had taken some male bonding time together and were picking out some comfortable shoes for Anmarie at the store when something funny happened.

Fred was paying for the shoes when the female clerk asked him, "Is the circus in town?"

Now he knew that she was being an asshole with that question, so he responded, "No, no, not to my knowing, but from the looks of things around here, neither is the sun. Have a good one anyway."

She was so lame and duddish that she never even got the return insult on her color of skin. When the boys had come back with that story, everyone fell out laughing, and Rainia really had to admire how Fred would never let another human being get the best of him for being dark-skinned.

Rainia had kinda tucked that attitude neatly away in her mind for the perils of Milwaukee. When they returned to the Brew City, she waited for the day to retaliate racial slurs and injustice with quick-witted humor like Fred had done.

Another hilarious moment had been when Fred tried to take them all out to eat at the Grounded Rounded, an upscale Milwaukee, superb steakhouse that rarely ever had Black people in it who could afford the prices on the menu. The waitress seated them all and looked them over strangely. She couldn't get past the Blackest man that she had ever laid eyes on, sitting there with a red-headed White lady and three Latino-looking kids. She finally broke from her trance and brought them ice waters and three big bowls of popcorn with a smile, "Just to let you guys know, we don't have any specials, and our menu is really pricey."

Fred looked at Anmarie, and then back at her, "Well, we'll see if we cain't split us a hamburger or something fancy like dat."

The woman went to get another table's order in the smoking section. The family ate the popcorn and drank the water. When the lady came back with the menus, walking away to get more popcorn, Fred took one look at the prices, and they all had to get up and leave. Anmarie was embarrassed, "Fred, it's bad enough that were are different and broke, but you coulda at least left a tip. We did eat up the popcorn."

"Anmarie, that popcorn and water was free! Ok! You wanna make her prejudiced ass feel better with a tip? Well, go back in there and tell that bitch to get used to niggas in her neighborhood then, cuz that's the tip of advice I got for her ass. Now maybe the kids won't be able to come back, but me and you gone be back. Just as soon as I get my bonus."

Fred did get his bonus, and he took Anmarie back there. They came home with a nice, fat doggy bag full of steak fries, garlic biscuits with cheddar cheese inside, fettuccine alfredo, and popcorn. No steak though. But they did go out often on the weekends. They went partying together after work, and afterward they would stop at little restaurants which they *could* afford, like 'Steve and Kris', getting hamburgers and corned-beef sandwiches, bringing back the leftovers that tasted so good at two and three o'clock in the morning.

Rainia would always be trying to stay up late, waiting on the food from her favorite spot, 'Steve and Kris', and watching every TV show that was on cable. She would even spend a few minutes trying to see through the squiggly lines of the sex channel that they obviously didn't have, but Steve and Kris got into a fight, and then the place was called 'Kris', with the 'Steve' crossed out. Steve must have been the cook, too, because the favorite haunt of after-bar-time eating had suddenly gotten real shitty. Hamburgers and fries tasted like perchy fish that had been overcooked in burnt grease. Needless to say, the place closed completely down, but it was small moments like that which made Rainia start to really feel like she had a family. She was ready to live a normal life with the simple moments, like being content with babysitting her brothers.

When it came time to go back to John Murial Middle School, Rainia had slowed down a lot. She'd become somewhat of a nerd, who laughed at all of the people who wore 'The Jack N. Markus Bommer' checkered jackets. The coat was a sure sign of being on welfare, which was always considered to be shameful. Kids like that would have to go to the store with a book of food stamps and buy little things like a pack of gum for 35 cents just to get the change in physical coins. Rainia was no stranger to this procedure.

Once, while living with Piggy Patty, she had to go to the store eight times in one afternoon just to be able to break enough stamps to make change for gas and cigarettes for Patty and Anmarie. She was remembering the incident while at a gas station that was close to the school. In the store were two boys who would talk about her yellow, bright skin everyday. They were at the counter paying for chips and candy with food stamps. The boy with the red and black checked 'Bommer' coat that had the stamps in his hand was trying to be secretive and conceal the book by sliding it to the clerk. The clerk didn't give a damn and held the book up high to his eyes, looking underneath his glasses to count them, "One, two, three, there's only three food stamps in here. I need seven or you put something back."

The boys had no idea that Rainia was even there and that she had seen the whole hilarious embarrassment. When she walked back up to the school and lunchtime came around, those boys didn't even think or know about her being in the store that morning and had made the mistake of starting it up, "You, big mella-yella, bright as the sun face ass, zebra-control, master of the zoo-looking ass, what up tho?"

Rainia let loose, "Oh! So u wanna play pimperish politricks about racial personalities? Witcho ol', illiterate, can't even read a book a food stamps, 'let's play chess and king me,' coat-wearin', breaking county dollas for bus fare, broke as yo joke, so Black you makin' everybody get ready for bed in third hour, sleepy go nite-nite, crispy, Black-ass-looking-ass nigga." She did a stupid tap dance, "Face-ass. Yeah! What up tho?"

That kilt him, and that was how she got into ribbing, and she discovered that she was funny as hell. The old followers from last year had clung onto her new lineup, and even though things at home were stressful, she still managed to laugh out loud. She had some good times in the eighth grade. That 8th grade year had flown by so fast that once again, b4 she knew it, she was graduating from Murial and on her way to West Divisional, a.k.a., "The Milwaukee High School Of Artists."

At 15 years old, She stood 5'5" and weighed 120 lbs. She was stacked like Halle Berren, from the *Karma in the Boomerangs* movie, with a little less breast. She wore glasses for reading and looked like Lisa Bonnel, the famous *Crosby Show* kid in the face. She dressed like her, too. For the longest time, she stuck to herself and didn't make friends, not even in theater class. Her plan was to keep her legs closed and stay in the books. She accidentally made three friends. A White girl named Reneé, a Black girl named Stef, and a light-skinned chick named Punkin, only because they were so damn goofy like her. She had no idea that Punkin was the niece of a famous talk show hostess. That information wasn't revealed to her until she got to the end of 10th grade.

But up until then, Rainia's mother let her exercise more freedom and work after school at a store called 'Lizzy D's' in the Grand's

Avenue Mall. It was in that store that she got her first taste of the racial injustice of colored people in the workforce in her city. The White assistant managers and employees were always watching her every move. It had made her feel uncomfortable. Then, they did shit like make her follow the Black customers around the store to make sure they weren't stealing. She worked there for over a year and put up with all of their shit, only because the original manager had decided that Rainia was worthy of the assistant manager promotion. Then, that woman had found the love of her life and up and quit on her. Corporate office then sent some 19-year-old blonde bitch from college to take the lady's place, and she hired her friend for the assistant position instead. Everyday that they were there, the more shit they were wearing from the store's inventory. *Those hos are stealing the company blind!* Corporate came in to investigate, noticed that the 2 White girls were wearing Lizzy D items from head to toe and still assumed that it had to be Rainia causing the retail loss but just couldn't prove it. So they cut her pay way down to starters and hired a Black lady to partially manage the place to see if Rainia was letting her friends boost.

    One day, during a lunch break, the new Black lady just came flat out and told her, "This whole thing is so damn ridiculous, Rainia Harris. Find a new job while your record here is still clean. You can use it for a reference. Do it now b4 they fire you, because even though I know, and corporate knows that those White heffas are the sticky fingers, they are gonna sack you. Stingy White America has reared its ugly head up in here. Come outside with me while I take a cigarette break so I can further explain."

    The teen escorted the woman to the food-court terrace to hear what she had to say that could not be said in the store. The woman called Terry Watts continued with what she knew, "The truth of the matter is, well, Rainia, I'm from Atlanta, Georgia, and down there, well, things are easier on the colored in retail than they are here. Believe it or not, though, Milwaukee, WI. was the place to be around from 1920-50! It started with Negroes escaping their masters, and then being free to prosper as businessmen and land owners. It was called the Bronzeville District, and it ran up and down Walnut Street and all the way to Martin Luther King Drive. Back then, our people took damned good care of each other as their own dentists, barkeepers, restaurant owners, and tailors. Yall had your own social clubs, bankers and nightclub owners hosting for guests such as Cab Calloway. And not to mention that the churches were the hub of the community. There were no gangs, and the Blacks spent their money among each other strictly! Then it all fell apart in the fifties with the Freeway Sytem conveniently crashing through ol' Bronzeville, and the Government promising to rebuild housing for Blacks that was never completed as promised. Ever since then, Blacks have gone downhill. Yall been down too long over here! Brainwashed into being nuthin'-ass niggas. But it's only the late 80s, and maybe one day Milwaukee Blacks will re-unite with their minds and dollars and get Bronzeville back. But until yall do, that's what I know fo sho! I have a sister who moved here with her White husband. She's a school teacher. At first, she couldn't even get a job for the longest time. And when she did find work with a school who was being questioned about their lack of minority staff, she had to walk on eggshells around the White staff all the time. The administrators were dirty, too. They would watch her through the cracks in the doors and follow her around, just snooping to find a reason to get rid of her. She was pregnant and was starting to show, so they tried to make her job more uncomfortable by making her do playground duty in the dead of winter, while a White pregnant teacher was treated like a pampered queen. They even took away certain materials from my sister's class, like books and chalk, just trying to make her job fucked up. She still hung in there, so they took away her classroom and made her a floating assistant, causing her to drag books and papers from class to class all day. When they couldn't find anything good enough to keep her from getting unemployment if they had fired her unjustly, they came up with a plan to give her all negative classroom evaluations, never acknowledged anything that she did right, or accredit her for any extra, positive efforts in spite of all of their sabotage efforts to make her quit. Their reports on her instruction had been filled with bashing verbiage, like, 'Teacher yells at students' in place of her voice being made loud and clear, and 'No real lesson plan made clear,' in place of her unique strategies that proved to be useful. In short, they were just prejudice, acting like they were following a procedure, when they were simply flat-out weeding her from the teaching workforce. And today, White people are doing this bullshit all of the time in other professions. Look at your situation right now with those two lil' girls in the store. Oh, yeah. Whites in charge will play over your livelihood. They don't care about you needing to pay the bills and support your family. Hell, most of them don't even give a 2 week notice anymore. They just can you. Greedy, pale, and cold as they wanna be. You will learn that White folk here get a job and things go so swell for them that they work that position for 30 and 50 years, all the while getting raises, upgraded training, promotions, and awards. Blacks can hardly keep a middle-class paying job or get patted on the back 4 shit. They can't even go to the top in states like this unless they are the owners of the operation. Ever since Bronzeville died, Wisconsin has always had a reputation for its educational and other professional divisions doing bullshit like this. They weed Blacks out. They pay top dollar for the Whites to work, but they cut salaries towards minorities even when they try to make it look equal by hiring one or two minorities for the same positions as the higher paid Whites. Then they have a high turnover rate for minorities because they fire them over the smallest thing that they can find. That's how greedy and uncomfortable they are about working with us. Now, if you are wondering what my sister's personal story has to do with you, then pay attention. How did you go from being the next candidate for assistant manager of this store to being a suspect in employee theft? You are only a Black 16 year old who was about to be promoted, until your new, White, 19-year-old manager demoted you and gave your position to a White girlfriend of hers who is really studying to be a librarian, and who has no prior retail experience, mind you."

    She flicked her cigg butt to the sidewalk and stepped on it. She looked like she wanted to cry, "It was all a setup to lock you out. They done met their nigger on the payroll quota for the paperwork, now, they don't need you anymore, because they don't want you thinking that you're actually going to have a lifelong career with them so close to their corporate office. The only place where they can't avoid Negroes is in their branch store out in Georgia. And the really fucked-up part is that these White folk in many office settings across the nation are always trying to get someone of color to assist them in their wrongful strategies. They think that by sitting the house nigga in on the meetings justifies the dirty, greaseball weeding system they're used to using in almost everything in the professional world. My sister has given a name for this strategy; the 'Whitesconsin White Wash,' or 'The Triple W Tactic'. Shit! I don't know what else to tell you, Rainia. Maybe, oh… in 2007, Whites will let Blacks in on everything. Or better yet, maybe yall will stop being niggas, and folk like you will somehow prosper to get the Bronzevilles of the world back. But that's what — Ten years away? What I can do is give you a great reference using your old boss's last entries about you, and I will also give you her home phone number to inquire if she would possibly write you a personal review. I will also include that I observed no foul play from you as an employee during my investigation. You're a good girl. Take this experience with you and leave WI as soon as you can. They'll never let you get ahead here, not even when you get a degree. Hell! Black folk hate on each other here. Whitey got yall asses trained! You might as well leave this job with your dignity. I'm sorry to have to ask you to leave, but I see where this shit is going. That's just how things work."

    The advice was taken, coming from whom Rainia agreed was a modern 'House Nigga'. *Why didn't she stand on a soapbox and use her voice telling the world this same shit, instead of just to me? If I ever did do something great, I'd use my voice and bring up as many people of all colors as I could here. She's right though, so fuck it! I'll quit b4 them snotty bitches fire my ass.* If anybody knew about Black folk being sacked on the job, it was *that* lady. Being no stranger to racism, Rainia quit with a 2-week notice, taking the review information. She tried to get a job at Merry-Go-Round and Chess King, but everyone of any kind of color had jumped on those. They were the only two stores that would hire kids from different cultures. It was sort of the store's niche to have different faces selling a new line of hip-hop clothes. Rainia had missed out on the opportunity while hoping to make assistant manager at her old job. Once a colored kid got a job in one of those two stores, they stayed until they were grown or caught giving unauthorized discounts. She left her resumes and cover letters anyway with discouragement, "Aw, fuck it, then. I'm sicka pushing around clothes racks, ballin' up thousands of plastic, see-through sacks that the damned clothes come in, gathering up a million hangers with rubber bands on them, tagging clothes, taking off anti-theft clamps that leave big-ass holes in clothes that I have to give discounts for, picking up broke-ass earrings and buttons, explaining long-over-with sales to snide White bitches with their noses in the air, threatening to 'Have my job', and ignorant Black hos yellin' at me, creating a distraction, so their booster partner can steal on the first and fifteenth any-fuckin' way. But now what?"

She was jobless and therefore without the means to do shit for herself. She couldn't even give her momma gas money, and she somehow wanted to more than ever, now. She continued to fill out job applications at the other stores in the mall everyday, but, everyday, more and more White kids got the positions, instead. She walked that mall in high hopes, occasionally eyeing the bear on a unicycle up over the shoppers heads, balanced by two frothing mugs of beer on the ends of his balancing pole, cycling back and forth. And then, during one Friday afternoon of early-school-dismissal job hunting, a man called out her name. *It can't be! Mr. Hard Dick!*

Chapter Thirteen

Guess Who Got Out?

"I said, wait up a minute, Rae! Damn! You ack'n like you don't know Daddy no more. Give me a hug, and let me look atcha."

She didn't even have to turn around to see who was there. She already knew who it was. He was the only person to ever call her Rae. When she turned around, Meechie was staring her in the face with open arms. He looked like he had aged at least ten years. *Leathery, ashy, different colors of skin on ya face, thinning hair on the sides of your gay-ass fade, and skinny! Damn! Nigga! What the fuck happened to you?* His hair was cut short, he had a gold hoop earring in his ear, and he wore dress pants and a big, leather Jirbow jacket on. He still had money. "Hey! When did you get out?" she reluctantly asked.

"Last time — or the time b-4 that? It has been a few years since I last saw you. When did you get so fuckin' fine? What, you one-a-dem college-bound girls now? Looking like Lisa Bonnel. What's up with them shot-ass hippie clothes, though? Daddy not diggin' that part. Com'on! Let's go to Merry-Go-Get-It and hook you up."

Rainia was thinking, *Right! And where can your dry ass get hooked up with a facial, some moisturizer, and a plate of soul-food, cuz you shot beyond gear, asshole!.*

He grabbed her hand and dragged her to the store. Once inside, he made her try on biker shorts, tube tops, and 'Used To Jeans' outfits. "Three, Five, Seven, get'n loose!" he shouted. "We gonna have to take you to get your hair cut right and get your nails done, too. You're too pretty to be looking so whack, baby girl. You gotta look fly when you roll wit me. Yea! We back on!"

By the time Meechie was done with her, she looked like a video vixen for M.C. Sledger or Keith Cry. On Saturday, she agreed to go out of town with him, faking like she was going over to Eva's house to babysit.

He picked her up in a Benz, and while driving her to Sheboygan, he bragged, "So, as you can see, I haven't lost my touch, Rae."

But you sho the fuck lost your good looks, "Why do you call me Rae, anyway?"

"How did you get the name 'Rainia' anyway, smart-ass?"

"Well, my momma went into labor with me during a storm and had to catch a city bus up to the hospital. The power and the phone had gone out and she couldn't call for an ambulance, and nobody around her would answer their door. She walked over to 27th and Locust, and the bus pulled right up. Right after she paid her fare and sat down, a car accident occurred right at the curb where she had just been standing. My mother was so grateful for her fate that she named me after the first thing that she saw next to mark that day forever."

"What the fuck was that, a rain cloud on the bus driver's head?" queried Meechie.

Rainia snapped, "Naw, smart-ASS! The house that still stands on the corner of 27th and Locust has these rocks placed over the grass. They are all painted brown and yellow now. But back then they were all painted different colors, like a rainbow. Momma figured that rainbow was a little flamboyant to use for a name, so she shortened it and named me Rainia. Then, if you can believe this shit, I didn't want to come out once she got to the delivery room. They ended up butchering my poor momma, cuz I did not want to bring my caramel-colored behind into this world. She still has the terrible scars that always make me feel guilty for living whenever I would see them across her stomach. The shit that me and my momma been through, boy, I tell ya! Sometimes, I look back on bad times and feel like I know why I never wanted to be born, and then — other times — like after a storm, I see a glimpse of a rainbow and know I'm important. Like I was sent by all means necessary."

"That's real nice, and deep! Who woulda guessed you were so deep, miss Rainia? I think I like your name shortened down to 'Rae' betta though. In fact, more than ever since the last time I laid eyes on you. But thangs are a lil bit different now. I got two kids." He pulled out an alligator-skin wallet and opened it up with one hand. It unfolded, revealing a photo of two light-skin babies, maybe a year apart, and holding colored eggs. "Yeah, that's Terry, the boy, and his lil sista, Rae. I named her after you. You don't believe me, do you? Well, take out the picture and turn it round. Read the back — out loud!"

Rainia took out the photo and read it, "Rae and Terry, Easter Picture. They are really cute. So, are you married now?"

"Naw, they White-ass momma be trippin'. In fact, you gone meet her real soon."

"What? I ain't tryna meet no damned babies' momma, Meechie. Fuck that, cuz that's out!"

Meechie just laughed, "Girl, puh-leeze. That's my babies' momma and shit, but she ain't nothing else. She know betta than to ack up. Besides, we already here. If I leave you in the car, girl, somebody gone snatch you up. Come on." He got out and came around to make Rainia go inside, which was easy, because some serious, hard-looking pimps were gambling in the parking lot right next to his Mercedes Benz.

"Seven, mutha fucka, and it's lady luck walkin' by, looking ev-ah so fly." The man speaking with a toothpick in his mouth reminded her of someone she hated.

Meechie gave the dude five and pointed at him, "Watch out now, Pimpin'; don't get nothing on ya!" then he hurried her inside. The door opened and Rainia realized that she was in a strip club. On the stage was a White girl, ass naked, with her bare pussy spread open with two fingers. Niggas was all around her trying to look inside, as she finger-fucked herself. There was a fat White broad bartending and a couple of Black and White chicks giving private lap dances at random tables. *Ooh, this is some stanken-ass shit goin' down in here! Damn, why I let this ho-ass nigga talk me into comin' here? Can't just leave, either. Them niggas outside look like a whole pimp team of Billy's. FUCK!*

"Com'on in the back to the VIP section."

She followed him to the back of the club through red velvet curtains. Once opened, she could see a pool table off to the side that had a Chinese girl being fucked on it while she gave head to another guy. In the corner, a Black girl was sucking a light-skinned dude off in a big, red chair. He started to bust a nut in her face, and she was laughing. "Meechie, what the fuck kinda super-duper ho shit is this? Why the fuck you bring me here?"

"I came to collect; that's all. Don't worry; we ain't staying. I don't want you to get no ho-ass ideas."

Like my life's dream is to be the bitch on the pool table for your lanky-shifty-eyed ass! Dick head! A White girl with long, blonde, straight hair came up to him and kissed his cheek, "Hey, baby, who's your beautiful lil friend? She come out to play, or is she startin'?"

"Hell, mutha fuckin' naw! This is gone b my wife. Nobody touches this good pussy but me. But *WE* will have some seven and seven over here in the office."

This nigga is crazy! He must have left his mind in the same place that he left his face and body behind at. He took Rainia's hand and walked her through a tinted-glass door marked 'Private'.

"What's so private in here? People in here getting pissed and shit on, or are there fag-booty orgies back here?"

Meechie giggled, "You a mess."

Then the door opened after them, and the White girl set their drinks on the table and said, "Well, holla if you need me." She walked out of the room, pushing up her titties in her bra, but Meechie never even looked up.

"So, was that your babies' momma?" asked Rainia.

"Naw, the loose bitch with her pussy spread wide open was her." Then he took out a white brick from under the floor's carpet where he had a hidden, secret stash and threw the plastic-sealed block onto the table. "Do you know how much this is worth? When I got out, I had six of these stashed away. Ol' girl in there on stage had a clean record and a bar license and moved my shit, opening this club for me. When I got out, I was richer than ever. I thought that I loved the bitch, until I caught her fucking my guy in here one night. True enough, she had made me a lot of money and kept shit flowing. She had already had my kids and shit, but she admitted that she was just a fuck-crazy ho and would never commit to any man. *That* fucked-up all the personal love that I had for the bitch. Now we just business partners, and my kids stay with my momma in Milwaukee."

He looked really hurt, as he stared at the cocaine packaged neatly on the black, marble-topped desk. Then his eyes trailed from the block of cocaine to Rainia's chest, up to her collar bone, and then locked in on her eyes, as he spoke with a somber voice, "I need you to be in my life, Rainy — our lives. I dreamed of getting you back at least a thousand times. Now, here you sit. You know you can never forget about me, cuz I'm the first dick you ever had."

Rainia thought, *He was the only one,* and then she cleared her throat, "Meechie, I am only Sixteen. Why would you think I am ready for, or, for that matter, even want a life like this?"

After he pulled about seven-hundred dollars from his pocket and threw it on the table, he gestured for her to take it, "Because I can give you everything in the world. Stop trippin' and ack right. You gone be my wife and have me five kids. Watch."

Yeah, right! Watch me have five kids with somebody much smoother than you, old man!

Then he pulled out a switch blade and stuck it into the cocaine. He licked the knife and took a little more to his nose, "That's ice cold! I'll be right back, baby girl. I gotta talk to the bouncer about letting those hard, leg-ass friends of theirs into my establishment for free." He took the brick with him and stuffed it and a glock in his pants.

Rainia put the money in her bra and knew that it was time to go. She could hear "Pimp'n The Hos" by 'Really Short' beating in the background and niggas yelling, "Yea, Black pussy on stage. Big booty, big, titties! Shake that ass, girl!" After two more songs, she got up and tried to walk outta there, but Meechie wasn't having it.

He was coming out of the men's room and ran up to her, "So, you ready? Let's go then, baby." He drove her to a nice hotel and walked her up to a room. The inside was immaculate and decorated in mauve and gold. He made her lay in the bed with him and watch "The Devil and Mista Jones" on the Playerman Channel he had ordered for the well-lit room. Then he started to try and have sex with her. He was feelin' on her and kissin' on her neck and stood up by the side of the bed to unzip his pants. He pulled out his flakey dick and it had blonde hair wrapped around it.

This mother fucker had his dick sucked and fucked already at the club! Nasty-ass, stanken-ass bastard! Then, good! My mutha-fuckin' excuse outta here with this nasty man's money; I am so happy about this. Now all I need is a way out. Think, Rainia, THINK! Just thinking about all of the filthy, freaky shit that Meechie was probably into, *And now he has the nerve to want me to suck it all off for his dirty, bitch-ass, worn-out-looking cock* made Rainia almost gag, so she told him, "I wanna make this extra special for you. I wanna put some ice in my mouth and chill out. You can be the first dick I ever sucked. You want that?"

"Hell, yea, girl! That's what I'm saying! Suck it, please!"

She got up off of the bed, "The ice machine is at the end of the hall. I'll be right back."

"OK, but undress and put on that robe in the bathroom, cuz I want my pussy as soon as possible."

Damn! she thought. She went into the bathroom and put the robe on, putting the seven hundred-dollar bills in the robe pocket and grabbing her school ID and her underwear and shoes, placing them into the ice bucket under her arm. She came out and flashed his nasty ass, and he didn't suspect a thing. When she got out in the hall, she walked towards the ice machine with the bucket in her shaking hand. She was about to drop it and hit it down the exit stairs, but she paused, thinking about how Billy first tried to front her life off when she was a pre-schooler, *That shit didn't count, and neither does Meechie. Fuck him, 2!*

Meechie was shot. He was a coke-addicted, dick-n-ball head with crazy ideas for her. Just as she was about to take her shoes and ID out of the bucket and run, their hotel-room door opened, "Hey, baby girl, come get this change, so you can grab me a 7down Soda out the vendin' machine, too. I got some licka up in here to party with. Hold on; wait right there."

"OK, Meechie, baby." She waited until his head went back in the door and took off to the exit door with the bucket in her hand.

She ran all the way down the steps and out of the parking-lot door. She didn't stop until she got to a coffee shop, about six blocks away. She walked up to the door, panting heavily, and straightened her robe, fluffed her hair, and dignifiedly re-situated her ice bucket. Then she opened the door and went inside.

"Hey, little lady, can't you read? No shoes, no service." The chubby White waitress only had one customer, and he was paying his bill to leave. Rainia held up one finger, pulled out two black flats, and slipped them on. One of the shoes had brought a bra and panties out with it.

"No underwear, no service either. Hey, you in trouble?"

"No, but where's the ladies' room? And I need a cab a.s.a.p." said Rainia.

The pudgy lady said, "Back there, and the phone and phone book is back there, too. You want sumthin' while you wait?"

Rainia liked the sound of that, "Ah… yea. I'll order and eat in the back by the phone."

The woman slapped the counter, "Hot damn! I knew it! Runaway hooker!"

Rainia gave her impressed eyes, "Almost, but not close enough," declared the lucky but frightened, sixteen-year-old girl. Rainia went into the bathroom and walked to one of the two stalls. She closed the door, sat the ice bucket down, took off the robe, and put her underwear on. The bathroom door opened and her heart raced, *I hope this ain't Meechie's withered-face ass up in here looking for me. God! Please help me get outa this shit!*

Two busted, black orthopedic shoes that were leaning over on each side, underneath white-stockinged, coffee-can ankles parked up under the stall door, "Here, you look like about a size seven. It's a uniform, but it's more normal than a robe; let me tell ya." The chubby hand of the greasy-haired woman reached over the stall, tossing a waitress outfit at her.

"Thank you, dear lady. I'll be ready to order in a minute."

Large Mardgie added with, "You ain't from around here. The only people with your color are the Mexicans working at the factory and the few whores at the many strip clubs. So, what's your story, because you can't be anymore than 17 or 18?"

"Well, if you must know," said Rainia, dressed like the woman as she came out of the stall, "I'm sixteen and from Milwaukee. I ran away from this man who was trying to get me to do coke and have sex. But I ran from him, and here I am. Now, I gotta get home before my momma starts looking for me."

The woman said, "Well, shit! Lets get you outta here before the creep comes looking for you. Those fucking pimps think they're so got-damn slick. But I'mma lil bit slicker! Lucky for you that my sister is a Greyhog driver, and a bus is about to leave to Milwaukee in 20 minutes. How's a ham sandwich and chips to go soundin'? We got chocolate cake and oatmeal cookies, too. Or was it chocolate chip? Oh well, no matter. You are running away from the devil, and I'm gonna see 2 it that you get clean away. Don't worry about paying for anything. We got you covered."

Rainia stuffed the $700 from the hotel robe pocket into her bra, as she followed the woman to her car after the lady had locked up the restaurant. The woman drove, and when Rainia spotted Meechie's Benz going the opposite way, she quickly ducked down.

Just as promised, the big White lady hooked her up with a clear, plastic bag containing the victuals and handed them to her as she pulled into the bus station.

"Thank u so much. I'll never forget this!" Rainia told her.

They almost missed the bus, but the shiny-silvery door opened up like the gates of Heaven, revealing yet another guardian angel in human form. The chubby lady patted Rainia on the back and spoke to her sister, "Janine, this here is a good girl. Take her home for me, will ya, and make sure she gets off in Milwaukee?"

The driver of the coach just shook her head, "Sorry, sis, but this one is packed. No room, Mardgie."

Just then a woman started running to the front of the bus, yelling something, "Oh, my goodness. We're on the wrong bus. I'm so embarrassed about this, but could we get off? All we have is this one bag, so there's no need to open the luggage compartment." The woman was very frail, and she had an adorable, two-year-old boy with her. The sight of the both of them walking down the bus steps reminded Rainia very much of two people she had known for a short moment when she was about 6 or 7. The woman stopped on the last step and looked at the see-through plastic bag held by Rainia, "Chocolate-chip cookies, huh? Here, take one of ours, too. We've been eating and eating them. Now we're sicka them; ain't that right, lil buddy?" She picked up her giddy tot and kissed him on his beautiful, golden hairs, handing Rainia an unopened, vendor-machine-sized bag of rainbow-sprinkled, chocolate-chip cookies.

Rainia felt a brush of cold go through her, as she watched the woman and toddler make their way back into the terminal, and the little boy blew her a kiss before disappearing inside, closely snuggled in his mommy's arms.

The woman from the restaurant playfully slapped Rainia on her back, "Well… you better git!" She winked at her sister.

The other lady looked just like her, but was skinny, and said, "Come on, lil lady, before whoever is looking for ya catches us. Nice outfit." She laughed while Rainia made her way back to the two empty seats that awaited, and pulled the bus out into the street, heading to a few places on the way.

The little towns they went through reminded Rainia of being a little girl, traveling with her mother up North. Rainia opened the plastic sack and eyed a meaty ham sandwich, cheesy and ruffley potato chips, a slice of chocolate cake, a stack of chocolate-chip cookies in clear wrap, and three cans of Peach Knee-Slap soda. Everything in the bag was her favorite. She took a bite of the delicious ham sandwich and cracked open a pop, catching a glimpse of her own image in the bus's tinted window and thought about getting a job as a waitress. She even thought about leaving for a whole new life for real. She thought about her momma trying to go to school after all these years to become a nurse. Her mind finally settled on school and graduating. Rainia wanted a normal life so bad that she could taste it. On the way to Milwaukee, she thought about how she wanted to grow up to be somebody. She opened the rainbow-chipped treat and thought of angels.

Once she got back in town, she took a cab to Eva's house. The cab that drove her to Eva's pulled up, and Rainia remembered that all she had was $100 bills. "OK, ok, I'm a runaway. I don't have any money, and this is my Auntie's house," she said to the Arab woman.

The woman chuckled to herself, "You are very lucky girl that I am the one they sent. I ran away, too, but from my country. Where I come from they circumcise the baby girls so they can never know what an orgasm is. So, having said that, enjoy the rest of your life, and stay safe."

The teen was bewildered, "What does that have to do with cab fare? OK? Never mind. Thanks." Rainia thought that all of her troubles with sexual experiences were the worst until she heard that. She'd made herself cum plenty of times, but she didn't have an orgasm with Meechie that one time. "Thank you for the advice, cab driver, and thank you for the ride."

She closed the cab door and walked into the building's locked lobby. It smelled of a good-quality, burning, sandalwood incense, and the faintest hint of freshly-cooked collard greens and hot water bread. She spotted a row of mailboxes and approached them, running her fingers across names until she found Eva's. She pushed the tiny, dirty, white square and waited.

"Who is it?" asked Eva.

"Bitch! It's Rainia! Let me up; it's cold down here!" The door buzzed for her to get in, and she went up the stairs and around the corner. Eva opened the door, "What the fuck you got on, 'Flo'? Where's 'Alisson'? At work on the TV show 'Melvin's Diner', or what?"

Rainia cracked up laughing, "Fuck you, E-val! I'mma tell you all about it. You got any liquor, girl?"

Chapter Fourteen

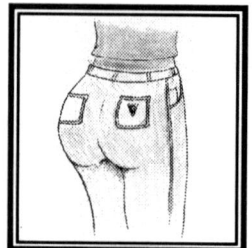

Is This Love, or Racism?

MHSA, or, The Milwaukee High School of Artists, a.k.a., West Divisional, never looked so good. Her weekend extravaganza had turned out to be a very weird sham. Rainia decided that she was gonna walk a straight line from that point on. She didn't want to go with nan-nodda nigga ever again, so she got a White boyfriend. His name was J.C., and he was a cutie. He was all into her body and talking about other people. The boy was like a brotha and could rib extra good. He was real popular, too. He would catch the bus with Rainia to school and from.

One day he asked her to come by his house. She got to his house and it was a nice little crib, but it was in the hood and about twenty blocks away from her house.

"So come in the garage and see the car I've been working on," he suggested.

She followed him into the garage, but there was no car, just a lawn chair and a blanket. "Hell, naw. You just want some pussy? That's all you niggas think about, and yes, you are a nigga, J.C."

He walked up on her and started doing his seduction thing. He could kiss very well. Rainia hadn't had sex in years, but she felt that maybe it was time. Just when they were getting into it with his blue condom on, another boy started looking in the small window off to the side. "That's my little brother. Don't stop; he ain't nobody. Come on, and let's finish this. Witcho fine, yella ass!"

Rainia pushed him off of her, and while she pulled her clothes together, she said, "That's alright. I'd rather not. I'm not a slut, you know."

She broke up with him after only a few, short weeks and started talking to another boy. He was light-skinned. His name was Gary, and he worked at a pizza parlor after school. He bought her everything and was always trying to get some. One night he took her to the roof of the pizza parlor and talked her into doing it, "Rainia, you are the most beautiful high-yella girl I have ever seen." His dick was so big that it was pointless to try and get it all in. He got his rocks off, but the shit hurt her so bad that she couldn't enjoy it.

He tried to have sex with her every day after that. At his parents' house, a friend's house, in a hotel, or in a borrowed car. All he wanted to do was try and jump her bones.

One time they were in the backseat of his cousin's car, and the police tapped on the window with a flashlight, "Get your bright ass out of the car, now." It was a Black cop and a White cop, and they forced Rainia to get out of the car butt-ball naked. They ogled her, chuckled, shook their heads, adjusted their dicks, and wrote Gary a ticket. "Don't let us catch your triflelin' asses up here again."

Rainia felt triflelin', too. It started to seem like everyone was infatuated with her light-skinned booty.

It was that same tail of hers which got her into her next tragedy. Sometime before they had been caught, Gary's condom broke. Rainia's birth control pill would also prove to be useless. Not long after, a test at Planning 2b a Parent confirmed that Rainia was pregnant, *How am I going to tell my mother?*

But Gary said she didn't have to, and he paid for an abortion, only to wind up knocking her up again when his prophylactic busted after he had just cum during a later plea for sex, once she had healed. After the second trip to the clinic, Rainia just didn't want to be with him anymore, so she called it off after only eight months.

Every day she walked around with the most terrible secrets hanging over her head. Rainia longed to have better than the cards she was being dealt and the stupid-ass hands she kept playing, so she kept on trying. She tried to get back in with the good girls and be civilized. Punkin had invited her to go to a party for her

Grandmother at the Renaissance Fair Place on Prospect Avenue. It turned out to be a surprise party for Ophelia Windsor's mother, who was also Punkin's Grandmother.

O.W. was a famous Black reporter who had just started up a talk show in Milwaukee's neighboring city, calling the show, *The Windsor Show*, "Baddest in the Windy." Rainia felt like her life was finally looking up. That night she got to meet 'O.W., The Baddest' and O's guru boyfriend, Sterling Hauser-Grafton, as well. To see and meet a strong Black woman and her companion in power had made Rainia feel proud of her colored side. The woman was smooth, too. She had a flair with words that flowed as lovely as her hair. The young teen, desperate for a positive Black mentor, was star-struck with her demeanor as well as her articulate abilities with White people. There seemed to be nothing that could be said above laymen's terms that would coast over O's head. The woman could have been a part-time lawyer. She was so smart and fabulous.

Rainia didn't know whether to shake the woman's hand or go cry in the ladies room from all the excitement. She ended up going into the ladies room to slap herself and pull it all together. After she splashed some cold water on her face and fixed her emerald-green, floral, silk pants set, she went to look for her friend, Punkin, to thank her for the invite. It was the best thing that had ever happened to Rainia.

She hung with Punkin real tough after that, but then, people started to say that she was clinging onto stardom. It was true that Rainia had never really had shit in her life, except for whatever petty stuff she had recently acquired as a teenager, and that she didn't even know what to think about hanging around rich, wealthy Black folk, but Rainia was a true-hearted person. She longed to be more like Punkin, but she always felt so low about all of the terrible secrets in her past. Sometimes when she would hang out at Punkin's Grandma's home in the suburbs of Waukesha, WI, she felt guilty and beneath the beautiful family that had so willingly opened up their home to a ghetto girl. Rainia liked Punkin for who she was, not for who she was related to, but she could never prove that by being an ordinary broke-ass, and no matter what would have been what, she would always be considered as the clinger. Clinging onto stardom just seemed to be a fake-ass move to inflict upon such fine people.

She didn't want Punkin to believe that shit, so she started hanging around other girls just to prove that she wasn't a faker. She wasn't about to give up her friendship with Punkin; she just didn't want to seem like a beggar or something. So she slowed things down.

Anmarie helped her in doing that by refusing to let Rainia go to Chi-town with Punkin to be in the show's audience. Rainia could've sworn that her mother was jealous or something, because why would she not want her daughter to go places with upstanding individuals? Punkin was always leaving town with her aunt and didn't really have time for ordinary Rainia.

Left behind, Rainia totally got lost to the wrong crowd. Those other girls were real bad-asses, too. Some were dancers already, and some had kids. One of the girls who was into stripping even had a brand-new car that she claimed to have bought for herself. Once again, a very confused Rainia was surrounded by the bullshit life that the ghetto had to offer and quickly turned into a dumbass like the rest of the girls who were poor.

Punkin had started hanging around Rainia's ex-boyfriend, Gary, and Rainia totally felt betrayed. She really began to go astray then. She was seventeen and about to enter the 11th grade. No job. No privileges. *If my mother wasn't so damned strict, maybe me and Punkin would've developed a sisterly relationship, or at least we would've been able to stay friends.*

Rainia retaliated. She got hooked up with a Black dude named Odeus Brownston, who went to Custard High. She was skipping school to be with him. Her mother confronted her with Fred one day about their teen's school attendance, "What the fuck do you think that you are doing, Rainia? Running the streets with these stupid-ass kids is gonna mess it all up for you. Who are you skipping school to hang with anyway? Where you been going all of these days?"

Rainia snapped, "What difference does it make now? You never let me go anywhere or do anything but clean your fuckin' house, and you never give me an allowance. When I am working, I gotta give you money. I missed out on a chance to be a part of something good with Ophelia Winsor's niece, Punkin, but you would never let me go to Chi with them. All my fuckin' life you never let me do shit but suffer, you selfish, mean-ass bitch!"

POW! No quicker than she had spoken her piece than she was hit in the face with a telephone, and Anmarie and Fred were kicking the shit out of her once she hit the ground. Then they told her to pack up only the things that she had bought with her own money and get the fuck out of their house. Rainia was so got-damned mad that she did just that, and through a swollen eye, she did not even look back.

She stayed at Eva's house for a few days where she could smoke weed and drink as long as she babysat and cleaned up the house. She would also sneak to a bar with some of her friends and drink with a couple of boys from North Divisional named Boston and Chauncey, until Chauncey took advantage of her when she was drunk one night. Odeus Brownston found that out and had her move in with him at the spot where she was helping him to sell dope. This had her skipping more school and all kinds of shit. Odeus stopped going to school to hustle full time.

Odeus and his momma were at the dope house one night bagging up product when 'Boom', some niggas in ski masks kicked the door in, "Get on the floor, face down, and don't move, or we gone blast," said one of them. They took everything Odeus had on the table, emptied his pockets, and left. Luckily, Rainia was out buying a fast-food dinner for them down the block. After that happened, her boyfriend got them all a hotel room for a couple of nights until he found a new spot to sell from.

Rainia was only seventeen and failing the 11th grade. She dropped out when her birth control pills and condoms failed again. Odeus got her pregnant and moved her into his grandmother's house off of 6th and Ringer Street for her and the baby's safety. He was hardly ever at his grandmother's though.

His momma was a drunk, who just laid in the bed claiming to be sick all the time. She was a hypochondriac, greedy-ass, lazy-ass bitch who wouldn't even take care of her own little daughter. She drank Rhine wine all day and would cuss Odeus out and demand money from him as well as weed. From the way they would argue whenever he was around, Rainia could swear that those two were fucking or something. Rainia couldn't stand his funky-actin' Grandma or his crazy-ass momma, and they couldn't stand Rainia, either. In their eyes, she was White. They didn't like White people, at all.

But, aside from 'Evaleenie and Evirmeanie', Rainia loved her some Strawberry, her boyfriend's little 5-yr-old sister. She made sure that nobody messed with her. When Rainia was her age, she had been going through some of the most wicked wrong that a child could bear, which often left her feeling depressed from time to time for the rest of her life. In her eyes, Strawberry was a dark-skinned princess who deserved better. She was such a happy, little girl, considering her circumstances, that she had made Rainia wish for dark skin. Most of the hopes and dreams of her lifetime had involved wishing to be White, but now that she had met the famous 'O' and lil Strawberry, Rainia felt like she had been wanting to be on the wrong side of the tracks all this time. Maybe if she were all Black, like this little girl was, she would be stronger. She probably wouldn't feel sorry for herself from time to time the way she did. She watched the little girl often, walking her to and from school whenever she could. She bought her candy and did her hair, laughing, joking, and reading her kindergarten homework directions to her every school night. Rainia didn't care what problems the women of the house had with her being there; she knew that a girl child wasn't safe in the world and needed a guardian angel. Rainia always wanted a baby sister and loved being a big sis to Strawberry.

And Rainia loved her some Odeus Brownston. He was the first guy she tried to love. He could make Rainia do anything, including quit school, but he couldn't make her have an orgasm during sex. She never told him that shit, though, cuz the nigga looked like Roul Tresvantin from the group 'Latest Edition' and had cold, wavy, jet-black hair. Also, she didn't want to fuck with his ego or make him want to cheat on her. She always had a smile for him, no matter how bad things were for her while living with those witches. He was about 6'1" and was a slender, brown-skinned brotha with a tolerable-sized jimmy, but he didn't know what to do to make her feel good. They would fuck like rabbits whenever he was home, and even though she really wasn't getting shit out of it but a stanky, sore coochie, to her, he was all that mattered in the whole-wide world. Rainia would soak in the tub after sex with him and think about her life.

It was one of those nights that he was home and Rainia was in the middle of her tub routine, thinking ever so deeply. It seemed that in the hood there wasn't anything for youngsters in poverty to do but fuck and try to be in love with somebody, maybe even *anybody* who appeared to love you back. It was a lot like Eva and Reny's view of down South. It was a 'poor thang', but falling in love with someone helped her to stand the pain. She would never be like the White girl, like Punkin, or even like the stripper girl with the new car, out of town vacations, credit cards, and a choice of ballers coming at them, trying to foot the bills of their high-maintenance lifestyles. Instead, Rainia was another weakened, low-grade statistic. A minority teen who was pregnant, with a dope-dealer boyfriend who stayed at the 'Dope Spot', and she figured that she was unable to look forward to anything else, other than having a baby. She wasn't happy to be living with his granny and mammy, but she was happy to have Odeus' child.

Rainia looked around the bathroom and felt a sudden cold chill of disturbance as if death had entered the room. The red walls and mirrors were haunting her mind like visions of Billy Jacksin's red Cadillac. Rainia was beginning to feel trapped like in her nightmares about being locked in Billy's car from her childhood. She got out of the tub and dried off. Her clothes were thrown on in a hurry, as she went down the dimly-lit steps to get a drink of Kooljuice from the refrigerator. Odeus' grandma's house was real freaky, too. The old woman had portraits of White people on the walls which could stare a person down from any angle that you looked at them, like they were alive. Her walls were covered in fuzzy red and gold, floral, Dracula-like fabric, and she had a winding staircase that was covered in weird, ancient carpeting. The bottom half of the steps were wider than the rest, like the last few steps were reserved for entertaining in a spotlight. Perhaps for singing Liberache songs to the adoring crowd, and even then they might raise up to reveal a fire-breathing drag-queen living under there. *Ms. Jack woulda loved to peep in the windows of this house.* His granny had a cold, dark fireplace the size of a wall and well crafted cherry-wood molding on everything, including the big bookcase. The whole house was like being encased in a live play of 'Klues' the mystery board game of murder in a big mansion. *Who done it? Was it the nigga in the kitchen, with the ham hock? Or was it the nigga in the library with the Civics Book?* The readings consisted of White history. To be so hateful towards Whites, Odeus' grandmother was sure intrigued by them. She cleaned houses for the rich ones on Lake Drive. Some rich, old couple had even left her some big lion statues to put outside of her ugly, gray, stucco house on the hill, chillin' on 6th and Ringer street.

One day while Odeus was out selling rocks, and Rainia, then about three months pregnant, was arguing with his grandma about how Rainia needed to take her White ass home, when suddenly Rainia caught a cramp. She went into the red-walled bathroom and shut the door on the second level. She felt something warm coming down her legs. It was blood. Rainia called an ambulance and was rushed to the hospital. She had a miscarriage. Odeus was nowhere around to share her grief. He was spending most of his time at his dope house. When she got back to his grandma's house, his Granny had asked her to leave. Rainia ignored her request and locked herself in the bedroom she was sleeping in for the rest of the day, crying and praying to God for an answer.

Rainia wanted to move on from all of the tragedies and start fresh, *God, I know I've really messed things up with you, but I just wish that You would help me get right, because I have no idea which way to turn. My whole life seems to just attract the bad things, and I could really use your blessings right now, Amen.*

Two days later, mean ol' granny asked Rainia to go catch the bus to pay a light bill for her, and when she got back, Odeus' granny had all of Rainia's stuff packed and sittin' by the front door.

"What the hell is this? I can't go home, because my parents are pissed at me."

Granny just walked away, mumbling something about another stupid, dumbass White girl. The house phone rang and granny brought Rainia the receiver, "Here, house pussy, it's for you."

Rainia just knew that it was going to be Odeus, but, instead, it was a nurse from the emergency room, "I just wanted you to know that the test results confirmed that you have gonorrhea. That would explain the miscarriage. So please come back with your parents to get treated as soon as possible."

Baby girl's heart was broken when she put the phone back on the receiver-charger. *What kind of shit is this, God? I prayed for a blessing and got cursed even more. What the hell am I gonna do now that my baby died, and I know that Odeus don't really love me after all, while I'm lookin' like a complete fool?* Rainia felt like a car had crashed into her heart.

That boy was all she had left in her mournful world, and he wasn't even thinking about her. He didn't even know what had happened to their baby yet, because he was still at the spot. At least she now knew what he was really about. It was exactly like his granny had said, that she was nothing to him but a slice of in-house pussy — no more, no less — that, and Odeus was doing some outside fuckin'. It would later come out that he was doing two or three girls at a time. Some of the bitches had even gone to her school, according to the rich stripper girl, and he was running trains with his friends and selling dope in the meantime. 'The Dope Spot' was really 'The Fuck Spot'.

His granny came in the room looking like she felt sorry for her. Still, as bad as she felt for Rainia's horror, she didn't want no part of the terrible shame. She walked away, shaking her head, "Call ya momma, and tell her to come get you out my house, now!" yelled his granny from the kitchen.

I swear to God, man, I hate my fuckin' life! Rainia had no other choice but to swallow her pride and get out. She was clearly not wanted here, not even by her fake-ass boyfriend. So a devastated Rainia called her mom after she hung up on the nurse and begged to be allowed to come back home. Her mother picked her up and told her she could stay if she went back to school. Rainia was so depressed and sad that she wanted to die like her baby had, but she kinda felt like she deserved every bit of her torment for having abortions. She also had to confess that she was a diseased idiot to her momma.

Anmarie took her to the hospital to get treated for the STD. Rainia then told Anmarie about the boy and the miscarriage. Anmarie had a heart-to-heart talk with her about life and death and having the strength to move on after that kind of double heartbreak.

Since she was already a suicidal mess, Rainia bit her lip and even disclosed the sexual abuse of Billy Jacksin.

"That dirty mother fucker! If he was still alive, today would be the day that I woulda killed him. I really hope that he is burning in hell. Why didn't you ever tell me?" asked a teary-eyed Anmarie.

"I tried, when I was about seven, but you whooped me and made me pray from the Bible, naked."

Anmarie could not recall the moment, "That's a damned lie. I ain't never did no shit like that."

Rainia thought it pointless to argue, so she dropped it. Rainia tried real hard after that to stay focused on school. It was hard, though, because she was sad about her babies, the ones she had denied, and the one she had lost. The hos who Odeus was picking up in his new car that he had saved his dope money to buy, that he had a shined up waiting on them after school in front of Rainia's view, were being extra mean and writing, 'Dead baby up in Rainy's boring, diseased pussy' on the bathroom walls. Rainia couldn't stand them bitches, couldn't stand Odeus, and couldn't stand the bad feelings that she just couldn't shake.

Death was everywhere around her. The kids were dying at her school left and right. One girl was hit by a car right out in front of the building. Another boy drew a picture of a boy being shot on the bus stop for a pair of tennis shoes and was killed that same way a week later. Another girl had a weird aging disease that she died of no sooner than she got into the school, and another girl died of heart failure linked with anorexia, and also, a couple of boys turned up in the freezer of a serial killer.

One day, a White boy from her theater class said hi to her at the mall while he was with his White girlfriend. No one knew that the girl had brothers in the Nazi Nation gang, who, in turn, beat up that White boy so bad for speaking to Rainia that he died in a hospital bed about three days later. The shit was so depressing that she couldn't even look for a job at that mall anymore without feeling guilty for that boy's death.

By the time she turned eighteen, she had finally found a job at a different mall. Capital Corner was the mall for Black folk. Rainia got a position with a clothing store and was only working there for a few days when Odeus came strolling in, wanting to talk. She went straight to the back and begged the manager to get rid of him. She didn't want to hear his shit. He kept coming by the store, and she kept going to the back. She was about to get fired when another guy came up to her one day as Odeus was approaching the store. Rainia grabbed the boy and started talking to him like they were together. Odeus turned around and went the other way.

The unknown fellow asked her to lunch, and she went with him, arm in arm. After that, the new boy came by to see her everyday. She didn't even see Odeus again. Since the new guy seemed to be alright after having lunch with him a few times, going to the movies with him, meeting his family, and going to church with him, she went with him as boyfriend and girlfriend for about a month, and eventually, they had sex.

The fucking condom broke the first time and Rainia was instantly pregnant. She wasn't about to have another abortion, so she kept her baby this time. The boy was an asshole, too. He dropped out of high school to get two jobs, but he wouldn't come and see her or check on the baby's growth. He claimed to always have something else to do. Before the birth of their child could even occur, the boy had left her completely alone after only five months of pregnancy. He said she was getting too fat and walked away from her in the middle of the street, on the way to the doctor's office to get an ultrasound. He didn't want shit to do with Rainia, or their developing daughter.

Rainia was so embarrassed by the pregnancy that she left West Divisional and started going to an alternative school. As a high-school senior, she graduated with honors, then she continued to stay at her parents' house until she had the baby. Rainia knew that she had played herself with the detour boy, trying to escape Odeus, but she felt like, *Fuck it!* Her and the baby didn't need the daddy's sorry, drop-out ass, anyway. The nigga never did come back by her mom's house to check on them once the baby was born, either.

Rainia didn't give a fuck about shit anymore, except for her daughter, and eating. She let herself get up to 267 lbs., convincing herself that *no nigga would want me anymore anyway, so why not be a fat ass?* At least she managed to graduate on the honor roll.

Odeus saw her with the baby one day in the mall parking lot, just after she had picked up her check and was getting into her momma's car. He decided to try one more time to get Rainia back. He was ringing her parent's doorbell later that day and begging her daddy to try and get Rainia to hear him out, "I realized that I love your daughter, sir. I messed up, and now she's stuck with a baby by herself with some strange dude, because she was trying to run from me. I don't care about her having a baby with another man, or being heavyset; I just want to marry her. Can't you talk to her, man?"

Rainia was listening to his plea from the livingroom, and she felt so vulnerable. She couldn't even think about the ho shit he had done to her, because she was the stupid bitch who had just gotten left with a kid, not him. There was no way she felt any better to judge him anymore. She wondered if he really loved her. He certainly had no alternative motives that she could see, as fat as she was now and carrying another nigga's baby on her hip.

Odeus laughed and continued to talk to Fred, "I even got my own house, and I'm working a real good job. Can you please take my new address and phone number and give it to her for me, please?" He handed her stepfather the info and walked slowly down the steps, as he kept looking back to see if Rainia was gonna come 2 the doorway. He got into his Nissan and slowly drove away. She thought of how many times she had watched him go down the street after he had scooped up his train sluts from her school and never even called to apologize for giving her that fucking disease. He never consoled her for the loss of their child, either. She felt like he had killed their baby, and that was probably the reason he was so desperate to be with her and the living baby girl she now had. *The nigga musta finally got into his feelin's? Fuck um!*

Her step dad closed the front door, "You can come out now; he's gone. Here, come get this boy's number if you want it, or else I'm gonna toss it."

She eased her big behind up off of the couch by the front hall, straightened her oversized T-shirt over her men's sweatpants, and picked up her newborn, kissing the baby's lips, "Toss it."

He did, and she ended up getting it back out of the garbage later that night. She never would of done it if it were not for the sermon on Channel 30 about forgiveness. The pastor was an old White man who reminded her of her grandfather. She put the baby in her crib and turned the volume up, "The Lord said to forgive your brother. God forgives us all of the time. Some of us have even done the unthinkable and desperately wanted to be forgiven. Yes, sins such as murder may seem far worse than adultery, but they are all sins and no less. Some of us walk around like we are better people, when we are just as bad as the people we judge. I want you to look me in my eyes from your TV set tonight and do something for me. I want you to forgive the person or people you are so angry with tonight. Then, and only then, will you lighten your own burdens. From there you will move on to joy and bigger things. I promise. All you have to do is trust God and forgive."

Rainia got down on her knees and forgave everyone she could think of for everything that had ever hurt her, then she forgave herself. After heavy tears of redemption, she went back to the garbage, took the number from the trash, and put it on the dresser in her room. Now she could sleep with a clear conscience.

Chapter Fifteen

Is It Racism, or Sexism?

The next afternoon she called him around 2:30. His answering machine took the call, "This is O. B. I can't get to the phone, but you can leave me a message."

"This is Rainia... I guess I'm calling to see,"

"Hello? Rainy! Hey! I was just walking through the door when I heard your voice. What a pleasure. So how you doing, baby? You and little Rainia ok ova thea?"

"We are just fine," Rainia stalled.

"Well, just fine and fine. When can I spend some time with yall?" asked O. B.

"That depends on you. I'm not working anymore. I was too fat too keep the store image, so they fired me." She wanted to change the subject.

"What? That's some bullshit. Why the fuck don't women's stores sell cute clothes for big chicks, anyway? You're so pretty, girl, that you would set a new line of clothing for the big girl's off! Don't worry about them. I got you covered in the cash department. You need some bread right now? Or maybe the baby needs somethin'?" he wanted to know.

Rainia huffed, "Well, since you're asking, I do need a couple a dollars, but I don't want to burden you like that. We'll be ok."

"Rainia, I know that I did some dirty shit, and I hope you can 4give me and at least let me be your friend? I'm willing to bet that the nigga ain't even man enough to step up to the plate and help you with the baby. I can hear it in your voice. Are you crying right now?"

Rainia sniffled, "Ah, naw, I'm just a lil sick."

"Bullshit! Be ready with the baby in about a half hour. I'ma go scoop her up a car seat and stroller right quick, and then you n me n the baby are going shoppin' and out to eat. Deal?"

Rainia thought about how she needed some of the things that Odeus was offering, "OK!"

"Cool, and tomorrow we are going to see about getting you a car, and I'm going to teach you how to drive, so yall ain't gotta ever ride no bus or wait for rides. Rainia, I really do know that you are my heart. See you in thirty."

She got her baby dressed first. Taking off her light blue and yellow-flowered housecoat and combing her unruly hair, she thought she looked strange with her skinny arms and legs, but big ass. Rainia became discouraged, then she threw together her typical sweat-suit attire with her wiped-off, somewhat-white tennis shoes, placing her hair in a ponytail with big, used 2b gold earrings adorning her ears. They were faded. She went to the top of the dresser and put on her new pair that she had painted with clear fingernail polish to try and preserve the life of the fake gold hoops. She tried to make her face up a little bit, but her face was chubby and looked terrible if she had on too much lipstick, so she wiped the red tint off and opted for clear gloss and just a touch of brown eyeliner. She thought back about a year ago, when she thought that she was so cute. When she first hooked up with Odeus to defy her parents with the nigga she thought was the baller who was going to save her from the ghetto. She wondered what working job he supposedly had, because dope dealers usually never quit, even when caught and let out of jail. They go right back into the game, because no punk-ass job around Milwaukee is gonna pay a nigga the same way he can hustle and pay himself. As strange as it felt, she wondered what Meechie's old ass was into by now? *I wonder if he's even still living!* Grabbing the diaper bag and her child in her arms, she walked down the stairs to Odeus' car.

Fred laughed at her, watching her get into the young man's car, and then he locked the security door to the house.

O.B. had reached over to open the door for her and pulled the passenger seat back to allow her to put the baby into the brand-new car seat. It was so pretty. Pink, with blue and purple flowers and blankets to match. The stroller matched as well, standing up on the other side of the car seat in back of Odeus' seat. He must have had subs in his car, because the base was vibrating even though the volume of the song was turned way down. He put the seat back and smiled, as he took a moment to look at the baby who was looking all around her with her squinty eyes, and he wondered, "Rainia, she looks like she's Black and Asian. What's her name?"

"Ciara Pashan, but we call her Cee-Cee."

"I like that. That's real slick. She looks like a 'Boo' 2 me, though. I'ma call her 'Boo' — if you don't mind?" O.B. said.

Rainia laughed, "Damn, nigga. You actin' like we getting married cuz this your baby or something."

O.B. turned the radio up a bit, "I feel like she mine. You know, kinda like a second chance. Like maybe our baby was gonna be deformed or something, so all of the events had to go down the way they did to bring her to us normal. That shit sounds corny though, don't it?"

Rainia felt her stomach turn and didn't respond. She was trying not to be mad with him anymore. *Forgiveness and friendship; that's all there is left, right?* At the mall, he bought both mother and daughter a new wardrobe and shoes, Baby Jordins 4 the baby, and Lady Jordins 4 the lady. Rainia thought that it was a good time to pry, "So, what's this job you got? You ain't sellin' no more?"

O.B. became alive with excitement, "I do airbrush art, and I'm in business for myself. I spray paint jeans, T-shirts, nails. Shit! What-eva! In fact, here goes my spot over here. Most of my clients are females from my former gig at my Auntie's salon. They like the nail art and come see me like everyday, 3 to 10 girls some days, at $20 a pop. Sweet huh? I've been trying to get you to come to this side of the mall since forever, but you wasn't trying to hear a nigga out, and I do understand. Once I started making money doin' the shit at my auntie's salon, I decided to do my own thing. I'm now renting this space. I decided to use that equipment you see all set up over there under the plexi-glass that a hype had given to me as a payment for some dope money he owed to me. You didn't even know that I was so cold at drawing, did you?" He was as conceited as he was extremely talented. He pulled the tarp cloth off of the partially covered cart and displayed some of his art to her. There were T-shirts with memorials on them, couples' faces on canvas portrait frames, fancy free-styled names in elaborate cursive with sparkles on a white board, cartoon airbrushed jeans, sets of fantastically extravagant nails of all colors and themes under glass, and champagne glasses on designed license plates.

Rainia was impressed. The last thing her eyes had landed on was a wall-sized portrait of a girl lying on a couch. Rainia took a double take of the mural. It was her body b4 the baby and her face when she was thinner. The portrait was the ultimate compliment that had lifted her heavy spirit.

Odeus pulled it from the back wall and brought it closer to her, "Yeah, baby, that's you. This White guy is coming to buy it on Tuesday for $900. He's n2 Latino chicks and wanted me to draw a mystery woman for him. I ended up taking the class photo of you from your yearbook and using your face for inspiration. I know you ain't Latino, but you damn-sure are fine like a Rican girl. Are you mad? Cuz if you are, then just think about this, that money is gonna help me pay for your car. I've been looking at this cute, little, white car, and I always think of you. Wanna go see it?" he asked.

"Yea! Where's it at?" she wanted to know.

O.B. went on with, "Way out by Waukesha, in Brookfield. We can go to the Italian Garden out there to eat. You ever been there?"

She was intrigued, "No. That's that new place, ain't it? I heard that the food is good, too."

It was final, as he walked with several bags, "Well, let's go then." He grabbed her hand and held it all the way to the car, as he struggled to carry all of their bags twisted around his other wrist and cutting off the circulation to his hand. Once he had loaded the stuff in his car, put the stroller away, and strapped the baby in the car seat, he closed the door for Rainia and jumped in, booming a song about, "Baby, U Can Have a Piece a Me", by 'The Guys'.

On the way to the restaurant, he pointed out the car he had been referring to. It was a cute, little hatchback sitting on the corner lot of a strip mall. Rainia liked it but really didn't want to stop and check it out fully, because she didn't want to get her hopes up too high, *Maybe it was the words to the last song he had just played that are reminding me of how he's such of a slut?*

At the restaurant he ordered for her, "She'll have the 'Italian Tour Situation' and I'll have the 'Fettuccine and Shrimp Tosser'. I'll take a glass of your best red wine, and she'll have a cola."

"Diet cola with a twist of lime, please," she corrected her order to the waiter, and then asked, "You drinking wine now? I thought your momma was the only one who was into wine? She still drinking that fart-smelling shit? What was it — Rhine wine?"

O.B. looked down at the table napkins wrapped around the silverware, "Yea, she the one got me to drinkin' wine, but I just can't get with the stinky stuff. Maybe you wanna try mine when it gets here, or are you breast feedin' lil baby Boo over there?"

Rainia flopped her boobs with her hand, "Yeah, but I gotta pump it out, cuz she don't do the titty thing."

He chuckled, "Yeah, your titties are bigger than I remember, but I don't wanna seem like a pervert. Uh, you got some leakage there on your T-shirt. Maybe you can put some toilet paper in there, because it seems to be spreading fast."

She looked down to see what he was talking about, "Oh, shit! I'll be right back!" She excused herself from the table and went to the ladies room to tissue up. After washing her hands and blow-drying them and her wet T-shirt spot, she rounded the corner to find Odeus feeding her baby her bottle and then burping her over his shoulder. The baby puked down his expensive dress shirt, but he just cracked up laughing like it was the cutest thing. He gently placed her back into her new car seat and tucked the blanket around her, then he attempted to wipe the spitup off of himself. Rainia discovered that she still had love for him.

After dinner he wanted to take the girl's to see his new home. Odeus had bought himself a house off of Teutonia and Hampton. It was a cute, little house with a small yard and garage. His homebase was a two bedroom, single-family brick-style with a decked out basement. Upon entering through the front door, Rainia could see that he had white furniture and a white carpet.

Odeus looked so proud, "With all of the white jumping off in here, I usually make people come in through the back door." He took her through the whole house tour. One of the bedrooms was decked out in black lacquer and had his momma and lil sister's pictures on the dresser. "This is my momma and Strawberry's room. I don't know where them two are at, though. Probably at her man's house. Yeah, my momma's old ass done found her some nigga that gives her everything she wants and keeps her stocked with Bayport's cigarets and the Rhine wine. She comes home whenever, so this is their room."

Then he walked her across the hall and showed her his personal quarters. He had a mattress in his room on the floor, "I'm looking at some white bedroom furniture. You wanna help me pick it out?"

"Sure, when?" asked Rainia.

He closed the door to his room, "How about this weekend? You and Boo can spend the night if you want. I get lonely up in here by myself."

She'd entertained the idea for a split second, "Naw! We better get home. My momma's probably looking for her grandbaby right now."

O.B. didn't press the issue, "Ok, well then, I guess I better get yall home. When am I gonna see you again?"

Rainia reassured him, "Soon enough. You know, it took me a long time to even talk to you again. I just need some time to see if you are for real. I don't wanna rush and get my feelings hurt again. I need to see if you are cool with just being my friend, cuz that's all I think that we got left."

O.B. let his conceit take over him, "Yeah, aight! But I think we both know that I want you back. I'm gonna win you back. Let's go before I do something to you."

Rainia thought about him looking at her fat nakedness and rejected the vision, *Nigga, Puh-leeze!* She rolled her eyes and shook her head in pity for him.

Rainia walked through the front door of her parent's house with the baby in her arms, placing the takeout box on the end table by the couch. Odeus came in behind her with the baby stroller, car seat, and the bags. He put all of their things down by the front door and came into the living room to properly introduce himself to her mother and twin brothers. Her mom said hello and snatched her grandbaby up like she had been worried sick about her. Odeus shook Fred's hand for re-approval from their private, man-to-man conversation that he had with him the other day, "Well, I brought your daughter and granddaughter home safe, so yall have a goodnight. Rainia, call me when you're ready to go test drive that car, ok?"

    She stood by the door, "Alright! Thanks again." She closed the door and her mother was peeking out of the living room shades.

    Grandma laid the baby down on the couch next to her, "Who in the hell was that? I don't know no Odeus. What the fuck kinda name is that anyway? And why is the nigga tryna butter you up with all this new shit for? I don't get this scene, and I want you to tell me what the hell is going on, Rainy. Fred, hand me that bag with the baby clothes sticking out of it, honey."

    "Mom, this is going to sound really stupid, I know, but that is the guy who gave me a disease. He's trying to be my friend now, and I guess he wants to help me and the baby out in place of all the rotten shit he's put me through. He said he wants to buy me a car, too."

    Fred interrupted her, handing his wife the bag she had asked for, "Is that boy sellin' that shit, cuz that was a new car that his skinny ass hopped into and took off in."

    Rainia felt pressure to redirect Fred's opinion of O.B., "No, he has his own business. He airbrushes art on things at the Black folks' mall. I guess he makes good money, because he does nails, too."

    Fred had found a weak spot in Odeus' occupation, "What? Anmarie, you hear this shit? That nigga is sugary?"

    "Naw, Dad! The girls come to him with their nails put on already, and he just spraypaints a design on them for $20 a set. He gets like 3 to 10 clients a day from that alone."

    Her dad was offended as a man, "Oh, really? It still seems like a pretend job, if you ask me. What happened to men carrying heavy loads and getting dirty? Nowadays, men wanna wear earrings — and have long hair — and sit on their ass all day long — and play with finger paint like a bitch. That nigga almost tripped up these steps with all that shit. I wasn't gonna help him either. He supposed to be stronger than that, anyway."

The twins giggled their famous Weenie woodpeckit laugh, "Ha-ha-ha," and J said, "He had a big-ass pear head with a tail in the back. Dude is extra skinny. You shoulda let him keep your take out box so he can gain some weight. Where did yall go eat at, anyway?"

"The Italian Garden," laughed Rainia.

"*Oooh*, big-time baller, balling out-a control. What he want with *you* though? *You* so fat now. Let *us* have those leftovers. *We'll* help you loose weight by taking this good food off your hands for you," quipped Jo, as he helped himself to her takeout box. J snatched a hunk of lasagna from the box like a dog and ran.

Her mom got pissed, "Cut it out, you two! You're both acting like scavengers! Oh, Rainia, these are some beautiful baby dresses in here. He just might be the friend you need. Just watch out, and remember what I told you. I think a new car *is* a bit outlandish though." Her mother looked at her like she was stupid, "Well, *get* the damned car if you want it so bad, but you better watch it with him, cuz he's nasty, ain't he? Besides, don't be bringin' me no more damn grandbabies; one's enough. Bring the rest of that stuff over here. I wanna dig in it to see what else you guys bought."

Rainia felt glad to have gotten something out of the nigga, but now she had to hustle him for the car without leading him on. The weekend came, and just as he had promised, Odeus pulled up to her house in the afternoon, but with his momma in the car.

"Hey, Rainia, long time no see. How you doin', baby?" asked his phony-assed momma. She had made it clear on many occasions that Rainia had no business with her son.

So why the fake niceness all of a sudden? she wondered.

His momz got out to let Rainia into the backseat, and when she got back in, she shut the door on her brand-new manicured fingernail, busting it down to the meat. "Ow, bitch, got damn it, muther-fuckin', shit-ass fuck. I think I'm gonna be sick," she announced, as she sucked on her hot, throbbing, slightly-bleeding, bald middle finger. As Odeus stopped at stop lights on the way to the awaiting car on the lot, people at bus stops kept yelling out, "Fuck you 2, you crispy, black-ass bitch," and putting up their middle fingers at his momma. She wasn't trying to offend anyone; it just looked that way, because that was the finger she was re-examining over and over. Rainia was trying real hard not to laugh out loud. The woman's bird flipper was indeed fucked up. "I don't see why we gotta go get her White ass a car, anyway. We need to be gettin' *me* a new car," exclaimed Odeus' mother.

"That's what you got a man for," he told his momma. "Make *that* nigga pay for that ass. Shit! All you gettin' is squares and drank. *Maybe* a couple dollas here and there. So what? And I ain't giving yo Black ass no more credit, Ma. You be wantin' too much. I'm your son, not your pusherman or husband."

Rainia's mouth fell wide open in the backseat, and she realized, *So ya punk ass is still sellin' dope? Ok, I'ma havta quit fuckin' wit you already. Lying-ass niggas! I swear, I remember when I asked you if you was selling, and you didn't exactly say no either, witcho deceitful self. And yo momma is a crackhead? That would explain the fake concern and the flip-flop attitude. And this sorry-assed, drugged-out woman got the nerve to disrespect me like I ain't even here? Always calling me White like I got it so good. Yeah, right! The White people reject me, and niggas like her do, too.*

Rainia repressed the urge to choke her prejudiced ass but was satisfied that her finger injury was as bad as it was, because his mom was still saying, "Ow, Shit!" Rainia grinned like a sly fox, *I'm glad that bitch broke her nail. I hope that shit aches so bad that her asshole starts twitching. Ha-ha! Now that's a crack twitch 4 that ass.*

His mother started making sounds like she was continually clearing snot from her nose and throat while adjusting her wig, revealing that her hair was in nasty, stinky, unkempt knots up under there. Rainia squinted her eyes at the back of the woman's head in disgust. *Bitch, you betta not drop no lice on my lap, or I'ma kick ya ass when we get out.* Rainia was looking down at her lap, hoping that there was a cootie so she could start some shit. She was a big, angry, light-skinned bitch right about now for some reason.

They pulled up to the strip-mall parking lot to find that the owner to the vehicle was in a truck, next to the little, white, foreign hatchback, and waiting on them. Odeus got out of the car, and so did his moms. Her pussy was stanken, and she had the nerve to be scratching it in public. She was definitely doin' some crack activities. Rainia had no choice but to get out, too, so she could avoid the blowback wind of funk that she did not want to be enclosed in a car with. His momma walked her musty, itchy cunt around the car and looked in, "This is a mutha-fuckin' stick? Rainia, yo fat ass can't fit in here, and you cain't drive no stick, either."

Odeus grabbed Rainia's arm and turned her to face him, "Look, my momma is coming down from her high. Please forgive me for asking this, but can you just ignore her?" Then he turned to the man, "Sir, I have the whole $1,100. We'll take it! It drives real nice; it sounds nice and quiet, and you have given me all access to the most recent repairs receipts and the original owner's manual this morning. Most one-owner cars are the good ones, so my baby here will take this one off of ya hands for you."

He turned to look at the crack fiend who'd shat him out, "Momma, I need you to drive my car home, and I'ma be home later. Make sure you take a bath, too. There's something in the cookie jar for you on the kitchen cupboard, so go straight there."

He then grabbed Rainia's hand and walked her to the little car, paid the man, took the keys and title, and they both got in. He was in the driver's seat showing her everything that he could, but Rainia already knew how to drive. Her parents had helped her on the weekends, and she'd taken Driver's Ed during her last year in high school. She even knew how to drive a stick-shift.

She smiled as he explained it all to her, then she said, "Oh, yeah? Well, can I switch seats with you and get the feel of it?"

"Shit yea! That's what we here fo." He got out and made the change with her.

Rainia got into the driver's seat and put it back a bit to accommodate her bigness, then started the engine and drove around the parking lot like a pro.

Odeus laughed, "Damn, girl! Why you just let me go on and on if you already knew the deal?"

"Because it was entertaining." She tried to change the subject, "Now, would you like to go somewhere special?"

A lightbulb went on in his head, "Yeah! Let's go to the D.M.V., because they gone be closed by 2 P.M. I want you to have the title in your name."

Rainia felt real good now. *Yea! That's what I'm talking about. Some compensation for the bullshit you and yo momma and bald-headed granny done put me through. Like Nee-nee's daddy once told me in Pine Bluff, Arkansas, "The shit you gotta do to make amends with the people you hurt!" I definitely feel amended! Me and my baby girl gone be straight in this car, boy! No more footin' it!*

Odeus was proving to be a real good friend. The following week, she had finally agreed to go over to his house to visit around 7 p.m. He told her to knock on the back window, because the front doorbell didn't work and his room was in the back where he could hear any knocking. She had left her daughter in her mother's care b4 going over there. As she approached the back of his house, a furniture truck was leaving the alley. Odeus' dream white bedroom set had just been delivered to his house, and he asked her if he could make love to her on it, breaking it in for the first time. She, for some reason, cringed at the thought, but she agreed to go to the movies with him to catch the last show after he had come back from a customers' house real quick. He left her sitting over there until 1 a.m., waiting on him to come back from a dope run. She would have done some snooping around, but there were too many good movies on his cable.

When he finally came back, he wanted her 2 go home, "Aw, man, I'm so tired. Those dope fiends will spend a check with you, but you gotta wait until they smoke it up, rock by little-ass rock. I made $900 for the night and I'm beat. Can I get a raincheck on that movie to make it up to you, Rainia?"

She had a plan, "Sure, it ain't like I got somewhere to be besides being with my baby."

He sheepishly agreed, "Yeah, that's right. Your baby probably crying for you right now. I'ma follow you home, so I know you got there safe, ok?"

"Thank you. That's real nice of you, Odeus." She wanted to see it with her own eyes this time. So when he watched her go into her house and then he pulled away, she got right back into her car and went to a late-night drive-thru, getting herself a snack and giving him some time to get into whatever the fuck he was up to.

She sipped the last of her vanilla shake on her way to Hampton street, as she carefully drove to his house. She parked right in the alley after circling the block to see that his car announced that he was back at home. The music was bumping slow jams loudly and he wasn't answering his back door. She was pounding on the kitchen window and didn't realize how hard she was knocking. The low-set window cracked and fell completely out of the pane. She climbed in, hoping to walk up on him fucking. Rainia crept up the stairs, following the source of music coming from his bedroom. She pushed the cracked door open all of the way.

There he was, doggy style, butt-assed naked with a super-duper Black girl who was eating out a stark White girl. There was a camcorder propped up by the bed. He couldn't take Rainy to the movies because he had gotten a sudden proposal to be in one. Rainia was real happy about it, too. They were so into it that none of the three even noticed her standing there. She called out his name and he jumped off of the bed and skinned his ass cheek on the pod-stand's adjustment lever, sending the still-filming camera to the floor.

He didn't have shit to say but, "Ouch! My ass!" so she yelled it loudly yet calmly out for him, "That's gonna be a funny-ass movie. I might buy it when it comes out. What's it gonna be called? I know, America's Funniest Home Pornos! That's a good title, right, girls?" The two hos were letting a little bit of an embarrassed snicker out as Rainia photographically remembered their faces with her mind's eye. She was relieved to be standing in the presence of the truth, "I guess that's the way you break-in bedroom sets. Do carry on, my friend. I have no business here, anyway. Nasty mafucka in the mix — take 2," she slammed his door shut and yelled, "Action!"

He re-opened the door, holding his ass and calling her name. Odeus had something he wanted to say, "How the fuck you get in here?" He was trying to be angry, but his booty hurt. Rainia felt relieved, because she had a free car to go home in this time around. She didn't even argue. She really didn't even care.

The next morning, a basement window was kicked in at her parent's house, waking up everyone with a start. Fred went outside to find Odeus' crazy, crackhead mammy out there trippin' and yellin', "That's for breakin' our shit, bitch!"

The front door was snatched open, and the barrel of a shotgun pointed through the screen door crack, "You ugly Black bitch! If you don't get yo raggedy ass from round here, I'm gone shoot it off," yelled Fred.

Homegirl took off runnin' down the street, putting Flowy-jo to shame. Fred then went to holler at Rainia, who was already dialing Odeus' pager with 911. The teenaged boy called back and agreed to bring by some money to replace her step dad's window. $200 was put into an envelope and dropped in her parents' mailbox that led to the inside of the hallway where it lay on the floor, with the words 'Window Money' marked on it.

Two days later, Odeus was arrested by the Feds for having 7 lbs. of dope in his freezer that he was mostly holding for an associate. It turned out that his own momma had given him up for a five-hundred-dollar snitch reward. They sent him to Black Brook Falls, a Wisconsin Federal Prison. He had the nerve to keep calling Rainia collect and begging her to write him. A few days after that, she saw the Black chick from the threesome, that he was caught fuckin' in just days ago, cashing her check at the bank. She gave the actress the address for the prison 2 be able to keep in contact with him, and that was the last time she dealt with him, ever again! He had made it clear, more than anyone ever had, that she wasn't White enough, nor Black enough for this fucked-up city.

Chapter Sixteen

Jack-Pot; Whore Pot!

Finding a job was much easier this time around. Finding her keys and things were not, *Where's my got-damned purse? I'm so sicka being broke as a joke. I gotta find a better way for my daughter. I do not want to be late for this test.* She found her stuff scattered on the dresser and scurried out the door.

Rainia had scheduled a driver's test and had passed it the first time, but the ID she got back was the downer to the exciting, uplifting moment of victory, *Weight, 267 lbs, two to three chins, and I'm still wearing a size twenty. I need to be walking to look for me a job, but I ain't got time to waste.* She had transportation and could fill out many more applications than she could by making her rounds on the bus. All that she had was a high-school diploma, and she was heavyset. The only places that seemed to want to hire her were fast-food places. Rainia was asked to come back to work for the youth center as a supervisor again, and she also got an interview at Kentucky Style Chicken as a cashier for the weekends. She'd gotten both jobs, and the lady next door, 'Big Momma', had agreed to watch lil Cee-Cee in the daytime for free. That was Big Momma for you. She loved and helped to raise all of the neighborhood kids, and now she was willing to help look after the next generation. Cee-Cee stayed with her grandma at night and on the weekends, as Rainia's hours picked-up at her fast-food job.

One Saturday morning, Rainia and another girl were at the 'Counter Service Only' restaurant waiting for a customer to walk in.

A man came into the small lobby from off of the bus stop and wanted only one thing. He strode up to the counter, cleared his throat, bent down, and pulled a few crumpled dollars from his crispy-new sock, and then laid the ball of notes on the counter, "Yeah, ahh... lemme get 6 corns, a lot of butter, and plenty napkins." The man had one tooth in the top row and three spaced out on the bottom row.

Rainia gazed at him with a straight face, fixed her stupid-looking visor, and turned around to the warming oven to prepare his order — but there was no corn left. Trying so very hard not to laugh, she replied, "I'm sorry, sir, but we are fresh out."

The would-be patron bent over again, slapped his knee, and stood up quick, "Maaaan — DAMN! Ev-er-y time I come in nis raggalee motha fucka... What the fuck you mean, fresh out? Go check in the back freezer, babygirl."

"Sir, I know for a fact that we have sold the last ear in our afternoon rush," said the other girl.

"Yall ain't got no corn? And you for real with this shit, too, huh? If yall ain't got no corn, then you need ta shut this mutha-fucka down, then!" He snatched his money off of the counter, went to kicking the store's entrance doors several times, and left out. Then he came back in pulling off his cap, scratching his head, and putting the hat back on to sit up on the back part of his head. "Why yall ain't got no funky-ass corn? Yo big, mulatto, zebra, mutt ass been back there snackin', ain't ya?"

Rainia became offended and snapped instantly, because it was bad enough that she had been ridiculed for all of her living years because of her skin tone, but she'd be GOT damned if a bald-mouthed nigga was gonna knock that and team it up with her size right to her fucking face, "Mutha fucka, the sign say 'Kentucky Style Chicken' not 'Kentucky Style Corn', and with a mere four teeth in your mouth, how in the hell can you eat it, anyway? Slap butter on it and gum it into corn oil? Now you can either order something else from the menu — or step!"

He looked at her for a good minute, twitching his fat mustache under his strained lip, with his receding new growth and curl sparkling with curl spritz catching the sunshine coming in from the big windows in back of him with his foot stuck out, his slip-on, black, knit-meshed shoes that people on the street named, "Winoes,"(The preferred shoe of the constantly drunk), tapping the dirty tiled floor with his white, knee-high socks pulled way up over his knees, and a pair of old-school loc shades on, a red-crocodile-print short outfit on, swinging his boney hands to his sides, the one decrepit hand still gripping the dollars that he was prepared to spend on his original desire, pondering the possibility that she was being truthful with him, and then he continued, "I like you. You big folks, but you is a cutie. Alright then, sista! I'ma quit fuckin' wit yall!" Once he had left, they thought that he was gone for good, but a minute later he came right back in, "Are you sure? OK, well then, lemme get a few napkins. I gotta take a shit."

The other girl gave him a stack and said, "You betta not be shittin' out back, either!"

Later on that night, Rainia snickered about the toothily challenged 'Corn King' and got the notion that she should probably do something about her bigness. She had tiny wrists and ankles and little-bitty calves, which gave the hint that she was not built to be fat. She had developed Asthma, and she got tired from walking up just one flight of stairs. She couldn't even play with her baby the way that she wanted to. She was tired of being heavy for the fuck of it, so she decided to go back to being the way she had been.

Turning on the cable, she watched an infomercial about a stepping system that was easy to use while a person watched TV. Rainia watched a lot of TV when she had the time, so she thought that she could try out their method. The only problem was, she didn't have a credit card or a personal checking account to order with, so she did the next-best thing. She made up her own shit by stacking up phone books and stepping up and down off of them for at least 4 hours a day, 2 hours in the morning and 2 at night. She also cut her meals down to just 1 real meal a day with salads replacing the other 2 meals. She also started drinking large quantities of diet sodas and glasses of ice water.

A couple of months later, she had gotten herself down to about 160 lbs. and into a size 14. Her ass was still big, and she now had cellulite, but at least she could make it to the gym where she had gotten herself a membership. Her ID card that she had taken had inspired her to step her game up. In the gym ID picture, she noticed that she was back down to one chin and looked way better than she did in her driver's license photo.

While taking her daughter grocery shopping to buy some fruit, she ran into her ex-boyfriend from high school. It was the beginning of the rest of her string of foul relationships to come, "Hey, J.C. What's been up with you?"

"Rainia? Damn, girl! How you doing? This your daughter? She's a little cutie pie. Somebody told me that you were big and fat-nasty and had a kid now, but I paid it no mind. You done got big though, ain't ya? You ain't fat-nasty, but I'ma start callin' u 'Big-draws'."

"Aw, fuck you, you Black man stuck in a White man's body, witcho long, beautiful, golden hair. Why you gettin' perms and shit like a fair maiden, you repugnant, repunzle-rumple nigger-skin? It's so long, blonde, and curly. Pretty boy! You look like a golden poodle. Shouldn't you be buying dog snacks instead of cereal?"

He looked at his box of apple cereal and shrugged his shoulders.

Rainia continued with, "This bitch is slower than my balls growing!"

J.C. chuckled, "You ain't got no balls growing!"

She looked dead serious, "Exactly! And we ain't gonna never get out of this line. Look at all the stuff that the lady in front of us has. Aw, shit! Now she's writing a check."

The check cleared, the cashier pulled off a three-foot receipt and gave it to the woman, who said, "Geeze! I didn't want all that."

Rainia glared at her and mumbled, "Well, now you got it. Now git b4 I have to buy birthday supplies for my baby's fourth birthday, cuz she just turned three while we been waiting behind your stockin'-up ass!"

J.C. giggle-grunted, "You still funny. Hey, you still with your baby's father or what? Where the nigga at?" He was looking around the store, as if some man was gonna step up and say, "I dat baby's pappy," or somethin'.

Rainia bit her lower lip, "He left us when I was still pregnant. He ain't even never seen her yet."

Her ex-boyfriend had felt bad for her and the baby, "Damn!

That's fucked up. I'm real sorry to hear that. Well, how do you feel about going out with me this weekend? Well, actually, I'm a professional drummer now in this band called 'Project', and we been getting a lot of gigs. I would love to see you come show some support to ya boy." He placed his hand on his chest, revealing the fact that he had been working out.

Rainia then looked at him real good. He was a cuter White guy than she could remember. She needed to get out, so she said, "Yeah, sure. That sounds really exciting. Where yall gone be at?"

J.C. thought about it, "I think the place is called 'Jamies' or 'Karenz' or some shit. Why don't you give me your number so I can call you with the right name, address, and showtime." He put down his box of cereal and pulled a receipt from his pocket, writing his name and numbers on the back of it. Then he ripped off the rest of it so that she could do the same for him.

After this exchange of numbers, they paid for their groceries in the checkout line and left the store. J.C. got into a black Toranado and peeled out of the parking lot, booming his subs that were playing the new 'R-ruh Kellyman' songs.

Rainia arrived at 'Jamies' around 7 P.M. that Friday evening, dressed in a jean outfit and tennis shoes. She was still a lil on the fat side and didn't want to come out in public looking 45 years old wearing fat-lady dress-up clothes that the stores sold to heavy women.

The show was about to start, and J.C. walked up from behind her table and sat down, "What you drinkin' on, girl?"

"Diet soda and rum."

"Well, I don't drink, but let the bartender know what you're havin'. The rest of your drinks are on me." He got up with his drumsticks in his hand and went up to the stage to perform with his band. He was the only White person in the band — and in the whole bar. The band was tight, and he was so cold on the drums. They played all R&B cuts that sounded better than the originals. Once their third set was over, J.C. was asking Rainia to go out with him the next day.

One date turned into many, and soon they were back together and living together. It lasted a year and a half. It would have worked out fine, if he hadn't talked about her like a dog everyday, trying to be funny. Rainia got tired of his shit. She'd had enough of his punk-ass 'Big-draws' jokes, so she lost all of the extra weight, wanting to be a model. Her second defense was enrolling herself into modeling school, and J.C. was jealous. Then she started to meet a few important people, and suddenly she was part of the 'In crowd'.

One woman from her modeling class in particular, 'Yaphiela', who was eleven years her senior, but didn't look a day over twenty-five and knew of all the best contacts in town, had asked her to travel with her. Yaphiela was trying to get Rainia's portfolio to be seen by all of the major modeling agencies.

J.C. didn't like that idea, so Rainia turned the offer down. J.C. protested every outside opportunity that was coming Rainia's way and liked it better when she was fat and at home with her baby daughter and fixing him dinner every night, waiting for him to get back from a show, kissing his ass, and giving him glory for his successes in life.

When her step-brother from her real father's side invited her to come to California for two weeks, she jumped on the family invite, only to come back home to find that J.C. had his ex-girlfriend calling their house. He had been seeing her behind Rainia's back just that quick. Foul! That pretty much did it 4 her, and it was over. Rainia packed hers and her daughter's things and left him, allowing him to keep all of the furniture that they had put together. She'd even gotten the help of her old friend, Chaz, to get the job done of quickly packing the little shit she did have to get the fuck away from him.

Then she moved in with her childhood friend, Ginny, for a month or so, until Rainia got a place in Brown Deerville, by the rich folk. It was really an apartment roommated with a homosexual jogger. She had gotten pulled into this strange deal because a White classmate of hers from John Murial was to be her original roommate, but that girl ended up getting married to this homo's brother the week after Rainia moved in. The brothers had stayed two doors down in the same apartment building, so it was convenient for the friend from John Murial and the gay brother to switch apartments. That way, the newlyweds could be together, and Rainia would share the girl's old apartment with his gay brother 'Frenchy'.

This homosexual sibling was a very strange character, too. He had bright-orange hair and a mustache to match. He was a chef at a local suburb restaurant, and his favorite things to do were go running in the morning, cook all of his dishes with turkey meat, and take photographs of the neighborhood flowers. Rainia never saw him with a date the whole, entire time she lived with him. Instead, he would always ask her about Chaz, "Where did you go? What did you see? Who did you meet?" It was as if he was trying to live his life vicariously through her experiences. Either that, or he was in love with her guy.

Rainia was working three jobs just to be able to afford rent, gas, and the cost of living. White people sure know how to keep the minority folks out of their areas by jacking up the rent so high that they can't afford it. She also had been trying to keep up with her new contacts, so that meant staying in the nightlife and the 'In crowd'. Rainia was cool with keeping up appearances as long as she could drink free beer. She discovered that she had a become a beer connoisseur.

All of the extra kicking-it left little time for Rainia to spend quality time with her child. She felt like she deserved to have more freedom, especially since she'd missed out on many important events, like the prom or spring break, to become a young, single mother. The baby was being left over her mom's house more and more, so she took her daughter to live with her momma for the next 9 months.

During that time, Chaz had found himself wanting to hang around Rainia's apartment more and more. He would bring friends over and make parties out of ordinary days. Whenever there was a party, though, the gay guy would either leave or stay shut up in his room. Chaz practically moved in and would give her all kinds of money to pay her bills and to go shopping, so she quit two of her jobs and knocked it down to one. The two had become real close, reminiscing about their childhood, declaring how right he was about them hooking up once they were grown. Chaz made her happier than any man had ever done in her lifetime. He was an upper-class White boy, indeed, but he was funny as hell, loved beer, too, and everyone wanted to be around him. She believed him to be her soulmate, sharing the bills and her bed. They had even started talking marriage, until his ex wanted him back. Rainia had been so happy with him that she wanted him to be happy. Even if that meant he had to do it by being with someone else. So he went back to his ex. Foul! Rainia and Chaz's relationship had only lasted 6 months.

Rainia didn't have the financial support of Chaz anymore, so the rent had gotten hard to pay. During that uneasy heartbreak-breakup from her supposed to be soulmate, Rainia got mixed up with some crazy activities. For one, she had met this girl named J.J. at one of her parties who lived down the street from her. This girl was a Philippino, high-school graduate, and popular rich kid from a nearby neighborhood, who was only seventeen but carried herself like a twenty-something year old by working two jobs and smoking a lot of weed in her spare time. She and Rainia had this strange marijuana bond where she would only come over to her house to share her smoke sack and talk about fucked-up men issues. They never did anything else socially except for that, but, in a funny kinda way, it made them as close as family, so they started calling each other 'Cuz' whenever they would re-connect.

J.J. was from a wealthy family and really didn't have to work. Both of her parents were doctors, so she just worked her jobs to piss her parents off. Rainia only wished that she had the new car and college opportunities that J.J. had but thought it pointless to be so envious to tell her so.

Rainia had major money problems that she kept bottled up inside. She was pressed for cash and couldn't find work to fill the monetary void, so she started stealing for a living. It was an instant rush to come home everyday with hundreds of dollars. Working for a clothing store in her youth had proven valuable for her criminal occupation. She knew where to look for cameras, which stores took back items for cash, and the best times of the day to lift. It was so damned easy that it was wrong.

One day she was in a department store, doing her thing, and she could've sworn that she heard the voice of the Lord speaking to her, "Ok, you are a cleaver thief, but u will be caught one day because of someone else. You will see things more clearly because of someone else through My Good Grace. Then I want you to try it My way and live your life trusting Me. When I finally get all of your trust, and you have done My work, only then will you be wealthier and happier than you have ever dreamed."

She asked herself, What does that mean? I always steal alone, so I'll never be caught.

Rainia dismissed the thought. She was grabbing all of the high-priced clothing and slipping them into the shopping bag she had fixed up at home to appear to be tied shut, but there was an opening on the side which allowed her to take a hefty load without being noticed. She turned down a paint isle and pretended to look at a color of glossy matte blue. As she bent down to get a gallon of paint, she dumped all of the hangers from her pilfered items behind the paint cans on the bottom shelf, selected the blue paint, and went up to the home-improvement register to pay for it. No one was there except for a pregnant girl digging in her purse, waiting on a sales person to appear, as well. The girl looked up, and Rainia almost died laughing, "Well, I'll be damned! Your high-maintenance, dancing ass finally got pregnant. Now you can't talk shit about me anymore for having a kid, bitch! How the fuck are ya?"

Rainia had run into an old friend from the bad crowd back in high school named 'Teela'. This girl was one of the females in her school that had stayed in fresh gear everyday, had a new car at seventeen that she'd bought herself, and had sworn that she would never have not even one kid.

Teela looked around at her and whispered, "I'm cool, but you gone get me caught, ho! This is a fake pregnant belly, and I'm out here stealin'. Just take down my number and call me."

Rainia whispered and giggled back, "Girl! Is that a wig... or what? Hurry up and tell it to me, cuz I'm gonna call you 2night so we can catch up on old times." Rainia quickly scrambled down the digits and acted as if she didn't know her. The sales lady appeared at the register from the back of the counter with a smile. She rang up Rainia's paint and put it in a bag with the receipt. Rainia walked out of the store with $2000 worth of clothes.

On her way across town to the next store, like the one she'd just left, to make a few returns, she thought about how coincidental it had been to run into Teela under the same circumstances. She wondered if she was still dancing. Rainia was a slim thang again and looking pretty good. She thought about dancing, too. As she made her way to the return register with her bag of clothes and a ripped-off receipt only showing the date, she ran right into an elderly woman wearing tinted glasses, almost knocking her over. "Opps! I am so sorry. Are you ok?" Rainia nervously asked.

"Bitch, are you following me today... or what?" asked the old dame.

Rainia did a double take, as she looked a little closer, "Teela?" she whispered.

Teela fixed her glasses and dusted off her moo-moo, "Yea? U got me. But let's just get our money and meet up at the steakhouse across the street — Cool?"

Rainia accepted the offer, "See you in about twenty."

Teela extended it with more directions, "And order me a cosmopolitan cocktail, honey, cuz after today's run in, I'ma need one right away."

"Me, too." Rainia had even thought about getting drunk after the day she was having.

The steak house was packed with couples. It was a Saturday night and Rainia found herself feeling like she had found a new sister. Teela had been a bad bitch in school, and Rainia had always wondered how Teela had the nerve to dance naked for money back then. Rainia was now a professional criminal, making more money than she'd ever had, and now all she needed was someone to egg her on to do something else to make her life more interesting. Teela was the perfect antidote to all of her pressed-down depression from loosing the wealthy Chaz. Teela had come into the establishment dressed to the casual nines. She had on a Nautical jean set with brand-new, crisp tennies, a full, fresh set of nails adamantly displayed with diamonds on every finger, as she talked to the hostess to find her place at the bar sitting next to her high-school chum. She tossed her head and her hair was a long and silky, flawless weave. Teela looked like a cool million dollars. She sat next to Rainia, and the bartender handed Teela her new cosmo. She smiled and winked her eye at him, turning to Rainia with her eyes all lit up like they had just run into each other at the bar instead of at the stores, "Damn, girl! I ain't seen you in years! How you been? I see you are into the same thing I'm up to. How much you hit em for today, girl?"

Rainia responded, "About a couple hundred. What about you? You seemed to have had an awful lot of room in that fake fetus!"

Teela slapped Rainy's hand, "Oh, listen at you? That's funky-ass chump change, and you know it! Girl, you should come dance with me outta town this trip coming up. Now there's where you will find your college funding and the down payment on a new home. Shit! I got a brand-new beemer outside, and I own my own condominium at 23. Hell, I know I'm doin' good. I'm travelin' back and forth to D.C. and the niggas over there will love you. They are all ballers up by New York, girl. It will only be for a few days. I bet you can make about a good eight thousand where I work at. What do you think?"

Rainia was intrigued, "EIGHT? You bullshittin', right? When you leaving?"

Teela continued with, "I plan on arriving by tomorrow night. All you need is about $400 to fly and share a hotel room with me. You can make the rest as you go. How 'bout it, ho? You wanna go make some real money and have some real fun? Come on! Go with me! I need a partner in crime, and you look like you need some laughs to remember when you get too old to do this shit. You better do it now while you're still young and fine."

Rainia considered the thought, "Well, I've only returned about $400 worth of shit over there at the store, and I have got to pay my rent. What time u leaving tomorrow? Maybe I can return some more stuff I took from this other place to make up the difference."

Teela sealed the deal with, "You ain't got no time; our plane leaves at 8:00 in the morning. and I got some frequent flyer miles I can throw your way. All you need now is about $200. Can you come up with that? I would loan it to you, but I ain't seen you in so long, hell! You could be a crack head and smoke up my money, hell!" The girls laughed together as one of them pondered the thought of dancing.

Rainia knew that all she would have left after she paid her rent was about fifty. So she excused herself from their conversation, went to a payphone, and called Chaz.

"Hey, Chaz, it's me, Rainia. I need a favor."

He agreed to loan her the money with no problem, feeling

guilty for having left her to go back to his ex. He even brought it out to her apartment the next morning, leaving it in her mailbox at 4:00 in the morning.

But Rainia and Teela did not get any sleep once they caught up on old times over dinner and talked about, "What ever happened to so and so?" They were like best friends getting all excited about the slumber party of the century. They rushed to Teela's apartment with Rainia following Teela's brand-new, drop-top BMW to gather up her stuff that was already packed in matching designer luggage that was awaiting her in a super-condo. Inside Teela's house were the most fabulous pieces of furniture and art that Rainia had ever seen. There were $6,000 paintings, mauve-berry walls, mahogany tables, and leather sofas in the spacious living area. Her dinning area was connected to her kitchen and boasted black-marble counters, black-marble floors, leather bar stools, all of the latest chrome appliances, real zebra-hide rugs, and a pricey, designer, glass dinning set to match. Her bedroom was of master-sized proportions, displaying a phenomenal wood-crafted canopy set with a matching vanity and a cute, little, silk-covered seat for her to sit on and powder her face in the filagree mirror. The bathroom was crème and gold and had a huge whirlpool tub with beige marble surrounding every curve, also matching counters and basin, gold handles, and a small crystal and gold chandelier hanging from the ceiling. The bathroom connected to a dynamic walk-in closet which could be entered through the bathroom or the bedroom. Inside Teela's closet were thousands of dollars worth of beautiful clothes, boots, jackets, and shoes to match. The girl had every wig and fur coat imaginable. Teela was living it up like a real, live Barbara doll, except the Black version, and Rainia wanted in on the shit.

On the other side of the massive closet was an area unseen, until Teela turned on the light for her. Glitter and shine hit Rainia's eyes like a diamond and gold mine, and she had the g-string-rush fever. She quickly fell in love with all sorts of stripper outfits, hot-pink sequin bras, thongs, black leather, red, patent leather, baby-blue lace, Vicki's Secret, Freddy's of Hollywood Blvd. Hell! Here was everything a stripper could need to come out looking like high-class eye candy, and it all called to Rainia's soul. A lot of things still had price tags on them and had never been worn.

"Go ahead, girl! Pick you out some shit and try it on. I wanna see how you look and if you can dance."

"That seems a little gay; don't you think?" worried Rainia.

Teela thought her to be ridiculous, "Bitch, we been seen each other naked like everyday in gym class. You remember that lesbo, butch, man-brawd gym teacher that used to come up from behind us and blow her whistle? Now, if she were here with us, then I'd be worried for ya. But, seriously, I need to know if you will be alright. I'm telling you this because there will be an audition, and you'll be up in front of everybody all by yourself. And if you ain't body-fine or just can't dance, then you won't be working. Now pick you out some shit and let me see what you gone be up there working with."

Rainia thought about it, Back in the day, my momma used to be a dancer. Like mother like daughter then. Here goes nothing! She didn't know shit about shakin' her ass and stripping, so she picked out a few outfits, changed in the bathroom into the hot-pink number, and came out walking like a knock-kneed schoolgirl.

Teela sighed and shook her head in shame. Then she told her to do a full turn, approved her frame, gave her a drink, straightened her up to stand up tall and proud, and showed her every leg-wobbling, ass-bouncing, pussy-popping trick she knew. "Good! U are a natural at this shit. Now try doing the shit in these high-ass heels. You gotta be able to do this shit in high heels or it don't look as sexy." By the time Teela was done with Rainia, she had turned the girl into a video vixen, as she watched the clock turn over to 4:30 A.M.

Teela let Rainia have some outfits and her old, trusty, purple, leather luggage for the journey and told her, "Rainia, this luggage has been good to me. Treat it like I was handing you my heirloom, because it always brought me good luck, and now I'm giving it to you." She and Rainia neatly placed all of the new outfits that Teela had given to her in the big suitcase and trudged all of the baggage down to the back entrance. It was a one-car space down in the garage's main entryway, so they had easy access of putting the big stuff into Teela's car first, and then backing it out onto the driveway. The rest of their things were thrown into the backseat.

Teela locked up the condo, set the alarms, and they both jumped into their own cars, Teela boasting a smile in the beautiful car with the fabulous sound system, bumping 'Really Short' rap cuts. They were ready to take off.

Teela was pumped with excitement, "Now it's time to get fucked up! You smoke, don't you?" Teela lit up a blunt, and they got high before they cruised back to Rainia's apartment to get the money that Chaz had left in the mailbox, as well as a few of her belongings to take on the trip. Rainia parked her small Ford Escort in her designated, assigned parking spot, left some money for the rent in an envelope for her homo roommate to find, and split for D.C. with Teela.

They drove to the bus terminal, and Teela parked her car in an underground garage nearby. She said that the Greyhog bus would take them to the airport, because airport parking was way too high. They made it just in time to check in their luggage, purchase another ticket, and head to the East Coast.

On the flight the girls got drunk off of soda mixed with a bottle of Early Times that Teela had hidden in her overhead bag. They got real drunk, and Rainia had heard someone once say that being drunk is like taking a truth serum. They talked about what to expect once they had hit the streets, and Rainia couldn't believe her ears. She listened to Teela go on about her past experiences, "I remember when I made my first trip out here. It was about 5 years ago. I went with this older brawd I use to know, but she's dead now. Dumb bitch let her man shoot her in the head. The nigga was jealous. I miss that bitch, too. That was my girl. But anyway, like I was saying, I didn't know anybody out here except her, and for that first year, all I did was dance. Then the second year came, after she died, and I started to thinking, Hey? What the hell. I'll sell a lil bit a pussy. I didn't like selling my pussy, girl. I think it was that mutha fucka who wanted me to suck his dick and the shit was covered in herpes that had threw me off. But that's ok, cuz I got a new gig I do out here. Girl! I ain't even gotta fuck, either. Now don't freak out just yet, because I tried my hand at being a dominatrix, and I'm lovin' it. I fucking love it, Rainia. You hear me? All I gotta do is spank a couple a asses, pee on a few mafuckas, pinch a couple a nuts, and cuss mafuckas out. Maybe I gotta slap the shit outa one or two — but that's it. Well, I did shit on somebody once. OK, the craziest thing that I ever had to do was tie a muther fucker, covered in peanut butter and jelly up in a hotel room, and I left him there until the next day. Why are you looking at me like I'm lying? For real! That's what he wanted! He paid me five grand to do it. It was so funny, too. Me and my girlfriends was laughing at his ass. They didn't believe I had some White doctor tied up, and that's what turned him on. Shit! I had a fuckin' tour goin' on in that hotel room. Every time we opened that door to throw slices of bread at him and to laugh at his gagged and bound ass, he would buss a nut. Then it got even funnier the next day when I went to go untie him, because a few pigeons had found their way in through the opened balcony window, following the scent of bread crumbs. They had pecked his balls bloody. I felt kinda bad, but that didn't stop me from laughing my ass off. After that episode, everybody heard that story. It was an instant 'Urban Legend'. Whoo-wee, Rainia! Talk about some hilarious-ass shit! That 'Dr. Strange Lover' was so fuckin' grateful to see me when I came back to untie him, he busted a nut!"

Rainia couldn't believe it, "No shit... He busted a nut off of that?"

Teela rolled her eyes, "Girl, puh-leeze! You would be surprised what turns these assholes on. I knew a man who liked to be burned with cigarettes on the bottom of his feet. He paid $7,000 to get it, until he got diabetes. I miss his ass, too. Hee-hee-hee, you ain't too scared to go dance now, are you? Cuz you don't have to do what I do. This is how I make my real money."

Rainia had it twisted, "Then, if you make so much money, why the hell do you steal?"

"I guess that's what turns me on. The fear of being caught. I think it's sexy. Why do you steal, Rainia?"

Rainia went for the obvious, "Shit! Y do you think? I need the fuckin' money! But I ain't gone lie and leave it at that. I guess it gives me a certain rush, too. I made some big and easy money and got addicted."

Teela looked at Rainia and said, "Well, hopefully you'll get addicted to this hustle, too. I need somebody to travel with. Somebody light-skinned like me. Shit! You know how jealous bitches be gettin'. I believe that we can get together and do some SHIT! All you need to do is relax and have you some fun. The club we going to work at is called, 'MACONGA'S', and there's nothing to worry about except for the dyke bitches tryna push up on your titties. But they ain't gone do shit to you while you with me. So stay wit me, or if I ever have to dip out, just stay upstairs and give lap dances until I come back, ok?"

Rainia's head was starting to spin from the alcohol, "OK, I'll just dance and mingle then."

Teela had yet another 'Post It' memo to tack onto her friend's brain, "Oh! And never, ever, ever leave with nobody. Oh! And never let them mafuckas touch your pussy, face, or titties. If they been jaggin' off and have AIDS, they can give it to you through an opening. And people are crazy out here, so never leave with no one. Do you feel me? I would hate for something to happen to you, knowing I brought ya ass out here, ok?"

Rainia put a fluffed-up pillow behind her head and agreed with Teela.

A few short hours later, they arrived in New York City. The steward was a flamboyant homosexual with an extra-shiny pair of wings pinned to his lapel, and he had extra-shiny, greased-up, vaselined lips, "I said get up, ladies! Please! We have another flight to prepare for boarding, lil darlin's, and I don't have all my rows cleared yet. Please, peaches and plumcakes, get ya yella tails up and take all of your things with you from the overhead."

He shook them, but they were still drunk and drowsy. The steward breathed a heavy sigh, blowing a loose-wave nuveau curl from out of his face, put his knuckled hands on his hips, and stamped his foot. He clapped his hands, "Will you puh-leeze get the hell up?"

Teela opened her eyes and was at first frightened at the sight. Then she burst into a fit of laughter, "OK, Momma! Damn!" She shook Rainia awake and practically dragged her and their stuff to the exit door. Rainia straightened up real quick with anticipation, "We here? Where we at? What time is it?"

Teela waved her hands at the terminal ceiling sarcastically, "It's still daytime, so we are gonna see a quick piece of the town, jump a train, and then head on over to Chinatown in Washington D.C.

where I buy all of my specially-made stripper gear when I'm over this way. I had a special suit made for the client I got this week, and I gotta check if it's done. What you wanna see first? The Empire State Building, Times Square, or the Statue of Liberty? OK, pick one, cuz we got all this shit to take with us on the wheeled part of our luggage, and plus it takes all day to do just one."

Rainia didn't want to drag a bunch of shit around all day, because the airport was so big as they were leaving that it seemed as though they might never even get out to see New York, so she said, "Times Square."

"Good Choice! It's the quickest. Plus, I wasn't gonna do neither of the other two with all of this shit, anyway, bitch!"

Once they had made it onto the civilian streets, Teela took Rainia down on Times Square and then to a pizza place. They had pizza and beer, trying to have the hair of the dog that bit them, drinking that damn Early Times on the way over there. Then as promised, they hopped a train to Major Station, ran into the famous DJ, Kid Capri, found out he was staying in the same high-class hotel that Teela had the deal on rates for being a constant customer, and promised to stop at his room later for a get-together he was throwing for his album-release party.

Once they had settled with all of their stuff on the train to D.C., Teela pointed out a few strange people to Rainia. "Look, girl! He is dressed like a woman going to work. Yea! That's a man! Look at the feet. What bitch wears a size fifteen? And over there, her! See how she keeps rocking back and forth? I swear, that ho is on this train every time I ride. I think her ass is a ghost."

"You're still drunk. And so am I. I'm hungry again, and I gotta use it. How much longer, Teela?" Rainia looked at the scenery going by while listening to Teela's e.t.a.

"About three minutes. These trains are fast as hell. But you are gonna have to wait a little bit longer to eat, cuz we ain't draggin' all of this shit to no fuckin' China Town. First we go to the hotel and check in, then we go kick it, then you come back to the club with me to see what time you can try out. Bet?"

Rainia nodded her head and watched the lady rocking back and forth until the train came to a stop. The girls hailed a cab to the said hotel, checked in, put their things away, showered, changed into jogging suits and tennies, and headed to the Asian part of town. The hustle and bustle of the small hidden city was in full throttle of its day. Red, paper streamers blew in the wind, as long, slender, tiny wind chimes whimsically clanged like the foreign street chatter among the huddled masses. The mixture of oriental spices crossed paths with some very exotic incense and wafted through the air around the young women.

Teela approvingly inhaled, "Mmmm... smell that? Take it all in, girl. So, where do you want to eat at? There is Wong Fat, Chow Lee, Kim Sue's, or Chop Joy. Which one you feel like going to?"

Rainia drawed the scent of scrumptious temptation into her nostrils that was coming from the Chop Joy establishment. She turned around full circle and began to walk towards the storefront.

Teela shrugged her shoulders, "Personally, I like a lil bit of this and that from each place, but I guess you like your dog and cat prepared one way." She opened her menu and ordered the 'Happy Family' dish from the waiter.

Rainia ordered shrimp in lobster sauce and some Chinese chicken with sweet and sour sauce, "Don't play, Teela. Don't even try it. We ain't ordering nothing that I can't identify by sight, smell, and taste. Hey! I know when shit ain't right. Chinese mafuckas ain't that cold that they can fix up some cat and dog sooo good that I ain't gone know!"

The woman who had to pick up her specially-made outfit soon looked at her watch, telling Rainia, "Don't be so sure. Take a look around from the time that you leave here until you leave the city. You will come to notice that you have not seen, nor will you ever see a cat or a dog in the whole area. So where in the hell are they going?"

The waiter came back with a complimentary appetizer platter. The girls looked down at it in confusion. Neither one had never known an Asian person to give nothing away free. "So what's up with this free meat then, Rainia? It's Dog! Or Cat! They done fuckin' went crazy with them damned meat cleavers and got appetizer-platter happy and made way too much. I'm finna just eat your shrimp and lobster sauce when it comes out. Hell! I ain't fuckin' with these chinks today, girl. They on some bullshit!"

Chapter Seventeen

Weep-Deep in The Struggle

At MACONGA'S, the two young women were sitting at the main bar, waiting for Harvey, the owner, to come back from Mc Denny's to set up a time for Rainia to come and try out. She couldn't believe how extravagant the place was to be a gentleman's club. There were six stages, all of which had stripper poles and streaming lights. There was even a lightman who was placed for operation next to the dj booth. The décor was that of a jungle, bearing bamboo trees, rain-forest sound effects, tiki torches, and orchids blossoming in big glass tanks that had live scenes of enclosed alligators, turtles, and tropical fish. Central air was blowing a cool mist of a very light and lovely fragrance of jasmine into the air. Every now and then, a spritz of steam was released from the air ducts to keep a foggy feel of the themed surroundings. It was like something out of one of the finer hotels in Las Vegas.

Teela lit up a smoke and said hello to a hideous man who had just come in. She arm-bumped Rainia as the man turned around and started to walk back down the bar by them. Before the man could even introduce himself, Teela snatched up Rainia and their drinks and said, "The downstairs! That's right! I forgot to show you the place, girl! I am sorry!" Teela pressed Rainia to move her ass down those steps. The walls were thick like they had been made out of paper mache, were painted bright red, and were sweating as if they were alive, as Rainia and Teela sailed down the staircase, sloshing drinks and cracking up laughing. Teela's arm rubbed up against the slimy wall, causing her to lose her footing. What was left of her icy rum and cola gushed onto Rainia's back, making Teela laugh harder, as Rainy belted out, "You prostitute!"

Teela was rolling, "We both gone be some dead hos if Candyman catches up with us. That nigga was so ugly he almost made me fall. I betchu he introduces himself as, "Hey baby, my name is Raaaaaahhhh! Like a monster and shit. Keep going until you get to the pink door with the green 'Yucky Face' poison stickers on it."

Rainia opened the described door and was amazed. It was nothing fabulous like she had imagined, *How could the club be so beautiful and go downhill in appearance, starting from the upper steps?* Two women were standing at dressing-room tables across the room from each other, preparing for later on. The one who was wearing a strappy, black outfit screamed, "Princess T! Hey girl… I missed you last time I was here. You had me worried and shit. You look good, girl, in this weave. Is it real hair?" and she ran across the room, giving Teela a hug and a kiss.

"Princess T?" prodded Rainy.

"Yeah, *girl!* That's my stage name. And this here is Trinity from Trinidad. She only comes over here to dance a few times a month. She has a husband and six kids back home that need their mommy. Ain't that right?"

Trinity, who aside from having six kids and a flawless body, had a Jamaican accent. She bobbed her Shirley-Temple-curled weave in agreement while she was swigging from the remainder of the rum and cola from Teela's hand.

"And that mean, rugged, sexy butch over there is 'Juciy Ju'. You gotta watch out for her. She'll try to lick you when you ain't looking."

Juicy Ju was finishing up putting the lotion on her legs. She stood up and smiled with a mouth full of gold teeth, walking towards Rainia, smoking a joint, and eying Rainy up as she strode in glittery neon-green stiletto heels, "Yeah… youse a pretty-fine lil Indian girl. What you mixed wit? Black and Indian? What kinda Indian, Navaho?"

Teela grabbed Juicy Ju by her electric-yellow, thong-string bathing suit and gave her a wedgie, "Naw, but you from the tribe

'Nappy Ho'. You need to go shave your cho-cha, cuz that peekaboo, ju-ju-nap-ball, knotted-up afro shit ain't even fresh."

As Juicy gritted the joint between her teeth and peered down at her crotch, pulling the G-string up while facing the girls so they could see the full of her unkempt vagina, she talked through her clenched, Fort Knox smile, "Well, fuck me hard in my ass wit the cheap grease! Looky there! I can't dance up there with crazy, jungle-man pussy now, can I?" She realized that Teela was right, and then she smoked the last of her regular ciggy that she had going in the ashtray at her dresser and hurried into the shower to handle that unruly, ridiculous, south-of-her-golden grill.

"Well, now that we got rid of her crazy, jungle-man *DICK*... what is your stage name?" asked Trinity.

Teela said, "Aw, shit! I forgot to give you a stage name. Well, what kinda Indian are you mixed with, cuz you do look Indian."

Trinity furrowed her brows, "I woulda guessed Puerto Rican, but I *can* see the squaw."

Teela toyed with the idea but changed her mind, "4-get the Rican thing. Cain't get no good or catchy stage name outta that. It would sound stupid, like tamale, and make the paying customers hungry for Spanish rice and cinnamon churros."

Rainia stopped the conversation, "I'm mixed with Blackfoot and Cherokee Indian."

"Well, it damn sho cain't be black foot; ain't nothing sexy about no bitch with black feet. I don't care if she is naked and oily. So, how about 'Cherakee'?" proposed Trinity.

"Then Cherakee it is," expressed Juicy, who had come back into the room glistening wet, but somehow smoking yet another item, a black and mild this time. She grabbed something off of her dresser, "Here, yall. Harvey said that it's 'Condom 'n a Cosmo night'. Yall gotta help pass these things out, too. Here, Cherakee! Yo ass ain't to new and cute to pass out condoms. Take a whole roll of these bitches off of my hands for me."

Just then, the dressing room intercom came on, and the owner, Harvey, was speaking to them like the wizard behind the curtain on the Wizard of Id movie, "All girls up top! All girls up top!"

The four women made their way upstairs, as Juicy was throwing on a floral silk robe, walking behind Rainia who was stuffing the row of condoms in her jogging suit jacket, too embarrassed to meet the owner with them in her grip. *He might want to shake hands or something.* She turned around to look at Juicy and thought, *She should change her name to 'Wolf Pussy' and maybe go make a lil extra money having scary sex with that 'Raaaaah!' monster-man up there waiting for the show to start.*

    Harvey turned out to be even uglier than the frightening bush left on Juicy's razor. His appearance told a story of a red-eyed man who probably never slept a wink since the day that he first opened MACONGA'S, trying to watch the doorman's hands, the bartender's hands, and all of the dancer's legs, titties, and asses for his cut of tip percentage. He even had a cocked, googalee gaze to vouch for his insomnia. As he sat at the first barstool waiting to talk to all of the girls, he leaned in to listen to the Brazilian, waxed butch's secret. His eyebrows raised and he extended his right hand to Rainia, "Cherakee! Nice to meet you, babygirl! Why don't you get on up there and let me see what you working with? Hey, DJ Top Scotch, put on that old 'Princey' cut I like. You know the one. Is it called "Erotic Village"? Yeah, that's it! The one about fucking a strawberry in the dawn. Ha-ha! Get on up there center stage, Indian woman. We wanna see you pow-wow!"

    DJ Top Scotch threw on the requested cut and introduced her over the mic, "Ladies and gentleman, MACONGA'S would like to welcome a very sexy squaw to the center stage. Let's give a big, warm welcome to Cherakee. Show us a rain dance and make me cry, baby!"

    Harvey was enthusiastic about seeing what Rainia had to offer to his exotic show. Rainia looked the man in his left eye, and then the right, because she didn't know which one was the correct one to look at so they could see each other eye to eye. It was pointless, so she gave him the once over. The man had on a red and silk short set with a piss stain by his barn door. His melted, chocolate, egg in the grass hairdo was clipped low with sprinkles of salt and pepper strands. Harvey was a bulky man with a huge pot belly who wore a beautiful platinum Byzantine chain with his name in diamonds. He was also a man who had asthma, and caveman sandals. The very noticeable breathing problem could have been aggravated by the awful cologne he wore, 'Loud by Doused N It,' followed by an inhumane faint of stench she was sure that she had smelled somewhere b4. He had chunky, beefy toes like that fat, big-mouthed character off of that popular stone-age cartoon, and he had the nerve to extend his big toe out to try and touch her leg as she finally turned around to look at Teela to see if she thought he was serious.

She pressed her eyes at Rainia indicating that it was now or never. Suddenly, 'Indian Girl' could identify the strange scent that was underlying the cologne on Harvey's presence. He must have just gotten a blow job or something, because his whole body reeked of dirty ding-a-ling, sweat, spit, and pee-pee all slobbed on a hot upper lip. Rainy walked her inappropriately-dressed self on up to the stage, took a deep breath like an ice-skating competitor about to perform on live television, and went for it. Once on stage, she moved her body to the beat as sexy as she could with the jogging suit on. She shook her rump like a tender, tempting rump roast and then dipped low, popping her coochie and then jumping right back up to dance around the pole. Rainia bent over to touch the floor with her legs spread open and then shook just one leg back and forth like a piece of jelly-meat for a dog to come and sniff. She then stood up to swing around the pole and slid down, coming back up smoothly while keeping the beat. The gyrations that she was doing with her pelvis, while her big, hard nipples were showing through her bra and jog-jacket, prodded the few men and the lesbian that were in there to yell out to her, "Take it off and shake it!" Rainia unzipped her top, and out fell a whole row of connected condoms. It was too late to grab them up. Everyone had seen them come out like 'The old snake in the can' trick. The embarrassment alone would had been enough to make her hop the next plane back to Wisconsin, because she knew that her square, country ass wasn't going to be working for Harvey now.

The music came to a stop, and everyone just kinda looked at her, and she just kinda stood up there looking at all of them. Teela's eyes were wide open as both of her hands covered her mouth and nose in shock and disbelief. Trinity had her curly head down over her folded arms on the bar like she was standing up while taking a nap, just-a shaking her whirled mop in pity and shame 4 the girl. Mr. Raaaah! Wanted a date with Cherakee for later on. DJ Top Scotch and his lightbulb twistin' sidekick were snickering on the microphone in the dark of the club's shadows, "Let's hear it again for Cherakee," said Top Scotch with a smooth, melodic, deep voice and then burst into hilarities with his homeboy, 'Lightboy'.

"I knew she was a ho!" exclaimed Juicy. "Sorry, Pocahontas, but he doesn't hire no hos."

"Your hired," said Harvey with quickness. Rainia smiled real big and jumped down from the stage to go celebrate with Teela and Trinity by throwing back a few shots together sponsored by Harvey himself.

Less than three hours later, it was time 4 her to have her first night up. Cherakee was a little on the tipsy side. She had chosen to wear the baby-blue, patent-leather outfit, and Teela was kind enough to straighten Rainy's hair out for her. Once she was confident with her look, she towered the dank stairwell to go check things out in the club. The new girl watched as the other girls were up on stage or giving guys lap dances. There were girls of every kind of cultural background and shade, mixing and mingling with the customers. White girls, Asian, Black, and now Mulatto were lighting the lives of the district's politicians on the Lower Eastside. As the dj was announcing Rainia's turn to dance, she felt a flurry of butterflies drop into the pit of her stomach. She approached the stage and the lights quickly found her body, as the seductive music began to come through all seventeen speakers of Harvey's elaborate sound system.

Cherakee emerged center stage with grace, while the rhythm took her to the top. The whole performance had men giving her five, ten, twenty, and even fifty-dollar tips in her attire and garter belts wherever there was room. One man thought that it would be funny to put a book of food stamps in her thong and then had the nerve to try and take it back. She pulled it out to flip through it and said, "Un-uh, honey! That's mine now; that's how that's gonna go," because it was a nice, one hundred and seventy-five dollars.

Across the room was Teela who was now dancing on top of two tables that were pushed together. She was totally drunk, and Harvey was yelling at her to get down. The men at the table were egging her on, and she did a low bounce, causing the tables to slightly separate. Her heel wedged down in the middle of them, and her left leg had skidded on the edge of the table all the way down to the floor, followed by the rest of her glitter-lotioned frame. She was instantly scraped from her ankle to her upper, inner thigh. Rainia rushed down off of the stage and ran over to her friend, "Teela! Oh my gosh! Are you alright?"

Teela was in too much pain to talk, so she motioned for her partner in crime to help her up off the floor, extending both hands out like a small child. Finally, after grunting, moaning, and rubbing her leg while trying to touch-therapy the pain, Princess T's voice had surfaced, "Aw, shit! Cherakee, did I fuck up your set? Can you just help me get back to the hotel before I pass out?" Both of the girls made their way down to the dressing room to put their street clothes on to leave, with the owner following closely behind.

Harvey, who was very impressed with Cherakee's natural talent, was trying to watch Rainia take the money off of her garters at a dressing-room table and turned around to look at Teela, "I told you to get the hell down, woman! Now, are you going to be able to dance tomorrow night? You just found me a good crowd bringer, and now she has to take your drunk ass home? Who's gonna go up next? Somebody go find Trinity and Juicy. Get Juicy upstairs, somebody! Cherakee, I get my two-hundred dollars now b4 you leave. That's my cut for letting you perform here."

She gave him the 2 and helped Teela upstairs to head back to the Plaza Place Hotel. Harvey called them a cab, and Rainia discreetly counted at least $900 by the time it had arrived. Inside the taxi, she managed to add up a full one thousand and thirty dollars, plus the food stamps, then she put the money in her bra so that she could free up her hands to help Teela out of the cab, pay the man, and get 'Princess Tipsy' to the room safely. She allowed Teela to hobble, using the support of Rainia's shoulder to the elevator and all the way to their small suite.

"Ok, I got it from here. I'm really hurt, girl. Stay here with me, Cherakee. Don't leave your old friend like this. I could die from this," she sighed, and then let the good side of her body drop onto the bed.

"Yeah, you could die from that if this were a bad 1970s flick, where the characters die from stupid shit like a paring knife in their shoulder, but I'll stay," she laughed. There was nothing for Rainia to do now except go into the bathroom and silently scream in excitement. She really didn't trust Teela with her money in Teela's usual hotel safe, so she put the majority of it into the sole of her gym shoe.

There was an abrupt knock at the door. Rainia opened the bathroom door and quietly tip-toed across the plush, seafoam-green carpet, trying to let the now sleeping 'Princess of Pain' rest, while Rainia stood on her toes to look through the peephole, "Yes?"

There was a guy clearing his throat, but he was standing somewhat off to the side, "Ah, hi, Cherakee. Ah, hmm… I saw you at MACONGA'S 2night, and I was wondering if I could take you on a date? You are so extremely sexy." The man moved into view of the peephole. Rainia could see a very-attractive, well-dressed, young Black man on the other side of the door, fixing his tie and moving his hard penis around through his dress pants, trying to get comfortable.

Teela instantly came awake and sober, "Bitch, don't you even think about opening that door! He could be a serial killer, or he could have a gun and try to rob both of our asses. MUTHA FUCKA, GET AWAY FROM OUR ROOM! SECURITY! I'M CALLIN' MUTHA-FUCKIN' SECURITY!" she hollered.

Rainia kept watching, as the man scrambled away in a frustrated panic, trying to adjust his hard dick.

Teela pulled the edge of the bed's covers over her butt, "Goodnight, girl. A bitch like me needs her rest. I got that crazy dildo-in-his-do-do-hole customer for his scheduled appointment tomorrow evening, and I gotta find some good make-up to cover up these bruises on my leg."

The next evening, Rainia stayed at the club by herself, while working her sets as her turn came up until Teela had come back from her appointment. The dancing dominatrix was happy to tell her about the insanity, "Oh, my goodness! This fool-ass nigga is stupid, *girl!* He wanted me to dress up like 'Tarzano from the Jungle' and fuck him with… oh! You are never gonna guess what else he brought with him. A crazy, white, Jungle-Man DICK! Isn't that shit ironically hilarious? 4 real, girl, it was complete with long, wild hairs connected to the rubber balls. That was the funniest strap-on I have ever used on a man. He decided to change his request for the outfit I had made in Chinatown, which was like a lady cop. Well, you saw it, and had surprised me with a cave woman getup. He has a fetish about chicks with dicks. He even gave me a five-hundred-dollar tip. You and I are going shopping tomorrow to celebrate. You do know that tomorrow is our last day, don't you? So, enough about me. How did you do tonight?"

Once Rainia stopped laughing so hard, she lied and told Teela that she'd made less than half the real amount. And when they both got back to the hotel, she hid the whole amount in her other shoe.

Their last day in D.C. was the best. They went to the local mall and bought several regular fashion outfits, got their nails done, and even went to the spa. Then, to cap off the going-away party with Trinity, they all went to go have dinner at a well known lobster and steak house in the metropolitan district. Teela and Rainia never did find time to go kick it with the famous DJ Kid Capri. Rainia had made a full $3,780 in only two days of dancing. Teela had scored at least a total of eight grand, but she had worked hard for it by pumping and sweating.

They made their way back to the D.C. airport and were soon arriving in Chicago's airport in no time. After their arrival Rainia had a question, "Why does it always seem to take a faster time to get back home when you don't wanna go back?"

Teela gave her a small armpit to shoulder hug with one arm around Rainia as they talked, "Aw, girl, you'll be back for the next trip out. Don't look so sad! Yo ass had the time of your life, didn't you? I know! I had a ball, too, except for my fucked-up leg. Oh, yeah! I hope you got your money on you and not in your bags, cuz people steal luggage on these flights. Personally, I like to keep mine in an old-school place, in my bra."

As the girls were walking through the airport to go and reclaim their luggage, Oddly, Rainia somehow lost Teela at the baggage claim belt. She grabbed the *trusty*, purple, leather set and stood there looking around for Teela or her bags. After about six or seven minutes with a no show, she walked to a payphone to page her.

As she was waiting for the line to connect, two hard-looking thugs were making their way toward her with stern faces, "OK, bitch! Give up the money! I know Teela is here with you, because this is her luggage. Ain't nobody got this purple 'Princey' looking shit but her and that little, high-heel-wearing, high-pitch-singing nigga, so don't try to act like you don't know the deal," said the tall one with the curl. He grabbed Rainia's big bag, and the other guy grabbed her arm real hard with one hand and went into her shirt with his free hand. He pulled out a roll of cash from her brassiere, and the two men walked away satisfied.

No one in the terminal had seen her just get robbed. Security was nowhere to be found, and Rainia was now re-dialing Teela's pager number in shock and dismay. She stood at the phone for ten more minutes and decided that she had been set up. Teela had come up with yet another hustle, *Take a naive bitch out of town to dance, then set her up to get robbed once back in town by the identifiable, trusty, purple luggage.*

As bad as her feelings were hurt, she was glad that their short-lived, fun but *Foul* friendship didn't end up with her being a total sucker. Rainia was standing on about $3,600 in her *trusty* tennis shoes.

Rainia cried all the way back to Milwaukee on the Greyhog by herself. She wasn't crying because she'd been robbed of a funky roll of singles wrapped with a few $20s; she wept because she'd thought that she had a real friend in the struggle. It was so hard to trust anyone in town, and that was why Rainia stayed off to herself, except for family. After that day, Teela's pager was turned off, and Rainia never saw or heard from her ex-friend from school again.

Once she'd gotten back to her shared apartment in the taxicab, she was wondering about her gay roommate possibly having company over, because she'd never told him that she was leaving town, *Frenchy's car is out here in his spot. Maybe he had the courage to have someone over during the privacy? I hope so, because if he doesn't get into a relationship soon, he might end up being the next gay serial killer.*

Coming in through the rear entrance made her feel somewhat good about being home, as she watched a young couple and their two small kids dressed in aqua gear heading to the poolhouse for a swim. She turned the key and opened the door of the apartment to find the most shocking surprise. She instantly heard the loud grunts of men having sex. She started to respectfully re-close the door, saying, "Good for you, but shouldn't you guys be in the bedroom? I'll just go to my cousin J.J.'s house down the street. Sorry to interrupt," but then she had already seen what the source of the sexual moment really entailed. Rainia re-opened the door with a serious double take. There sat her roommate in a chair, ass naked, jagging off to a fag porno. It was even more fantastically horrifying that there was a big picture window in their front room that people could look into their house from, if a person was leaving or entering the front entrance of the building. He had all of the curtains drawn back as if he had wanted someone to see him. There was an old man walking up the walkway, and he had noticed the naked man with his erect, pink cock dripping with lotion in their living-room recliner. The elderly fellow started to go into a coughing spell and grabbed at his heart, falling to his knees on the front lawn outside of the big picture window. *Oh, heeeelll naw! Now this sick mafucka is really desperate for a friend!*

'Gay Guy' jumped up and started to try and explain, but she was not trying to hear him, "What the fuck do you think that you are doing, Frenchy? Do you know that you have just probably killed a man right outside that window? You sick, twisted freak! You know what? Never mind," and she slammed the door shut as she left.

Rainia, fully embarrassed and pissed off at the same time, stomped back out of the rear entrance and started up her car, driving to the gas station payphone down the street to call her momma, "Mom? How's the baby? That's good. I never knew how much I missed her until now. Can I move back home, like today? I'll tell you when I get there. You are my only friend."

Rainia moved back home and told her mother everything. She was twenty-three and had been doing very bad things. Ignoring the needs of her daughter had a very serious price to pay on Rainy's soul, as she blindly searched for fun.

One day, a lady from her modeling class, Yaphelia, had called Rainia to go out of town with her for a job that required modeling and selling fur coats. The weekend trip would allow her to make a couple of thousand dollars. Yaphelia asked her to meet her and her daughter at a department store to pick out a few outfits for the trip. Rainy agreed, but when she got to the store, Yaphelia was leaving out, "I just need to go across the street to pick out a few pairs of shoes to match these dresses. You've met my 'Always got her hand out for some money' daughter, right? *No?* Well, Hadaria, Rainia, Rainia, Hadaria. There, yall met, and she getting on my last nerve about these damned tennis shoes she wants — that this store doesn't even carry. And I need a new pair of black heels for this trip myself, so, would you mind staying here with Hadaria to see that she fills out her job application?"

Rainia thought about how she should fill out one for herself, "OK, I think I'll fill one out, too, for when I get back. Hadaria is your *daughter?* Dang! Yall look like sisters, not mother and daughter!"

"Yes, we do, don't we? Hell, I know I look good. But thank you for the compliment. She's a teenager who needs too much shit. It's time that she gets her own job and buys her own stuff. Right, Hadaria?"

Hadaria smiled, waving around two of the three shopping bags that her mom had her carrying and sniggled at the thought. Yaphelia went to do the shoe shopping, and Rainia and the teen went to the service counter to fill out job applications."

So, you know my mom from modeling class, huh?" asked the girl.

"Yeah, this is true," Rainia responded.

"Well, how old are you? You look like a teenager," Hadaria asked.

"I'm twenty– hey? What's so funny?" she wanted to know, as the girl instantly burst into laughter.

"It's funny that my mom has found someone to hang out with who also looks younger than her real age. She's thirty-one and could pass for twenty-one. And it's even more super-hilarious that you and I are filling out applications for the same job," Hadaria remarked.

Rainia thought of an even deeper coincidence as she gazed around the store, "What's even more funny than that, ironically, I used to rip this store off blind. Now I got the nerve to want to work honestly for them."

Hadaria really went into a spell, "Oh, really? And when was this? You don't look like the type. Did you ever get caught?"

Rainia tried to divert the conversation, "That's not important. I can't glorify doing the wrong thing by telling you about my past. What matters now is that I'm trying to do the right thing by helping you fill this out correctly. Now let me see... Everything looks pretty good! Oh! Sign here! That's a question I always forgot to sign at, too."

Rainia waited for the customer service man to take the apps, and then Rainia walked around the store to find a few things for herself, to pay cash for them and not steal them. She found a couple of outfits, while Hadaria went to the teen section to look for a double-buckled belt. When Hadaria walked past Rainia as she was looking at a long, jean skirt, Hadaria gave her the thumbs up for approval on her selection. Rainia went to the checkout line to pay for her stuff, got her change and receipt, and spotted the teen walking her way.

As the two were leaving the store, Hadaria asked Rainia to hold one of her mother's shopping bags that she had been keeping for her. Rainia reached for the bag and opened the door for the girl to get past her. No sooner than the girl could get out of the glass door, than a bald-headed White man wearing jeans and a forest-green turtleneck grabbed them both by their arms and escorted them to the security office. The woman inside was waiting for them both with folded arms and a stern face, "Well, well, *well!* What do we have here? Two teens with sticky-icky fingers?"

Rainia rebelled the notion with, "No you don't! I didn't steal shit! What the hell are you talking abou–"

The security woman was agitated by Rainia's voice, "Shut the hell up! We have it all right here on tape; now watch! You see right there? That's you passing her in the Junior's department. Now look right here; that's her walking past you and giving you the thumbs up as you were looking at that jean thing you bought. Nice touch! You thought that by paying for something that you could decoy my sharp eye, didn't you? WRONG!! This store has been getting ripped off by teams of thieves like you for a while now. Some of you even have the gall to dress up in phony wigs and glasses. Bauser, open those damn bags and let's see what we got. If it's more than one-hundred-dollars worth, you two are going to get a free ride to jail in the police car that's on the way."

The two security personnel dumped the things out on the floor and counted one-hundred-fifteen-dollars worth of clothes stolen from the Junior's department. Rainia rejected the evidence, "Now this stuff is clearly not mine. It's all from the Junior's department, and I can't fit into those clothes!"

The security woman grew impatient, "Shhh! Watch the tape again. See right there; your accomplice is passing you the bag, and there you are trying to walk out with the stolen goods. It's all right there! Now I need to take your pictures and see some IDs," the woman demanded, as she took poloroidal instant camera pictures of their scared faces and pinned them to the corkboard wall of shame with brightly colored thumb-tacks, right in with the other shoplifters that can no longer shop with them. The police walked in to arrest them both, handcuffing them, and rolling their index fingers in black ink for booking purposes. Hadaria went in one car, just as her mother was re-approaching the store in utter shock at the sight, and Rainia went handcuffed in the other, running back in her mind what the voice had predicted, *"You'll be caught because of someone else."* God was right! Rainia hadn't tried to take a damned thing that day. In fact, she was just trying to get a job and find a few things for the job with Yaphelia that Rainia had paid for.

They took them both downtown, but because Hadaria was a minor, her mother was able to get her out of the situation right away. Rainia had to sit in jail for three days and then go to an 'Action Justice' class to renounce the stealing activities. Those three days in jail were hell on her, too. The bullpen was filled with other shoplifters, dope fiends, prostitutes, and dykes. Rainia played crazy and didn't answer anyone's questions, nor did she engage in any of the conversations around her. On her last day in, one of the discussions was about this girl who used to run 'West-Lawnery Projects' over by her old school, 'John Murial,' who was notorious for being the first female-lesbian gangster to serve large amounts of drugs and could fight like a man. The woman who they were referring to was named 'Killa Queen', and she really was a true urban legend in Milwaukee, WI in the late 80s. Rainia remembered hearing about how she would knock grown men out with one punch.

The gay girl who was talking about her said, "Bitch, puh-leeze! Killa Queen was cold! She could whoop yo daddy's ass then turn around and mack the shit out yo sister. She had some pretty-ass bitches on her team. The brawd was a true player, pimp, gangster, and pusherman. She was "The Shit", and that's why they kilt her ass. They was hating on her because she was coming up to damn fass. They said that she was set up by her ex-girlfriend. Yeah! Some light-skinned ho! Looked kinda like that bitch over *there!* That's not her though. This girl was straight-up Mexican and was in the Latino Queens Gang. Look at homegirl over there. She's more scared than a mother fucker; can't you tell? The bitch ain't ate or said shit since she got in here. Say! What's yo name, babygirl?"

Rainia started to slobber and rock back and forth to avert their interest in her, but the guard had come to let her out, saving her ass. Rainia was glad to leave that place. She had lost a few pounds, too, because she had refused to eat prison food, as a vow to never return.

Needless to say, Yaphelia didn't have shit to say to Rainia after all that went down. The ex-model had lost her chance at making the same kind of money honestly that she had made stealing or dancing. Rainia was a damn shame, going nowhere fast.

J.J., her 'Cuz', had come over to laugh at her bit in the pen, "So, what was it like?" she asked, as she passed the blunt to Rainia.

"It was fucked up! *Man!* Them big-ass bitches in there was plotting on my coochie. I'm just trying to get high and forget about the whole fucked-up situation," said Rainy, passing the chronic back to J.J.

"So you mean to tell me that you went to jail for nothing? Your ass didn't steal *shit* that time?" she choked and passed the blunt back.

"Naw, Cuzzie Cuz, I told you how it happened. God showed me that shit awhile back, but I dismissed it. Now I'm missing out on some good, clean money. That's what my ass gets." She passed the blunt.

"Yeah! That's what your stupid ass gets. Now you two wanna tell me why the hell are you both standing in front of my house and smoking weed?" asked Anmarie.

"DAMN! Sorry, Momma. How long you been standing here?" asked Rainia.

"Long enough to know that marijuana makes you two some stupid asses. Y don't you two go somewhere with that bullshit before your dad gets home, Rainy? You need to stop doing that shit anyway, and get a fucking job! Why don't you guys go to college while you both are still living with your parents, rent free?" Anmarie asked, as she went back up her front steps, sweeping them off with the broom that she had laid down to go and bust the girls who were smoking.

Rainia wasn't thinking about no job. She had a place for her and her daughter to stay, and she had her kickin'-it buddy to hang out with. J.J and Rainia had a routine of getting high and going to the store for Little Sidney's Gin and Juice, a Sneaker's Bar, Chips, and gum suckers. Now she was a true blunt smoker with her friend, turned cousin, J.J., who was willing to ride down to the hood every other day to see her. As the turmoil of the streets dug its claws into her brain, making her more and more magnetized to the riskiest of situations, Rainia had developed a bond with J.J. She was the only girl from the hood that wasn't really *from* the hood. And the most unbelievable part about her not being from it was how much more respect J.J. had for her associates in the hood than for her own family.

J.J. was from Brown Deerville, and the two of them would get into her mother's Toyolla Camery and drive around deep in the streets just looking for weed. This search for THC had allowed the girls to make acquaintances with some of the most thuggish fellas in the ghetto just to get the very best marijuana Milwaukee had to offer. They would end up at crazy-looking houses, filled with teenaged Black youth who couldn't cut it in school. They would get high with them, and J.J. would go back to Brown Deerville to the crickets at night, to the peace and quiet and security of White-people land. Rainia went back to her parent's house and had to try and get her sleep while listening to gunshots being fired, people arguing, police and firetruck sirens zooming up and down the street or off in the distance, all night long.

The next day, she would get out of bed, play with her daughter all afternoon until J.J. would pull up. Then, Rainia would turn her baby over to her mom, get in the car, pull off, and repeat the process. There they went, back to the grimiest of the hood the next day and doin' the same shit. They made friends with some real gangstas that lived like real impoverished individuals. Their homes were filled with sixteen young people or more, including the infants and children that usually had at least one old mom, who doubled as a grandmom and tripled as a great grandmom who was so tired of yelling and preaching, and working two or three jobs, only to come home to the same-ol' shit, that she basically became a 'Mute'. Old Mom just didn't care anymore. The teens could fuck in the house, have people spend the night, allow the nigga from down the street to move in rent free, gamble on the kitchen floor, live in a dirty house with broke-up furniture and roaches, stay on the porch ribbin', drankin', smokin', and sellin' dope all night. Hell! The old Mom just didn't give a damn anymore, so all she did was come alive once a month. That was when she went to Aldin's to get groceries, cook good for about two to five days, until all of the strange people in her house would take over everything in it, including the refrigerator, and never even compensate her with one dime, or even clean up one mess. One boy named Snoopie had clarified it all to them, "See, niggas like us, we hustle. Ey… lemme hit that blunt, J.J."

"But your mom is right there in the livingroom, watching TV!" exclaimed J.J.

"Aw, fuck her old ass. She ain't gone say shit. She don't even know what the fuck is goin' on. That's what she get for havin' all those damn kids and droppin' out of school, chasin' after my daddy's dick. Now we are bad-ass kids who don't give no fuck either, except for hustlin'. We ain't neva gone be intrigued with school. Who the fuck Black wanna hear about a bunch of rich-ass, thievin' honkeys, who have always stole and taken over everythin' since they got here? They stole the mutha-fuckin' land from the Indians. Then they stole Blacks from Africa to work their punk-ass crops. Then they stole all of our good inventions and patented shit that changed the world and kept all of the bread. They stole the fuckin' lottery idea, too. The niggas out in Chicago and over in Harlem had straight got ripped off, and White mutha fuckas is still jackin'. Why the fuck they get to have our lottery? And we can't even have the shit. We need to get a lotto for broke niggas, that's what! Fuck White folk! I ain't talking about you, Rainia, cuz u are half-White. Cuz everybody knows that if you even got a quarter-teaspoon of nigga in you, White folk say you are Black anyway. They still think they is 'Massa' up in this piece. In the fuckin' jails, and out in the gotdamn streets, and they start us niggas out learnin' some shit that we will never relate to in the mother-fuckin' schools. So, fuck it then, like '2 Packin' said in that one song called "Fuck This World". We fucked already, so we might as well keep hustlin' and strivin' to survive till they really acknowledge our Black asses in the fight. Until then, we gonna go out in a blaze a glory! And don't get me wrong, cuz I would rather die like a soldier than to be a honkey's bitch up in the system. I'm talkin' bout lockin' our asses up for cheap labor, cuz I ain't gonna do that part. It's bad enough they punkin' us out here by makin' us hustle, cuz they keep all the real jobs for their people. They overcharge us on bills and make sure our credit is bad. Either way it go, we can't get out. Our kids can't get out. We fillin' up the graveyards and overcrowdin' the jails. Maybe one day one of us will make a real change."

    Snoopie wasn't lying. He was like the chief of the chiefing session. The things that he would say would infuse a fire among the other teen boys who had all felt like they deserved to live so much better than that. They knew that no one was coming to save them with a job or a second chance. They knew that there wasn't a place for them in school, because of the very little respect the education system had for the way they were forced to live. They knew that their chances for survival were as slim as their hungry waistlines, so they did what they had to do; they stole; they fought; they sold dope in their dingy, white T-shirts and dirty, baggy jeans with ran-over tennis shoes and cried when no one was looking. They were children who were not allowed to enjoy childhood, because one of their very first goals was to cop a gun to ward off the anger and the danger of each other. They would watch each other like dogs to see who was a little more happy than the others, and like a game of survival in the wild, take what the other guy had — because he could, including a life, if the mood felt right. Snoopie sold rocks on the block, and he was exactly that nigga to be scared of. He was so gangsta that he would sell dope to his customers, and then put on a ski mask and catch them around the corner only to pistol whip and rob them before they could smoke it. Then he would act like the proud lion of the pack and buy Rainia, J.J., his closet guys, and the little kids Kentucky Style Chicken with the extra money. He had done it at least seven times while J.J. and Rainia were with him, and on that seventh time, one of those hypes came back with some gangstafied people from his family.

Snoopie and company were all upstairs, high as hell, when they heard several car doors slamming. By him always being on a keen alert for the karma to come back to him, he instantly knew that it was going to be a gun war. He ran downstairs with his strap, yelling, "Aw, yall, get the girls and the kids out now! We at war! Yall niggas grap your straps and get ready to buss shots! Mafucka, get your ass down here and help me keep these niggas from running up in here!" Rainia grabbed J.J. by her arm and ran into the bathroom, as four or five children ran around the living room screaming. Shots were fired in a hailstorm, "PAP! PAP! BUCK< BUCK< BLAST!" went the gunfire, as everyone hit the floor.

Rainia and J.J. knew that they had to brave the possibility of being killed and crawl out to save those little kids. They both gathered the children as quickly as possible and ran with them, dragging a few by their arms down the back steps and out of the back door. They kept on going, while the bullets continued to fly past them, "PAP! POP! BUCK!" heart's racing and praying to God like a mother fucker until they were two blocks over. Somehow, by the grace of the Almighty, none of them were hit, but one of the little boys was crying in pain because Rainia had drug him across some glass in the dirt field, and he'd cut his leg on something causing it to bleeding pretty badly.

A boy by the name of Reese was riding his bike up the block, doing his special, drama call, "Ooo-a-wit!" when he saw the girls standing on the sidewalk with the kids, checking them over for gunshot wounds and scrapes in a frenzy. Reese brought his stolen bike to a stop, "Hey, yall! Yall ok? Yeah, they just shot some nigga in the chest, and them other niggas stopped bustin', put his ass in the car, and smashed out. I think that nigga is gone die, too! Why don't yall come into my uncle's house right over here for about an hour, until we sure that them fools ain't gonna come back? I can see if we got some peroxide and bandages for the shorty's hurt leg. If you want, J.J., I can go back over there and get your car for you and drive it over here so yall can leave. Yall don't belong over here, no way."

"Neither do you, Reese. You are only thirteen, and everyone knows how smart you are in school. What about you? How are you gonna get out the hood?" asked J.J.

Reese tried to man up, but it was sad because he was just a boy. He had watery eyes, as he seemed to go back to a painful moment in his life, "I guess I gotta do like everybody else and pray. Cuz my uncle is the only guardian I got left. My momma is dead from the hand of her ex-boyfriend, and my baby brother got killed last summer right up the street while walking home from the bus stop. I was the only child after that. Ain't nuthin' to do for a nigga like me but to weep about being so deep in the struggle. Gimme your keys, J.J., It's time for yall to go back to your safe place."

They knew that Reese was right. He was placed on this Earth in the situation that he was in, and there was very little that he, as a child, could do about it. He had no choice but to stay in the meanest part of the ghetto. However, Rainia and J.J. had the choice to leave. So they left, and that was the last time they saw the corner of eleventh and Keefe street.

After that, twenty-four-year-old Rainia decided 2 write songs about the things that she had seen in the hood. It was because of these songs that she wrote that she ended up hooking up with a guy she once knew from North Divisional named "B" to try and do some songs together.

B had just lost his baby's mother and had a few of his own songs to sing. They got more involved, and Rainia ended up getting p.g., but B talked her into getting an abortion, because he said that his living other two kids by her would be hurt.

Rainia was in cosmetology school one day, reading a paper in the school cafeteria. She had just found out that she was pregnant again and was considering having yet another abortion for B. When she turned the page to the Campus Times, she saw a picture of an adult hand holding a tiny pair of feet, and the caption read, "Abortion is not birth control; it's murder. God forgives you, so keep your baby this time."

Rainia refused to have the procedure for B again, because she felt like an angel had sent a very clear message for her to have her second child, but B, while drunk off of his ass, beat shit out of her at seven months pregnant, trying to kill the baby before it could be born. He begged for forgiveness from her, and she forgave him. She loved him dearly.

For the next few years, after that, she reminded herself of her mother, with her black eyes and broken bones. She tried to stay with him, hoping to change him into a good man. Rainia was scared to death of him. B would hit her everywhere they would go, in the car, on the street; it didn't matter. He would pull out her hair, give her black eyes, and then take her to dinner.

Once, while they were celebrating her birthday at The Lobster House, Rainia's makeup must have been coming off from sweating, and the waitress was bringing her a cupcake with one candle in it, singing her "Happy Birthday", when suddenly she stopped short, "Girl! What happened to you? You got two black eyes!" Then the lady looked at B who was smiling like nothing was abnormal about beating on a woman, because that's how he had grown up in his house. Rainia put on a fake smile, herself, as she blew out the candle, letting a painful tear escape one of her blackened eyes and wondering, *If I don't leave him, will I ever see another birthday?*

After a few years, she planned to leave him after seeing Chaz's friend at a carwash. She told his guy, Jimmie, where she was working at and for Chaz to come rescue her again like he did from J.C. She even gave him her job number, cuz she couldn't leave her house number while living with B. For what it was worth, in one week, she had her hopes all set up to leave him and go back to Chaz, but Chaz died in a boating accident. Rainia didn't find out about it until after he was buried, and she almost had a breakdown. She missed the funeral, but ended up going to see his momma in Sussex. Rainia told his momma, Maggie, of how she saw him at her job but didn't know he was dead, and that people think that's crazy, "I swear, he was standing right there at the end of my register, saying, 'Goodbye, Rainy. See you on a Rainy day'."

His momma believed her, and she told Rainia of how she sometimes sees signs of her son's presence in the house, "Sometimes I'll go in the bathroom, and there will be a breath of fog on the mirror with the words 'Happy life now' written inside. Or sometimes he'll draw hearts with 'Mom' inside. I know that there is life after death, Rainia. Don't feel like life is over for you just because he's gone and your dream was sadly interrupted. You are still here to live the rest of yours. You are just going to have to find a way out of your situation by using the guidance of The Lord. You have tried it your way, and look where doing stupid shit has gotten you. Chaz told me how you went out of town to go strip. How did that turn out for you?"

Rainia put her face in her hands and tried to speak through them with utter embarrassment, "Bad! Just like my mom's attempt. I only did it for a weekend, and that was all. But that personal battle was awhile ago. I have been going through a different kind of personal battle with my son's abusive father. I was hoping that Chaz and I would get back together so I could get away from him, and then this happened."

His mom put her understanding hand on Rainy's shoulder and said, "Well, fucking leave his ass! You don't need that shit in your life! Why don't you go to college? Why don't you start praying to God for a better life and get your act together while you're still young? You can have a nice house and a good man one day if you start to change the things around you into a positive view."

"Yeah, I know you are right, Maggie. It's just so hard to raise children on your own in the ghetto. With Chaz in my life, I would have had a better chance at getting all of us out in one piece."

Chaz's mom lit up a cigarette and paused for a minute, smiling at her, "I know how you feel, but don't think you still can't. I had to go into the service to find my dream man, and for a while, we were all happy in this house. I know that if I had never taken a chance on my husband, I would have lost Chaz a long time ago. I also know that you saw my son that day in the store at your job like you said you did. I'm about to tell you why I believe you so intensely, so don't get all freaked out on me, ok? I went to go see a psychic because I was so distraught at first. I was hurting so bad inside that I needed some kind of message or contact, even if it was a phony one. The woman had several messages for people that he had known, and I knew for a fact that she didn't even know these people that she spoke of. These were messages from beyond the grave. She had one for you, too, Rainia. Chaz said to tell you not to cry about his early departure, because he cries for you still being here. He also said to not worry about the hundred and fifty dollars he loaned you to go out of town. And the jacket you wanted is upstairs in his room, under his 'Marilyn Montgomery and James Decan at the diner with Travis Elvis' poster."

Rainia had never told anyone, not even Chaz, how much she wanted that rainbow colored, leather jacket. The candle on the table started flickering, and a man's shadow zoomed across the patio, as the light hanging over the kitchen table went off and then back on.

"He's here," said his mom.

"I'm gone," said Rainia, who was standing up to leave.

"Not so fast! Take this lady's info! Now, let's go get this supposed jacket for you before you go. He really wants you to have it."

Rainia took the name and number of the psychic from Maggie's rolodex and walked with her up to his room. They opened his closet door and observed. There were many new clothes and shoes inside and all were stacked neatly like a store display. They moved the things until they saw the edge of the said poster. Underneath it was the multi-colored 'Pelly-Pelly' that Rainia held up and hugged to her sorrowful chest. She wiped away her tears and put the psychic's number into one of the coat's pockets. The messages from the grave were real.

They went out to the front where Rainia's car was parked and spent a moment to laugh about shit back in the day on 43rd, like the humor of Ms. Jack the cross-dresser. Then his mom revealed that they probably would never see each other again, "Yeah, those were the good-old days. I just want you to know, Rainia, that I am moving to another state. This house is cursed. It takes your first born, you know. The last family that lived here lost their son to a freak train accident. So I really can't take the chance of loosing Cid, or my youngest son, Mitch, either. Why don't you give me a big hug, and tell your mom to call or come and see me before we leave. We will be gone by the end of the summer, so make sure you tell her, ok? Take care, pretty girl. You can start by taking your ass to college. And, Rainia, I'll always remember how happy my son was with you. Thank you for being a part of his life."

After she left, with Maggie waving goodbye to her, Rainia got really depressed because she had to go back to baby daddy number two and the feeling of being stuck with him. She did take Maggie's advice and went back to college while she tried to work things out with B. In total, her and B stayed together for about six years, until she found out that he'd had another woman for the last two years they were together, and finally, weep-deep and weary in the struggle, she let B go.

Chapter Eighteen

One Peace

    Rainia went with a friend of hers from her schoolbus job, because she thought that she could trust him. They were together for a couple of years, and she ended up having a child for him as well. The man had lost his mother and swore that a Junior would make his life worth living. Rainia was even more vulnerable to do this for him, because of something terrible that had just happened to her. It was something that she had refused to face because it was too unbelievable to have occurred. Rainia believed that her third baby's daddy lost interest and respect for her, because while she was with him, she was raped.

    Rainia was robbed and raped at gunpoint by a teenaged boy who wasn't even on her schoolbus route. He was a desperate stranger. She had just finished doing her morning route and had decided to stop at a Jule-Oscar Store to buy a book of postage stamps so that she could mail off her bills. She parked her small bus with the tinted windows across the side street of the store and put the keys to van number 0044 in her purse, as she locked the bus with the lock-unlock knob and closed the door. Then she went to the back of the bus and made sure that the emergency door was locked and was unable to be opened from the outside. After that, she observed the people on the street, outside the store. There was a T-shirt vendor, three garbage men standing by their garbage truck with coffee and doughnuts, engaged in early morning banter, and the Jule-Oscar customers either leaving or entering the store. Rainia crossed the street to the walkway leading up to the stores automated swinging doors. A young man was approaching to pass her with his head down and his hoodie pulled way over his head. He was apparently trying to avoid her, so she turned around to look at him again, only to find that he was walking backwards and was smiling at her.

These funky teenagers are always looking me over like I'm their age or something. That child is supposed to be in school, but here he is, skipping class, up to no good, and nobody cares. Damn shame!

Inside the store were some scraggley and scruffley-looking customers. Although there were only a few, they all looked frightfully like hard times, like they all had stepped off of a food drive commercial for Third-World Countries. Rainia walked past the in-store bank and went to the customer-service desk right next to it to get her mailing stamps. Even the ladies who were at the counter and the two open check-out lanes appeared to be ghetto-monstery, mean-mugging, and snatching cash and cards with short patience, agitatedly answering questions with one-word sentences. The service-counter chick had given Rainia three dollars in change, along with her stamps, saying, "Have a nice day," like it was pre-recorded, as she closed her eyes and smacked on gum during the departure phrase.

Outside, it was a clear, fall day with the beauty of the sun slapping all unhappy faces with a smile. The faint smell of the Milwaukee breweries was swimming in the occasional breeze going by in the crisp air. Rainia felt so good to just have a job and to be able to pay her bills that she had 4gotten about her angry conversation in her head about her babies daddies number two and number three. She walked around the bus to check for strangers, but none were found. She tip-toed up to look in the window, but no one was aboard. *Men are assholes, but it sure is a beautiful day,* she thought, as she stuck the key into the lock to let herself in.

A cold object was suddenly jammed into her temple from the side of her, "Open the door, bitch! Get in! Hurry up, and don't try and look at me or I'll kill you in front of all of these people," demanded a whispery voice of a teenaged young man.

Rainia's heart was racing out of her chest as she got up into the driver's side, allowing the young teen to climb over her legs, hurting her at the same time. He had then reached over her to close the driver's door and told her to start the bus and pull into the alley right by the store. She did as she was told with the gun still in her face, in total shock that no one was paying attention to what was happening. Probably less than thirty feet from the crowd, Rainia was forced to stop in the middle of the alley on the side of the store and empty her purse. The thief became angry with her, as he swished her belongings around on the schoolbus floor, "Where's the fucking money, bitch? All that's here is three dollars. I saw you go into the bank, so where's the fucking money, bitch?" he questioned.

"I only walked past the bank in the store. I stopped to get a book of stamps at the customer-service counter. All that I had was a ten-dollar bill, so three dollars was my only change back."

"Why u ain't got no money, bitch?" he asked, as he walked up on her with the gun. Then the boy put his hand in her shirt to ramble through her bra. Once he could tell that there was no cash in there, he began to fondle her chest. Rainia knew what was coming next. He stood up straight, "Come and sit in this second seat and suck my dick, before I fucking kill you for not having any money." He pulled it out in front of her, as she sat down in the seat that he wanted her to, tears falling down her face in total humiliation. "Suck it, bitch!" he demanded, as he jammed the nine millimeter into her cheek. She unwillingly opened her mouth, trying not to gag, as he forced his dirty, musty, super-black penis into her mouth. She tried really hard to hold back the vomit that was rising in her esophagus, letting the slob fall freely to the floor. She didn't want to swallow a got-damn thing. He became frustrated with the terrible blow job that she was giving him, so he changed his order, "You light-skinned hos cain't even suck no good dick. But yall got some good pussy. Get the fuck up and get in the back. Go to the middle of the seats and take your pants off. Panties too. Matter a fact, take off everything."

Rainia was scared as hell, noticing that the gun was still aimed at her. She did as she was told, trying not to look at her aggressor.

"Get up in that seat doggie style and look out that window. If you try to turn around and look at me, I'm gonna blow your mother-fuckin' brains out." She faced the window and could see a garbage can overflowing with baby diapers, forty-ounce bottles, and someone's stack of unpaid bills and disconnect notices, all blowing about in the gentle breeze. The boy was putting on a condom, "I gotta cover up my soldier, cuz your nasty ass could have AIDS or some shit."

Rainia was insulted by the rapist's last comment and realized that he was attempting to go up her butt, as he asked her, "You ever had a dick in your ass?"

"No, I ain't never been interested in that. I was molested as a child, and I have a hard time enjoying regular sex, much less backdoor action."

He was trying to force his way into her booty, but he must have felt sympathy for her, "Well, I ain't gonna do you like that then," as he took the head out. "I'm just gone fuck the regular way, then I'm gonna kill you because I know you saw my face."

"How? You won't even let me look at you? You don't have to kill me for no reason. My kids ain't got nobody but me, cuz they daddies ain't shit. I know that times are tight, but I used to be in the street to get my money. I once was a stripper, but that lifestyle wasn't for me. Now I work this punk-ass job. But honest to God, and I know I still ain't shit, but this is the first time that I could pay my bills on time in my whole life. By you being so young, you'll have a better chance at a better job if you go to school now. I was a drop-out once, too. So I know what I'm talking about. If you try things in a positive way, there's room for change and room to like who you can become."

He hit her in the back of her head with the gun, but he was careful not to do it so hard that he'd knock her out, "Shut the fuck up while I'm trying to fuck!"

She was thinking about her whole life, and how devastating it all had been. She was pretty sure that she was going to die, ass naked, on a short, yellow bus, raped and robbed with her brains blown out in an alley. Her kids would have to live with that in their minds forever. *All I was doing was getting fucking stamps to pay these mother-fucking bills. This is fucked up, God, I came all this way, lived through all of that bullshit, and now I'm gonna die by the hands of a teen-nigga who is not only raping me, but who tried to cop my ass virginity. My kids are gonna know that their momma died, ass-bleeding naked and with her brains blown out, in an alley, on a fucking little-ass school bus with tinted windows, all over just three dollars and three cigarettes. Hell, I gave the little, dirty mutha fucka what I had. I know, myself, that times are tight. Shit! I couldn't even buy my kids a decent Christmas this year because Lovell 'Cheap ass' be short on the bills and shit. It doesn't even matter that I'm being raped. I've been raped b4. All I ever wanted to do was succeed in life. I wonder what my kids are doing? They gone b fucked up for life off of this. God, I won't question why I gotta go like this if it is Your Will, but I can't help but wonder why Black men and boys seem to hate me so much? After all that I have been through with them, from birth to the present, I still love them and wish Blacks real freedom and dignity. All of this bullshit that goes on in cities like mine are coming from poverty, and a lack of jobs. Hell! I even saw a special on channel 10 about a few hoods in France, Saltruville and Alnae Sue Bois. People over there are trippin', too. God, we poor folk need You. I need You now! If You let me walk away from this, I know that I am gonna help make a change to ridiculous shit like this; I just know it! This boy started out robbing me, now he's taking me, and if he don't get to kill me, I have got to respect Your gangster on this. If I die like this, please give me the heart to respect Ya gangster on this. I'm a heathen and a sinner; I know, God, but I love You.*

Rainia wept deep into her soul, silently, *Use me, God, use me. Right here in the presence of the Devil and the Grim Reaper. Lord, use me and change this boy's mind.* The boy was pumping his way up to coming, jabbing the gun into the back of her head with each stroke, and with each stroke, she was sure that he was going to slip up and shoot her. Every time the steel touched her neckline, Rainia could hear the shot blast to come. She kept wondering how bad it was gonna hurt. She wondered if it was gonna hurt at all. She thought about the two-year-old baby that had died at the hands of his father's blast to his sweet lil face on State Street so many years ago. She thought about the little girl that had come up missing who used to ride the very bus she was being victimized on. She could still see her smiling, waiting for the older Black lady to come on the bus and walk her off and into the Head-Start four-year-old daycare off of Lisbon Street. Rainia wasn't her school bus driver anymore when she came up missing and hadn't been since the girl was about four, but Rainia had helped to search for the nine-year-old child for at least two months. They never found her, either. Rainia had often wondered what had happened to her. Thinking about such a tiny victim to crime on the very bus she was on, Rainia felt like she was being a punk and tried to stop crying like a bitch and just take the shot like a big girl.

She wasn't no different from anyone else that she once knew who was murdered in this fucked-up world. She even thought about her gay friend from school that was dismembered by a true madman when she was just nineteen, and she realized that shit just happens. *It can happen to any of us at anytime, and it doesn't matter how old you are, how much shit you been through, or whatever. The Devil is everywhere! People are fucked up because somebody fucked with them.* Rainia could have been a serial killer, too, targeting Black men. Or she could even be a female child molester, or maybe even a rapist with a gun, herself. *Fuck it then, shit! So be it! God knows who He wants to live and who He wants to die. Billy died in a shameful way, and, now, so will I. A lot of people have. Whatever the fuck it all means, whatever... because I'm tired of living in this punk-ass world, anyway. Just kill me, nigga.*

Rainia faced the fact that she would go out like that, with her brains and thoughts all splattered on that window in the middle seat of the bus, doggie style and looking at a garbage can filled with the evidence of poverty.

The boy had taken the condom that he had used on her and put it in his pocket, "I don't want you to take the evidence with you, so I'm taking it with me."

He's gonna let me live, Lord? The boy zipped up his dingy pants and forced Rainia to go back up to the driver's seat to start up the bus. She still didn't have any clothes on. The seat was cold when she sat down. She could feel the rip in the seat that was scratching her behind as she turned the ignition key. Her heart was still pounding at an extremely fast rate. She was hoping to walk away alive and with no further harm.

The young teen directed her to continue up the alley and drive around the neighborhood naked, trying to search for an unsuspecting place for her to let him off. He insisted, "Turn here! Make a left! Go straight! Make another left! Keep going! Stop up here and let me off. I still should kill you because I know you saw my face."

"No, I swear I didn't see you," she lied. She knew that it was him. The same little nigga from the store who she had passed on her way in. The clothes were the same, and she had seen his face really good as he had walked backwards while smiling at her before she had gone in. Only now she knew that the real reason he had been smiling was because he had found his target.

He seem to struggled with letting her live, "Well, I'm gonna have to rip this radio out, just in case you try to call for help. I'm also taking your clothes, and this." He bent down and picked up her checkbook, snatched out a blank check with all of her info on it, from her full name and address down to her house phone number and driver's license number. "That way, if I see anything on the news about this, I'll know which house to come to and what kids to come and get. Now, when I get off, I want you to go left, and don't even think about turning to look at me. I'm pushing your overhead mirror up so you can't look at me like that, either. If I see you turning around, I'm gonna fire every bullet I got in here at you until I hit you." He stuffed her balled-up clothes into his hoodie's big middle pocket, then he wrapped something black around his hand that held the gun. "That's in case I got to fire this. It will confuse anyone that sees me. They won't be able to say I fired a gun, and I won't have residue on my hands or clothes. Now, I'm getting off. Don't turn around, or you'll never even see another face again." He backed down the stairwell slowly and off the bus. Then he backed up to the corner and watched her turn left.

Rainia could feel her hands trembling to turn the wheel. Somehow, from the sideview mirror, she had gotten another glance at him as she was turning. He was cracking up laughing at her, probably because she was in the nude and driving a schoolbus. Rainia could also see him turn around to walk the other way and down the street, probably to find another victim. Oh, how badly she wanted to whip that bus around and run his fuckin' ass over, but he still had a gun. She re-played the whole ordeal in her mind and rewound his laughing. She suddenly broke into a screaming rage. The radio was gone, and he had her clothes. She really needed a way to contact someone while she emotionally fell apart.

There, on the compartment console, over the handle to open and close the sliding passenger door, was her slim, black cell phone. She had forgotten that she had put it there earlier that morning. The teen had never seen it, nor did it ever ring. Rainia picked it up and the phone rang in her hand.

She answered it, and the voice said, "Rainia! Where are you? We've been calling you over the radio for fifteen minutes. You are late checking in for your second route. What's wrong? Are you crying?"

"I've just been raped at gunpoint on this bus! I'm going home! I don't think I'll be doing anymore routes today," she tearfully confided to the dispatch lady at the schoolbus company, and then she drove herself home.

Lovell, her boyfriend at the time, was standing outside of her house by the time she pulled up. The dispatch lady had called him immediately to tell him of Rainia's condition, and to watch for her arrival. Lovell had called the police, and they were pulling up, too. Lovell walked up to the passenger door and could see that Rainia was naked through the long, slender, glass doors. He told the cops to wait up and went to get her a robe and some house shoes.

Rainia didn't even get a chance to cry it out, because she had the cops in her face, asking for details and dusting her bus and the contents of her purse for fingerprints. Then, she had her mother walking through the front door to take her to the rape center, to try and salvage any DNA that may have been left behind.

At the rape center, the nurse made her take a morning-after pill just to make sure that she wouldn't become pregnant from the rape. Then they scraped her insides of her vaginal walls for DNA, diseases, or any kind of anything that might help identify her attacker in the future that they would keep at the crime-lab storage. On Rainia's way home with her mother, in her mom's car, Lovell called, " Well, what the fuck did they say? Did he cum inside you or what? Fuckin' tell me something here. I mean, I don't know no man who is gonna stay with you after this, but I gotta know if you're tainted with the nigga's taint."

"Lovell, do you have to cuss me out right now? I've just been through hell!"

"It ain't my fuckin' fault yo dumb ass got raped!" he yelled at her. Rainia threw her cell on the floor of the car and tried to open her mother's car door to jump out and kill herself, but just as the car door swung open, her mom grabbed her arm, digging her nails into her daughter's skin for dear life.

"What the fuck did he say to you? Close that got-damned door, and give me that phone." Anmarie called Lovell right back, "What the fuck did you say to her, you asshole? Well, she just tried to jump out of my car! Aw, fuck you, too! I hope you get raped one day, and someone treats you like this right after. See how you like it!"

Lovell must have felt bad after that, because once Rainia returned home, he jumped in his car to go and look for every young dude in a hoodie on the street where everything had went down. He never found him, and he seemed to let it go after a week or two.

They didn't talk about it anymore, but Rainia now had two nightmares; one of Billy's red Cadillac, and now one of this kid with his gun to her head, ready to blow the stars out of her dreams of midnight sky.

Months had passed of her being tempted to kill every kid she saw wearing a hoodie, but it was never him. Then, one day after Rainia had returned to work she was at a stoplight, waiting for it to change, when she looked over at the teenagers playing tag at a bus stop on the side of her bus. It was him! He had noticed her looking at him and made a break for it. She chased him in her bus down two blocks. He tried to cut through an alley, but he tripped over a garbage can and tumbled to a stop. His ankle was twisted so badly that when he tied to get up again, he toppled over in helpless agony. It was too late for him to get up. Rainia had that bus right on top of his pants leg, pinning him to the ground.

She threw the bus into park and revved up the motor, then she exited the vehicle and walked around the front to where he was lying on the ground, begging her for his life. She didn't even give a fuck if he still had his gun, because if he shot her today, she vowed not to die until he was nothing but a ground-beef-looking memory. Rainia bent down to look him dead in his eyes, "Where's your gun now, bitch?" she said to him as she went through his pockets.

"My uncle took it from my momma's house. I only meant to rob you; I didn't mean to rape you, too. I was on some extra bullshit that day. Those condoms I had were for me and my girlfriend to have sex with. Are you gonna kill me now? That would be fucked up, because I think about you everyday. I'm going back to school and I'm living right. I even go to church with my uncle, and he even gave me a job after school at the store he owns. Please don't fuck me up, even though I know I deserve to die," he quickly pleaded.

Rainia laughed like the big, red devil with bright, yellow eyes portrayed in the movies with the gigantic, black bull horns, "Ha, ha, ha! You expect me to believe that, you foul, pussy-stealin' son-of-a bitch? Now I get to fuck your mind up. I'ma do that by taking that leg that's so close to being underneath that tire, bitch-ass nigga! I remember that day you and I shared. The stank off your nasty dick in my mouth wakes me up at night. I told you that I had kids to live for, but you kept fuckin'! I told you that I was molested, but you kept right on fuckin' rapin' me, didn't you, bitch? Do you know how many times I thought about you? I think about you when I go shopping and write checks, or when I get home with the groceries, dropping and breaking my shit, because I'm always rushing to all of the windows in my home, checking to see if you're coming for me and my babies. I think about you at night, when I double lock the doors. I think about you in my sleep, when I dream of you coming to harm my children. Now, why in the fuck should I let you get away, bitch?" Rainia calmly asked him as she grabbed him by his nappy hair and slowly leaned into his ear with a death-wish whisper that only he could hear.

The boy was crying a river of hot, desperate tears, talking ever so fast, so sure that he was about to die. He could see in her face how badly she wanted to kill his ass, and he knew that he was about to pay for everything that every nigga in Milwaukee had ever done to her. He sniveled back the snot, as he tried to convince her to spare his life, "Because you're a good person. You don't want no jail time for killing me, ma'am. I ain't worth it! I swear to God, I don't even know your name or where you even live. I ripped that check up that I took from you and threw it away on my way home that day. I'm just learning how to read! Please don't kill me! Let me go! Please let a young nigga live! I know I ain't shit, but I plan on getting right with God. At first I thought that I didn't have shit to live for, but now I got a little baby on the way. Miss lady, I understand what I put you through. If you don't believe me, check my ID."

She thought that he was full of shit, remembering him hitting her in the back of her head with his gun that day, and threw his head into the pavement, causing him to chip a tooth, "What the fuck else you got in these pockets, lil nigga? You got some money for me, mutha fucka?" Rainia felt like a real gangster as she went into his pockets again and pulled out his school ID. It said, 'Jerry Austin Middle School, Seventh grader, Mathew Thompson, age 16.' She put his card into her bra, "You 16 and still in the seventh grade, dumbass mafucka? How did that happen. Don't answer that. In fact, don't say shit else. Y your broke ass ain't got no money?"

He was about to answer her, but she kicked him in the ribs, " I said shut the fuck up? How do you like being the scared one?" He didn't dare answer her. She kicked him again, just for the hell of it, or maybe because he was broke, "At least you got three dollars off of me. I would rape you back, but you're ugly and you was stanken, from what I can remember. Boy! I wish there was something out here in this alley that I could shove up your ass — Damn!"

She thought about killing him long and hard. She wanted to crush his genitals, his chest, and then his head, for at least one victory from all of her rapes compiled into one revengeful moment, but a voice kept saying, *Don't you do it! DON'T YOU DO IT!* She stood up and ran her right hand down her face with her decision, "Ok, bitch! I got your information. And if I see anything suspicious around my house, anything, or if I even see anything on the news about this and you snitch on me… me and my people are coming to get you. Understand?"

"Yes, ma'am, I do. And I will never forget your kindness. I promise you that I will never rob or rape anyone else again. And I know that this is some stupid shit to say, but you saved my life."

Rainia agreed to let him go on one condition, that he strip, ass naked, and give her his clothes and shoes. She made him limp through the glass-ridden alley, butt naked and injured, watching him try his best to hurry on his badly-twisted foot. The shit made her feel good, too. After all, he coulda been lying about some of the things that he told her just to get away.

On the bus, she inspected the contents of the rest of his pockets one last time and found an ultrasound picture that had just been taken the day before, bearing the name of 'Thompson Fetus, Female, 18.5 weeks development' in the upper left hand corner. In the same pocket was a flyer to a church near where she had dropped him off that day. It was called New Faith Tabernacle, and the program flyer looked like he had been carrying it around for a while. On the back of it was a drawing of a schoolbus with an angel driving it. Underneath that was a heart inscribed with 'LaTisha and Mathew 4 ever' with an arrow through it.

Rainia dropped everything to the floor in the same place that her purse had fallen when he had robbed her. She was flooded with the Holy Spirit of the Universe and broke down into a deep prayer, for something deep had clicked in her mind. Rainia opened her eyes, and it was all so clear to her now. She talked to God inside her head as she backed out of the alley and went on to her afternoon stops, *Dear God, I now realize Your purpose for me. You want me to help all of the people in the struggle. I'm gonna do like this boy and go back to school again. This time, I'm going to college for Human Services. And I'm gonna follow through and graduate with honors, then I'm gonna go out into this world some kinda way and help change this mess of poverty that has been made. I'm gonna break up with Lovell, but first, I'm gonna help him save up some money to find his own place, because I know that he's been seeing someone else. I'm gonna find me a new church home, even though every church in this city seems to start with 'New Faith' something. I don't care if it's called 'New Faith Word' or 'New Faith Hope'; I'm gonna go. I'm gonna do Your Will, God. Use me anyway You would like.*

After that, Rainia did everything that she said she would. She went back to school. She earned a degree with honors. She allowed Lovell to save up to move out but found out that he was still with his other baby's mother, so she put him out. She became a teacher for 18 thru 21 year old, Second-Chance Students needing life skills. She became somewhat of a martyr. She did everything except try and have a goodtime for herself. All of the long hours at school made her weary. Her days were hectic, as she gave the class lessons from her heart and soul. Then she would go home and give her children all of the love and guidance that she had left to muster.

    Each and every single day, Rainia Dae Harris ran herself into the ground. In the morning she would wake up, get the kids dressed, get herself dressed, make some kind of breakfast, or pour some kind of cereal around the table into bowls, take everyone to their bus stops, and then make her way to the daycare. On the way, she would stop at the Mc Denny's to get breakfast for herself, share it with the baby in his car seat, try to eat what she could at the stoplight, spill stuff on her clothes, try and put her make up on, comb her hair, go into the other lane, answer a call, loose her eyeliner down the crack between the seat, and then loose the call, fight for a parking spot at the daycare, get the baby and enough diapers and wipes out of the car to take into the daycare, try to convince her crying baby that she had to go to work and that she would be back later, zoom off to her job, run into the building to punch in on time, go back to the car to get her stuff, teach class, associate with her colleagues at lunch, teach class again until the busses pulled up to the school, send the students off, meet with her colleagues and punch out, go get her baby, sit in the irritatingly slow, end-of-the-work-day traffic, go wait for her other kids at their bus stop, get everyone in the house safely, fix dinner, feed the kids, help them with homework, send them to do their chores, do her own chores, get the kids ready for bed, wash and iron clothes for the next day with her daughter's help, get herself ready by running a bath, get in the tub and sit her tired ass down, suddenly have the urge to shit, get back out of the tub to take a dump, answer a question from her son knocking on the bathroom door by responding, "Damn, I am tired, baby! No, I don't know what happened to your wrestling man with the huge, green head. I'm happy that we all made it back home to have seen another day together in one piece, but can I shit in peace?" Then she would wash up with toilet wipes b4 getting back into the tub to experience total exhilaration. The bath had always seemed to wash away the fatigue of her mind. When Rainia's head finally hit the pillow, she was already asleep.

Chapter Nineteen

Mind Vacations

Rainia was at her desk after school one evening, thinking about everything she had survived, *Poverty is such a cold-blooded thing to do to even just one person, let alone a whole race. It's like being on punishment, everyday of your life. You can't afford to go anywhere or do anything to get away from it, and it hurts us. We cry behind the stress. We are bound to be stressed by struggling to survive, and yet, because of our poverty, still only getting the things we are entitled to. We have no enjoyable lives, yet we have more places to be and things to hustle for than a lil bit, such as welfare, W-2, the Quest Card's Doc 1 form, W.I.C., childcare, housing, court appearances, doctor's appointments, the dentist, optometrist, and the school meetings concerning your stressed-out, disturbed child. Believe me, I know! That is why we take the mind vacations that we can afford. We smoke, drink, do drugs, and cheat, just to be able to deal, and then we either kill each other or die behind the foolish circle that we just can't seem to escape all at once. It takes a lot of time 2 be able 2 see through the smoke and mirrors, so it's not our entire fault. Dear God, please put all of our names on the prayer board this Sunday, Amen.*

Things were so bad 4 her at the time that she even attempted suicide, but her momma was there to deter her from the act. Rainy was also thinking about God turning her life around, *God, You have done so many beautiful things for me. I guess I don't need a man to feel worthy of happiness. I'm happy serving You, even though You forgot to send me a soulmate, but I'm cool with that.*

And, just like that, God heard her loneliness and blessed her life with Ade, pronounced Ah-day. His full name was Sumburu Ade Hasson — or 'Pooh' for short. Formally, he liked to go by his middle name. He didn't like his first name at all. He was a college student who used to be a thug that she at first thought was out to get her in a bad way. She was so sure that she was done dealing with Black men, because of all of the things that more than a few had put her through during her whole, entire life. In fact, she was supposed to be contacting J.C. from an 'Old Class Mate's Dot Com' email he had sent her, claiming that he was doing really well for himself, working on a popular cruise ship in a headliner band.

She tried hard to push Pooh away and get with the White guy, but Pooh ended up stealing her heart instead of wasting her time. Their relationship was unstoppable, because it was blessed from the start. He was everything that her life was missing, from their deep passion for one another, to the telekinetic energy and the laughs that they shared, all the way down to having someone to serve The Lord with at his church, aptly named, 'New Faith Ministry'. The man could read her thoughts and put a fire in her body that she never knew existed. He was "The Love of her Life" and the only man to ever make her have an orgasm. She'd always had a hard time with sex because of flashbacks from her past. But with her fiancée, Rainia couldn't have been happier. Together they had prospered from the wretchedness of the ghetto, because both of their past relationship disasters had inspired them to write a screenplay that was turned into a movie. Rainia and Pooh had instantly became very wealthy and were planning to marry. They even had a child on the way. She was four months pregnant. And when the devil tried to test their love for one another, love had sent yet another message of victory.

Rainia was upset about the circumstances around Pooh's baby's momma, who was trying to keep them from getting married, *God, why is this happening to us? We just wanna be married and live right by You. And You know that I am proud to do Your Will to use me to help those in our society who are misfortunate. So tell me, Lord, how can I continue if I don't know which way to turn now?*

Her whole life's mission was to help correct the problems of society and poverty. And from this striking revelation, she had

become so wealthy that Rainia decided to take a great deal of her own profit 2 take steps and help to start a city lotto for poor people.
But how? Rainia kept wondering.
Rainia needed guidance, a sign from God. She got down on her knees and prayed for something clear to come to her, something as clear as day or the 'DAE' of her name, something directly related to her name to assure her of her purpose on Earth. Later that day, God sent a sign through Pooh and a coat. Pooh was coming into the kitchen with a colorful, old leather jacket, putting it on and asking her about the number in the pocket, "I was looking at this number in this coat, and I really think that you should give this lady a call. I don't know why I feel so strongly about this. Baby, just call her for me, please?"

Rainia called the woman, wondering if she was still even in business. As the phone rang, Rainia realized that just about every single African-American she had ever laid eyes on, especially in the hood, was a direct descendant of someone from the birth of America who was hung, burned alive, tortured, raped, beaten, and was ripped off for their prosperity, childhood, and Black cultural identity in some way. The phone stopped ringing, "Hello, this is Rebecca Daniels."

Rainia was about to introduce herself, but the woman stopped her, "I've been waiting a long time to hear from you. You're the girl with the dreams, right?"

Rainia tried to laugh it off, "Well, everyone has dreams, but I was wondering–"

The woman cut her off again, "But not everyone has dreams of a red Cadillac, or should I say — nightmares?"

Rainia put the phone down with widened eyes and silently mouthed the words, "This bitch is for real — for real!" to Pooh, who was standing next to her, trying to eavesdrop.

Rebecca Daniels said, "I *am* 4 real, and don't you be calling me no *bitch*. Y don't you and your friend standing there come to see me tomorrow. My address is still the same. 7:00 P.M. should be fine. I've been looking forward to this, so there is no charge," and she hung up.

Pooh just stood there in confusion, "What nightmares about a red Cadillac? Where do you even know this lady from?" he wanted to know.

Rainia opened the 'Milltown Blackopoly Game' that the kids were playing with on the kitchen table, "My dead-ex's mother, Maggie, gave me this lady's number before moving to another state. That was, like, a hundred years ago, it seems. I'd forgotten all about it. The only reason I even took the information was because Maggie had insisted. That, and this Rebecca woman had passed on a message from Chaz in the afterlife that we would find that coat you have on up in his room, stuffed way down in the closet. He kinda left it to me from beyond the grave. She has a weird accent that I can't place."

Pooh shuffled the cards and threw the dice, "You mean 2 tell me that I have on the coat of a dead man? *Kewl!* It goes good with the dress shoes that I got from the grave guy."

She picked up a card and laughed as she read it, "Yeah, right! I just hope that you didn't kill him and take his shoes. Now, you must play this game with me! It looks funny, even though ain't shit funny about the bullshit on this card. The kids can't play this piece of work no more, honey." She turned the card over so that he could read it: *You just got pulled over by the cops for driving while Black. Go back nine spaces.*

Pooh giggled and passed the small game figures her way, "Ladies first, boo. Which one you want to be: The Ho, The Man, The Baby Momma, The College Student, The Business Owner, The Bar Owner, The Preacher, or The Pimp? I'm going to be The Thug," he smiled and snatched up the game piece of the little dude with the platinum toothed, angry facial expression.

Rainia pinched The Pimp between her fingers and then flicked it across the room, "That one's face looks like someone's ass. I'm going to be The Business Owner." She rolled the green dice; it was a two and a five. She yelled, "Seven!" and moved her figure of a briefcase seven places and landed on 'Nigger Rock'. She picked up a card from the Nigger Rock pile, and it read: *You are at the lake, and you see your name on the biggest rock out there, and under your name is your phone number and address for a good time. You get mad and try to cross it out by using a piece of charcoal left over from a cookout. The police see you and write you a ticket. Go back two spaces!*

It was Pooh's turn, and he rolled the dice, "Eleven! Naturally, baby," and he moved his Thug dude up to the place that read: *Church and Liquor Store Boardwalk.* He picked up the card from the pile: *You have just found the wallet of the neighborhood drug dealer who was kidnapped. Inside is the unsigned deeds to the property he owns. Assume he is dead and claim his property. Collect two project apartment buildings and move up ten spaces!* He moved his Thug up ten spots and hit the table with his hand, "Dammit! I landed on 'Ho Corner'." He picked up a card from the 'Ho Corner' pile. It said: *You just got caught getting a service from the dope fiend on a dead-end street. Sell a property to get out of jail time, if you have it. Go back fifteen spaces! Otherwise, go straight to the pen!* Pooh pushed the Thug dude back to where he was instructed and set up his remaining project apartment on the empty lot space, "Every time a nigga try to come up, some ho is trying to bring him down. I'm sorry, baby, but Blow Job Betty ain't got no teeth, and you heard how she can boss a nigga up!" he laughed. "So... Rainia? What about this red Cadillac?"

She was enjoying the game with him, "Baby, I promise I'll tell you everything tomorrow with Rebecca Daniels."

He didn't want to press the issue and ruin her fun, so he let it go.

The next day, after Pooh and Rainia dropped off the kids to their grandma's house, they headed straight for the address on the paper somewhere up on Fondulac Avenue, by a strip club called Star-Studded. They pulled up in the driveway of an ordinary, brick ranch house with a huge, glass-enclosed, indoor patio off on the side of it. They both got out of the Nissana Armada truck and scoped the property as they walked up to the door. Pooh looked at his 'Jacoby the Jeweler' watch and it read 6:58 P.M. As he was about to ring the bell, the door opened with a lovely, middle-aged Arabic woman holding a baby on her hip.

"I'm Rebecca Daniels. Please — come in and sit."

They both walked into her living room that had toys strewn across the floor and three cups with saucers waiting for them on the coffee table by the expensive-looking, crème-colored, rounded, pit living-room set. On the walls were pictures of her with her husband and family, and one gigantic oriental fan that flared out in back of the pit set couch like a wall centerpiece. She had two massive oriental and intricately decorated vases with gold filigree on either side of the room. The cream-colored carpet on the floor was spotless. A nice, big portrait of a lakeshore at night on the opposite wall, framed in gold, was turned on by a remote control to reveal the fact that it was one of those cool TVs. A DVD was played to show Rebecca's accreditations, some of the famous people who she advises, and a few crime cases she has helped to solve.

Rainia held on tight to Pooh's hand, as he said, "We believe that you are for real. Now, what can you tell us about what we need to do to start this inner-city lotto? Are all of the answers hidden in an old, red Cadillac, or what?"

Rebecca Daniels set the baby in a playpen and then settled across from the couple. She poured some steaming water into all three of the cups and opened a bag of Dorities from underneath the coffee table. "Want some?" she offered, and Pooh took a handful of the cheesy tortilla chips and shared them with Rainia, waiting for Rebecca's mystic response. The physic put several chip into her mouth, "Good, good, good, these chips are. Betcha thought that I was Arabian, didn't cha? Well, I'm actually Jewish. I know, I know; who ever hearda-ah Jew who predicts the futcha?"

Pooh laughed, "Oh, I don't know, ah, Jesus, probably, maybe, pretty much?"

The woman cracked up laughing, sending small pieces of chips across the floor, "Oh, my gosh! You are funny! The spirits told me you two were the new comedy couple of the century since Desimond and Lucillia from that old black and white TV show. I'm honored to be in your presence. You two are going to be a huge icon in the entertainment business. And what's really wonderful is that you'll always stay togetha — and you'll always be in love with each otha. Now! Down to business! What I have ta do now is get you two centad."

Rainia tried to clear up the word, "You mean, centered?"

Suddenly the woman became all serious, "Yes. Some people like to drink the chamomile tea for the calming effect it brings, so if you need to take a couple of sips b4 we begin, go right ahead."

"Ah… that's ok. We're good. Now, what can you tell us?" inquired Pooh.

The lady closed her eyes and scooted closer to them. Then she reached out both of her hands, suggesting that they both put a hand into hers. They agreed, and the lady parted her lips to speak as soon as theirs hands touched, "I see a little girl. She's locked in the backseat of a car. The seats are white. There is a pair of evil eyes in the rearview mirror, but no one is in the car with her. She's crying. She's trying to unlock the doors in the back by her, but they won't unlock. I see a woman. She is quite beautiful. She is trying to help the little girl get out of the car by trying to break the windows. They won't break. Rainia, now is the time to tell the little girl to climb up to the front seat and start the car with the keys from the sun visor," Rebecca tells her and continues with more, "Good! Now tell her to let the top down on the car and get out. Good! Now, do you see yourself in the dream? Wonderful! Now grab the little girl by the hand and walk to the corner to where the African tribesmen are ceremoniously dancing. Walk up to the kettle and look inside. Do you see your own reflection in the water? Good! You should see two reflections: that of a girl and a woman. Now watch them meld into one vision. Rainia — tell me what you see in the water now?"

Rainia was in tears, "A queen."

Rebecca Daniels spoke again, "Now, tell me, Sumburu... what do you see when *you* look in the water?"

Pooh let out a long breath of air from his lungs, "I see a lovely lady near three warrior kings, two with gold and mighty African headdresses on bearing a great amethyst of some sort and gleaming from an unknown light. Next to me is Rainia, my lovely lady queen. She is dressed in a purple and a gold head wrap. On the other side of her is my dead, identical-twin brother. I also see the enemy tribe's king, who was also my ex-best friend. We were as opposite as night and day. He sold his people who he ruled to the White man and murdered the innocent to gain power. He was plotting to take my wife as his own and then take my life. *He* is the wicked king of the Royal Bantu Tribe."

Rebecca gripped their hands even tighter, "You are correct. In your past lives, your wife Rainia was murdered by your best friend, the third king, because she would not have him. She knew that he was a dark spirit from the very start, and that is why she married you instead. Heartbroken, you sat many nights longing for your soulmate, and then, one night, your best friend drove a spear through your back and tried to strangle you with a slaver's whip. But it was not you who he killed, but your brother. You, then, in turn, killed *him*, hanging *him* with his own weapon. He, then, in turn, spewed a curse to follow your souls, hoping to disintegrate Rainia's spirit to the point that she would never recognize you in this life. He has reincarnated himself to be a pimp. One who drives a red Cadillac. I sense that he has passed already, years ago, when you may have been born, Pooh. Rainia, do you know this person?"

Rainia tried to pull back the frog in her throat, "Yes, I knew him. He was the father of my brothers, the twins, and he did terrible things to my mother, my brothers, his own daughter, and me. His best girl stabbed him to death when I was about 7 or 8. I put it out of my mind, but the nightmares have haunted me for years. I couldn't even have enjoyable sex with men because of the flashbacks of him. Once, he told me that I would never be happy with another man and that I would always be his. For the longest time, I believed him. It seemed like everything I did for whoever I was with was always cursed. He used to call me Judas, and I never understood that."

Mrs. Daniels rubbed her thumbs across the young couple's hands, "That's because… as you were dying in your past life at the hand of Pooh's evil adversary, you had enough strength to tell Pooh's brother, in a dream, who had killed you. That's why Billy Jacksin always called you Judas. You and Pooh, and his twin brother, were the invincible core to the African Tribes all over the continent. Once the queen was murdered, and the second king was killed by his brother's friend, the confused tribes went up against each other and fell apart. A stupor-curse was placed on the king and queen's people, so they were easily captured by the Europeans and brought to America to become slaves. The effects of the curse were so devastating that Black people still struggle with that curse to this day. The band of Zulu warriors dancing around you both are doing the dance of 'The Queen To Come'. Now, you and your king have arrived, and the people are being set free. The lottery will be started with the help of some very wealthy partners, and volunteers will come from all over the land to see it through. Rainia, all you have to do is 'speak it' into existence

— and it will be. All of the difficult details will be worked out from then on. Now… a few things you should know about your people. They know who you are and will remember you from long ago. In fact, every time you and Pooh have done things in your life, such as honoring the dead by pouring out a little liquor before you take a swig, you were reminding the souls around you of an old, ancient practice. Pouring out a bit of your drink first before you take a swig is an old custom from the African tribe called 'The Fanty People' meaning 'Come drink with us and pour out for the dead.' When you acknowledge the ancestors with respect, then they can protect your path and usually will, especially the royal ones who prove to be good natured through purity of heart during the struggle. The 'Howsa Gangster' of the Howsa tribe of today prays five times a day to avert trouble. Pooh, you should be familiar with this practice. It is still performed by drug dealers of today who pray every time they do a deal, to not be caught by the police or killed by enemies."

Pooh gave his answer with a nod.

"Now I will tell you both about the meaning of your names. 'Sumburu' means warrior, but in this day, warrior for Blacks means soldier or gangster, if you will. 'Ade' means 'Royal One', and 'Hasson' means 'First born of twins'. Rainia, because you are of mixed blood, from Black and White ancestors, in a battle between your Black and White Brothers and Sisters of today, you were aptly named from different regions. 'Rainia' means, 'Queen' in Latin, and 'Dae' or 'Daya' means 'Bird flying free' in Hebrew. You were the queen to come who the Zulu warriors were waiting for with their ceremonial dance. Your mother was an albino Rendille Queen in her past life who could move her take-apart, thatched hut at any time to escape famine or war. That would explain why you look the same light-skinned way as you did back then. I would guess that you and your mother moved a lot in this life as well. To this very day, from hundreds and hundreds of years ago, your White mother still has a Black husband. And your real father is the descendant of a Kiyuku King with many wives. That would explain why he married twice."

Rainia stopped her, "My real father was married only once, and his wife is dead. So that part of your visions does not make sense."

The woman laughed, "But your step-father was married before he married your mother. He is your real father in this life. I know that it sounds totally unbelievable, but sometimes things happen unavoidably for a reason not yet clear to us. Rainia Dae and Sumburu Ade, your lives are the perfect example of synchronicity, and the act of watching for signs from a powerful source. You both have been searching for each other by trying to find your way back to destiny. Destiny found you two first and brought you both together again. Now, you can both reclaim your positions and save your people in this country. It is sooo damned deep that you might as well keep this information to yourselves, because no one will ever believe you two."

Pooh, or Ade, was so blown away with the mind's eye of this woman that he had to reveal how accurate her prophecy past and present really was, "It is true that I was the surviving baby from a set of twins. My brother died when I was born."

Rebecca told him why, "He is gone because he had to block the evil king, or Billy Jacksin from trying 2 reincarnate himself again to do the same thing he did in the past; kill your wife. Billy and Pooh's stillborn twin have the same hour of death, therefore preventing another attack. God wasn't having that, because you both had already forgiven the evil, ex-best friend king from the past the first time. It's like double jeopardy. A soul can't be forgiven twice for the same sin, against the same souls. He would've had to have come back as the soul who was seeking forgiveness and accepting it as the daughter or son or something. He chose to be Billy Jacksin, and when that man was killed, he couldn't re-enter the world. Sumburu's brother, once again, gave his life to defend what is, this time, yours and Rainia's future together. It was too late 4 him to choose to be someone else."

Pooh cleared his throat and opened his eyes, "And all this damned time, I thought that I killed my brother in the womb."

"No, you didn't kill him, God made him move on to do His Will in a new life, and what that is, where, or who he is now, I do not know. I see you two are expecting. What will it be, a boy or a girl?" asked Rebecca.

Pooh told her that he wanted another girl.

"I know you do. In a few short months, both of your lives will change forever, but that is all I know," Rebecca said and smiled. She let their hands go and told them one final thing, "That damned red car from your dream! All you had to do was let yourself out, huh? Now you can even drive it if you want to, Rainia. You hold the power; nothing and no one can stop you. That is all there is. I have nothing else to tell ya. You are both free to go. Come back to see me only when you need me. Right now, I have to get ready for my last appointment of the evening." Rebecca Daniels walked them to her front door and opened it, bid the couple farewell, and closed the front door to her home.

Sometime later, Rainia and Pooh were at home in their beautiful new surroundings, debating the meat and potatoes of the possibilities of reincarnation and the terrific way that the lottery had started 2 come into existence in such of a short time. It only took about 2 months of e-mailing possible sponsors, important people in the city, and a few parties thrown by Rainia and her future husband, while showcasing the finest of Milwaukee's talent, to pull up the right cards for play. Rainia had such wealthy, heavy hitters on her side that the lottery was 2b up and set for running after the gala kickoff. Her and Pooh had witnessed what money and the right contacts could do, especially if God was willing it to be. The media was on their side, due to an extensive documentary about the nation's corporate world being silently racist for so many years.

Rainia turned down the volume to the gold-framed portrait television that Pooh had just recently bought and commented, "Our government needs to be ashamed enough to make it right. They would do right to give every Black adult in this country the cash-profit of forty acres and a mule at today's value, multiplied by the years that it took to do it! All of that money they toss around 2 each other in every division of White America from the courthouse to the welfare building. They've really taken good care of each other over the years — with our money. They act like they don't have anything to give to Blacks like they have given to the Native-Americans or immigrants. Welfare is a sham and another way to entrap. It's like stealing the foster baby's check, turning around and calling themselves feeling bad, and then giving the foster baby a few dollars of their own money. They thinks it's a big deal that they give out Energy Assistance and the way that they do it is demeaning. 200-300 Blacks lined up outside the Welfare building in the cold, only to get turned away because they were missing a document, a check stub from 13 years ago or a picture of their dead Uncle Ronnie in a monkey costume to qualify. They know good and got-damn well that they owe us, but they refuse to treat us right. You would think that the government would have felt bad by now and given reparations alongside of Indian reservations like they gave back then. You would even think that they would have felt bad and extinguished welfare and helped Black men and women attain a real education, for FREE and get real jobs that pay REAL money! Not this old, stupid-ass, demeaning, 5-dollar, 2 and 3 jobs to get by, never can get ahead, bad-credit bullshit! That report on the corporations in America having an employment grudge against Black America with a high minority turnover rate was fantastic! And I know for a fact that the same information holds true in the retail world, in the hospitality business, and in the educational system. You wouldn't believe how many Black teachers are fired on bogus terms and replaced with White instructors every damned school year, just in Milwaukee alone! Yet at the same time, Black, Asian, and Latino children fill up the schools and make all kinds of grant awards possible for the pedjudiced administrators to benefit from. They only re-certify and continue to educate their White staff, but are quick to fire minorities for lacking on their job skills and methods. Now we can open our own schools again and instill some culture and pride! I'm so glad that we have figured out a legal and peaceful way to finally take care of our own without all of the racial red tape. We needed her help, because that woman has caught the attention of America with her powerful voice. She understood that this was not a Black thang; it was an equal opportunity for the still-suffering descendants of the many captured, enslaved, forced-immigrant, African-natives denied for so long until now in American thang. She always knows how to put difficult situations into gripping conversation with so much style and grace. That's why so many people of so many races, including Whites, look up to her. Did I mention that Ophelia Windsor helped us out by sponsoring all of the difficult measures, and has single-handedly picked a research and financial team that helped put this lottery together? I've got to raise a statue in Johnson's Park in her honor. That's the park where the real 'Underground Railroad' had run through back in slavery times. You listening to me, baby?" Rainia was talking to Pooh who had been locked in a deep thought, as he sat on the floor by her feet, writing his poetry.

Pooh put down his pen and asked her, "Listen to this, please, and tell me what you think? It's titled, *We Know Better; We Know How.*" He stood up and retied his do-rag, cleared his throat, gathered his notepad, looked it over one more time, and recited what was memorized.

"*We Know Better; We Know How*

We've been tricked to sic each other in a fenced-in yard of pestilence and pain,
Black pits with the silkiest coats ready to dash, with clean feet, still wet from the rain.
We rise to stand up on hind legs, together in a pack, at the federal table 2 place sure bets,
Like the famous big dogs in the gambling portrait, we've come to eat with all breeds, making dollars with sense.
No more shabby doghouses with bright colors of paint, and empty dishes laughing at us,
For we are not dogs, but we are men, no less.
Now we have what you have; let us laugh and be blessed.
Take off your seeing eyeglasses; you're not too blind to smell this mess.
We are all one in the same, and we serve the same Book of Names.
I'm talking about the one God wrote, combined with common sense and self-conscience.
Urban wisdom has survived the street and has broken equality down to a science.
At last we arrive not late, but just in time for the effects of justice, poetically set,
In the form of lifting up one another in this struggle,
By what is ours that we haven't seen yet.

And as each family wins the lot, planting the crop that only we can plow,
We will sow our seeds with fields of love in these communities proud,
  while singing,
'We Know Better; We Know How'."

    Rainia stood up and clapped, "Hey, that was nice! How would you like to open the lotto ceremony that's coming up with that poem? You think you could have it down pat within a week?"
    Pooh smiled and sat down on the lush, forest-green carpet of their sitting room, "Anything for my queen and our people. Besides, I want our baby to know that we did this thing together."
    "Yes, we did," replied Rainia, as she bent down to kiss his warm, grinning lips.
    He put down the pen and pad, pulling her head down and causing her body to come down to lay back with his. He was careful not to disturb the unborn child within her womb, while he easily pulled her across his body to lie next to him. Pooh turned her over on her side, as he lay behind her, kissing her neck and rubbing her swollen breasts. He untied the soft, pink ribbon to her gown's silk robe and groped her breast in a tender motion. His right hand held her forehead, pressing the back of her head up against his forehead, as his left hand reached down her pregnant body and raised the nightgown up her thigh. His hand went in between her legs, as she widened the gap for him to massage her joy-spot, and then, slipping his long finger up inside her. She was pregnant, horny, and ready. He was expecting this child, horny, and ready, too. Pooh grabbed Rainia's body and allowed his manhood to find its way home to where his baby was coming from, making love to his future wife so gently, right there on the den floor of their awesome, brand-new, beautiful home.

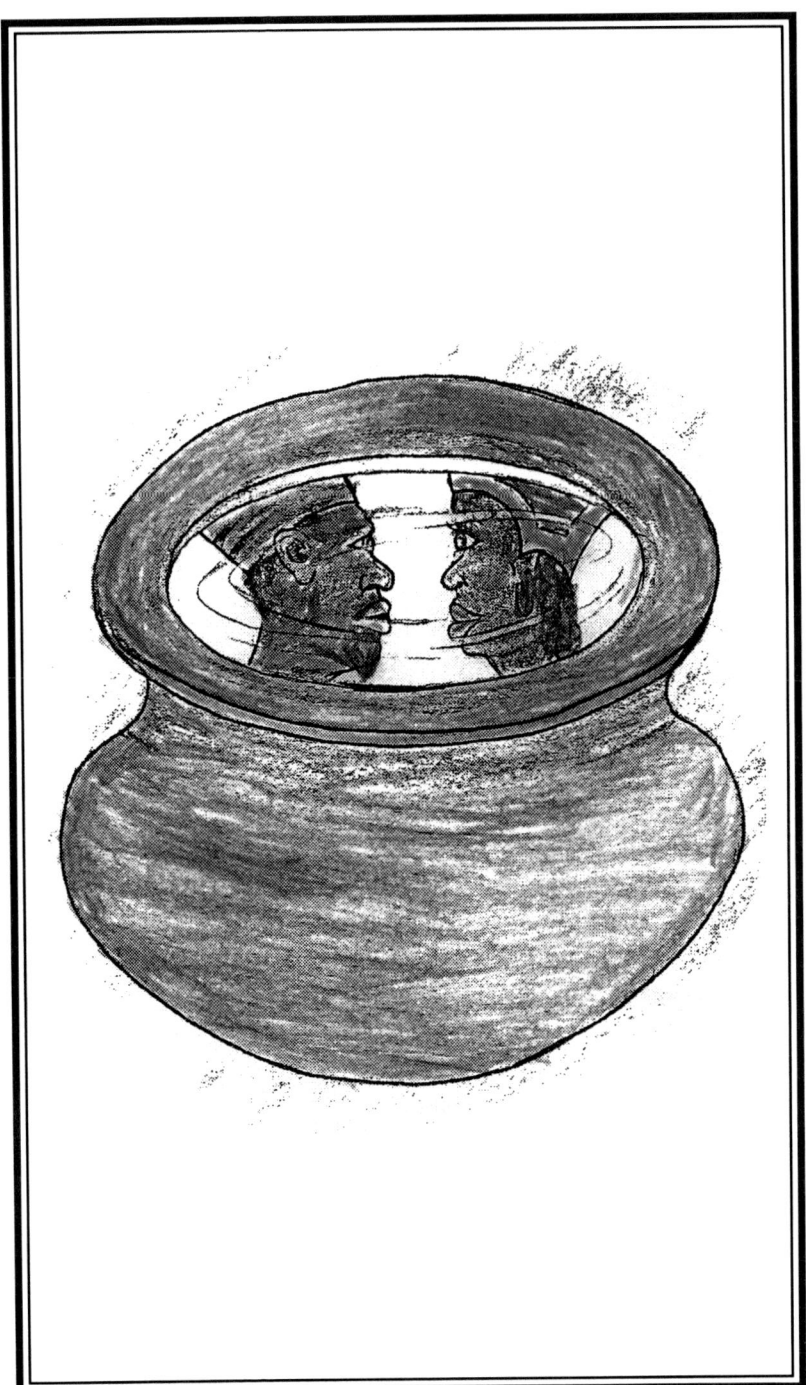

Chapter Twenty

G'dom in the Kingdom

Why couldn't Rebecca Daniels warn us about this? So what! Rainia had gotten pregnant! It really ain't none of Kiesha's damned business! Why don't she get her a life of her own? Why is this crazy-assed woman trying to ruin us because we are changing the world?

Pooh's ex-girlfriend, who was also the mother of his first child, was starting to cause major problems. The loony woman had called him to say that she was going to take Rainia off of the map during her 'City Lotto kickoff'. Pooh had spent most of the gathering searching the parking lot for any sign of the nutcase, so he could try to stop her from hurting his lady love and unborn child. He was going to take her ass out, if he had too, b4 he'd let her take away his new, happy life. He was sure that the hateful woman had shot her at the gala when everyone had heard that first crack of loud thunder. Pooh felt uneasy, as he recalled the panic in his chest when he ran in the lavishly-decorated banquet hall only to find that his dear, expectant fiancée was laid out on the polished marble floor with people screaming around her body. He just knew that it was too late.

But because God was so good to them, the lunatic had never even showed up to be able to harm Rainia. Luckily, his ex had been pulled over by the police as she was speeding on her way to the affair, just as she had threateningly declared. The lady cop that got her said that the goofball dame had run a stop sign and was doing 45 mph over the speed limit. When the officer pulled her over, thinking that she was a drunk driver, and asked her to get out of the car to walk a straight line for her, his ex had dropped her purse, and the gun inside it had gone off as the weapon hit the pavement, accidentally shooting the woman in blue in her foot. Immediately, the cop called for backup, as she held her crazy, armed and dangerous driver captive.

Pooh thought, *I'm so glad that lazy, crazy woman is in jail! Now I can finally get my daughter that she has been keeping from me.*

When homegirl went to jail, Pooh finally got sole custody of his child. The devil had been trying to use his baby's momma to interfere with their wedding, which they had to call off temporarily. Kiesha Wellington was a tricky, flippy one. At first, she wanted to meet Rainia, and she tried to act all nice and sweet to her. Kiesha would go out of town all the time, leaving her daughter in Rainia's and Pooh's care with no problem. Then Kiesha changed, once she found out that Rainia was pregnant, and she started to keep Pooh's daughter away from him.

Once she found out that they had become wealthy, she was demanding all kinds of money, as well. She was the reason that Rainia and Pooh couldn't get married. The wedding was all planned out with invitations and all, and here comes Pooh's baby's momma with all of her legal and very expensive drama. She did it big, too. She would come to their house in the middle of the night and want to fight and shit. She would show up at his momma's house with the baby and then leave with her once Pooh and Rainia got there.

Rainia had bought his daughter some Christmas gifts, and the hateful woman took every present except for the stuff that Rainia had bought for the little girl she adored as if she were her own. The woman was so hateful that she had even changed her religion to try and keep Pooh's daughter from them on the little girl's birthday and on holidays. Then God stepped in on Kiesha's mad toes and broke her down, little by little. First, The Good Lord allowed her money to get so messed up that Kiesha lost the cottage she was living in.

Kiesha's family wouldn't allow her to live with them, because she had started too much shit with them over the years, as well. They only person that let her and her daughter move in with them, ironically, was Pooh's Grandmother. There Kiesha was, living with Pooh's Grandmother, rent free, collecting child support, and still doing silly shit like locking their child up in the backroom with her during an Easter Sunday meal. She had her own baby crying tears the size of her own head, all because Kiesha wanted to be an asshole, claiming a religion she wasn't even true to, herself, but was gonna make her daughter true to it by taking all of her birthdays and holidays away from her. Kiesha's aim was to hurt Pooh, but she sadly couldn't see that the only person who she was really hurting was the baby that they shared. Rainia couldn't imagine how the woman even had the heart to have their daughter celebrate all of her holidays and all of her birthdays up until this point, and then take them away just to be spiteful, in the name of religion, no less. That woman was truly playing with God, by trying to play God.

She celebrated everything herself coming up. Now she wanna flip Gods on my child and threaten my unborn child's life? And let's not forget that night she came over my house to fight Rainia, Pooh thought, as he recalled the night that Kiesha really showed her ass. Rainia was asleep when someone started ringing the doorbell. When she went to go answer the door, Pooh stopped her, "Don't answer that; it's 'Dummy'. She found out that we are getting married and she's pissing, shitting mad. In her sick mind, she thought that we were getting back together or something."

Rainia moved away from the door, "How do you know that it's her, baby?"

Pooh giggled as he peeped through the keyhole at her, "Don't you hear the song playing in her car, jacked up all loud? *'In my mind, I'll always be his girl*,'" he sang. They were on their way back to bed, totally ignoring her, when they heard the back patio door slide open. Pooh turned on the hallway light and could see Kiesha coming right at him, swinging and scratching up his face. Rainia was so confused at the level of rage coming from someone who had been so nice to her earlier that summer at Pooh's daughter's tap-dance recital that Rainy blurted out, "Kiesha, what the hell is wrong with you, breaking and entering? Are yall still fuckin' or somethin'? Who the fuck gets that mad about another woman unless it's that, or maybe the person is crazy!"

Pooh tried to push Kiesha away, "The bitch is crazy! That's it! Ain't nobody this way fucking her crazy ass. Rainia, call the police, now!" Rainia was already on the job, but Kiesha fled before the cops could get there. Pooh filed a restraining order, and so did crazy-ass Kiesha.

She claimed that she was coming from a four o'clock in the morning Hall Service, and, supposedly, Rainia and I both had agreed to let her get our daughter from us. Then, when she complimented us on our relationship and our home, we supposedly jumped on her. She's so far gone in her head and lies so much that she will stand in front of you and lie about what color shoes she has on, Pooh laughed at the dumbest lie that she had come up with that night for her side of the story. *Then she never came to court for neither of the restraining order complaints. That girl is so mentally struggling; I truly believe that she woulda tried to kill Rainia if God hadn't interfered.*

Pooh hadn't seen it coming. He'd thought that Kiesha would have realized her fate, and maybe leave them alone, and even consider serving true to The Hall when her car broke down, and then she had to share joint custody of their daughter with Pooh, ending with the judge not making him pay child support, but sending her to therapy.

Kiesha waited for the right time to finally snap, months later, at the City Lotto Gala. She had even planned an escape from the asylum through the morning bakery truck at 'It's Alright Acres', the newly required residence of herself and her assigned group of 'On Campus and Board Certified' therapists. Rainia had received Kiesha's death text on her cell phone right before her speech. Her blood pressure went up and she panicked, searching the room for either Pooh or Kiesha Wellington. Rainia simply couldn't handle the stress. She had passed out during the lottery ceremony and gone into some kind of weird deep sleep, due to an old, undetected brain injury, but was reawakened by the thunder of that day. They rolled her right across the street to the hospital, in the rain and thunder, and there, Pooh spent his days and nights waiting for an answer to his prayers.

He was in the hospital room, staring at his fiancée who was still lost in a deep sleep, after she had given birth to a beautiful, premature baby girl by c-section. It had been three months now of prayers and tears, and Pooh wanted nothing more than to take his queen and princess home. He touched her forehead and smiled at her beauty.

Rainia could see him up ahead of her while her eyes were closed. It was like she was out of her body. She wanted to reach out to him.

***

"You know he's waiting for you, don't you?" asked her Gramma Marie.

"Who?" responded Rainia to the orbs of light.

"Your fiancée, Pooh. You know... Sumburu Ade Hasson. He's reading the book."

"What book?"

"The book about your life, the hate, the racism, with the meanings of the names about you guys, duddish girl! Rainia means Queen in Latin, and Dae means bird flying free in Hebrew, remember?"

"Huh?" Rainia asked.

"Miss Queen of Freedom, I'm talking about the book you already wrote, silly," said Chaz's voice. "Remember when I told you that I would see you on a rainy day?"

"Yea! Why?" asked Rainia.

All were silent for a mere moment, and then the voice of a man she swore she never wanted to hear again said, "Look around you."

Rainia's spirit trembled like a passenger in a rocket launch; she was paralyzed, as she listened to the man some more in disbelief.

"It rains in your mind, too. God and his Natural Forces are present where ever there is space."

Waves of light rushed through the dark memories in her like an ocean of renewal. She wanted to hate him, she wanted him to remain dead, but God was lifting her pain and wrapping her soul with a Greater Love, like the Love that God had for her. Rainia shut down all the way to helplessness, just like an infant in the care of another. As she drifted, suspended in time, all she could do was let go of her nightmares, piece by piece, like a puzzle of confusing madness.

The man said, "Why do you think that the universe keeps expanding? Once the dark matter is hit by light or life or love, that space is taken like a parking spot traveling together for all eternity. And since energy is neither lost nor destroyed, according to theory, thus began the art of forever moving forward. Since God is the beginning to everything, everything must come back to him when you question where you came from or where you're trying to go to find some answers. He is Omnipresent. Did you realize that even when you think you are moving backwards, you are still moving forwards? Technically, the point of origin you started from is always the beginning of your journey, even when you call yourself going back to the start. So, starting over really means to continue from where you called yourself leaving off. Freaky, huh? It was raining on the day you passed out at the Lotto Ceremony, as it is now. You see, Rainy, we are all stars and servants of Him, looking for our next big-gig to bring us a step closer to the solidarity of victory, and to 'The Love Everlasting'. All those times that you almost died, *you* were there to pull you out. All God did was slap the mess outta you 2 make u hold onto Him, to make you want more life. God only gave you the strength. You thought you were just another lil girl tryna find her way out of the perils of the ghetto, when, in actuality, you were sent to help destroy the ugly of it. From now on, there will be no ghettos. That's what your life story had the strength and the power to do. That's why there is *you*. Having said all of that, Rainia, do you forgive me? I am sorry for everything that I've ever done to you. And if you do, then this time, when I ask, I want you to tell the parts of this story between us the way it really all happened, and only then will I be free from what you have truly forgiven me for."

    It was a feeling of the greatest weeping that she had ever experienced. Cleansing her soul never felt so good. After all the years she had spent holding on and hating and blaming, the one man she feared most in life had come forth and had asked her for freedom. She felt glorious, as her voice danced across the Heavens in a piercing scream. It was long, strong, and oh so very overwhelming. Then... with a whisper... Rainia complied — "I forgive you, Dameon."

    His voice said, "I thank you, and I respect that. And no matter what people may say, there is a God. There is a reason. Tell it!

Write it all! Move somebody! This is the part of the pretty-much-all-true story that is the most important. The part where u wipe away my tears with a sentence which I've waited so very long to hear. Thank u 4 letting 'Billy Jacksin' go with love."

    They had let each other go and be free again in the light. Rainia looked around, and there she was, in the middle of space. Different colored stars glowed all around her as she was now sitting in the driver's seat of the red Cadillac that had tormented her mind for ages. Out in back of the car were Milky Way trails of memories which made it possible for her to get her to her destiny; in the back seat was the smiling lil girl, proud, emotionally well, and finally free to get out at any time. Rainia saw her own eyes as she adjusted the rearview mirror. The fuzzy, green dice had a cross on one and a question mark on the other. She turned it over and saw a happy face on the other side of the question-marked die. Rainia took a gamble on happiness in God, and won! She turned on the radio, and soft music played to the sound of Chaz's and her fiancée's voice in unison, as she saw the raindrops fall across the windshield. The top was down on the red Cadillac, and the little girl in back of her pointed at the brightest blue star just freshly born to the nearest nebula and said, "Look! Here comes the future."

    Gramma Marie chuckled her hearty laugh, as Chaz spoke in unison with Pooh's voice one last time through the speakers of the radio, as the star got closer and closer to the Caddy, "Think of your tears as the washing machine that is spin-cycling the dirt out of your soul. Every time you felt pain, down came the rain. The rain is equivalent 2 all of your tears, and you are beautiful like a rainbow at the end of the shower, Rainia. Good bye, Rainia. Today is that rainy day."

***

    Pooh's voice stood alone now, "Your mind-vacation is over. Wake up, my love. It's drizzling outside, and it's time to come back and share your story with the world," said Mill in his head, as he closed the best-seller book that he had been reading, out loud, to the woman he loved. He kept the last few lines of the book to himself, because he was scared to end it, as if Coraz would slip away forever or something. She had been out for months in a diabetic coma. Mill had come home from the movie set to find his pregnant and future wife face down in butter-crème frosting, novella and fork on the terra cotta-tiled floor. *Fucking wedding cake! How much of that shit did you eat that day? Who knew your ass even had diabetes? That shit just came outta left field on us, boo. Seems like we are always under attack by Satan's stanken ass. The doctor's said it was because of the pregnancy. Look at my baby. She's so pretty lying there like a sleeping beauty from a storybook. Po, lil, lucky thang doesn't even have traces of the disease anymore. She gone be just fine. I'll just wait here until my baby gets her mind back. That's what I'll do.*

    His faith was unmovable, clearly because of the miracle of Coraz's condition. The doctor's had said that the longer a person was out, the more like a vegetable that they would become, or likely to just die. But all of Coraz's brain activities were normal. She was just locked in a deep sleep. The x-ray showed that some previous accident had made room in her brain for the small part that did not receive a slight deprivation of oxygen.

    The baby was perfectly normal after the c-section, just premature. This was even more protection from the previously-injured myelin sheath. Their daughter had been born premature, just like in the book. She was snuggly wrapped in an incubator down the hall from them, and it was time to take the baby home.

    Mill thought about how much Coraz had done for the community in the charity donations and jobs which she had created. 'Re-raise 4 Praise' was a real thing that was turning quite a few heads. He reached over to the table and fixed the vase of roses that had been sent by the real-famous, Black talk-show host from the book and situated the letter of interest from the real man who was said to be the richest man in the U.S. Both of the tycoons had read Coraz's book and were so inspired that they had an interest in helping her start up a real lottery for the poor, worldwide. The idea was spreading all the way to Africa and the Middle East, and the world waited for Coraz to come out of her coma.

    Mill got down on his knees and said a small prayer for her, "Dear God, it's me, Mill. Normally, right about now, I would be upset and depressed about the way that the chips have fallen for us. But I really do believe, more than ever, that everything — everything

— happens for a reason. I know that I have done a lot of things in my past to deserve 2 be hurting for the rest of my life, if You were to take her from me today. But I am very thankful that You love me enough, even through all of my mess, to have designed her for me. She is my soulmate, true enough, but give me the strength to pray for her safe return to either You or me. Thank You for our beautiful daughter. Oh, Lord, and thank You for today. Amen."

Then he pulled something from his back pocket. In his hand he held the nomination for the 'Nobility Prize of Peace' for his future wife's literary smash. He stared at it for a minute, then the nurse came in, "Excuse me, sir, but the baby is ready to go. I *promise* that we will take good care of your wife while you're gone."

"She's my fiancée. We'll be getting married as soon as she gets well, God willing."

"I understand, sir. Right this way, sir," gestured the nurse.

Mill kissed Coraz's lips and tucked her in for the night. "I'll see you soon, girl." Tears fell on her face, as he remembered how he had told her that same thing after their first meeting in Zarkalov's, just about a year ago. Mill straightened himself up, wiped his eyes, and put the letter back in his pocket before turning around to face the waiting nurse. He didn't want to appear to be an old, soft-ass nigga. After all, he once was a stick-up, dope-slanging, pimpin-ass gangsta who wouldn't be caught crying over a woman for a paying movie scene if it was required.

Mill pulled his shit together and faced the resident nurse. Then he reluctantly walked with the nurse to the baby's room. Although he was thrilled to be taking home a healthy daughter, he was sad to be leaving Coraz behind. He bent down to pick up his pink child. He recalled how some people had suspected that she may not have been his baby because she was practically White, and Coraz was supposed to be reconnecting with the White guy named J.C. at one time, right b4 she had hooked up with Mill. Somehow, Mill knew that Coraz wasn't even the type to cheat. He knew that she loved only him. Fuck whatever anyone else thought. The soulmate in waiting was so sure that the girl was of his flesh that he willingly signed the volunteer paternity form, in spite of the accusations of Coraz possibly having been unfaithful.

Another tear formed in his eye and fell to the newborn's sleeping face as he held her up, kissing her rosy and coffee with a lot of crème-colored cheek. It was like he couldn't stop crying. He was thinking about how the character 'Rainia' wakes up in the end on a rainy day, out in space on her way to live out the rest of her fabulous life with Pooh. Mill only wished and prayed that today was the same kind of day for him, Coraz and infant as well. "No weapons formed," he whispered to his pretty baby girl.

As he looked up at the windows outside, he saw a flash of lightening. Then he heard a clap of thunder. He felt a rush of warmth and love go through him like the wind, and his heart raced. He knew that it was God. With the baby in his arms, he flew back to the room where Coraz lay sleeping and said the same words that he had somehow memorized except for one part; the name. Standing next to Coraz's bed, he closed his eyes, held the baby with one arm, and held Coraz's ring-less hand with the other, whispering softly, "The rain is equivalent 2 your tears, and you are beautiful like a rainbow at the end of a shower, Coraz. Today is that day. Your mind vacation is over. Wake up, my love; outside it is drizzling, and it is time to come back and share your story with the world."

When he opened his eyes… she slowly opened hers. The thunder outside rolled through him like a steamroller, shaking him to the core. It was the Presence of God Himself, still dazzling from her eyes. It made him feel watched like the knowing feeling of the fear one feels when they realize a newborn baby's set gaze on you holds all of the knowledge of the universe, for babies are still so close to the Creator of all things. Mill knew that she had been somewhere talking to members of the highest power. He felt his knees go weak at the miraculous sight of the woman who was supposed to be a vegetable, fully awakened like an angel from a fairy tale. He played his princely part and bent down to kiss her lips that he had kept soft with the Anti-Chap Stick while she was out each time he came into her room to comb her hair, read her story aloud, feed the baby, or 2 pray. "Hello, beautiful. I've been waiting on you for a long time. Someone wants to meet you, Mommy," remarked an ecstatic Mill.

Coraz put her hand over her mouth, " You got some gum? Cuz I know my breath stank! I don't want to send our baby into the knockout coma I just got back from with this breath." She giggled, surveying the room with a dumbfounded expression, "I had the strangest dream, Pooh! Only, I don't think that it was a dream at all. The main thing that I remember is this: All of us, together, make up the complexities of God. The life-light which is never put out, is God. God is Love. Love is the final answer to all questions, even in scientific explanations." She sat up and expressed herself to him like a wise, old college professor, "Seriously, Mill, for example, negatives love to be around positives, otherwise there's no exciting, marital action. Instead of calling it a love affair, based on why the need to explain everything so everything has logic, they use the word research in its (Love's) place. Scientists do research on an old or new subject, and they hope, but really they are *praying* for an answer. The scientist calls his or her answer from GOD, *"The results."* Now, if the scientist's findings are to his satisfaction and can be successfully explained and accepted by the scholars of the world, then the prayer has been answered. If his findings are inconclusive, God wasn't ready for him to know yet. So we all are only at where He will allow us to be. Our passion is all for the same purpose of bigger, better, and eventually, good! Take my life story, for example. Everything bad that happened turned out to be for my destiny and my strengths, in the long run, 2 serve him. And, one day, baby, I'm going to be able to explain what I know to the rest of the world without sounding crazy, and I'm going to mess around and win that Prize of Peace."

Mill pulled the nomination letter from his pocket and shouted, "Halleluiah," jumping for joy, as he laughed and danced, causing the nurses and the doctors to rush in to see the dead arise. It was an impromptu celebration to the Heavens, for they were all witnessing a miracle.

Two days later, on a bright and early Sunday and after a few more medical tests, Mill and Coraz were leaving the hospital, and he was on his cell phone with his buddy, Zhantrel, about the Grammies that had been on TV the night b4, "What? 4-5 Mafia won a mutha-fuckin' Grammy? White people really are starting to come around. Coraz, Zhantrel finally decided to settle down with his baby momma, and they buying them a house. They were approved for a loan. Isn't that a blessing?" Mill made a face of understanding, as he chuckled and re-adjusted the earpiece to his celly while he listened to his best friend ramble on in excitement, "What? Nigga, don't eem trip! Shopping at Aldin's Food Stores, paying a quarter for a shopping cart and eight cents for a bag. Shoo... me and my baby still go there occasionally. Chili cheese fritters? Are they hood-good though? Cuz you know that shopping at Aldin's teaches broke folk how to cook really good, making cheap-ass macaroni hood-good. Ha-ha! All right, player, we gone have a double wedding. Bye, man, I got to go."

Mill made sure that the baby's car seat was secured safely, and then he kissed his new daughter on her nose. She looked exactly like him. He then laughed, because she even had his big nose, but she was rockin' it. It was amazing how much his baby resembled him and even favored his brother's infant daughter. Any fool could see that the babies were cousins. *Man, we Worthys got some strong genes.* There was no doubt in his mind that everything about his bundle of joy was meant 2b only his, as well as the woman who had birthed the child. Once he had double-checked to see if the door was properly locked, he then made sure that Coraz's seatbelt was secured as well, "Don't want your head going through a windshield again, do we?"

Coraz laughed, "So, you finally got to read my book? Well, what did you think of it?"

He shut the door to her side and walked around to get in on his. He put on his seatbelt and then looked at her strangely, "Am I really the only man to ever have made you have an orgasm?"

Coraz burst into a fit of laughter, "It's the number one book in the world, and I'm being nominated for the 'Nobility Prize of Peace', and you *would* pull from my life story only one particular detail that concentrates on something sexual between us?"

Mill grabbed her hand and put back on the engagement ring he had bought her, "I took this off your finger so that I wouldn't have to kick nobody's ass if it came up missing while you were under." Then he clasped their fingers together, kissed her hand, and sighed, "No, baby. That is not the only thing that I pulled from your masterpiece. In it, I found out that I needed to watch out for the signs of God all around us more closely. God speaks to us all day in coincidental ways. We just got to know how to spot stuff. I would have never guessed that you have seen and lived through so much. And to think that you are one of the nicest people I have ever met. Most people don't come through hard times like that, back to back, one tragedy after another. Folk go crazy and do crazy thangz. Look at you, though. You inspire us all to keep on trying and fighting for what's right. I also liked the part about our names in the book. And the Sumbaru Ade Hasson thing was brilliant, and yet a little freaky at the same time."

Coraz looked at him sideways, "How's that?"

"You know… I really was a twin. My brother was stillborn." Mill was about to feel guilty about being the one to survive, and then he had yet another question, "Say… we know our daughter's real name means 'Most Exalted One', but, Coraz, what do our real names mean?"

Coraz paused for a moment to jog her memory, "Well, first of all, don't eem trip on this, cuz it's just as freaky as the twin thing, which I had no idea, but here it all go. Milton means, 'The young family man from the Milltown'. Get it? Milwaukee? And although I couldn't find 'Coraz', I found that the root of the name, which is Cora, means, 'Dark-haired, older spinster'. Remember when we first met, and I told you of my fear of ending up an old maid. Get it? Dig that, huh? Was and is that us, or what? Let's go a lil bit deeper now that we are together and about to be married by investigating the rest our names' meanings. Sade, my middle name, is an African name meaning 'Honored by royalty', and since you have no middle name, I gave you one in my book. Ade, meaning 'royal one', wasn't something that I planned. I just picked Ade to match Sade, and your last name will be my last name, 'Worthy', which speaks for itself."

Mill was beginning to understand, "So, in other words, we started out like peasants, at first, and then moved into our genetic-born royalty, in the union of our soulmateness, recognized by our attraction to the lives that we were living when we met, in which we are aptly named? Damn! That's deep! Coraz, you moved the world with this book." Mill turned his copy of the new novel sitting on the dashboard over so that he could see the cover. "You know how the stars are sparkling in the background around Jacksin's car?" he asked her.

"Yeah. So tell me what your thinking, baby. Was it a bad call?" she worried.

"Naw! A genius one if you ask me, boo. You remember that movie, *The Mack,* starring Max Julian? Well, there is a scene when he had some hos in an observatory, looking at stars as he spit his game. That shit made every nigga in the States wanna pimp women. But look at you! You took a low-life of a pimp's choices, outcomes, and his car straight from the depths of hell, forgave the nigga with the truth by setting him free and pimped his ride 4 a higher power. That is strength. That is love, mercy, and what is most powerful. It is harder to forgive than it is to kill. Girl, u gave me new meaning to the phrase, 'Let go, and let God'!"

He loved the way the woman's eyes on the cover were determined in the rearview mirror. He also loved the way she took a gamble on faith in God, and won, even though she was a natural-born sinner and had been a victim, a heathen, and a culturally mixed-up and lost fool. Then he looked over to his real 'Entreprenubian' Queen, "You inspired a planet to truly put aside their differences, to accept one another, and, finally, to take care of each other, for Goodness' sake. Money was everything, but now your lotto will make it nothing compared to human compassion. You've inspired nations to reassemble on what's right for the human race, blamers to stop blaming, killers to stop killing, child molesters to stop molesting, all mothers to push on with a stronger love for their children, and all fathers to become fit enough men 2 protect the women and children. It's all about the perfection of a universal family, whether we like it or not. Everyone has a purpose that is far greater than the power of wrong against one another, blame, shame, and hate."

Coraz held his hand tightly, "I had been a victim by the name of Judas, a dancing Cherakee, and a useless living being. Who would have thought that there was finally love waiting for me in my search for my purpose here?"

Mill reached over to caress her cheek, "The only thing worse than getting used, is believing that there will never be anyone out there to honestly love you and not cheat on you, beat on you, or use you. You are worthy. U R WORTHY! I know that you convinced a G like me to quit bangin' and slangin' against my family's ancestors, and I can do nothing but respect you for that, and respect the universe and God for allowing us this time to live out our lives. Coraz, I love the way that we get down on our knees and pray together. We got a lot of life ahead of us. We both gotta stop cussin' and get right with God. But, man, oh, man, do moments in life make you wanna cuss! For instance, this new drama coming at us in the form of an envious woman. Now we got to deal with my baby's momma. I hope that she don't read your novel and get all 'Self important' to avoid fixing her own life by blaming me and trying to mess with ours, because she will most certainly loose the battle 4 good. I hope that she re-finds herself; that's what I hope. We'll continue to pray for her, right? God only knows that you and I wish her nothing but happiness in her life, too."

"Praise God," said Coraz. She knew, if anything, that the woman would read her story and finally stand aside with all of her self important, useless tactics. Although she didn't trust the woman's intentions at this particular time, Coraz, herself, knew how hard it was to let a man go who didn't love you no more, and with that kind of pain, Coraz sent out her real feelings on the matter of his baby's mother and all of her past spite, *I love you, sista gurl. Even though you have hated me and wanted me to hate you, I love you for everything that hurts you. Don't let past pain stop u from sending out your peace. Just like I send my love to this whole damned world, I forgive you for threatening our lives, disrespecting what we have, and I truly do send you my love and peace, for love's sake. Go and be happy. If I could tell u anything, I would tell you like I told Mill; U need to let that go.*

Mill broke into her thoughts with, "Speaking of exs, your kids' fathers might try to start some shit up, too. Damn! It's three a them niggas, too! But that's ok, about all of us people. We all need some help. And a whole lotta love. God knows we all do."

Coraz said, "Amen."

He started the car and kissed his finger, pointing and looking toward the sunny, clear sky outside the windshield. Then he fixed the rearview mirror onto his face like the Rainia character had done in the book when she had finally beaten all of her bad dreams. At first, the reflection of his image made him look down into his lap, as he thought about all of his dark nightmares, the ones he had beaten, and the ones that he and his new family had yet to overcome. Mill suddenly smiled dauntlessly about their future together and looked up at himself again.

Once he could see the powers of survival and nobility in his own eyes, he then spotted a man selling kentes type garments across the street from the hospital parking lot. There was a beautiful, purple one with gold trim blowing its magnificence in the sunshine. Mill rolled down the window, "Excuse me! Can I by that from you?"

The African man headed toward the car, rolling the garment rack with him and smiling like the sunshine above them, "You wand do buy kente?"

"What African descent are you from?" Mill investigated.

"In dese vee-ans run pure-wa Ashanti. All kentes here ah of powafoo Ashanti crawfmanship and gread pride, but I give do you 4 good price. Only 100 Amare-ican dollas. Wheech one?"

Mill pointed at the purple one, pulling from his pocket a bill to fit the price.

"Dees for a mon. ZULU, kingly mon. Purple represens royaldy." The man took the morado garment and handed it to Mill as they made the transaction. Then the man handed Mill the second kente behind it, which was also purple.

"Two for one?" asked Mill.

The African retail man spoke, "No, no. Dees is a seembolic set. One for de king, and de odduh for de queen do come. Hees bride do be should have dees." The man waited for Mill to say something.

Mill dug into his pocket, "Thank you, brotha; here's a tip." Mill slipped the man a few more bills and handed Coraz the garments to hang on the car hanger in the back, up over the door. Then he laughed long and deep, watching the man walk away, through the rearview. Mill focused on himself once more, "Ade and Sade, huh? Coraz, you are doing way too much! And now that I have joint custody of Imana, I know we are going to love living like 'Entreprenubian Royalty.' Hey! Do I hear the title to the on-going saga of Coraz and Milton Worthy Jr., my darling, sweetheart?"

She allowed her eyes to light up with anticipation, Entreprenubian Royalty? She could just see it now, "Baby, I think that's a great title for the next book, or maybe even our next film!" Just then, Coraz's cell phone rang from within her purse, "Oh! I forgot I even had an important call coming in. I hope it's who I think it is. Hello? Yes, this is she... mmm-hmm... You're kidding me, right? SERIOUSLY? THE NOBILITY PRIZE OF PEACE! I WON? Oh, my GOD! Thank you! Thank you, GOD! I RESPECT YA GANGSTA! Oh, sorry. I guess I got caught up in the moment! Thank you 4 calling."

She hung up and embraced Mill, who continued to praise and shout with her, "Oh, God! We have so much to do for You, God! In a world where so many people hate each other, thank You for loving us this much. Please continue to use us." Mill cleared his throat, held Coraz's ring finger, and said, "One more thing, if You would please just allow it, God? Please marry us in this lifetime. Amen, Lord!" Then Mill said, "As a matter of fact, Coraz, let's go talk to my cousin the preacher right now! I bet that his church's service is just about to end, so if we hurry, we can still make it!" As Mill drove on and was soon approaching the famous church on Good Hope Road, some strange and frightening things took place onece they pulled up to an empty parking space right near the front. # 1. The real, "Reese," from the book involved in the 11th Street shootout from chapter seventeen, came bursting through the front door of the sanctuary yelling, "I just broke all of you fools in the Name of Jesus!" # 2. The driver of his get away car parked right next to them rolled down the tinted window and pointed an A.K. assault riffle right at Coraz and Mill. It was another character from her memoir. Tracel TEELA Winters was back and Coraz and Mill sat in the parking stall with their hands up wondering to God what was His gangsta on this situation?

Teresa Rae's Questions and Trivia

Who were all of the people from the first book, Don't Even Trip, that had the same names in this sequel, God, I Respect Ya Gangsta?

What were Mill and Coraz's fictional names in this book, and what did they mean?

What was the negative, and, finally, the positive significance of the red Cadillac all throughout the story?

What do you think the author meant by, "God, I Respect Ya Gangsta?"

What were all of the conditions of the 'City Lotto'?

Name all of the helping spirits in the story. Are you sure that you named them all?

What was the guiding spirit's main reason for contacting the main character?

What was the name of the award that Coraz won at the end of the story?

Who was your favorite character, and Y?

What would you like to have happened to the main characters?

*Bonus

Many names and places were misspelled. Can you figure them all out?

This piece was obviously targeted at those who've had it rough, to help 2 forgive and let that go, but how did this story relate to your own life?

Although this read is very controversial, do you think that this fictitious book could help to bring certain people who either don't believe or have strayed away… back to some kind of positive, peaceful spirituality?

Were you offended by the language and tone of the book?

Why do you feel this way? Do you believe in World Love? Y or y-not? Please feel free 2 e-mail your comments, NOT your QUESTIONS, dear ones, to teresarae@text4mpublishing.com RE: GANGSTER GOD

A chat room or discussion board on this book can be found by using most search engines.

Soon to come titles from TEXT 4M PUBLISHING…
(For adults)
Ghost Talk- A Novel
Entreprenubian Royalty
Young Soul's Book of Poetry- Volume One

(For young adults 17 & up)
Temporary High "I Like Your Hair."

(For the children)
Duddish- A Tale Of True Friends and Not So Cool Trends
Gym Shoe Salad

The End?
Or is it?
Look 4 Teresa Rae Butler in your bookstore.
Bye 4 Now!

And, Thank You.

Printed in the United States
88270LV00003B/23/A